T0194223

# GALAXY KILLERS

Living Planets: Book One

*Amber Wokaty*

authorHOUSE®

*AuthorHouse*™
*1663 Liberty Drive*
*Bloomington, IN 47403*
*www.authorhouse.com*
*Phone: 1-800-839-8640*

*First published by AuthorHouse 4/26/2011*

*ISBN: 978-1-4567-5703-8 (sc)*
*ISBN: 978-1-4567-5702-1 (hc)*
*ISBN: 978-1-4567-5701-4 (e)*

*Library of Congress Control Number: 2011906535*

*Printed in the United States of America*

# PART ONE:
# A Doomed Assignment

"Push your enemies as far as they can stand. Execute them when they're down."
*- General Xavier Trellick, on combat*

# CHAPTER ONE

V'Let knelt down to the earth, sad eyes watching the horizon. The name of the planet was irrelevant, as its fate had been sealed. They had landed here almost a full year past, directed as such by those that had control over them. The dominant species had been judged to be below the Council's standard, bearing a malevolence that could lead to forceful and dominant actions once they had achieved space travel. By the Council's own bylaws, they could not be allowed to evolve that far.

Allowing her eyes to focus farther along the horizon, she spotted a shimmer on the air. It was very small, almost indistinguishable against the autumn sky, but she could see it almost too easily. Her brother would arrive soon with their spacecraft, allowing her to escape this act of finality. If he didn't, she would die with the planet and he wouldn't, couldn't survive that.

*Plant the device, sister,* D'Las's firm voice echoed through her mind. *It's time.*

*I wish we didn't have to,* she murmured to him before doing as she was bid. She reached into the many folds of her robe and pulled out a small gold mechanism that was barely large enough to fit in the palm of her own slender hand. It was three-dimensionally elliptical and covered with angry red numbers and dark black buttons. She punched in a complex series of buttons, making the numbers shift slowly until they read (OO:45). She then spun a dial on the bottom and plunged the device into the ground as a deadly electrical spike emerged from the dial.

She watched as the device became the color of no color, watched as the void machine grew at an exponential rate, soon to envelop the entire planet.

V'Let glanced up to see her brother in their small spacecraft speeding toward her, the rear hatch open for her.

Grabbing onto the edge and rolling inside, she punched the large button to close the airlock just before the planet completely disappeared beneath her feet. She sighed roughly, pulling herself to her feet. The death of yet another planet pulling at her heartstrings, she headed for the bridge.

As she passed through the far edge of the cargo area, she reached out with her mind and flicked very slightly. Across the room from her, a panel flashed white and then red as a series of numbers scrolled across its screen.

"Successful destruction of Planet Barti, residing in Galaxy Dark Sun in Alpha Sector. Sending report to the Intergalactic Council, care of Military Elder, Media Elder and Tactical Elder."

She sighed again once she was on the bridge, watching in discontent as they traveled farther and farther away from that empty spot. Slowly, everything that had been controlled by that planet's gravitational pull began to readjust to the new amount of room, filling into the space as if an unwelcome guest had finally left.

D'Las pulled up the navigational guide, obscuring V'Let's view with a different brightly-colored screen. "Let it go, Letta. It's gone. We have to move on."

"But it *hurts*, Lasso. It hurts when they all blip out like that."

A scowl covered his face, paling slightly. "I wouldn't know, sis."

"Sorry." She smiled gently, trying to cover her gaffe. "You could, y'know. If you opened up to everything."

His scowl turned upwards into a sad ghost of a smile. "Your pain is knowledge enough."

V'Let didn't try overly hard to get D'Las to uncover the power that was under his severe suppression to feel. The last time he unsnapped his control over their natural abilities, the resulting seizures had nearly killed him. She'd felt like someone had broken her in half when she'd used her own enhanced powers to knock him unconscious. She'd cried almost nonstop for two days, telling herself she would never hurt anyone again, especially her own blood.

Looking back, it had turned out to be quite stupid to make that promise to herself, considering what they did for a "living". Shaking her head at herself, she looked at her brother, willing the sadness to seep away. "I'll be in my bunk, brother dear. I'll take the next shift."

D'Las grinned at his sister. "It'll get better, I promise."

Her eyes darkened. "You can't promise a thing until they decide to let us stop." She turned on her heel and left the bridge. She felt his grimace even though she could not see it.

*They'll never let us stop,* she heard him think downheartedly as she drifted down the corridors of the ship, gracefully entering her bunk and walking straight to the wash station.

Sighing, she peered at the mirror on the wall. She poked at her violet skin, grimacing when the shadows under her bright blue eyes seemed to stretch in response to the slight physical touch. She knew she needed sleep. It seemed so difficult to find rest on the last legs of their missions.

She leaned closer to the mirror, examining her eyes. Her dark pupils were slightly dilated across the blue of her irises, denoting her exhaustion. Her eyelids narrowed slightly and she forced her pupils to dilate even further, causing them to expand and stretch across her irises. She lost her ability to see for a moment but she endured it, watching a mote of dust float between her and the mirror. When her pupils retained their normal size, a mere pinprick of black in a sea of blue, she noticed that the deep stress lines and bloodshot veins in her eyes had completely gone.

She pulled back, taking in the sight of her face again. The shadows were still there. No power in her brain could make the pain of judging a whole people go away. Thus, the shadows...

She turned away from the mirror in disgust and flopped tiredly on her bunk.

*D'Las?* she queried across the impenetrable link with her twin.

*Yes, dear sister?*

*I don't want to kill anymore.* Then she finally turned her mind toward sleep, finding her way there on a trail of tears.

# CHAPTER TWO

"Bloody stubborn wench! I know you see it!"

Rosalie rolled her eyes up at the intimidating creature that had forced his way into her very personal bubble. She arched an eyebrow at him and he took the required three steps back. "See what, Erik?"

Erik thrust his hands into the air. "That thing!" He pointed sharply but quite vaguely behind his person. "That overgrown marble you made. It went all… FWOOSH!"

The eyebrow stayed up, quickly joined by its twin. "First of all, I didn't make the orb. Second of all, 'fwoosh'?"

He sighed roughly. "Yeah, you know! It lit up real bright and I…" He looked down at the floor boyishly, seeming shy for half a second before regaining his composure. "I thought it was going to blow up."

Rosalie grinned. "It can't."

Erik was flabbergasted. "What do you mean, 'it can't'? Everything can blow up or melt or be otherwise kaput."

"That 'overgrown marble', as you so eloquently put it, is affected by neither temperature nor stress. It doesn't exist in this realm."

"But it's here, you moved it here."

She smirked. "What can I do that you can't?"

Erik pretended to think, his face echoing her smirk. "Lots of things, actually."

"That no one else can do? At least, not that I've encountered anyway."

"You mean, the planeswalking?"

"Yeah, that."

"Oh." Erik sat thinking for a moment. "But *why* did it do what it did?

Something had to have happened to cause that. Right?" He paused for a moment, his eyes widening slightly. "Did you say the Prince made that for you? Like a danger barometer?"

Rosalie nodded, gazing pensively at the now clear globe that hovered idly under the living room's bay windows. "Yeah. Something definitely happened. We just need to find out what."

He scoffed. "Oh, and how are you going to do that?"

She sighed heavily, reaching up to knead her temples. "Looks like it's time to talk to the Oracles again."

# CHAPTER THREE

V'Let opened her eyes slowly, idly wondering how long she'd been unconscious. She yawned and stretched, also wondering at the time. Was it time for her shift yet? Why didn't she know the time?

She felt so disoriented.

"They're here," D'Las said tonelessly.

V'Let looked up at her brother from her prone position. "Well, that explains the dreamlessness." She pushed herself up to sit on the bunk. "I thought it might be at least a week before we got another assignment."

D'Las shrugged absentmindedly, fingering the air around the hologram of their mother that sat on the edge of her bunk. "Said it was urgent."

She stood on firm legs, her eyes rolling upward momentarily. "You'd think that, just one time, it could wait."

He looked at her reproachfully. "You know the Adepts. Nothing can wait."

She harrumphed to herself. "I wonder what the Council would have to say about that."

D'Las smiled mirthlessly. *The Intergalactic Council could care less. Also something you should know,* he whispered psychically to her as they exited her bunk.

V'Let snorted softly to herself, her eyes having brightened after she realized the source of her disorientation. As they made their way to the bridge, she could see the image of the Council's Adepts, three very specific and very powerful members of the Council, overtaking what was normally their nav screen. Their snide smiles in place, they seemed perfectly content in their office millions of light-years away that was hidden in plain sight with that horrendously bright machine of theirs.

They called it their Separator. Ten feet tall and two feet wide, silver gleamed from every possible angle. There were a dozen titanium fans inside the metallic cylinder, all of them set at staggered speeds. The resulting sound made one's very teeth itch. As it was, it was all V'Let could do to stop herself from shielding their ears against the sound. It was supposed to mess with one's mind, to block what advanced mental capabilities one may or may not possess.

The design was ingenious, the machine itself marginally flawless when it was finally created. It really was too bad it didn't work.

Okay, that was an unfair assessment, really. The sound had had an effect on D'Las and V'Let the first two times it had been utilized against them. She had barely been able to refrain from weeping and he had barely been able to get their next assignment before ending the transmission. Now it didn't do much besides knocking their internal compass loose for a while.

That didn't mean they were incapable of pretending it still worked, however.

V'Let let her head fall down, allowing her flowing lavender hair to cover her face while she focused solely on listening to the minds of the smirking Adepts. She did not transmit what she was hearing to D'Las but she did do her best to listen to the spoken conversation as well.

D'Las swallowed visibly, making it look as obvious as he could. That damned machine did still grate on his nerves quite a bit. "How can we help you?" He ground his teeth together, reminding himself yet again that the sound would be gone soon.

*That's good, you peon.* V'Let clenched her teeth in anger at the first mental remark she heard. The audacity that was the Adepts was unmatched, she was sure. Mentally shaking herself, she cleared the bitterness from her mind and dug as deep and as far as she could manage before D'Las cut the transmission.

"There's a planet in a moderate-sized galaxy—the Milky Way. We believe you're familiar. It's in a small solar system we have designated SOL-634. The planet is the third from its small sun." One of the Adepts glanced down for a moment and cleared his throat. "We believe the natives, as well as the rest of the Council, call it Earth. It is a primitive backwater rock. You will have to cloak."

"Anything else we should know?" D'Las ground out.

"Just that the investigation should be started immediately. No time to dawdle."

D'Las nodded curtly. "Yes, sirs and ma'am. Good day."

*In the palms of our hands,* V'Let managed to catch before she lost the subspace connection to the Adepts. She groaned softly and hurried over to the ship's computer, eager to input the information before most of it faded away.

"What'd you get?" D'Las asked as he uploaded the bare specifications of the next planet that they might be destroying. Would probably be destroying. He sighed. There was probably no probably about it.

"A lot of arrogance, even more plans and finally something we might be able to use." V'Let grinned. She was glad that the day was starting to look up. "It's a name of a Council member they've been trying to coerce over to their way of thinking. You know, all that 'control the universe' crap. However, it looks they're going to be attempting murder instead."

D'Las arched an eyebrow. "Why?"

"He's too loyal to the Council and to goodwill in general, I guess." She sighed, rubbing her hand against her forehead. "How long?"

"Two weeks in hyperspace. It's quite a way from here. It's less than a day from our homeworld, though, which is a plus."

"Yeah." V'Let's happy mood drooped for a moment before she forced it up. "Did you check the database?"

"Checking it now. Cross-referencing the location with the Council's records and… Oh, God."

"Oh, God?" V'Let looked at her brother, concentrating on where his train of thought had gone. "Oh, God!"

"It's protected."

V'Let shook her head and set her forehead in her hands. "Gods above, not again."

D'Las gazed at his sister with concerned eyes before asking the other question weighing on his mind. "Who exactly is this person they've supposedly been trying to turn?"

She lifted her head and busied herself at the console again, inputting the search against the name she pulled out of the Adepts' minds. After she retrieved the results, she nearly hung her head in despair again.

"It's the Head of the Council."

# CHAPTER FOUR

Rosalie yawned, daintily lifting her hand to her mouth. She opened the door to the front of her house, well aware that Erik was long asleep, and was immediately attacked by the brilliance that was mid-morning sun on west coast America.

"Well, it's certainly a sunny day in the neighborhood," she muttered to herself as she stepped out into the world. Shaking her head at her own silliness, she closed the front door behind her and started walking down the sidewalk.

If anyone had paid close attention to her, they would have noticed her form slowly dissipating. They would have noticed that she actually fully disappeared at the near cross-street. However, no one really ever noticed Rosalie and she was comfortable with that. She had an Oracle to see.

*Aura or Senka?* she thought to herself idly as she attempted to concentrate on her location. *Ye Gods, I don't know.*

As a result of her untimely indecision, she coalesced as a wispy, semi-corporeal form in both realms. Standing before both Aura of the Plateau of Light and Senka of the Valley of Shadows, she cursed herself vehemently.

"You did it again," Senka declared in her bored tone.

"I am aware," Rosalie replied evenly through clenched teeth.

"I'll never understand your inability to choose, human," Aura intoned haughtily. "We both know I am the superior being."

Rosalie felt herself strain a muscle trying to avoid rolling her eyes. "You have a tendency to lie, Aura."

The Light Oracle had the grace to look affronted. "I do not."

"Really?" Rosalie arched an eyebrow.

"The truth merely has a scope that you obviously cannot comprehend, mortal."

Rosalie pressed the tips of her fingers into her eyes harshly. "Whether or not you actually tell the truth, I need answers. I've recently had problems with the Reality Globe that the Prince of Realms conjured for me."

The Dark Oracle grinned slyly. "Oh, that? A planet died."

"Destruction abounds," the Light Oracle murmured, her voice having reached the airy quality that Rosalie hated. It usually meant that she was "giving the truth scope". However, this time fear put a serrated edge into her statement.

"What are you talking about?" Rosalie ground out in frustration.

"The Galaxy Killers," they declared as one.

"The Council of Realms wants them to stop," Aura added.

Senka grinned happily. "They have destroyed several planets."

"But—but why?" Rosalie spluttered. "Why would they kill planets?"

"Because they are bound." In unison, again.

Rosalie stood still for a moment, her mind awhirl with questions, but she knew quite clearly that the Oracles would most likely not answer her inquiries clearly. At least not in a way that she would be able to understand. She sighed heavily, realizing she would have to sort through the answers at hand herself. "Well, I guess that answers my question, huh?" She turned away from them both then. "See ya." She faded from their respective sights before they could say anything further.

Aura turned away but Senka stared pensively at the planeswalker's former position. "And they're coming here," she whispered to herself, her wry smile forming across her dark face. "What fun."

# CHAPTER FIVE

V'Let sat on the bridge as her brother slept, twisting her hands in frustration as she tried to figure out how to not destroy a planet even though it would probably give her countless reasons to do just that.

"Of all the primitive planets in this whole wide universe, why did this one have to be protected?" she asked herself softly. Her brow wrinkled gently as a thought occurred to her. "*Why* is it protected?"

Restless, she pulled up the navigational screen, which showed the approximate time of hyperspace travel remaining. There were roughly thirteen galactic cycles left. As she was about to access the Galactic Information Database, she heard a low-pitched chime echo throughout the ship.

"Incoming communication from Beta Sector, Freti Galaxy, Planet Wraven. Identification blocked."

V'Let smiled at the sound of the computer's hollow voice. "Accept communication."

The face of a tall humanoid male filled the screen. He had a longish, gently formed face and a full head of auburn hair. His skin tone, however, was a near-ivory color that made V'Let vaguely nauseated if she thought about it too much. "I take it they gave you another assignment?"

Her smile twisted into a wry grin. "Hi to you too, Mallik. And that's an affirmative to your oh so subtle inquiry."

Mallik at least had the grace to blush, which created a bright pink shade high on his cheeks. "I apologize about my greeting, V'Let."

"Or lack thereof."

He continued as if he didn't even notice her interruption. "I received the information during a planet merger. Is this true about Head Council Member Gralug? This is a very serious accusation."

"Everything against them is a serious accusation, Mallik. That's how huge this is." She peered closely at the screen, reaching out with tendrils of her mind to skim over the surface of Mallik's. "They don't believe us, do they?"

"I'm sorry, but it's kind of farfetched, my little mentalist. The three most loyal members of the Galactic Council have secretly been planning for years to take over the universe? And they're going to kill Gralug? Of all people!"

Everything seemed so odd. Just two days ago, Mallik had been aboard the Crush-the-Adepts train—heading it, in fact. Now he was so skeptical.

Suddenly, it all clicked together like a brand-new jigsaw puzzle. Of course, it took her a moment to realize she wasn't reading him properly, despite her ability to read minds across subspace. His mind read like fragments, telling her the truth as always but pieces were missing. Certain thoughts had been reconstructed crudely but with enough sense to convince the owner of their authenticity.

"Mallik! You didn't!"

He faltered slightly before continuing in a stammer. "Didn't what? I don't know what you're talking about."

"You went to see them, didn't you?"

"Maybe…"

"And they put you in front of that damned Separator and now you can't remember any of your time there properly and you think everything my brother and I have told you is 'Galaxy Killer lies'. Right?"

Mallik looked taken aback. "How did you know?"

V'Let tapped her temple. "Nothing can hide from me, even if it's being hidden." Furrowing her brow slightly, she continued. "Not that that makes sense at all." She sighed and relaxed into her chair. "And I should have known this new assignment was a punishment."

"Why? Where is it?"

"Another protected planet." She sighed. "You should remember that's what really got us in trouble in the first place. Stupid Council couldn't care less that we're destroying planets and billions upon trillions of people as long as it isn't one of their precious protected planets."

Mallik got thoughtful then. "Just out of curiosity, which one is it?"

V'Let arched one lavender eyebrow at him. He never asked anything "just out of curiosity"; there was always some purpose or connection on the edge of his mind. "A planet called Earth, Milky Way Galaxy, Zeta Sector. Why?"

"Oh, Gods above," he swore.

"Mallik…" she warned.

"Would you believe it's classified?"

V'Let peered at the screen closely again. A few seconds passed and then a grin broke out on her face. "Oh, no way! No possible way. That would make it the perfect planet."

D'Las stumbled onto the bridge just then, his hair in an extreme state of disarray considering its length of one inch. "What's going on?" he mumbled sleepily.

Mallik ignored the brother momentarily. "The average inhabitant is not aware of the protected species. The 'humans' are probably why you've been assigned this particular planet."

The smile fell off her face as she glimpsed vague things from his mind, bare facts about the world. "They've had how many wars?!"

# CHAPTER SIX

Erik woke slowly, though his groggy awareness made it seem sudden. He rolled out of his bed and glanced at the clock across the room. 1:23?

*Did I oversleep or. . . ?* He moved over to the window and pulled aside the heavy curtains uncertainly. He hissed grouchily as bright afternoon light flooded the room. He flung the curtains shut and turned away, looking longingly at the bed.

After a moment of blank staring, he realized he could hear a low humming sound. Reaching out with his hypersensitive hearing, he realized that no one else was in the house. Rosalie had said something about going to see about an Oracle. He guessed that she probably phased herself over to one of their planes. Usually after one of the Oracles' "revelations", she would walk around the city for a while, trying to sort through what she'd been told.

However, there was still that odd humming. It was almost like the idling of a machine, except for the fact that it was steadily, incrementally getting louder. Trusting his ears for the tracking, he followed the sound.

It brought him to the living room in front of that blasted overgrown marble. He sneered at it briefly before looking at it more closely. The sound was coming from it but he couldn't figure out how or why. He concentrated harder, folding himself into the lotus position before the globe.

He thought he could hear words. Words like "planet" and "wars" and "punishment". Words that started to leak an irrational fear into him. The globe seemed to have some sort of light show going on inside, like the crackling of a lightning storm. The light itself was odd, its color a deep purple. If someone would have asked him, Erik would have said that whatever was going on inside this thing, it looked very, very angry.

The globe then seemed to crack and the word "xenocide" blasted through his mind. Then everything went dark.

# CHAPTER SEVEN

"Xenocide?" D'Las asked softly, glancing back and forth between his sister and the Council member on the screen. "Don't you think that's a little rash?"

V'Let shook her head harshly. "They've had more wars than I've ever seen on the face of any planet. They use nuclear devices as weapons of mass destruction. They're even killing the planet so very slowly themselves."

"But it's protected, right? All of it?" He glanced back at Mallik, who was rubbing his temples. "Wait, what happened to Mallik?"

V'Let calmed a bit at that. Glancing at their liaison, she replied, "He tried to investigate the Adepts himself. The effects of the Separator are finally wearing off."

D'Las shook his head and smirked at Mallik. "Bet you won't be doing that again anytime soon."

"I admit that the pain is a good enough reason to stay away."

D'Las glanced at his sister. "I don't think he's told the Council anything."

V'Let sighed, pulling her fingers through her long hair. "He hasn't. *They* were sure to screw that up." She looked up at the screen again, locking eyes with Mallik. "You need to send us all the information you have on this particular planet."

"But... It's classified! I can't." Mallik looked torn but resolute.

V'Let stood suddenly, her back straight and her fists clenched. She felt helpless against the rage that surged through her. "Then make it unclassified. Or... give us clearance or something. Because I need every nasty little fact about that planet that you have *before* we get there."

"Why before?"

A righteous fire lit in her eyes and she smirked mirthlessly while Mallik cringed at the sight. "I need to deal with my anger before we get there and have as few surprises while there as possible. If I'm there and get this angry, I might just destroy the planet out of spite. The Intergalactic Council be damned!"

D'Las's eyes widened almost imperceptibly as Mallik gasped. "Fine," the liaison ground out after a shocked moment. "I'll have it to you by next cycle." With that, the screen went blank as Mallik shut down the communication.

"It must be bad," D'Las declared, "for you to be talking about just destroying a protected planet like that."

V'Let sank back into the chair, her eyes troubled. "It is, Lasso. It's very, very bad."

D'Las looked at his sister in sympathy, knowing that when her own emotions hit her, they hit her hard. "Why don't you go meditate and try to calm down? I'll make sure we stay on course."

V'Let's mind was already far away. "Yeah, okay." She seemed to float away.

D'Las shook his head, grimacing at the few facts he'd gleaned from his sister that she'd gotten from Mallik. "It's gonna be a long mission."

# CHAPTER EIGHT

Rosalie sat on the pier, gazing into the middle distance as the sun set. None of it made any sense, really. The Prince had told her that the globe would only show her things that would somehow affect her or Erik, things that would endanger them. She felt as if she were missing something... very important.

She felt it keenly as someone decided to sit themselves next to her on her bench. She glanced over, nearly falling off the bench herself.

Sitting there as if it was the most natural thing in the world was a Kres'Fol demon. Of course, this particular demon was familiar, known to many as Quin. But the pale blue skin and flat black eyes would always be a bit of a shocker.

"Heya, doll. What's happening?" The demon grinned good-naturedly at her.

Rosalie inhaled deeply, followed by two more shallow breaths. It was her get-calm-quick method. "Nothing much, Q. Just saw the Oracles and now I'm stewing in my own juices."

Quin settled back into the bench, just barely abiding by Rosalie's personal bubble rules. Dressed in the latest style for any college fraternity rich boy, he was regardless severely out of place no matter the venue. Except for exactly where they were.

"And you decided to do this 'stewing' in the demon part of town, a mile out of Luna Morte's territory?"

Rosalie looked at him out of the corner of her eyes. "Yeah. So?"

"So... you should know better," he drawled.

Rosalie shrugged. "I don't see why. I've no quarrel with any of the demon community."

Quin looked at her sharply. "Doesn't mean they haven't got a quarrel with you, darling." He glanced back and forth, concentrating on the people walking on the pier. "The remnants of Erik's old gang are still out and about, darling. And they're out for blood."

" 'Out for blood'?" she mocked. "Whatever for? It was Erik's decision to leave that Godforsaken gang, not mine."

Quin grinned grimly. "Blood in, blood out, sweetheart. Our dear Erik may have been their leader but vampire gangs are for life." He snickered for a moment at his choice of words. "Or rather, for eternity. He had to resort to killing off most of them to protect your precious derriere."

Rosalie looked away for a moment, her gaze returning to the middle distance. "Yeah, I know." She stood, having decided maybe it would be safer at home.

"Why did he leave Luna Morte? Just out of curiosity." Quin had stood with her.

Rosalie smirked sweetly at the demon as she started to walk down the pier. "You'll have to ask him yourself."

Quin gazed at her as she walked away, his eyes seeming to glow against the remaining sunset. "Wait, dear Rose!"

Rosalie paused and turned to look back at Quin, sighing heavily. "What?"

"That's not why I'm here." He took a deep breath. "The Crone wants to see you."

Rosalie's eyes widened ever so slightly. "What for?" she asked, awe mixing with her curiosity.

Quin shrugged his shoulder. "No clue, was just told to fetch you."

Rosalie turned again, facing the park and gesturing Quin forward. "Lead the way."

Quin grinned toothily at her as he swept past. "Follow close, Rosie."

At that nickname, she grimaced but followed nonetheless.

# CHAPTER NINE

V'Let sat in the cargo area, a big space that took up very nearly two-thirds of the ship. It was a wide, mostly empty space and it was the only place that she would meditate. Both she and D'Las had a habit of collecting bits and pieces of the cultures of the planets they were commanded to destroy. There was the plaque from the main distillery from Planet Voo, the only piece of anything their population had ever cherished. There were statuettes of gods and goddesses, both benevolent and otherwise. There was also a hermetically sealed container that only contained currency. The history surrounding her somehow managed to calm her mind.

She calmed her breathing first, trying her best to think of the culture that surrounded her, to realize that no matter how much they killed there would always be places that would thrive. Though she knew it would return, she pushed the anger aside, feeling the tendrils of worry emanating from her brother's side of the bond dissipate with it.

"It's time," she murmured aloud, sinking deeper into her meditative trance.

*Are you sure?* D'Las queried softly. *You were so angry.*

"It has to be done," she replied. "Before the anger returns. This is important." She tried to stress that fact to her brother mentally.

*So be it. I'll let you alone.* He sighed and let their bond fade down to a dull murmur.

V'Let began to hum softly to herself, a tune she remembered very vaguely. She knew it was something her mother used to sing to them. She couldn't remember the lyrics very well anymore, mainly something about beauty and hope. She knew the tune, however, and it did well to calm. She let her eyes drift closed, letting the melody mellow her further. She was only harmony, she was only sound. She was only notes on the air.

She grinned lazily when she opened her eyes again. Her mind was flowing along a line that led directly to their destination. Looking around, she could see countless other lines flowing above, below and beside her. Different courses, she knew. These were all different paths she and her brother could take instead, places that didn't lead to destruction.

*This path will not lead to destruction,* she told herself, forcing her attention back to the line in front of her. *I know it doesn't. And if it does, well...*

She gulped, pushing distraction and indecision out of her mind. It would not help anything at this point.

V'Let sank deeper into the trance, casting aside certain thoughts as they came to her. Thoughts of regret and guilt, of anger and pain were all pushed to the very back of her mind. Vague memories of a smiling woman in bright colors followed closely by images of fire and explosions, vague memories that even V'Let tried so hard to forget were squashed down in the effort to forget.

Sometimes she hated this trance. It brought up every little thing she refused to deal with in the light, the bad memories and the feelings of shame and fear. Sometimes all of it was so strong that it was all she could do to not wrench herself out of this deep, silent state of mind. As a matter of fact, she had done that very thing. Once. There had been pain, so much pain, like something trying to rip off her skin, and then there had been nothing. For what had seemed like days, she had heard nothing, saw nothing, *felt* absolutely nothing. She hadn't even been able to move. She'd been afraid, so very afraid, until D'Las came. He had already tried several times to pull her out of her accidental catatonia. All of it had been to no avail. Then, she'd heard a quiet sobbing followed by a whisper. *"V'Let? I love you. Be strong, please?"* A shuddering sigh had followed this just before the words became sharp with righteous anger. *"I promise you—I'll find a way. We'll be free of them. I will find a way."*

V'Let smiled softly then, having followed the line to its end. She was aware of being in a structure that was well-insulated with comfortable surroundings. She turned in a circle, reaching out with her senses. She felt beyond the house first, trying to ascertain if she was actually on Earth. She scanned the brains of some, noting the distinct lack of mental ability, and grimaced. Then she stumbled upon an astronomer when she reached a bit further, one that was contemplating Einstein's theory of relativity, specifically the curved time-space continuum, and how it would relate to Earth and things approaching the planet.

Nodding to herself decisively, she smiled slowly. She knew it was no good to connect with an animal on this planet. If the "humans" were so dull, what kind of mind-numbing torture would she be putting herself through by connecting to a native animal, which must naturally be a baser species? Besides, she was on a protected planet. She wanted to connect to a member of a protected species.

She closed her eyes and concentrated, forming a diamond-like crystal in her hand. She then reached out with her mind, looking for differing brain-wave patterns, looking for the rarities of the universe that seemed to breed so naturally on this planet.

Surprisingly, her mind butted up against a different mind in a matter of nanoseconds. Her eyes snapped open. It must be there, in that very structure in which she stood. She turned slowly, her eyes taking in everything.

She noticed a corridor that seemed to be in the correct direction, so she began moving that way. It was a short corridor with one entryway blocked by a door on each side. V'Let ignored these and continued into the large room at the end of the corridor.

The first thing she noticed was a medium-sized semi-transparent globe. It looked big enough that, if she were to try to pick it up, she would need both of her hands and possibly her arms as well. She blinked and looked away from the globe, noticed that unlike the rest of the house, the floor in this room was hard and the room itself was empty. Looking down, she gazed at the person on the floor. It seemed distinctly male and he seemed dead as well as unconscious.

She smiled and uncurled her hand, letting the crystal drop to the floor. As it made contact with the wood, it solidified and took on a purple tint before bouncing toward the man. On its last leap, it bent on an axis and dived point first into his forehead. It burrowed in, causing a small bleed.

V'Let watched in amazement as the small wound healed almost instantaneously behind the crystal. That had definitely never happened before. She smiled to herself as she turned away, allowing herself to follow the line back to her actual body. This mission might actually turn out to be interesting rather than just depressing and difficult.

Just as she returned her body, Erik's eyes snapped open, his normally dark blue eyes now having an inner ring of V'Let's own cerulean blue. His pupils flashed deep purple as the small connection crystal reached one of the targeted regions of his brain. He stood quickly, sensing another presence, but calmed minutely when he didn't see anyone.

On the spaceship, V'Let wilted into unconsciousness with a soft *thud* as her head hit the cargo floor limply.

Erik frowned to himself, feeling that something was very off. He stalked through the house several times, searching for a clue of anything amiss. The air seemed disturbed but there were no signs of someone having been there. It felt like there was something crawling under his skin, violating his person and causing him no insignificant amount of unease. He clenched his fist and growled low in his throat, knowing something was wrong but having absolutely no idea what it could be.

After a moment, he forced himself to relax, thinking it was possible that he needed to feed. It was also possible that he needed to find Rosalie, though that would happen in due time. He vaguely remembered a large amount of fear, though he couldn't pin down the source for the life of him. Not knowing seemed to make the feeling build, adding fuel to the sense of something being off. Knowing himself the way he did, though, he knew he did not deal well with not knowing. It was a flaw.

He grinned viciously, thinking he could take out some of his frustration on the remaining members of Luna Morte. He could turn this into a good night.

# CHAPTER TEN

Rosalie followed Quin along the shoreline, wondering the whole way what the Crone could possibly want with her. She knew she didn't have the talent to be a witch. Whatever power she did possess was all diverted into the damned sanity-stealing planeswalking. She ground her teeth together, trying to keep all of her attention on the Material Realm as the mere thought of the other planes attempted to drag her mind away.

Ahead of the petite planeswalker, Quin walked briskly, wanting to get this part of his night to be over. When the Crone got involved, it meant things were getting serious. When things got serious, well… that was when Quin usually decided it was time to hightail it out of wherever he happened to be. Serious happenings meant death and bloodshed and violence and there was no way he was getting caught in that.

No way.

Quin shook his head slightly, concentrating on his task once more. For now, he was the Crone's whipping boy, for however long that lasted. He would take the young planeswalker with the weird power to her and he would do whatever she asked him because she paid him. Then, when things shifted from merely dangerous to inevitably deadly, he would leave before he could get killed.

He heard a throaty chuckle on the air suddenly, causing him to focus again. The Crone's house was just up ahead and she was standing on the porch, laughing. The house itself was a brown A-frame structure with an unstable-looking porch. From experience, Quin knew the house was quite sturdy and much bigger on the inside than out. Much like the Crone herself. The witch herself was slightly hunched with age, making her height slightly above the five foot marker. Her skin was deeply wrinkled and the color of chalk and her silver hair was pulled back into a loose bun today.

Even from several yards away, Quin could see the cloudy blue of the Crone's eyes, denoting her blindness. If she hadn't ever practiced magic, he knew her eyes would instead be a milky white because he had seen it that way in humans and nonhumans alike. Her particular brand of calm, balanced magic infused her eyes with that unnerving blue color.

Quin rolled his eyes imperceptibly at himself. *Says the demon with the flat black eyes.*

"Welcome," the Crone called out to them cheerily. As they reached the steps to the porch, she seemed to look hard at Rosalie. "Good, planeswalker. You've seen the Oracles." She smiled to herself before turning to enter her home. "At least two of them."

Rosalie cast a sidelong glance at Quin. "How'd she know that?" she hissed.

Quin shrugged, holding the door to the house open for the girl. "Same way she knows everything else, I'd gather."

Rosalie seemed to sigh. "This is going to be weird, isn't it?" Then she gasped as she stepped inside the doorway, having seen the inside of the house and the impossible size of it.

Quin grinned and closed the door with a click behind him. "It always is for me."

They passed out of the foyer into another room, one in which the Crone was sitting at a table with a calming smile on her face. Quin shook his head lightly to himself. As serious as the woman could be, she had a tendency to act more like a Maiden than a Crone the rest of the time.

The Crone's smile brightened as they came closer. "Welcome, planeswalker, to my sitting room!"

Rosalie smiled shyly at the old witch. She sat down gingerly in a chair at the table and waited. Quin noticed idly that she seemed to have a strange amount of focus on the here and now.

The Crone's face hardened and Quin knew she was slipping into a severity that scared some witches, the very persona of the Crone Witch. He hoped it didn't scare Rosalie away; he hoped she was made of sterner stuff.

"Do you know me, planeswalker?" The Crone's voice seemed to echo ominously through the room.

Rosalie gulped, her eyes shifting to Quin for half a moment before concentrating on the witch in front of her. "Yes, you are the Crone, the Matriarch to all witches current and past."

"I, Matlinda Bethlyn, Crone of All Witches, have called you to me, Rosalie McGrath, Walker of the Realms. Do you know why?"

"I do not."

"There is a cataclysm coming. You are somehow at or near the center of it."

Rosalie's brow furrowed in confusion. "How? Does this have anything to do with what the Oracles told me?"

The Crone tilted her head at the planeswalker. "What did the Oracles tell you?"

"They called them the Galaxy Killers, someone that's destroying planets. But they said they were bound somehow. Could someone be forcing them?"

The Crone nodded, as if to herself, tapping some of the crystals on her table. She picked up a rather large crystal, seeming to gaze into it for a moment. "That much may be true, child, but it may well not. Much of it is very clouded." She turned the crystal in her hands, looking at it from a different angle. After a moment, she finally set the crystal back on the table and rested her eyes directly on Rosalie. "I'll need you back here in a few days for some protection amulets. Until then, you should stay close to your pet vampire. Whatever is going to happen, these planet destroyers may be fast approaching."

Rosalie shook her head and stood, attempting to sort through everything the Crone had told her. "So, they're coming here, then?"

The Crone smiled mirthlessly. "Yes, they are. That much, I do know. They may very well be here within the month." She sighed, her face creased in worry. "I wish I knew more."

Rosalie reached down and laid her hand on top of the old woman's own, desperately trying to tamp down on her own panic. "I'm sure you'll be able to find out more." She looked at the door leading to the foyer, knowing it was already well dark outside. "Erik has probably gone hunting. Do you think you can tell me where he is?"

The Crone nodded, picking up a much smaller crystal. She floated her hand over it, closing her eyes in concentration. "Looks like he's coming up on Luna Morte's territory, on the edge of the bay. He seems angry."

Rosalie furrowed her brow, concerned for a moment, before clearing her face. She turned to Quin. "I have to go through a section of their territory on the way home from here anyway. Can you take me to Erik, Q?"

Quin nodded in resignation. He wasn't exactly the best demon to be protecting a young woman from those vicious vampires. He had to concede, however, that he did have some demonic powers of his own. Erik could probably protect them coming out of the vamp territory anyway. Quin had seen what he had done to the vampires that got near or threatened Rosalie.

"Sure, if it's all right with Crone Bethlyn."

The Crone nodded. "I'll need to speak with you when you return, Quin."

"Yes, ma'am." Both Quin and Rosalie exited the house as the Crone went back to examining the crystals. Once they were both outside, the demon looked down at the petite planeswalker. "You know, Luna Morte's territory is quite large. How will we find Erik? Because there are some pretty nasty characters, especially in the bay."

Rosalie looked up at him, a twinkle in her eye. "I have an idea." She grabbed Quin's hand and they blinked out of sight.

# CHAPTER ELEVEN

Mallik stood at the Council's mainframe console that was stationed in the Freti Galaxy, staring at the screen absent-mindedly. He had searched down every bare fact of Earth that he could find, everything from their own reported history of the Anglo-Saxons to their most recent use of hazardous or toxic weaponry. He also included a list of the eight hundred and nine protected species that resided on the planet, as well as a footnote of hybrid species that may also qualify to be protected if the Council would bring their attention to them.

He rubbed his temples idly, still suffering from the painful "hangover" from his personal encounter with the Separator. It was so utterly odd, now that he actually bothered to think about it. He knew his strong suspicions about the three Council members that the Looran twins called the "Adepts" had firm ground upon which to stand but in front of that large, formidable, annoying machine, all those thoughts had seemed so silly and preposterous.

Of course, the guise that this particular subspace message stood behind had to be Mallik's best idea yet. Every protected planet had to have an annual report submitted to the Council. It would be submitted to every member of the Council as well as the scribes but there was a hidden recipient in the message, all traces of which would disappear once one of the twins actually received the message and uploaded it permanently into their ship's hard drive.

He knew that it would look suspicious to both Head Council member Gralug and all three of the Adepts, especially because he had decided to send it while he was supposed to be busy with the somewhat vicious political disputes that were currently running rampant through the Beta

Sector. It seemed to concentrate from the Freti Galaxy, so that's where he was. It was times like this that he was supremely glad to be the Diplomacy Elder. It gave his freedom to be away when that was the best place to be and the state of mind to think through all sides of an argument.

This Adept business, however, kept him quite flummoxed. Why were they demanding that the twins destroy planets as a whole and what exactly did they have to gain from it?

# CHAPTER TWELVE

Erik stalked through Luna Morte's territory, something nagging at his brain the whole way. Something was off, something was wrong. That was all he could think. He needed to kill something and nothing could be more effective or productive than a member of his old gang.

*Stop. Breathe,* a soft voice whispered inside his head. He halted abruptly then, just stopped almost mid-step. After a moment of absolutely no thought caused by pure shock, he moved to a nearby shadow as a human couple crossed what would have been his path almost three seconds prior. He leaned against the brick building next to which he found himself.

"Who are you?" he asked softly, so softly that he barely heard the words.

*Relax.*

His brow furrowed as he concentrated on the voice. He could feel the burning need for violence fade away, realizing with a sigh that some pressure inside his head was lifting. "You sound like the globe, before I fainted earlier." The anger was gone, replaced with curious wonder and an odd giddiness. Now that he thought about it, he could remember the fear, though he still had no rational cause. However, like the anger, it was long gone in the presence of this voice.

There was something that sounded like a laugh. In the back of his mind, Erik thought to himself that this was very odd. He was talking to himself, maybe a feminine version of himself. Maybe this was the kind of crazy that Rosalie felt when she was seeing too many planes at once.

*I'm real. I'm not you.*

"You can hear my thoughts." It was a solid enough argument for him.

*I made a Connection with you.*

Erik could hear how she capitalized the term, even mentally. "Do I know you? Rosalie couldn't do that, wouldn't do it anyway."

*Rosalie? A planeswalker? That's interesting.* The voice fell away, making slight sounds around Erik seem deafening. About a mile away, he could hear a faint *pop* and somehow knew it was important. *You don't know me yet.*

A few minutes passed and Erik knew the voice was gone. He didn't know whether to be disappointed or relieved and it occurred to him that he may have imagined the whole thing. He tried for a moment to regain his angry momentum toward his old gang but the frustrations were gone as if carried away by the wind.

He stood away from the brick, idly brushing bits of dust off his clothing. Earlier, he could remember the rage in his blood, the absolute *need* to feed. Now, however, everything seemed quelled, as if he would never need to feed again. It was disconcerting, being a vampire without the bloodthirst and all the things that came with it.

He stepped out of the shadows and bumped into someone almost immediately. He shook his head, berating himself for not paying attention. "I apologize," he started, automatically slipping into the kind of language from when he was human.

"So much for unearthly grace, huh?"

Erik snapped his focus then, seeing Rosalie's familiar face and the fidgeting blue demon behind her. He let a smirk slide on his face. "You know me, I was just thinking."

Rosalie smiled. "And, of course, that takes all of your concentration."

"Of course," he replied good-naturedly. His smile drooped slightly when he remembered exactly where they were. His forehead creased as he looked at the unlikely duo. "What are you two doing in Luna Morte territory?"

Quin laughed nervously, his eyes darting around and every inch of him quivering in obvious fear. "Looking for you. The Crone said you were near the bay."

"Ah, Madame Bethlyn. How is she?"

Quin tried to smile but failed, giving the vampire a trembling façade instead. "Fine. She wanted to talk to Rosalie about some upcoming nastiness."

"Oh?" Erik arched an eyebrow at Rosalie, the question clear on his face.

"I'll tell you when we get home," she promised.

Quin squeaked timidly. "Speaking of, can we go there now? Preferably walking and not on other planes?"

Erik chuckled and clapped the demon on the shoulder, leading them out of the vampire gang's territory in the same move. "Don't worry, Q. I remember what it's like. Rosalie just can't see that dark void between the realms."

Quin shivered slightly, remembering the lack of senses and lack of himself. "I don't ever want to do that ever again. Ever."

Rosalie looked at the vampire and demon. "What is this void you speak of?"

Erik shook his head. "Let's just get home, okay?"

Rosalie harrumphed but nodded nonetheless.

# CHAPTER THIRTEEN

V'Let laid flat on the floor of the cargo bay, staring at the very high ceiling. As soon as she'd become aware of herself again, she knew that the connection crystal had somehow gone wrong. She hadn't anticipated this being's healing capacity properly, mostly due to the fact that she had chosen a species with accelerated partial-regeneration ability.

*Stupid, stupid, stupid!*

She'd had to force herself immediately into another deep trance, though this one was much more controlled than the one she use to connect with another being. The connection crystal had gotten stuck in his limbic system, just barely far enough into the cerebrum to afford her his vision. He had been running off instinct and anger and memories that fueled both. She'd locked herself deep in his brain, concentrating on pushing the crystal past his center for self-awareness and nearer to his pleasure center. For a moment, nothing had happened. She knew it was because he was so angry, which kept absolutely everything on that particular emotion.

Then she had spoken to him. Boy, would that have been so completely stupid if it hadn't actually worked! It had, though; it had shocked him into completely stopping, into pushing himself physically into the shadows, which in retrospect was an odd reaction. From there, the crystal moved smoothly to the back of his brain. She hadn't pulled out then, though, and that had been immensely foolish. She couldn't resist sifting through a complacent mind after all. She'd learned a few things, mainly about his personality and the planeswalker he had for a friend.

She sat up abruptly, shaking her head. It could have been a complete disaster and it would have been all her fault. She was trying to forget about it but shame was a familiar friend and guilt a confidante.

V'Let resigned herself to going back to the bridge to relieve her brother. She'd technically been unconscious for five hours and it would be several hours yet before she would be calm enough to sleep.

When she reached the bridge, she steeled herself and brushed aside the shame and guilt once again. She came up behind her brother, placing her hands on his shoulders, and focused on the navigational screen. It read that they were closing in on twelve cycles remaining but there was also some activity happening below the destination countdown.

"What's going on?" she asked softly. She focused on the seemingly random numbers flowing across the screen. "Is that an upload?"

"Yeah, Mallik came through." D'Las entered a few more commands into the console, finishing the upload. He stood finally, stretching, before turning to look at V'Let. His eyes drilled into her own, both a perfect reflection of the other. "You did something bad," he whispered.

V'Let cast her gaze at the floor beneath her, openly displaying her dismay. "I had to. It was the only way."

D'Las grabbed her hand with one of his own while using the other to lift her chin. He gave her a small smile of encouragement and led them to sit on the floor of the bridge. "What happened?"

"Well, you know I wouldn't be able to resist making the connection to one of the protected," she started, pausing when he chuckled. She rewarded him with a wry smile and continued. "It was surprisingly easy; he was even already unconscious. Maybe it was too easy. He healed almost immediately after the crystal cut into his skull. It was so… interesting at the time." She took a breath, letting her eyes meet her brother's again. "I was most of the way out of the trance when I realized that something had gone wrong, really wrong. Because of these abnormal healing abilities, the crystal had stopped halfway to the pleasure center, had gotten stuck in the anger center of his brain. I had to go back under and force the crystal, guide it manually."

D'Las arched an eyebrow at her when she stopped. "Is that all?"

V'Let shook her head slowly. "I had to talk to him."

D'Las's eyes widened, alarm seeping into his eyes. "What? Why?"

"The crystal was lodged in the anger center of his limbic region. While he had all his mental capacity aiding all that anger—which, by the way, he had a lot—the crystal would not move. I don't have much telekinetic ability across that much space!" She stopped, breathed once in through her nose and out through her mouth. "I had to shock him."

D'Las whistled a long, low note, his brow furrowed for a moment. "Did it work?"

V'Let grinned. "Yeah, it worked. I'm pretty sure he thinks I'm just a voice in his head."

A laugh escaped D'Las suddenly. "I've heard your mental voice, sis. There's no way you can sound like a male, no matter the species."

V'Let shrugged her shoulders. "He thought I might be his feminine side or something. From what could pick up, there's a lot of psychology running around that planet." She stood up and moved to the console. "I know it's not really that bad, just bending the boundaries of a bond a little. But I still feel bad, like I ruined his privacy."

D'Las came up behind his sister, circling her shoulders in a tight hug and pecking the high point of her cheekbone. "It'll be okay." Knowing his sister like he did, he knew that she needed something to distract from her massive guilt complex. "Why don't you decrypt the upload?" He gave her another encouraging smile as she sat at the console, the centermost point of the bridge. "I'll start the report and then get some sleep."

"I'll be awake for a while," V'Let told her brother, most of her mind already navigating the program to decrypt the information that Mallik had sent them.

"I know," he replied. He stifled a yawn as he started the report on their secondary console. The report would consist of all the things illegal of which the planet Earth could stand accused, not that they could ever attempt to contest these accusations. That was the purpose of what the Adepts were doing. They found planets that were subpar, technologically speaking, and could easily be accused of abusing the planet or a reportedly violent species that needed to be rooted out and punished. Killing the planet, however, removed all traces of everything and the fact that he and his sister were the ones to obliterate these places left the Adepts guilt-free in all senses of the word.

Not for the first time, D'Las wished they could be free of them and that damned contract.

# CHAPTER FOURTEEN

Marina DuPont traced the edge of her wineglass, her mind far away from the half-empty bottle of Voo wine. It was from one of the planets that she and her male counterparts had demanded that the twins destroy. It had been a planet of complete indifference, the likes of which she had never seen. Being immersed in the media and having almost daily contact with the worst publicity whores of the universe, she had seen plenty of indifference. Planet Vow's wine was superb; the fruits they used had just the right balance of stinging sweet and puckering sour. The wine seemed to be all they cared about.

She sipped demurely from her glass. It was good wine.

She felt she was getting old. She had now seen over seventy rotations and she was the youngest of the Adepts. Dmitri was just over seventy-five rotations of age and Xavier was eighty-three. They had been lucky with the decimation of the planet Lora twenty rotations ago. They had razed the surface of that planet, knowing it was filled with a species known for their mental capacity. They were a very large threat to the ultimate goal of the Adepts. She was thankful that that particular species had never been politically inclined.

It had actually been the destruction of a species to which a member of the Council belonged that made the Intergalactic Council stop their "well-meaning" campaign against the "threats of the universe". It was the reason the Adepts now believed in research, despite the mistakes of their youth.

The twins, oddly enough, survived the razing like some kind of Messiah. They were so young, so malleable when the Adepts had found them. As the Looran attempt had actually been a last hoorah, the Adepts stopped attacking species with "reports" of violence to train the twins to continue in their footsteps should they... expire.

If not for their genetic memory and the strict morale of their culture, it could have been done easily. Marina herself had almost persuaded them over to the Adept way of thinking in the beginning. It had ended like a dream, though, with the twins supporting each other in doing the right thing. It had been a disgusting display.

Marina grabbed the bottle of wine, tipping it to refill her glass. The dark red liquid flowing into the clear container reminded her of blood, such as the blood that bound the twins to them. The twins had been resolute in their decision to stay away from the killing business, which they had known was under every explanation the Adepts had used from the very beginning. There was no hiding anything from the little beasts, their abilities being what they were. In the end, there had to be some very complicated subterfuge.

The twins were sent away with Dmitri, who had wholly objected to the idea. He felt it would all be much easier if they were agreeable. His idea had been to keep them on strong drugs, drugs that would keep them easily controlled. These drugs were much too easily tracked, as they were not yet approved by the Medical Elder, and the side effects were unpredictable.

While the twins were training on whatever deity-forsaken planet Dmitri had taken them, Xavier and Marina came up with a plan. The plans for their Separator in all its massive glory were years from fruition but they did have some prototypes that could do roughly the same. It interfered with the communication on the same general wavelength on which the twins could hear the thoughts of others.

When the twins returned, they attached the devices to the napes of their necks. The devices themselves seemed insignificant—small and silver, they clasped onto the nearest nerve ending to tap into the entire system. It would hinder their ability to "hear", making everything they did pick up sound muffled and distorted. They could only hope that they didn't notice.

Marina was disappointed when it was all over. The contract was complicated, a document that she had taken pains to word very specifically in the twins' absence. They were charged with the responsibility of the universe, ridding it of threats to the safety of all; they had to pursue every assignment they were given by the Adepts; they had to follow the bylaws of the campaign that had recently been headed by the Adepts, which made punishment unbelievably harsh. The contract itself was a Blood

Contract. They were illegal now but it was the last reasonable resort to make the twins do what they wanted. It was signed using fresh blood, the contract tying every aspect of itself into that person's very being. The Blood Contract was a living, breathing document and a harsh mistress.

The girl had persuaded the boy that it was okay to sign it. Marina never knew why and most days didn't care. She didn't know how far back the genetic memory stretched or how much of everything either of the children actually knew and understood. She wondered if they'd signed up for this on purpose, if they were dead inside with the thought of being the last of their kind, of a strong and proud species.

Marina moved to refill her wineglass again, realizing with a numb kind of wonder that the bottle was empty. She had more, many more, but she just set her glass down and leaned her head back on the couch. Their plans were coming to a slow boil, she thought, but there had been some unforeseen interferences. Like that man, Mallik. He had come to investigate the "Adepts" and thus the twins had to be punished. They were sent to Earth, the protected planet, the one to be protected above all others.

She massaged her temples as she felt herself losing consciousness. Things were becoming quite complicated and she thought, not for the first time, that they were running out of time.

# CHAPTER FIFTEEN

Three days had passed and the time had come for Rosalie to go back to the Crone's house. She supposed the talismans would be ready but she waited patiently for the sun to drop below the horizon, taking a seat on their porch swing. It would be a few hours, she knew, before Erik would appear. It may not kill them but she knew vampires hated the brightness of the sun. Erik usually got grumpy every single time he accidentally woke up before sunset.

"Usually" was the operative word there. Lately, he had been different. There was lightness to him now, like he was content. She wasn't sure where it came from, though she was sure that it had come on the heels of some deep-seated anger. Because his anger was a large part of who Erik was, it was like he was a completely different person.

The front door creaked open, catching Rosalie's attention. Erik peeked his head out the door, cringing slightly at the light. Rosalie watched in amazement, as she always did, as his pupils shrank to the size of pinpricks, letting his irises almost completely overtake his eyes. He exited the house in one fluid motion, closing the door behind him, and sat next to Rosalie on the swing.

"So, when do you want to go to the Crone's?" he asked her mildly, his eyes calmly watching the horizon.

Rosalie glanced over at her vampiric friend, suspicion marring her face. "Is there something wrong with you?" she blurted out suddenly.

Erik looked at Rosalie curiously, tilting his head at her. "What do you mean?"

She stood, a clear sign of an oncoming rant. "My god, Erik! You're happy. And your eyes are weird. You came out in the sun!" She made a wide gesture at the horizon, noting that sunset was still hours away.

Erik shrugged, his face a good-natured mask. "It won't kill me, you know that as well as I do. Lately, it doesn't even seem to bother me that much. And is it really so bad for me to be happy?"

Rosalie sputtered for a moment. "Well… no. But… you're never happy! Ever!" She paced in front of the vampire. "I haven't seen you feed in the past few days either."

Again, that nonchalant shrug. "Haven't needed to."

Rosalie stopped her pacing to breathe for a moment. "Fine, whatever. Let's go to the Crone's."

Erik smiled brightly at his friend. "Jeez, Rosalie, calm down. Everything will be fine."

She grumbled to herself before responding. "If you don't recall, there is a possible alien invasion headed this way. Aliens that even the Oracles know very little about."

Erik chuckled. "Well, there is that."

Rosalie suppressed her urge to shriek in frustration.

# CHAPTER SIXTEEN

D'Las trudged on to the bridge, rubbing the sleep out of his eyes. He felt extremely refreshed, as if he had slept for days.

"You have," he heard his sister declare as she jumped from the central console to the secondary console. "Nearly three whole days, in fact." She turned her gaze to him, her fingers still flying across the keyboard. "You must have been tired."

"Three days?!" he exclaimed, looking at the destination countdown to be sure. It read just short of nine cycles. "Are you sure you just didn't find a way for us to get there faster?" He knew sometimes his sister relied on the countdown for time.

She arched an eyebrow at him before turning her eyes back to the secondary console. "As our trajectory, route and speed have not been altered, I would say yes, I am quite sure. You sleep too much."

"Ha ha," he muttered in response. He sat at the central console, the dregs of sleep leaving him. "How could you let me sleep so long?"

V'Let scoffed at him as she sank into the chair at the secondary console, spinning to face him as she finished entering data. "When we aren't entering data, this ship could be run with half a person with an arm tied behind their back. Especially when we're in hyperspace."

D'Las smiled at his sister. "I imagine you took the encryption off Mallik's message and went through it already?"

"That and I sifted through the memories of my bond."

"You've been busy," he remarked. "You want to brief me on it?"

V'Let nodded a little over-brightly and walked over to the central console, pressing a button. Their countdown was replaced with a satellite image of Earth. "Earth is seventy percent water, most of it saltwater, with almost every type of terrain you can think of: tundra, desert, jungle, swamps and so on and so forth." The Earth was then obscured with pinpoints of lights, some yellow or white but mostly black. In fact, there was so much black, it was like someone had blighted the surface of planet. "Most of the inhabitants of the planet can be split into one of three categories: fey, demon, or human. There are some exceptions and some hybrids, I imagine," she murmured as an afterthought.

From the way his sister had said *human*, D'Las guessed that they were the blight of black and the main reason why this protected planet could become an assignment for them. "The humans first, Letta. Let us air the dirty laundry."

V'Let smiled at her brother, the smile turning to a grimace as soon as the screen changed. The screen was filled with numbers and notes, most of which made shame and sadness fill her at once. "The humans are corrupt, like the Adepts are corrupt. They seek power—over the soil, over the species they consider lesser, even over each other. They have split the planet's land into over two hundred separate sovereignties. They have had countless wars, some over a nonexistent catalyst, most over religion. Religion is a great motivator, it seems, for violence and strife." She took a breath for a moment. "According to Mallik's report, they have even destroyed massive amounts of their own human culture in the name of these wars."

D'Las bowed his head, his mind swimming in a deep pool of rage. He could see things in V'Let's mind, the things she wasn't saying. He could see explosions, a mushroom cloud of destructive radiation. He had the knowledge of genocide, of mob mentality becoming a cruel and vicious weapon. He imagined he could see into the eyes of these humans, see the darkness that abided there. They could not know that they had passed the point of no return.

"It's enough," he declared hoarsely. "I don't want to hear about them anymore."

V'Let walked up to her brother and ruffled his fine lavender hair. "I know this rage, brother, but you have to step down on it now."

He shook his head violently. "We should just destroy it from here!" he exploded, a dark destructive force now present in his blue eyes.

She hugged him tightly, holding him down with her own embrace. "Sh-sh-sh!" she hushed him calmly. She blasted his mind with wave after wave of clear memories of their mother and father, calming and happy images that seemed to tamp down the rage.

"We should, Letta," he said again in a much smaller voice. "They're too destructive, too malicious."

"We can't, Lasso." She let go of her brother, smiling encouragement at him, and returned to her briefing of the planet. The screen now showed a massive, dark red creature with fierce horns and cloven hooves. "This is a 'typical' demon. They tend to be a fierce species in both appearance and behavior and are very territorial." The screen changed again, showing a lithe figure with flowing white hair and silver eyes. "This is a 'typical' fey. They are long-lived and also quite territorial."

"I assume these take up most of the protected species?" V'Let nodded to her brother's question. "If they're so territorial, how did the humans manage to take over most of Earth?"

V'Let smirked. "It seems the humans can breed much more with much quicker gestation periods than the protected species. In the millennia since their evolution, the humans have managed to take up every corner of this planet and they're actually starting to run out of room."

D'Las furrowed his brow, concern washing over his face. "Do they have the technology to inhabit other planets?"

V'Let shook her head to the negative. "Not yet. They've been trying, it seems, for a while. Once they reach a certain point, disaster strikes—sometimes in unusual ways."

"Really?"

"I think the Council has been hindering them from too much progress. Especially the way they do progress." V'Let grimaced.

D'Las arched an eyebrow at his sister, urging her to explain.

"Yet another thing that is destroying their planet." She breathed in and then out, pulling more information about Earth and its crimes from her mind. "Their technology uses almost strictly metal, the mining of which hurts the atmosphere. They also use combustion over fusion because, apparently, they want to run through all their fossil fuels before using anything they would have readily available. They rip up the land and tear through the atmosphere just for the sake of progress."

"Gods above," D'Las muttered. "What are we going to do?"

"Well, there is a piece of good news," V'Let chirped, trying to force a happy tone.

"And that would be?"

"You know that species of growth that was on the other protected planet?"

"You mean those insanely tall trees?"

"Yeah." V'Let reached and pressed another button on the console. "The Earth inhabitants call them redwoods. They generally grow on the west coast of a country in the western hemisphere. I thought we might land there."

D'Las grinned momentarily and nodded, actually happy for this particular turn in events. He blinked then as something clicked in his head. "Well, that makes sense."

V'Let cleared away her presentation, taking the screen back to the countdown. "What does?"

"We never got a heavy punishment for destroying that protected planet. We just stay out of the Central Planets on our own. And the Adepts want us to stay away, of course."

V'Let shrugged. "They must have known they had backup."

D'Las chuckled. "Indeed." He steepled his fingers and rested his chin against them, trying to settle his brain a little bit. "What about your bond?"

She laughed to herself for a moment. "That was a little hard for me to get through, actually."

D'Las looked at his sister closely. Now he was beginning to see the wear of heavy research and hard truths on her face. "Why?" He decided that after she explained everything to him, he would make her go to sleep.

V'Let cast a knowing look at her brother but continued in the original vein anyhow. "What I connected to isn't actually a protected species at all but a hybrid of a blood demon and a human. They call themselves vampires. They need to drink blood to survive. They're very nearly immortal, it seems, and can only die if someone or something sets out to kill them purposely. They're extremely photosensitive and generally vicious. I believe that's the human in them, mixing its own brand of cruelty to the demon's territoriality."

D'Las furrowed his brow. It seemed the hybrids could be dangerous, almost as dangerous at the humans themselves. "And what about this particular 'vampire'?"

"His name is Erik von Telford, born a human more than three hundred years ago, turned into a vampire about twenty years after that."

"Wait, wait. Three hundred years?!" D'Las exclaimed, a high note sneaking its way into his voice.

V'Let rolled her eyes. "Do the terms 'long-lived' or 'nearly immortal' mean nothing to you?"

"Well, yeah, it means something. But I thought you meant a hundred and fifty years at best."

V'Let massaged her temples, sighing in frustration at her brother. "We have been around species with shorter lifespans for too long. Most of the species on Earth are long-lived like we are long-lived."

"But… Loorans can live for millennia, if we so choose. We were just not prepared for what happened… before."

Both V'Let and D'Las flinched visibly. Neither one liked to remember the decimation for their species, the razing of their home planet. As such, they moved past it again without a word and V'Let continued. "Erik has knowledge but not actual memory of the wars before their second World War."

"Second?!"

"D'Las, let me finish."

"How many have they had? World wars are serious business, V'Let."

"They had two. May I continue?"

D'Las grumbled to himself but nodded.

"Okay, for most of his existence as a vampire, he lived in a secret vampire community, hidden from the humans. He did become rather vicious, as some vampires seem to have to be to survive. He killed the vampire that turned him. He ruled over this vampire community until the force behind the second World War began to encroach on his area. Instead of striking back at the humans, he dispersed the community and escaped to the Americas. He and some of his former subjects formed what he calls a 'vampire gang', overtaking a good portion of a beach city in northern California. He met a planeswalker and then abandoned his gang, which seems to have been a bone of contention ever since."

"A planeswalker?" D'Las asked.

V'Let nodded, her eyes rolling up as her mind searched for the details again. "Yeah, he's not entirely sure how she can do it—something about a curse, I think? But this girl can visit the planes of existence that run parallel to our own."

"That's new."

V'Let yawned largely, realizing that the three days of doing too much was quickly catching up with her. "I imagine you or I could do it but it seems like something that's not really worth the concentration it would take."

D'Las smiled at his sister and stepped down from the central console.

He began to guide her to her bunk. "Did you take care of the crystal, then?"

"I sent the command for it to dissolve across his brain a few hours ago but it still might be a bit before it reaches their area of space." She yawned again and pushed on the door to her bunk. "Oh, and they know we're coming."

D'Las had turned to go back to the bridge but quickly spun to face his sister again. "What?! How can they know? They don't have the tech to receive those transmissions. Right?"

"Yep," she responded blearily. "Rosalie, the planeswalker, talked to some Oracles or something." She smiled at D'Las. "Relax, brother. All they know is the Galaxy Killers are coming to Earth. Being what they are, they're thinking some huge alien invasion, for some unknown reason. We're flying low and quiet and we're not invading."

"Well, sister, what are we going to do?"

She giggled softly, losing parts of her conscious mind while on her feet. "I will figure that out. Y'know, after sleep." She disappeared into her bunk, the door thunking closed behind her.

D'Las knew that, for now, their discussion was over and he continued back to the bridge.

# CHAPTER SEVENTEEN

"What do we need these talismans for again?" Erik asked Rosalie, blinking quickly against the brightness of the sunlight.

Rosalie looked at her friend, noticing his rapid blinking. "You know, we could have waited until nightfall, you big galoot."

Erik blinked hard, his eyes watering now. "No, I'm good. It's just kinda bright. How far away from Matlinda's are we now?"

Rosalie looked around a moment, noticing that they had in fact passed the pier. "It's still about another mile. Erik, are you sure you're okay?"

Erik visibly glanced around, trying to ignore the tears running down his face. He wasn't embarrassed about this display at all, nope. All he could see was everything around him covered in too-bright yellow, the edges of his vision becoming dark red. Everything was definitely too bright, perhaps he should have waited, and he thought maybe someone had set fire to his brain.

Rosalie watched Erik's face, knowing that despite the fact that the sun hadn't been hurting him lately he was definitely in pain now. "We could take the Dark Plains. Erik?"

He could see a fire and explosions in the distance. What was going on? Why would someone try to do that? He could hear crying and there was a woman screaming. He heard words in a strange language but he could understand parts of it. However, his pain was too great and everything was trying to fade into dark gray until all feeling was numbed.

Rosalie grabbed hold of Erik's hand, her brain panicking in worry. She concentrated on the shadowy plains and valleys of the Realm of Darkness. She knew it would be better in the dark, even if what looked like pain across his face remained.

The solidity of their bodies wobbled and disappeared, transferring completely from the Material Plane to the Dark Plains. Rosalie stood very still, thinking for a moment that this might have been a very bad idea. She normally only came here to talk to Senka and, half the time, she didn't even materialize completely. There were very dangerous things in the shadows, she knew, and she was probably out of the range of the Oracle, even if Senka would deign to protect a mortal in the first place.

She turned back to the vampire, attempting to judge his state. He was focusing on her again, though she could still see a large amount of something in his eyes, something that was either pain or anguish. "I could hear screaming," he murmured.

"There was no screaming," she replied. "What's wrong?"

"Something was happening, I don't know." Erik sniffled and she realized that he was still crying, though it had slowed. "My head hurts."

"There's someone in there," a voice whispered softly.

Rosalie snapped attention back to her surroundings. "Senka?" she called out.

A woman coalesced before them. She was tall with dark olive skin and long, shiny black hair. There was a cruel smile in her face, shining with sadism that could only be the Oracle of Darkness. She walked up to the vampire, tilting her head ever so slightly and reaching out to tap his forehead lightly. "Isn't there?"

Erik pulled back for a moment before Rosalie reached out to grip his arm to hold him in place. She didn't want the Oracle to be offended. It was an honor to be touched by an Oracle. She then nodded at him to answer—not answering could also be quite offensive. "I'm not sure," he ground out through clenched teeth.

"Oh," Senka purred. "You lie." She looked at Rosalie, smirking. "I can smell it," she stage-whispered conspiratorially.

"Tell the truth," Rosalie hissed at Erik.

"Well, this voice did speak to me. And I feel like someone's watching me."

Senka turned to Rosalie. "He's got one of them in his head, keeping him in a happy place."

Rosalie narrowed her eyes at the Oracle. "One of who?"

"The destroyers. She's trying to see from far away."

"She?" Rosalie exhaled roughly but she could feel panic ramping up in her head. "What are you talking about? Are you saying the Galaxy Killers are in his head?"

Erik glanced back and forth between the Oracle and his friend, his eyes narrowing the whole time. Anger mounted in his head until he almost couldn't stand it. "Whatever is or isn't in my head is not destructive!"

Rosalie looked at Erik, her gaze piercing. "How can you know?"

Erik glared back. "I just do. I know this more than I could ever know anything."

"She could be making you think this thought, know this knowledge."

Senka shushed them suddenly. "You should go back now, younglings. The light takers are coming." She made a shooing motion with her hands. "Stupid children," she muttered before fading away.

Rosalie sighed and grabbed Erik's hand, fading them out of the Dark Plane before the light takers could find them. When they were back on the Material Plane, they were standing in front of the Crone's home. Rosalie let go of Erik's hand quickly.

"Why didn't you tell me?"

"It didn't seem relevant, okay?" Erik rolled his eyes. "Whenever I would get angry, there would just be this voice calming me down. It was a good thing, right, I thought. It just wanted to know things sometimes."

"About us?" Rosalie demanded. "About Earth's weaknesses?"

Erik's brow furrowed. "No. About wars and humans. It would get angry at humans, I could feel it, but it doesn't seem to want control."

"We should talk to the Crone about this."

Erik looked at the house, seeing the witch-woman smiling at him through one of the windows. "There is a possibility that she already knows."

Rosalie turned her head to look at the house as well. "Let's go in, then." She turned on her heel and stalked into the house ahead of the vampire.

Erik shook his head and followed her. He could see images flashing just behind his vision, overlaying what he was actually seeing with horrible images and he was quite sure he could hear screaming. He did his best to push all of that to the back of his mind, though, as he entered the Crone's home.

Walking through the witch's front door, he saw Rosalie talking to the Crone, gesticulating wildly. The girl already had three amulets hanging around her neck, one of which was clearly to keep one from harm. Matlinda was trying to hide a grin as Rosalie talked.

"Did you make one for the house?" Erik asked when he met the Crone's eyes.

Matlinda held up a small satchel, shaking it playfully in his direction. He moved toward her and took it from her without comment. "Rosalie tells me you have an alien in your head?"

Erik shrugged, knowing full well that the Crone could see it in her own way. "That's what the Oracle said. I suppose you could check for yourself."

Matlinda smiled warmly at the vampire. "Yes, I suppose I could." She moved until she was fully in front of the vampire. She lifted her aged hands in front of his eyes and he dutifully closed them in response. He could feel the heat of her hands move over his eyelids, across his forehead and finally settle hovering less than a centimeter away from his temples. He could hear a low-level humming, exactly the same sound he had heard a few days prior. It jumped in pitch very slightly before settling down again.

Erik opened his eyes as he felt the Crone pull her hands away from his head. He saw that her brow was deeply creased in a furrow and she was holding her body a little more stiffly than normal. "Something wrong, Madame?"

Matlinda shook her head slowly, her physically sightless eyes darting less than momentarily in Rosalie's direction. "It was odd. I couldn't feel anything."

Erik looked past the Crone to look at Rosalie. She looked to be shifting, very nearly hopping, anxiously from foot to foot. "Maybe your Oracle was mistaken," he commented, letting a small amount of hope leak into his voice.

"The Oracles are never mistaken," she responded automatically. She removed two of the three amulets around her neck and handed them to Erik. Her movements were jerky and rushed, so he knew something was up. "The Prince of Realms is trying to call for me. I'll see you at home." With that said, she blinked out of existence on their plane.

Matlinda sniffed indignantly. "That was abrupt."

Erik moved to the table at the center of her sitting room and sat down. "When the Prince calls, everything else has to wait." He smiled at her as she sat as well. "What did you really feel?"

"It was nothing," the witch conceded. She sighed, reaching for the large crystal. "There wasn't anything there." She picked up the crystal and looked into it again, almost obsessively. "Like when I look into this crystal, looking for them. I just see static."

Erik slumped down in his seat, gazing sightlessly at the amulets in his hand. "So... I'm just going crazy, then?"

Matlinda turned her head sharply to look at him. "Not at all. There's nothing *now*," she stressed the last word. "There was an impression that something had been there."

Erik perked slightly, looking the Crone in the eye. "The voice is real?"

Matlinda gave him a small smile. "It probably is, or was. I imagine it might be gone now."

The vampire shook his head vehemently, his face having brightened considerably. "No, I don't think so."

The Crone tilted her head at him. "Why not?" The way he'd said it, there had to be a reason.

"I've been seeing things."

She leaned forward, concentrating on the vampire in front of her. "Tell me."

"I can't make much sense of it. For a while, it was overlaying everything I was seeing. There's a fire and I can see explosions. There's screaming in the distance and someone's crying. I hear a word—I don't know the word but it sounds like it could be 'mother', maybe."

Matlinda grinned. "Interesting."

Erik blinked, coming back to the present. "What?"

Matlinda touched Erik's forehead and chuckled in a low sound. "I think you're picking up memories."

# CHAPTER EIGHTEEN

Mallik yawned widely, reaching for a cup of java juice near his desk lamp. It was the only light on in the room. He was better at going over reports in near darkness. During these long negotiations, it gave him the illusion of getting some sleep. As it was, he was in the middle of his second day awake, the negotiations of the Freti Galaxy having gone long into the night. He was also well aware that this long stint of extended consciousness would not end until at least sunrise the next day.

"Gods above, I hate treaty negotiations," he muttered, bringing the cup to his lips.

"But you're so good at them, Mallik," a foreign voice commented, slicing neatly through the silence.

Without stress and exhaustion laying over him like a blanket, Mallik was naturally a high-strung, jumpy individual. Now, he had layers of stress—from the three-day negotiations with a group of civilizations that bordered on too violent to the fact that the twins, the Galaxy Killers that were publicly notorious for destroying planets without a second thought, were heading for Earth, the one planet that had to be protected above all others. Thus, he was not in a state to deal with surprises overly well.

He shrieked, sounding very much like his niece of thirteen rotations, and inadvertently flipped his cup of very hot java juice in the air. He jumped up at the liquid hit his lap, retaliating for the sudden movement.

"Ow!" he exclaimed, the pitch of his voice slowly lowering back to normal. "Ow! Hot! Overhead lights on!" He went straight for the sink and grabbed a small hand towel, dabbing delicately at his now-sensitive thigh and groin area. He turned slowly to take in the sight of his visitor. "Council Member Andian."

The man waved his hand in a dismissive gesture. "Call me Dmitri, please." He sat back in a chair in a corner of Mallik's quarters, steepling his hands with a smile on his face. Dmitri's particular species averaged out at a height of about five feet. They were easily spotted by their cloven feet and glowing eyes, the Tactical Elder's own being a deep green. Dmitri, however, always managed to carry all traits of his species with quiet dignity. "That was quite entertaining."

Mallik arched an eyebrow, moving to brew himself more java juice. "What are you doing in Beta Sector, Dmitri?"

Dmitri barked a short laugh, adding a level of intrigue to Mallik's attention. "Getting away from the scene of the crime." The comment was said with a dollop of conspiracy, a ghost of a smirk gracing his face.

Mallik turned back to the Council member, arching an eyebrow at him. "What crime?" He took the towel he had used to dry himself and applied to the mess he had made on and around his desk, making a disgusted face at the slight stickiness left behind. He moved quickly back to the sink to wet the towel, well aware that java could solidify very quickly. Normally, the cleaning bots would take care of this for him but they weren't allowed to enter this room—in fact, no one was. The Diplomacy Elder was to be left to solitude outside of negotiations during times of treaty. Which obviously led to the question: how did Dmitri enter this room, utterly and completely without his knowledge?

Returning to the desk, Mallik shoved the question aside for later and concentrated on quickly cleaning the java juice remains. He glanced up at Dmitri, noticing his expectant and amused expression, and realized that he must have missed a question.

"I'm sorry, what?"

Dmitri grinned, showing white teeth that gleamed in contrast to his dark brown skin. "I said, we're a bit removed from the Central Planets in Alpha Sector. Why don't you check your news feed?"

Mallik nodded idly. "Okay, just a minute."

Dmitri leaned forward, watching as the other man furiously attacked the mess of java. "You give obsessive compulsion new meaning."

Mallik scoffed. "I have no idea what you mean." He stood and stretched, smiling slightly as he heard a hollow pop from the general vicinity of his back. Satisfied, he retrieved his new cup of java and tossed the dirty towel in the trash compactor. He sat at his desk, setting his cup under the desk lamp again, and began to put the reports strewn across his desk into neat piles off to the side. Under all the paper was a computer system laid into the line of the desk.

Dmitri grinned enthusiastically, his eyes seeming to have gotten bigger. "The Multi-Processor 5000?"

Mallik glanced at the other man. "The 5600, actually. You said the news feed?"

Dmitri nodded idly, standing to look more closely at the system. "Sneaky bastards," he muttered under his breath, a smile on his face.

Mallik turned his attention away from the enthralled council member and back to the Council's news feed. There was a breaking news bulletin—Council Member Xavier Trellick, brilliant military strategist and the Council's own Military Elder, was dead.

"You killed Council Member Trellick?" Mallik gasped.

Dmitri snorted softly and reached out to let his hand hover over the line of the computer. "Keep reading."

Mallik scrolled down the page. Xavier had been found dead in his sleep, the cause currently unknown, and it was assumed that he died of natural causes. The Council was setting up the promotion of his successor, his own daughter Railey Trellick, at the time of the bulletin. Of Xavier's five children, she was the one that had shown the most promise in bringing forth the same kind of military genius that Xavier himself had exhibited. There was more to the bulletin, mostly funeral appointments and litigation jargon.

"He was only, what, eighty-three, right?"

Dmitri shook his head, showing signs of sympathy. "Seven years earlier than the average lifespan of his species… but Xavier had led a rough life." He edged around the desk and sat back in the chair. "And that was before Marina and I joined him."

"The Adepts," Mallik murmured. A bit too loudly, it seemed, because Dmitri arched an eyebrow at him. In response, he hurried to remark. "The three of you headed the Intergalactic Strike Force before the order for it to stop was released. Right?"

Dmitri leaned forward, his gaze piercing into Mallik's. "You remember."

Mallik laughed nervously and couldn't keep his eyes from darting furtively. "Remember? Remember what?"

Dmitri grinned. "I just had to check." There was an electronic-sounding pop and the Council member disappeared.

Mallik squeaked in alarm and jumped away from his desk. He inhaled deeply for a moment, trying to calm him heartbeat. "Well, that's how he got into the room," he murmured to himself, having spotted the small, burned-out microchip on the floor near the chair. "Wait! What was the crime?"

# CHAPTER NINETEEN

Rosalie slid seamlessly into the territory of the Prince of the Realms. In most ways, this territory was beyond definition. It was what connected the realms, allowed certain creatures to transport themselves from one realm to another. Rosalie did it, of course, on pure power. This territory was semi-corporeal, everything in it lacking a clearly defined shape.

On a nearby knoll was the dais in which the Prince's throne and court resided. His palace was an opulent affair, all gold and earth tones. Some days it made her think of the Taj Mahal, other days Buckingham Palace. It was like that here, always changing, always fulfilling the Prince's every whim and need for variety. "The spice of life," he'd told her once, grinning falsely because he'd used a human phrase.

The walls of the palace flickered for a moment and Rosalie could see him in his throne room, waiting somewhat impatiently for her arrival. Unlike the Oracles, he couldn't sense when she fully materialized near him. The Oracles just knew where she would be when she became visible—because that was what happened. She would just shift her visibility on the Material Plane to that of another.

With a sigh, she began to crest the hill, knowing that the Prince's impatience could turn for the worse if she left him waiting too long. Upon reaching the palace, she angled along the walls until she was standing alongside the throne room. She waited there calmly until the solidity of the walls flickered away again, at which point she darted inside.

Rosalie turned to see the Prince looking at her, his silver eyes almost leveling a glare. She presented him with an overly deep bow. "How may I serve you, Prince Darrin of the Infinite Realms?"

She noted his grimace at the amount of sarcasm in her tone. "You took longer than normal. May I inquire as to why?"

She sneered at his back when he turned to his throne. "I was with the Crone."

He quickly turned back to face her, his countenance showing alarm. "Why were you with the Crone?"

Rosalie sighed, rolling her eyes at the territorialism that had crept in his voice. "I'm sorry, Darrin, but things have been a touch more dire on the Material Plane lately."

"Such as?" His right eyebrow went up, showing skepticism. Rosalie was well aware that he thought of her as a young child, most of her mind still on material things. He didn't know what she'd had to put herself through to be this sane this young, although the Gods knew she still had her moments.

Her gaze hardened, her words coming out in a deep low tone. "Well, there's almost certainly aliens coming to Earth, more likely than not to destroy it. That's a little more important than playing messenger for you, dear Prince."

Prince Darrin sighed, his eyebrow lowering to its original place and his face becoming serious. "I know."

"You know?" Suddenly, facts migrated together in her head to click into place: the Oracles had known about the "Galaxy Killers" and it hadn't been new knowledge, although knowledge never did seem new to them; the Prince's sources could see farther and much more clearly than she could; lastly, he didn't seem as concerned about the aliens as he was tired. "You know, you've known. Why couldn't the great Prince deign to tell his messenger, who resides on the Material Plane?" She was trying to keep her anger under control but it was hard with it already being accessible from the argument with Erik.

His anger, however, could not be controlled and it flared obviously across his face. "Because you're a child, that's why. I put measures in place so that you would be sure to mention it. But no, I had to hear it from the Oracles."

Rosalie thought for a moment, turning her eyes away from the Prince, and tried to pin down to what exactly he was referring. "Are you talking about the globe? The thing you said would warn me if harm would be coming to *me*?" She returned her eyes to him, the glare evident. "Are you telling me that the protection measure that was *supposed* to be for me is actually a barometer aimed directed at the aliens?"

The Prince nodded, his eyes searching hers. "And you couldn't even tell me when they destroyed a planet!"

"Yeah. That happened about a week ago. Obviously you found out." Rosalie stopped and took a deep breath, calming her nerves. When she got that emotional, she could feel her body trying to slip back to the Material Plane. "Because of that globe, probably, one of them found a way into Erik's head."

The Prince scoffed and made a dismissive gesture with his hand. "What should I care about the vampire?"

"You should care because these aliens destroy whole planets and leave nothing behind. You should also care that they managed to get into the head of a three-hundred year-old vampire without anyone knowing and now there is no trace left."

Darrin shrugged his shoulders, all concern gone. If there had been any there to begin with. "There's nothing we can do until they get here, maybe nothing even then."

Rosalie exhaled roughly, her face a mask of concentration. "There's got to be something."

The Prince chuckled at her and pointed idly at her amulet. "It's not like we can 'protect from harm' the entire planet."

Slowly, a smile spread across her face. "Maybe we can. I'll be back later."

Darrin grinned as the planeswalker disappeared. "That was a bit easier than I thought it would be."

Rosalie's smile disappeared, however, when she reappeared on the Material Plane. She smacked herself soundly on the forehead when she looked around and realized that she had regained solidity in the heart of Luna Morte territory. She glanced at the horizon and noticed the sun was setting. She imagined she could see hungry eyes peering out of every window. Whatever luck she had was quickly running out.

Randomly, she picked a direction and ran. Fear rather than oxygen fueled her muscles and she knew soon that would filter out as well. She took advantage of her own shortcomings while she could and pushed herself to go even faster.

"Rosalie!"

In her fear-addled mind, she didn't and couldn't recognize the voice. She didn't know what direction it came from but she knew she had to keep moving. She had to be out of Luna Morte territory before sunset and she absolutely had to see the Crone very soon to tell her idea—maybe the only idea that could work.

She felt someone, something grab her wrist and she felt herself react instinctually. There was a move that Erik had taught her just in case she ever got caught by a vampire that wanted to get back at him and she couldn't happen to phase to another plane. He had taught it to her over and over again, often attacking her himself so that he knew it was ingrained as a first reaction, as pure instinct. She reversed her momentum, going with the weight that was pulling her back, and used every ounce of strength she possessed to punch her attacker somewhere on his face.

The structure underneath the face that she hit hurt her hand in the process. She pulled her hand back close to her body, breathing heavily, and focused enough to glare at her attacker.

"Jesus, Rose." It was Quin. He was wiping the black blood off his face that was oozing out of one of his eyes. "What's gotten into you?"

Rosalie looked at the demon, remorse flowing through her very being. "Quin, I thought you were a vampire."

He spit off to the side, disgust flowing onto his face and then away again. "Do I look like a Luna Morte half-breed to you, planeswalker?"

She scoffed at him. "A little makeup and some contacts and you might." She sighed. "Look, I'm sorry, okay? I phased back to this plane and found myself in the heart of Luna Morte. I should have concentrated before leaving."

Quin shook his head and looped his arm around her shoulders. "You're always in the worst places around sunset." He chuckled softly and started leading her in a slightly different direction. "Come on, let's go see the Crone."

"Why?" Rosalie looked up at Quin, her eyes worried. "Does she need to see me again? Did something happen with the alien in Erik's head?"

The demon snorted, having laughed through his nose in surprise. "Are little green men talking to him?"

Rosalie punched his arm lightly. "No." Her automatic answer was indignant, but followed by a thoughtful pause. "Well, I don't know. Maybe." She focused on him again. "Why do you want to take me to the Crone, then?"

Quin grinned knowingly. "You have that look."

"What look?"

He shrugged. "I don't know how to explain it exactly but it means I have to take you to the Crone. So, technically, I think you should tell me why we're going to see the Crone."

Rosalie grinned back at him. As they made their way across town back to the Crone's A-frame house, she filled him in on what the Prince of the Realms had told her (which wasn't much) and her idea on what might work for protecting themselves against the aliens.

Roughly fifteen minutes later, they had walked little over a mile to the Crone's home. Upon arriving, they noticed Erik sitting on the porch. He was in lotus position holding a rather large amethyst. He was staring into the crystal, his brow furrowed in deep concentration.

Rosalie glanced over at Quin and he quirked an eyebrow back at her, shrugging his shoulders in response to her obvious question. "Hey, Erik!" she called out loudly.

The vampire twitched visibly and the amethyst thunked to the floor of the porch audibly. Erik stood gracefully and picked up the amethyst, holding it close to his chest as he pulled his dignity back together. He arched an eyebrow at Rosalie as she hopped onto the porch.

"What's that?" she asked perkily, trying to grab the crystal.

Erik stepped back, taking the amethyst out of her reach. "Matlinda and I are trying to get a grasp on the aliens, since I supposedly have some kind of a connection. Hopefully, if I can reverse it, I can try to figure out their motives."

Rosalie grinned at the vampire. "It doesn't matter anymore."

"Oh?" Erik turned around, leading both the planeswalker and the demon into the Crone's house. "And why would that be?"

Her grin just grew wider. "I have an idea."

"Oh, dear Lord." Erik shook his head. "Matlinda's looking at her collection of crystals, trying to see if anything in there would be better than the amethyst."

Quin peered around a corner at the edge of the foyer. "The crystal room?"

Erik shook his head to the negative. He moved toward the sitting room with the quartz viewing crystals. "She's up in the attic, she said. Tell her I'm going back to the exercises she showed me. I think I almost got it."

Rosalie grabbed Quin's arm as he passed her in the other direction for the pull-down stairs that led to the attic, stalling him for a moment. "Don't you want to know my idea?"

Erik rewarded the planeswalker with a soft smile. "You can tell me later. I need to do this."

She inclined her head in a slight nod and released her grip on Quin, allowing him to move forward. She followed three steps behind him as he led the way to the attic. A brief walk down a hallway brought them to the stairs to the attic, already pulled down.

"You up there, Crone?" Quin called, moving his neck in such a way that he seemed to be looking up into the attic entryway.

"Looking for crystals, yes. I'm sure Erik told you." They both heard a shuffling noise and then saw the Crone coming back down the stairs. When she turned to face them after pushing the stairs back up into the ceiling, she arched an eyebrow at her demon messenger. "Are you bleeding?"

Quin smirked and tilted his head in Rosalie's direction. "The little one's got a mean right hook."

Matlinda furrowed her brow for a moment and then smiled, her expression clear again. "So, Rosalie, how was the Prince? You weren't gone long."

Rosalie scowled, thinking about some of the revelations she'd made while in the Prince's Realm of Whim. "He was well." She shook her head, attempting to clear her head of the negative emotions. "While I was there with him, he kinda gave me an idea."

Matlinda made a vague gesture for them to follow her as she started down the hallway past where the stairs had been pulled down. She led them into a large room with a high ceiling. "This room is normally reserved for my daily meditations but Erik needs to be left alone," she told them by way of explanation. She spread her arms out around her and proceeded to sit cross-legged on the floor. "So, Rosalie, your idea?"

Rosalie fingered her amulet for a moment and then removed it, handing it to the Crone. "This amulet – can you turn it into a spell?"

Matlinda chuckled softly. "This amulet holds the protection spell, so yes."

Rosalie ducked her head, blushing at her lack of knowledge. "Oh." She cleared her throat. "I thought maybe we could do the protection spell around the entire planet?"

The planeswalker looked up just in time to see the Crone's eyes widen. "That would be quite an undertaking. I'm not sure I could do it myself."

Rosalie sighed, her entire body slumping. "Oh. Again."

Quin nudged Rosalie's shoulder. "Never give up hope, Rosie." He gestured with a quick jerk of his head in the Crone's direction. "She has an abundance of ideas."

The Crone was smiling, Rosalie noticed, and she could see a light dancing behind her eyes. "It will take a few days to contact the major covens that would need to be involved in this." Matlinda brought herself back to her feet, beginning to do a slow pace. "I need to formulate the spell. If everything goes right, we can do this soon." She stopped for a moment, her gaze going to a middle distance for a moment, and then she walked across the large room.

Rosalie noticed she was stopped at a large white device. Quin leaned over to the planeswalker. "She calls it her 'moon watcher'. It helps her track the movement of the moon phases for her spells." Rosalie nodded, though she only understood in the very basic sense.

"Yes. The ideal moon phase is near." Matlinda looked up and grinned at the petite planeswalker. "I think we can do it."

Rosalie grinned. "Really? We can save Earth?"

The Crone's expression faltered slightly. "Well, we can certainly try. In seven days."

# CHAPTER TWENTY

Dmitri arrived at the funeral with a happy song in his heart and a muted spring in his step. It wasn't that he'd wished death on the man when he'd been alive but he was certainly glad that he was now dead. He had been beginning to hit that age where senility and nostalgia had become who he was. Truthfully, it had been dragging down the plans of the Adepts.

He had been glad for it while it lasted.

He felt more than saw when Marina came to stand next to him. He didn't even look at her as she initiated the conversation. "Gods above, I hate military funerals."

"I can't disagree," Dmitri replied in a low voice. The military always made such a spectacle of themselves when one of their own died. The weeping, the color guard, the testimonials—he wasn't sure that Xavier actually deserved any of this. He was a cruel, hard man, barely anything outside of his ambition and his military status.

Dmitri and Marina stood quite a distance from the procession of death. To a lot of the public, the Adepts individually did not have a lot to do with each other. Marina was always fully in the public eye, guiding the propaganda. Xavier had spent most of the last ten years of his life guiding his middle daughter in the ways of the Council, military matters and the mission of the Adepts. Supposedly. Dmitri was very secretive about everything he did, giving him more tactical advantage in everything he attempted.

"Mallik remembers." Dmitri decided it was best to be out with it. It hadn't been a surprise, the revelation from the meek man the night before. After the newest report on Earth had gone up a few days prior, a good three months before the planetary reports were due to be released again and while the Diplomacy Elder had been busy in the Beta Sector no less, the red flags had gone up. Between Xavier's failing health and Marina's latest wine binges, Dmitri had been the only one to catch the alerts. Knowing that they would soon come back to themselves, Dmitri had sent them both a message informing them that he would investigate it himself. He just hoped that Marina would refrain from making a big deal out of it.

She didn't disappoint. "Was he in any pain?" Marina's tone conveyed boredom. Dmitri had a feeling that the binges weren't over, just on hold out of respect for their partner.

Dmitri finally looked up at his fellow Adept. She towered over him by two feet, coming from a species of delicate features and an average of a height of seven feet tall. She wore the dark robes of mourning native to her planet, a form-fitting dress that flared subtly outward at the elbows and knees. Her long black-and-silver hair was pulled into a complicated-looking bun at the back of her skull and her face was devoid of makeup, leaving behind only the mottled yellow skin. What he noticed most of all was the wrinkles. Every single one of them seemed to turn downward, as if every emotion that poured out of her was overlaid with negativity of some kind.

"None that was evident," he replied, turning away again.

"Perhaps the Separator needs to be overhauled."

Dmitri shrugged. "It's your invention."

"Based on your research."

He sighed. "Do what you want. The Separator's really your baby."

Marina stepped forward, coming back into Dmitri's line of vision. "Leave it be, then. It still seems to control the twins well enough." With the decision made, she moved to join the funeral procession. With an Elder dead, she had to be seen.

"Seems to," Dmitri murmured to himself. That was correct—to the untrained eye, the Separator still hurt them. He knew better, he could spot the signs of bland acting. The transmissions when they used the Separator were always so short that Xavier and Marina wouldn't have noticed anyway, not that they cared to notice the twins in any capacity beyond tools to an end.

Dmitri shook his head, sadness having etched itself across his face. He didn't know why they attempted to control them anyway—the Blood Contract did quite a job of that by itself. If they made any action that defied the bylaws of the Code of the ISF, they would feel it in their blood, in how healthy they were—or were not, as the case would be. He had no idea how the Earth assignment would play out.

"You're thinking about them again," a voice declared from slightly behind him.

Dmitri turned to face the person, though he already knew who it was. A member of his own species, shorter than him by half a foot, stood there holding a sheaf of papers. His eyes glowed pensive blue back at his own sad green. His hooves had a level of smoothness to them that suggested youth.

It was Dmitri's son, Marcus.

He grinned at him, trying to push back the sadness he felt when he thought about the twins. "How do you always know?"

"You carry negative emotions in the eye and mouth," Marcus replied, gesturing vaguely at his own face with a stylus he always carried. "Thinking too much about them would make me sad too."

Dmitri sighed. "It can't be helped." He moved closer to his son, glancing at the papers in his hands. "What have you got there?"

Marcus grinned. "I did some calculations involving the Contract and how far away they'll be this time."

Dmitri barked a laugh. "The Council psychologist delving into hard science? Armageddon is near."

Marcus rolled his eyes at his father, the one vice that always came rushing back when he was around either of his parents. "Well, from what you said you observed, distance does seem to have an effect on the Blood Contract. They'll be at least fifteen galaxies away from the Contract this time, five whole Sectors. Before now, they have only been two Sectors away from it. I believe that while on Earth, they may not have to abide by the Contract." He glanced up from the papers to look his father in the eye. "Their proximity to their home planet may affect it as well. I think they'll be much stronger while in the Milky Way."

Dmitri's gaze faded for a moment, becoming focused and hard as he thought it through. "Okay, you should leak it to Mallik when he returns from Beta Sector." He started to move toward Xavier's burial place, the funeral procession having long vanished. "Be forewarned—he might be a little jumpy."

Marcus scuttled after his father, being careful not to drop anything. "What did you do?"

Dmitri chuckled. "Let's just say I renewed his fear of the gods."

Marcus sighed roughly. "Dad, what did you do?"

It was Dmitri's turn to roll his eyes. "It was a harmless holo-visit. He needed to learn to be more careful. The new generation will be running things soon and he was being too obvious."

"He's protected by Gralug," Marcus rebutted. "Railey and Xen wouldn't dare."

"I wouldn't say that Xavier's children were gifted with an overabundance of brains, not even the queer one. They're exactly like Xavier and Marina were but without the experience to temper their urges. We do not want Mallik dead."

"No, we do not." Marcus nudged some of the dirt near the grave with his hoof. "Okay, I'll be going. I have information that needs to be leaked."

Dmitri watched his son leave and smiled. The Adepts, they were all different. Marina was barren (*like her soul,* he thought snidely), so she lacked the ability to create her own progeny. Xavier's five children had only cemented his need to take over and control everything. Dmitri had had Marcus less than a year after they returned from the Loora razing, a miracle for a species known for their common sterility. Looking at his son that day was like having light flood in through a bay window. Suddenly, everything was so clear. Their plan was wrong and flawed, not to mention what they were planning to do with the twins. His change of heart had been so complete that he'd even had the crazy thought of just freeing the twins. That was when he heard her voice.

{*Who are you?*

It sounded like the little girl. V'Let.

*You're the mean man, like ice is mean.*

Dmitri had been looking at his son through the glass screen of the nursery and barked a teary laugh.

*Ice melted. Sweet boy.* There was a pause and Dmitri could feel something like a push inside his brain. V'Let's voice returned with sudden alarm. *You can't free us!*

Dmitri reached to where her voice seemed to come from. It seemed so far out of reach but he spoke inside his mind anyway. *Why not?* Compared to her clear voice, his own sounded like a whisper on a breeze.

*They'll kill you. They've thought about it. They think you're weak but you scare them. You have to stay like ice.*

*Like ice?* he thought finally.

*Cold and untouchable.* There was a small, tinkling laugh that echoed through his head. *They're too dense to see past that.*

*You're only five?* His query had a touch of disbelief in it.

*Alive in the universe for six years in the coming season.* There was that laugh again. It made Dmitri smile. *If you really want to free us, we will have to make plans.*

That is what they did for the rest of the day—made a set of long and complex plans for the freedom of the twins. Half the time, Dmitri forgot that V'Let was just a child, infantile by Looran standards.}

Dmitri turned away from Xavier's grave, back-kicking some of the dirt in the process. V'Let had been right then, had been able to see everything in a clarity that he still didn't possess on his own. She'd known that as Xavier and Marina aged, they would lose their need to dominate and instead start finding things to make themselves feel complete. Xavier never really lost his need for dominance, just replaced the subject; Marina had lost herself in the media, the propaganda, the need to feel anything.

*Soon,* Dmitri thought to himself as he slowly made his way out of the Council's gravesite and its insane number of holographic grave markers. Soon enough, everything would change.

# CHAPTER TWENTY-ONE

V'Let sat down at the central console, watching as her brother reseated himself at the secondary console. She glanced at her brother and then at the navigational view screen, noting the time they had remaining.

"A little over eight days?" She let her gaze remain on D'Las until he nodded. "What are you doing?" She let her hands fly across the keyboard, bringing up the list of protected species again.

"Reading the news," D'Las murmured, his eyes roaming across the screen in front of him.

She arched an eyebrow in his direction and then cast her attention back to the upload of the protected species. There was one that she couldn't quite seem to understand. She cleared the viewscreen of the countdown and brought up the one species that seemed to defy description.

"Council member Trellick died," D'Las announced, his voice breaking into her concentration.

V'Let rolled her eyes and shifted her gaze back to her brother. "Which one? I think there's four of them now."

"Council member and Military Elder Xavier Trellick," he responded in a flat tone. "His middle daughter, Railey, is stepping up to take his place."

V'Let turned back to the viewscreen, tilting her head at the being on the screen. It was a vague image of what only she could describe as a glowing green ball. If the stats of the creature weren't even more confusing, she would have just thought that it was a puffed-up version of a will-o'-the-wisp, a very small member of the fey. "How did he die?" she asked her brother distractedly.

D'Las scrolled quickly through the news article again. "Cause unknown. Says they're assuming natural causes."

"Hmm."

D'Las turned to face his sister, fully intending to ask his sister what she meant by that particular answer. Then he saw what she was looking at, realizing her reply had been short because of her distraction. "What is that?"

V'Let reached her hand toward the screen, trying to get a feel in her mind for what this creature was. "Whatever it is, I don't know enough about it to reach out to it." She glanced back at her brother. "Its reported size is absolutely enormous, the size of a small to medium planet. Its abilities are guessed to be life-oriented. It's also extremely rare, only five reported in the entire universe." She paused, tilting her head slightly in the other direction as if trying to physically wrap her mind around this being. "Though the Council reports of the other members of this species say that they all have different abilities."

D'Las imitated his sister's pose and tilted his head at the viewscreen. "You suppose maybe it could actually be the planet itself?"

He glanced at V'Let in time to see a light dawn in her eyes. "Yes, that could be it." She turned and rushed to the central console. She pushed a couple of keys and brought up an image to be side by side with Earth's very large glowing ball. "The Council reported this same species to be on Loora. It's purple there."

D'Las clearly saw that it was. "Okay, so Earth's glowy ball is green, which means it's geared toward life, right?" His sister nodded vigorously. "So, that's probably where this extreme number of protected species comes from."

"That's a thought." D'Las could feel his sister getting excited and knew as she rushed from the central console to the secondary console that she was going to add to the report.

"Okay, then why is Loora's purple?"

V'Let didn't even look up as she quickly typed in their speculations. "Um, evolution."

D'Las nodded to himself. "That's right. Each generation made jumps and leaps, evolutionarily speaking. That's why the genetic memory is so important."

V'Let was smiling as she spun in the chair to face her brother again. "Because the Loorans as a species find it extremely difficult to conceive, to reach our peak in ten thousand years was truly miraculous." She grinned at him. "At least you remember your lessons."

D'Las rolled his eyes. "How can I not? When you've got a dozen scientists telling you the same thing, it's a little hard to ignore." He moved to sit at the central console and wiped the screen clean of the images of the planetary species. "I think we should go into stasis."

V'Let shook off the shock of her brother actively delving into his own genetic memory. "Stasis? I thought you hated being in stasis."

"Yeah, the dreams." D'Las shook his head. "It'll shave at least two days off the journey and I'm starting to get antsy."

V'Let nodded. "I know. The longest journey we've been on before was five days." She punched a few keys. "Put in the failsafes for the stasis and I'll put in this new route I found. It'll shorten travel by another day."

The two of them were silent except the sounds of their keyboards for the next few minutes. They stood from their consoles simultaneously, heading out of the bridge and toward the bunks.

"The failsafes are in place," D'Las told his sister as they reached his bunk. "The stasis will be stopped if anything goes wrong."

V'Let smiled at her brother. "The new route takes us a little closer to the Milky Way's super-massive black hole, adding some fuel-less speed to the ship."

He nodded at her and entered his bunk, sealing it hermetically behind him. She stared at his door for a moment, thinking that maybe they could try to awaken his abilities again very soon. Shaking herself out of her reverie, she hurried in long strides to her own bunk. Once inside, she hit the seal and strapped herself down into the bed. She watched as her lights dimmed to black and felt sleep descend on her as the oxygen levels fell to base levels.

On the bridge, the viewscreen was dimming to its lowest contrast, barely showing that the new calculations had brought travel time down to just below five cycles.

# CHAPTER TWENTY-TWO

Matlinda pinched the bridge of her nose hard as she set her phone back on the receiver. She had just finished talking to the last of the dozen very powerful covens she had decided to involve in this venture. As enlightened as all of the witches were, however, many of them found it difficult to believe that extraterrestrials were coming to Earth. Even the ones that did believe claimed to sense no danger from the near future. Matlinda had rebutted that there was nothing wrong with casting a protection spell on the earth. Not one of them would dare defy her, though. What the Crone commanded would be done, for the Crone asked for little that wasn't necessary.

The Crone closed her eyes for a moment and leaned back in her chair. She had been awake for the last thirty-six hours, just talking with covens and arranging their synchronization. It was tiring. After Rosalie had presented her idea, Matlinda had spent an entire day going over the details of this spell. The initial protection spell was quite simple but the immensity of what this was had made what she planned to do very complex indeed. The easiest way to tap into the energy of the earth to tie the protection into the planet was to be at or near a ley line, the nearest one being some distance south in one of the redwood forests. Secondly, they needed to do the spell near the full moon as it was waning to increase the potency of the spell. Lastly, they would be reciting the spell in Latin through a series of differing invocations, making for a very complicated spell of high magick.

Idly, she wondered if they truly needed this. Witches across the globe denied sensing any danger at all, beyond the danger that the regular humans presented daily. The feeling that she was being blocked every time she tried to reach for them was disconcerting, however.

She stood then and stretched, her old bones creaking and her joints popping loudly. "Better safe than sorry," she muttered to herself. She headed to her bedroom, the need for sleep emanating from her very presence. It was time for the preparations, beginning with a very long sleep.

In the hallway, she passed Quin, who was currently bedding in one of her extra rooms. He looked to be dressed for the day, clad in a t-shirt and fitted slacks. He arched an eyebrow at the Crone as he noticed her. "Are you just going to bed, Matlinda?"

She nodded lethargically. "Is it morning?"

"How is it you can see some things, like looking at me and probably knowing exactly what I'm wearing, and yet you don't know what time of day it is?" He sighed exasperatedly. "And yes, it's about ten in the morning."

"Could you make me some oolong tea?"

Quin inclined his head in subservience at the Crone. "You're taking it in your room?"

"Yes." She sighed a long, tired sigh. "We need to have that talk."

Quin winced. "In that case, I will make myself a cup as well." With that, he turned and disappeared to the kitchen.

Matlinda continued her slow shuffle to her room. Days like these, when the hours were so long that events seem to bleed into each other and she was exhausted to the point that she couldn't feel the sun in the sky, were the days when she most felt her advanced age. When she felt the heavy aura of her own presence, faded but repeated over time, she held out her hand and turned her doorknob. Even her preternatural sight was fading, she knew.

Upon entering her bedroom, she stepped very carefully to her bed. It had been a very long time since all sight she possessed faded to the point that it was useless to her. She thought that maybe if she rested herself for a moment, some of the sight would return, at least enough that she could have her conversation with Quin with some small amount of focus. After an eternal second of feeling air, her fingers encountered the cotton sheets and thick quilts that adorned her bed. She climbed atop the mattresses and just sat, closing her eyes and stilling the very inside of herself.

After about three minutes of this self-imposed nirvana, she opened her eyes and her world was filled with color again. Quin was standing beside her bed, staring at her with part-curiosity and part-worry. He handed her a cup of steaming tea and set down his own on her nightstand. He turned around and fetched a chair from a corner of the room. Upon returning, he sat down and fidgeted until he was comfortable, becoming very still even as he reached to reclaim his tea.

"I didn't want to disturb your meditation."

Matlinda smiled at Quin. "I understand." She inhaled the steam of her tea deeply and took a small sip. "I know you're thinking of leaving."

Quin knew he shouldn't be surprised. Matlinda was the Crone, after all, and not just any witch could have accomplished that. However, his face was a still mask of shock. "How did you know?" He couldn't even stop the words of an idiot from rolling off his tongue.

She smiled that demure yet knowing smile. "I just do. But I'm not sure I understand why. Is it about these aliens?"

Quin snorted. "Well, yeah." He stopped, reined his disrespect and took that moment to sip his tea and regain his composure. "We've talked to Rosalie a number of times and she has spoken to the Oracles and the Prince of the Realms, whoever that might be, and it sounds important. These aliens destroy whole planets. What chance do we have?"

Matlinda sat her tea on the nightstand and looked her demon messenger in the eyes. "You must understand that running can't help you, Quin. Where on Earth would you run to?"

He sighed roughly, breaking the eye contact. "I am a runner, Matlinda. It's what I know to do. It's what I'm good at."

"If it's any consolation, I do believe this protection spell will work. Even if the other covens do not believe in the existence of aliens, they still want to protect the earth against all harm."

Quin looked at the Crone again, connecting with her cloudy blue eyes again. "You really think it'll work?"

Matlinda rewarded him with a wide smile. "I really do." She cleared her throat. "So, will you do me a favor?"

The smile that had graced his face at her affirmation of their pending success faltered very slightly. "Whatever you need, Matlinda."

"Keep composed until this blows over." She held up a finger when he moved to speak. "And it *will* blow over. Also, I'll need you to housesit while I'm in the forest performing the ritual."

Quin arched an eyebrow. "I won't be going with you?"

Matlinda's smile turned mischievous. "No, I'll be taking the planeswalker and her pet vampire."

Quin nodded for a moment and then tilted his head very slightly at the witch. "Erik for protection, I know, but why Rosalie?"

Matlinda shrugged. "She asked to go. And this was essentially her idea."

Quin nodded and moved to stand. "All the better, I guess. You know how I get around magic doings. You get a vampire bodyguard and I get to sit around and safeguard your crystals."

# CHAPTER TWENTY-THREE

V'Let came to consciousness slowly as the oxygen level began to rise. She blinked for a moment and then proceeded to roll herself out of her bed. She crossed the room to her sink and splashed water on her face, shivering instinctively at the temperature. Looking at herself in the mirror, she grimaced. All signs of exhaustion were long gone, her eyes and hair having taken on their natural shine again. Her skin, however, had faded to a pallid mauve.

"Gods above, I look sickly." She shook her head and turned away from the mirror to head to the bridge. D'Las was probably already there. He was always quicker to wake than she was, something to do with his obsession with all things physical to maintain the repression of his powers.

As she passed his bunk door, it whooshed open and he appeared, his hair slightly mussed but his clothing as neat as a pin. She arched an eyebrow at him. "Did you just get up?"

D'Las scowled at his sister. "Yes. I overslept. I was dreaming."

"Oh?" She walked ahead of him, briskly making her way to the bridge just out of his arm's reach. "Oversleeping, dreaming, freely accessing your genetic memory? Looks like you're losing your knack at blocking absolutely everything, Lasso."

He growled and reached out to grab for her hair, which was the only thing halfway in his reach. However, she reached around and pulled her hair out of the way half a second before he could reach it.

"I don't block anything, brother dear, especially not you."

D'Las huffed as they reached the bridge, hurriedly taking the central console to enter the codes for entering planetary orbit. "That's a lie."

V'Let inclined her head slightly as she took the secondary console, punching in her own set of codes. "Okay, yeah. But not nearly as much as you."

D'Las stood and stepped down from the central console. The destination countdown read just over two hours. He reached around him and pushed a button. The viewscreen changed to transparency, a seemingly clear screen that simulated what they were facing outside of the spacecraft. There was now what looked to be a very large, highly water-logged planet dotted with tan-and-green and white landmasses, a planet that they were still approaching at high speeds. "So, that's Earth?"

V'Let stood as well and nodded. "The home of an abominable people."

D'Las grinned tightly, causing the skin of his face to stretch unflatteringly. "And more. We've got to tread lightly here." He sighed and turned back to the central console, hopping back into his seat. "You're the Earth expert on this vessel. What side of the world are we looking at?"

She craned her neck to scowl at him for a moment. As she faced the viewscreen again, she forced her pupils to dilate fully, causing her eyes to look black with a thin ring of blue. Her view of the Earth as D'Las saw it was multiplied over two thousand times. "I can see the Wall of China. I think we're facing the eastern hemisphere."

D'Las narrowed his eyes at the planet. "A wall?"

V'Let allowed her eyes to relax, the pupils pulling back in to near-pinpricks. "Yeah, another separation thing, I think. We need to be over nine thousand miles east of there."

D'Las punched vague coordinates according to her instructions. "Language?"

V'Let perked up at that. She glanced at a dark corner of the bridge where their translators sat dormant and then started punched commands into the secondary console. The translation console slowly lit up and showed two small devices that fit into two thumb rings beside them. These devices together became force fields that surrounded the wearer and translated both in and out. The devices themselves were microchips that housed the translation program and all languages the users stored in them. The rings housed a program that created semi-permeable force fields. When the microchips locked into the rings, the two programs melded into symbiotic involvement with each other.

As a matter of course, the twins could learn the languages but that took time. The Adepts had long since decided that time was not a luxury they were allowed when "judging a planet for destruction". They said it that way, as if there would never be any other solution. Thus, they had found the easiest and most reliable way to translate a language so the twins wouldn't have to. They were called Linguistics Rings.

"Mallik sent some of the major languages with the file on Earth. It's about seven different languages, I think." Her eyes scrolled through the information from Mallik's very large file. "No, I was wrong. It's ten different languages."

D'Las arched an eyebrow at his sister. "Ten?"

She shrugged. "Still only a fraction of the actual number of languages spoken on the planet." She punched in a command to overlay the image of Earth with a translucency of the protected species. Looking up, she noted they were quickly approaching the western hemisphere. She could see the edge of the landmass that the humans had dubbed "North America". She glanced back down at her console screen and noted their time had decreased to just under an hour.

D'Las cleared his throat to get his sister's attention. When she looked at him, he queried, "What's the green there?"

On the viewscreen, there was a concentration of dark green dots on the western edge of approaching landmass. "The dark green marks a protected species that is plant life. I believe those are the trees."

"Those are the redwoods?"

"Yes. Unbelievable, right?"

"There wasn't near that many on the other planet."

V'Let nodded. "We need to start planetary entry." She punched coordinates into her console and a purple ring appeared on the viewscreen slightly to the north of one of the concentrations of redwoods. "We'll need to land there."

A musical hum echoed through the bridge then, followed by the computer's sterile voice. "Languages uploaded. Linguistics Rings ready for use."

The twins stood simultaneously, D'Las to look closely at the viewscreen and V'Let to assemble their rings. With two subtle clicks and a low hum, the rings were assembled and V'Let moved to join her brother, handing him one of the rings.

"Why here, particularly?"

She smiled at her brother. "There is a concentration of demons and hybrids in this particular city, with fey ringing just outside the city."

D'Las turned around to return to the central console where he punched in the commands for the entry sequence. "So, what's the plan?"

V'Let fiddled with her ring for a moment before she forced herself to stop. "You'll drop me discreetly at the edge of the city." She moved back to the secondary console, punching in the cloaking commands. Anyone who happened to look directly where their spacecraft happened to be would only see a shimmer in the air. "I'll gather information. If you can, you need to skim the planet and scan as much of it as you can."

D'Las nodded his acquiescence. "I'll scan it. It'll just take a few hours, I'd imagine. The long range scanner can reach about five thousand miles, right?"

She nodded back at him in affirmation. "I imagine I'll have to talk to a human first." She pulled a scowl on her face. "Lovely."

D'Las chuckled at his sister. "I'm sure you'll find a nice one."

She rolled her eyes and turned to her console again. She typed a few more notes into the report file, noting the time and date of the initial landing. She stood then and headed for the cargo bay. On the way, she stepped up on the central console and pecked her brother on the cheek.

"Be safe," she whispered to him, as she always did when they were separated for any period of time.

He smiled at her gently. "You too."

V'Let rewarded him with a bright smile and continued to the cargo bay. As she passed a vaguely shapeless statuette, she reached her hand toward it and smiled. An incarnation of a Goddess of Creation for a planet that no longer existed, it still incased a lot of the goodwill that planet had directed toward it. She knew in the coming days, these artifacts and what feelings they represented would keep her more stable than anything else.

Without thinking further, she punched the large airlock button to release and open the hatch. The change in air pressure and flow forced her back a step. She took a deep breath of clean planet air and looked to see what they were flying over. Looking toward the horizon, she could see the edge of the very dense forest they were currently above. A bit farther, she could see the signs of a city.

As they quickly left the forest behind, V'Let could make out scattered shops on the edge of the city. She allowed her pupils dilate halfway to be able to see through the window of the shops. Inside of one was lined with books. She knew she wouldn't get much information there; most book-readers tended to keep to themselves. Another shop was filled with clothing, something that was another no-go. Sighing, she looked into the next shop. She grinned. It looked promising. It might not be java juice but it was worth a look.

*The shop of heated beverages?* D'Las queried through the link.

V'Let arched an eyebrow. *You're getting stranger and stranger, brother.* She could feel him laugh inside her head. His mental voice was getting stronger, she noticed, and she hoped that his control wouldn't break while they were separated. That alone could be disastrous. *Set down between the clothing shop and the book shop. I don't wish to be obvious.*

*Don't forget to cloak yourself to their eyes,* he replied before setting down in the shadows between the two stores. V'Let peered out of the spacecraft to make sure there were no humans in sight. There were none. She punched the airlock button again and took off at a dead run to escape the airlock doors and the hatch before they fully closed.

*All right, I'm out,* she told D'Las as she flattened herself against the brick of one of the shops. *Go forth and scan things.* There was that laugh again and she watched the spacecraft leave, watching it fade into a shimmer when it was more than a few feet away from her. She focused on the sky then, trying to gauge the time. From the sun's position in the sky, it seemed to be late afternoon. She couldn't be too sure, though – the last planet they were on had had two suns, had made gauging time a pain.

V'Let sighed and concentrated on the task at hand. She needed to make a glamour to lay over her person for now. Mallik had sent pictures of the different races of humankind and that was what she needed to be right now. She filtered through her memories of what humans looked like and what they tended to wear. After a moment, she smiled and walked into the light, striding confidently to the beverage shop. The few people that she passed that happened to glance in her direction would jerk and just have to look at her again but then look away and forget. The first glance gave her true form of big blue eyes and very purple skin. However, when they looked at her for more than half a moment, her skin became light olive, her eyes a deep brown. Her long lavender hair became a loose dark brown braid that barely reached her shoulder blades and her full-length ivory chemise became a white-and-red floral sundress. Despite the very weak glamour, she now looked perfectly human.

She inhaled deeply as she approached the third shop with the seemingly sole purpose of serving beverages. The scent on the air was pungent, so similar to the java juice that they served in the Central Planets, and yet cloying in a way. V'Let frowned as she felt the scent invade her head, seeping into the cracks and trying to press apart. Unlike the java juice, this scent was inherently unhealthy and she knew she would not drink it. Something about the scent... hurt.

She entered the shop, allowing the cloying scent to wrap around her. She stepped to the counter where there stood a woman with pale skin and tired eyes. The term *barista* leapt into her mind unwittingly. It was followed by *coffee*, which she gathered was the unhealthy thing in which this shop seemed to specialize.

"Can I help you?" the woman asked. V'Let arched her eyebrow. There was something slightly off about her voice, which was low and lilting, and her dark eyes.

V'Let did her best to smile, showing the barest hint of bright white teeth. "Do you have anything that doesn't have coffee in it?"

The woman smiled brightly at her then, the expression making her seem much younger than moments before. "Awful stuff, isn't it?" she replied in a conspiratorial murmur. V'Let's smiled widened in response, an almost unconscious response to the woman's good humor. "I'll skip right past the teas because, while it's not coffee, it might as well be. There are the milk-based drinks, fruit smoothies and the like. I recommend the strawberry-mango myself."

V'Let nodded at the woman. "I'll try that one then. My name's Violet." She decided that her own name would probably seem slightly out of place but Violet was close enough that she would likely answer to it.

Even though the woman was now facing away from her, V'Let could feel her smile. "I'm called Cara. This shop is mine, as the sign says outside. I had to change the sign a few months back."

V'Let frowned slightly. "Why?"

Cara set down the smoothie in front of her, her expression having regained its blandness. "Three dollars for the drink."

V'Let pulled a piece of currency out of her pocket, noting the pale pink of Voo currency. She concentrated for a moment and it became the many green shades of an American ten-dollar bill. "Here," she said, handing the currency note to Cara.

The barista nodded agreeably back at her before turning around to make the change. "Anyway, I opened this shop for healthy beverages, milk-based drinks and the gentler teas. In a short amount of time, I realized that wasn't going to cut it. Everyone wants coffee, espresso, latte! I blame Starbucks."

V'Let nodded knowingly even though she only partially understood what Cara was talking about. The Central Planets had long perfected making drinks that provided energy to be healthy as well. She moved to the side as another person approached the counter to make their order, which consisted of a tall non-fat half-caf latte and a slice of coffee cake. She watched as Cara lifted her eyebrows and rolled her eyes before quickly letting her face relax again.

She silently moved into a corner of the shop to sit at an empty table. She did her best to cultivate an aura of solitude while listening to the surface thoughts of the other patrons and those people passing very near the front of the shop.

*How am I gonna fix this? I screwed up so bad...*

*That woman's such a bitch! Why is she so mean?*

*Coffee... coffeecoffeecoffee... Love coffee.* V'Let pulled a face at that one.

*Gotta get outta this mess. He's killing me...*

*What is she? She's not normal, can't be human.* V'Let's eyes narrowed and she concentrated on that particular mental voice, her eyes trailing an invisible line the entire way. She connected her gaze with Cara's once again, noticing that the woman's eyes had become bright and shining once again. Cara winked once before turning away to the next customer.

V'Let nodded to herself, deciding that there was definitely something very off about the shop owner. She was mostly human but it was possible she was a little bit of something else, maybe something protected. She settled into her seat and let a smile grace her features again. It wouldn't hurt to stay and find out.

# CHAPTER TWENTY-FOUR

Mallik paced jerkily outside Head Council Member Gralug's chambers, his mind awhirl with the many different reasons for which the man could have called him, most of them not good reasons. He'd returned from the Freti Galaxy late last night, exhausted and extremely nervous, to find the herald from Gralug waiting in his home messages. The message itself had been upwards of ten cycles old.

"Not good, not good," he muttered under his breath. According to the date stamp, it more than likely had to do with the planetary update on Earth, which was leagues of suspicious by itself. Not to mention the fact that he'd had to stay in the deity-forsaken galaxy of disputes a bit longer than planned. When Council Member Xavier Trellick had died, the Fretians had urged a rewrite of the treaty, one with stricter boundaries but gentler punishments. Mallik had found it odd but continued along with it anyway. This particular galaxy had become quite fierce in the past years and he felt the need to oblige them despite his obvious exhaustion.

He came to a spastic stop when he heard someone clearing their throat. He turned slowly on his heel to face the entrance to Gralug's chambers and saw the man looking at him, humor in his eyes. "You can come in now, Mallik."

Mallik smiled tremulously as he followed the Head Council Member into his rooms, quietly closing the door behind them. Gralug was a large, hulking figure, though a runt to a species that was marginally larger and of greater hulk and aggression. When he had first been appointed to head the Council, Mallik had had nightmares involving angering Gralug and those very large fists of his. Over time, Mallik discovered that while Gralug could be fierce and firm with the Council, he was quite jovial and kind in person.

Gralug eased himself into the massive black chair behind his desk and gestured for Mallik to do the same in one of the three chairs that faced the desk. Mallik nodded jerkily and fell clumsily into the middle one.

Gralug cleared his throat again and turned his attention to a report of significant thickness lying on his desk. "Roughly eleven cycles ago, you sent out a broad report of the planet Earth in the Milky Way Galaxy. Most of the information is something of which most of the Council is well aware. Most of it was about the humans, of which the Council has no care excepting hindrance of their tedious progress."

Mallik gulped through the large lump that seemed to be residing in his throat and forced himself to gather what composure he had remaining. "I know. I know that the report was very early." He snapped his jaws shut after that. He had a bad tendency to lie and embellish the lie when he was in a tight spot, which would have been fine had he not been such a horrible liar.

Gralug leaned forward in his chair, his eyes seeming to pierce into Mallik's own. "I just need to know."

Mallik smiled lopsidedly, his eyes darting to the side and then back again. "Know what?"

"Was this for the twins?"

Mallik bowed his head slightly in defeat. "Yes."

Gralug jerked slightly, casting a baleful stare down at the report on his desk. "They sent them to Earth? Why?"

Mallik watched as Gralug heaved himself out of the chair and began to pace smoothly across the area behind his desk. "I believe it was a punishment."

Gralug cocked his head to glance at the diplomat without pausing the determined pacing, though Mallik could have sworn he heard him slow just a bit. "Why would they be punished?"

Mallik looked away from Gralug for a moment before stoning his resolve and facing the head of the Council once more. "It was me." When Gralug looked at him again sharply, the diplomat only nodded. "I know they're trapped somehow and so do you. We still remember some of the Loorans that would leave that planet of theirs. They were the epitome of peace." Mallik smiled very slightly when Gralug fully halted his pacing and returned to his seat. "But that was over twenty rotations ago. Most of the new generation is convinced that the Galaxy Killer propaganda is true and most of our generation didn't even know they existed either until the razing of planet Loora or until the sole survivors of that planet started destroying other planets. Marina makes damn sure that the Central Planets are clogged with Galaxy Killer propaganda."

Gralug nodded sympathetically. "Yes, but like almost all other propaganda, you knew that it was not true."

Mallik shook his head. "No, I didn't. Not really. Yes, I met a Looran before the razing. Yes, at the very core of me, I believed everything the twins told me. But I had no proof. All Loorans are extremely strong telepaths. So I looked for proof."

Gralug arched an eyebrow. "Did you find it?"

Mallik's eyes flicked downward as he remembered. "Not then. Before leaving for the Freti Galaxy, I searched for the Adepts, a location where V'Let told me they could sometimes be found. I may have been a little too gung-ho. I don't remember a lot about being there except this very large silver device and then nothing. I woke on my ship halfway to Freti Galaxy. I didn't even remember anything about the twins until they sent me an upload during the planet merger that took place before the preliminary treaty talks."

Gralug leaned forward again, placing his elbows on the desk and his chin in his hands. "You said you didn't find any proof then. Does that mean you've found some since?"

Mallik smiled brightly at him. "It does." He pulled a holocube out of his left pocket and set it into a square device on Gralug's desk. "You know I've been monitoring Psychologist Andian's computer, correct?" At Gralug's nod, he continued. "He's been talking quite a bit with Tactical Elder Andian lately." The Head Council Member gave him a blatant look and Mallik ducked his head slightly. "Yes, I know, how odd for a father and son to be speaking. However, he's been doing research on this specific item lately." Mallik tapped a button to the right of the device. Above the device now floated a three-dimensional grainy copy of a legal sheet of paper.

Mallik watched as Gralug's lips moved, reading the simple but binding sheet of paper. "It has the same rules and bylaws as the Strike Force," he muttered idly. He saw Gralug's eyes widen as he got to the bottom and saw the twins' names signed in their deep blue blood. He glanced at Mallik past the holographic image. "This is a Blood Contract."

Mallik nodded. "Proof that they've not really had a choice in matters for a very long time."

Gralug glanced at the contract again. "I thought you said Dmitri Andian was an Adept as well?"

Mallik arched an eyebrow. "He is."

"I only see the signatures of Xavier Trellick and Marina DuPont here."

Mallik nodded and tapped the button again. The Blood Contract changed for a sheet with a short addendum, one that explained that Dmitri Andian refused to sign the contract for personal reasons, one which was signed by Dmitri Andian. "I think this might mean that he didn't agree with the method."

Gralug scoffed. "Well, I wouldn't either. The Blood Contract has been illegal for well over thirty rotations."

Mallik smiled and pushed in the left side of the square device to eject his holocube. "Also, you might be in danger."

Gralug jerked very slightly, scoffing quietly out of habit. "'In danger'?"

Mallik shrugged. "V'Let picked up something from the Adepts, something about a plan to assassinate you. But then, well, Xavier died. I think everything is in pieces for them right now."

Gralug nodded idly as Mallik stood. "I'm not sure there's anything to be done. The twins have likely landed on Earth by now and begun their 'process'." The Head Council Member sighed heavily. "You said before that they usually take a year for everything?"

Mallik nodded jerkily, gulping past that lump in his throat again. "Usually they do, yes. But it's possible that's not the case this time."

Gralug's forehead furrowed deeply. "What do you mean?"

"I mean that the humans on Earth are one of the most malicious species I've ever heard of. V'Let exploded when she found out just a few things, like the wars." Mallik sighed. "They are exactly the kind of species that we would endorse them destroying, the very reason the Strike Force existed to begin with. Time may very well be against us this time."

Gralug leaned back in his chair, hands firmly pressed into his temples. There had to be a solution, there was always a solution. He'd joined the Council because he truly believed that everything could be fixed... somehow. He let his fingers fall away as he shook his head. "I'm not sure how to proceed," he murmured just loud enough for Mallik to hear.

Mallik giggled nervously. "It's not like you could just go to Earth and stop them."

Gralug looked at the diplomat sharply, the light back in his eyes. "I could."

Mallik shook his head viciously. "No, sir, you couldn't. There's nothing that can make it to the Milky Way Galaxy in less than thirty cycles."

Gralug smiled widely, his thought transforming fully into a plan. "Does the research department still have the Looran vessel?"

"Well, yes."

Gralug rocketed out of his chair and led Mallik out of the office. "That's great, then."

Mallik attempted to smile at him but only managed a frightened mockery of a smile. "There would be a small problem with that, sir."

"Oh?" Nothing could bring him down. Everything could be fixed, after all.

"We have to go through Tactical Elder Dmitri Andian to get it. He's in charge of all research and development."

Except for that.

# CHAPTER TWENTY-FIVE

Dmitri grabbed his white lab coat as he entered the main offices of the Council's R&D department. This was the part of his day that he looked forward to. He didn't have to bother with the complicated politics of being one of the Adepts and his own very complicated façade that had to be held in place when he was near one of them. He could be happy here in this place of science. It also helped that his son was nearby.

"Good morning, Maya," he called out as he passed the receptionist in his fast pace to get in his office.

"Dmitri!" she called after him.

He stopped on the spot and turned to face the receptionist at the urgency in her voice. She jerked her head back very slightly and he moved closer to her in response to her signal. "What is it? Not Marcus…"

She giggled slightly. "No, your son's fine. But Gralug's in your office." She stopped when he cast a glance at his office, now seeing the two silhouettes clearly. "With Mallik. Gralug's been asking about status updates on the Looran speed vessel." She watched as Dmitri began to smile. She hated it when he smiled like that. Those particular smiles didn't convey any type of happiness but rather a type of calculation and maybe a little manipulation. It was a little scary. "I told them to wait in your office. They've been there about five minutes, give or take."

Dmitri focused on his receptionist again. "Thank you, Maya." With that, he turned and continued to his office. It was going to be an interesting day.

He entered his office gracefully, his face paved into a smooth mask. He nodded idly at the Head Council Member as he took his seat behind his desk. "How can I help you, gentlemen?"

Gralug straightened very slightly in his seat and cleared his throat. "I need the Looran vessel."

Dmitri arched an eyebrow. "I'm afraid that could be a problem." He smiled almost imperceptibly at Mallik fidgeting almost uncontrollably in the chair next to Gralug. "It's currently out on a test flight."

Gralug glanced at his watch to note the time. "This early?"

Dmitri inclined his head to indicate the affirmative. "Research and Development does employ a scant night crew and modifying the Looran speed glider for use is a very special project."

Gralug settled further into his seat and smiled wanly at Dmitri. "We can wait."

Dmitri sighed. "You can't just take it, you know."

Mallik stopped his fidgeting for a moment. He looked at the Tactical Elder in the eyes. "What do you want us to do?"

Dmitri flicked his eyes to the diplomat. "It's very simple." He leaned down to one of the lower drawers on his desk. He punched in a complex seven-number code and smiled when he heard the low click of the locks inside releasing. He slid the drawer open and pulled out a slim, round mottled grey device. He straightened back up in his seat and set the device in the middle of his desk and picked a seemingly random stylus out of the row lined up neatly on his desk.

"What are you doing?" Gralug asked, casting a questioning glance at Mallik.

Dmitri merely held up a hand, signaling their silence. Glancing at the tip of the stylus, he affirmed that it was the same mottled grey of the pebble-like device. He touched the stylus to the device at the lower left edge and madea swooping line up to the top center edge and then back down to the lower right edge. He lifted the stylus and made a horizontal line just above the vertical center of the first mark. He finished with an accenting mark to the upper right region of the device. After examining the accuracy of the character, he placed the stylus upright in the pebble's center lightly enough as to not make an actual mark.

The marks on the device glowed a very light blue for a moment before fading slightly. The thin device pulled itself apart, the top and bottom now two centimeters apart, and began to spin in opposing directions. It made a soft whirring sound as it spun, one that resembled a low-level humming. After about five seconds, it stopped suddenly and reassembled itself.

Dmitri leaned down to the device and blew softly at its surface. A layer of glowing blue dust detached from the device and flew into the air, where it remained to float without moving.

Gralug eyed the dust suspiciously. "What did you do?"

Dmitri grinned toothily at him. "It's somewhat technical. Suffice to say that no one can hear our conversation now, even if they stepped into the room." At Gralug's skeptical face, Dmitri's grin fell slightly. "Okay, I pushed us very slightly out of the normal time loop."

Mallik's eyes went wide. "How did you do that?"

Dmitri noted that Gralug didn't become alarmed until Mallik did and realized that Gralug didn't really know what had actually been done. In response, he just gestured at the device. "One of the many things that come out of Research and Development." There was no way in the Seven Hells that he would tell them that these devices were based off of Looran technology, that all of his current research on the mind came from Looran tech.

Gralug pinned his gaze on Dmitri. "Was there a purpose for this?"

Dmitri shrugged. "First of all, the speed glider not really on a test flight. It's locked down." He sighed. "Why do you need it anyway?"

Gralug straightened slightly. "I need to travel somewhere a great distance away and I need to be there quickly."

Dmitri's eyes glittered. "Zeta Sector?"

Gralug growled softly, the instincts of a highly aggressive species nudging at his frustration. It caused Mallik to jump and attempt to hug the far side of his chair but Dmitri just chuckled. "Would you please explain yourself?" the Head Council Member ground out slowly.

Dmitri sighed and settled back into his chair. "We all know I'm an Adept, not that the two of you are really supposed to know what an Adept is." He shrugged to himself. "Not that it matters. Xavier is dead and Marina is bordering on unfit. The next generation, those we have bred to take up the mantle, are stepping up."

"What about you?" Mallik asked, his voice momentarily firm.

Dmitri sneered. "I lost the taste for destruction a long time ago." His face smoothed out again, showing a neutral expression. "You want the speed glider because the twins are on Earth and you want to stop them from destroying your precious protected planet. Correct?" After a moment, Gralug begrudgingly nodded. "They probably won't destroy the planet, though the decision about humanity has already been made."

"It has?" Mallik squeaked. He paused for a beat. "Wait. How do you know?"

Dmitri tapped his temple, a knowing smile on his face. "You honestly have no clue what the twins can do. Too many people underestimate their power."

Gralug harrumphed. "As much as I'd like to believe you, Dmitri," he drawled, "I would rather hear this from the twins themselves."

Dmitri nodded then, repressing the smile that tried to blossom. "Then there's only one solution. We all go."

Gralug cleared his throat softly. "Why all of us?"

"The twins don't trust you, Gralug." Gralug glanced at Mallik, who nodded after a moment to affirm Dmitri's statement. "They trust Mallik, though he might be weak. As for me, I do not allow the speed glider to travel more than a parsec without me inside."

Gralug grunted softly and nodded.

"Good. It'll be ready in an hour." He gestured them out of his office, which they complied with after a moment. He noticed Mallik eyeing him strangely as they left. He glanced down at his desk and saw the device. Looking up again, he noticed the dust very still in the air. He picked up the stylus from its precarious position atop the stone-like device and tapped the device twice in its center, smiling in relief when the dust began to drift slowly downward. He turned to the phone on his desk and pressed a button marked "Maya."

"Yes, Dmitri?"

"I need you to file an administrative requisition for the Loora X25-JLM. Also, patch me through to Marcus."

"Yes, sir."

There was a pause and then he could hear the soothing instrumental that his son liked to use as the ringtone others heard when they called him. It clicked and then, "Marcus Andian speaking."

"I'm going, leaving in an hour."

Dmitri heard a muffled clatter and a slight gasp. "Today? In an hour?"

"Yes, Marcus. What happened?"

"I just dropped... my entire desk. Dad, I'm not ready."

Dmitri smiled. "Sure you are. You're a lot more prepared than I was."

"You were fifty, Dad. I'm only twenty."

"You'll be fine. Just listen, don't openly commit to anything either one of them says. If you think you need to, just call out to V'Let like I taught you."

He could hear Marcus beginning his breathing exercises. "Okay, don't commit, call the scary aliens that everyone hates and fears if I'm afraid. Got it."

Dmitri rolled his eyes. "Okay, I'm going to leave the personal communication device in my top drawer. Get it before you leave today. You can reach me if you have trouble."

Marcus exhaled. "Okay. I will." There was a soft knock. "Oh, I gotta go. My first appointment just got here."

Dmitri hung up the phone and smiled before starting one of the many tasks he had to accomplish before he could really leave. He really hoped the twins weren't going to destroy that planet.

# CHAPTER TWENTY-SIX

D'Las sighed slightly as he hovered over a continent the part of his brain connected to V'Let identified as Australia. As far as he could tell, it was the single smallest landmass this planet had to offer. It was also the last he had to scan before he could return to his sister.

It didn't take long. Australia was very small, compared to everything else. When the scan was completed, he noticed there was a large amount of yellow dots on this continent, almost enough to rival the black. There were no white dots.

He tilted his head at the viewscreen and tapped a command on the console. His view of Australia became three-dimensionally topographical. From what he could tell, most of the demons on this landmass were actually under it.

"That's interesting," he murmured to himself. "Underground demons... Something to tell V'Let."

*Some demons have relocated under the earth to escape the growing human plague...*

D'Las furrowed his brow slightly. *V'Let?* he called out mentally, hoping idly that he was close enough physically for her to hear. Not that that was ever an actual problem.

*Yes?* He heard her mental drawl clearly, much more clearly than he usually could at great distances.

*Did you just say something to me about demons?*

There was a mental scoff. *No. I'm talking to a human right now. I think she's a little bit something else, though.*

D'Las input a command for the spacecraft to start heading toward

V'Let's location. *So you didn't say something about underground demons escaping the human plague?*

He heard a soft giggle, one that certainly did not originate from his sister, and soft echoes of a conversation. The term "banshee" suddenly bounced around in his head. *I believe that was one of the comments about demons in Mallik's upload. A lot of the species have been underground, literally, for centuries.* There was a pause. *You think she's a banshee?*

*I don't know,* he hedged. *It was just there. I don't know what's going on.*

He could feel the worry growing on the edge of her thoughts. *You should get back, as soon as you're capable.*

*Will do. The alley?* He felt more than heard her affirmation as their connection dimmed down again. He wasn't entirely sure where the comment about the subterranean demons had originated but he wasn't going to pursue it further.

D'Las glanced down at the console and realized that he forgot to turn off the long-range scanner. He was well on a way back to his sister's location. Below him was a large expanse of deep blue water, which made him very aware of himself and his current location. Glancing at the viewscreen, he noticed that it was in the process of a deep scan on the water.

D'Las furrowed his brow again. The scanner only began a deep scan when it sensed something in or just outside of its range. Obviously there was something and the time it was taking to scan denoted that it was something unspeakably huge.

When the scan finished, it was covered in the bright green that was the planetary being as an overlay. Underneath was something completely different. At first, he thought the color of it was silver. After a moment, he stood from the console chair and moved closer to viewscreen. The color of the object of the scan was unknown; it was alternating very quickly from white to bright gray to black and back again. It was static and from its size and location, he could tell that it covered miles and miles of the ocean floor.

"Gods above," he muttered in awe. "What is that?"

# CHAPTER TWENTY-SEVEN

Rosalie stood on the Crone's porch, watching the darkness of night creep over the city. Inside, she was full of fear and nervous energy. The Crone would be performing the ritual tonight, one that was aimed toward protecting the entire planet. Rosalie knew that this had been her idea but it was all on the Crone. All the details, all that raw power that it required, all of that had been ironed out by Matlinda.

"You think too much, little Rosie."

Rosalie turned around to face Quin, who was standing in the doorway. She flicked her gaze past him for a moment to see Matlinda and Erik at the far end of the foyer, deep in a discussion. She shifted her eyes to look at the demon again. "And?"

Quin glanced back at the Crone, noting her soft expression as she spoke with the vampire. "Just because you don't have the available power for this ritual does not make it or you any less important."

Again, it was a moment in time where Rosalie only heard what she wanted to hear. "I don't have power," she murmured softly.

Quin sat down on the porch swing and sighed, patting the space next to him. Without a word, Rosalie sat down in the space indicated, turning slightly so that her full attention was on Quin. "First of all, you do have power. In abundance. What makes you think that you don't?"

Rosalie smiled sadly, gazing in Quin's flat black eyes. "Yes, I have power. But I don't have even enough control of it to do what a novice witch can do. This power that I have, it wants to destroy me."

Quin matched her sad smile and reached to hug the girl. She was barely twenty-two and had accomplished quite a bit in that time, as he had been told by the Crone. A family curse that spread insanity... Quin knew he couldn't be so strong.

"Are we ready?"

Quin and Rosalie looked up to see Erik looking down at them expectantly. Quin nodded and stood from the swing. "I'm prepared to babysit some crystals."

Erik arched an eyebrow at the demon. "You sound rather enthusiastic about that."

Quin moved to the doorway, mentally nudging them on their way. "Well, yeah. Releases of power attract evil, nasty things like winged insects to a flame and the Crone assures me that this is a rather powerful ritual. I am very comfortable being elsewhere."

Erik chuckled and Rosalie joined him as he stepped down off the porch to the ground. Matlinda looked at Quin seriously. "If anyone comes by, be sure to make them aware that I will not be available for the next four days."

"Four days?" he echoed. "The ritual's just tonight, right?"

Matlinda's lips curved into a small smile. "Yes, but it will almost completely drain me. I'll be useless to everyone that would seek me for a few days after."

Quin darted his gaze downward, blushing slightly. "Oh, right. Will do."

Matlinda waved idly at the demon and then joined the vampire and planeswalker on the ground. With the instructions given, she began to lead them toward the leyline that she had chosen. Quin watched them slip away into the darkness and then settled back onto the porch swing. It was going to be a long night.

Matlinda turned around to face Rosalie after they were about half a mile from her house. "So, Rosalie, are you ready?"

The planeswalker sighed softly. "As ready as I'll ever be." She looked the Crone in the eyes. "I'm not even really sure if this will work."

Erik snickered. "No, Rose. She wants us to planeswalk there. She wants you to take us there."

Rosalie arched an eyebrow at the vampire. "Why?" she asked automatically. Then, before anyone could answer her, she continued. "Wait! Is this what the two of you were talking about in the foyer?"

Matlinda chuckled gently. "Erik was trying to convince me that the experience was highly unpleasant. However, I still maintain that this particular venture can be quite useful."

"Useful?" Rosalie echoed. Matlinda merely smiled and held out her hand. Rosalie grasped it and looked at Erik. "Okay, then. You ready?"

Erik growled slightly. "No." However, he grasped her shoulder firmly. "Let's go."

Rosalie inclined her head slightly, which Erik accepted as a nod. She concentrated deeply, closing her eyes and slowly letting her surroundings mean less, be less. Mentally, she reached down and pulled at that part of herself that she hated to disturb. It was essentially her control center, a tightly coiled part of herself that kept her sane through rigid control of the planeswalking. This was the entire purpose of her daily meditations and she was about to have to put a crack in that control.

Matlinda looked over Rosalie in concern. She could feel power mounting below the surface and knew that it was Rosalie's trapped power being used. "What's happening?" she mouthed to the vampire.

Erik just shook his head and placed his index finger on his lips. "Just wait," he mouthed back. He knew the Crone was beginning to feel antsy and she wanted to experience the planeswalking with Rosalie to see if there was a way to unbind her power. However, he had seen Rosalie do this before, when she actually had to search something down on one of the other planes, sometimes when she had to collect raw materials for the Prince that no one else would retrieve for him. This process was hard on her system and nearly detrimental to her control.

Rosalie felt the crack grow slowly, could feel her sanity slipping ever so slightly. At that point, she stopped the pressure on her control, using her trance state to seal the crack as it was. Promising herself that she would repair it later, she pulled out of her trance and looked. There was quite a lot to look at. That small crack in her control caused her to see twenty more planes of existence on top of the Material Plane. She swallowed thickly, feeling a part of herself recoil in fear at some of the things she was seeing. Some of them she had forgotten because she had turned her mind away. The Realm of Pain, the Plane of Death, the Plaguing Unknown… She'd completely forgotten them and the things on them frightened her anew for a moment.

Erik could smell the fear on Rosalie and wondered in concern what she was seeing. He heard the small intake of breath and guessed that she was perhaps seeing something that didn't want to see, perhaps something that she had forgotten existed. He shook his head imperceptibly and reminded himself about her strength. After all, she had survived all of this for twenty years before he had vowed to protect her. He couldn't protect her from the other realms.

Mentally, Rosalie shook herself. This was no time to become a frightened girl that saw too much. She steeled herself and looked past the horrific images that the Realm of Pain served her to see the Plateau of Light. The skies were clear and everything gleamed like spotless silver and platinum. Coming back to the physical form of herself, she gripped the Crone's hand and smiled an honest smile at Erik. He nodded at her but she saw the discomfort in his eyes. She knew he hated this ride.

Matlinda inhaled to cleanse her mind and exhaled the moment that everything disappeared. Initially, she was only aware of darkness. It was as if she'd been stripped of everything. It reminded her of times before she'd received the title of Crone, when spells and rituals would drain her of power so completely that all that was left was this awesome awareness of her blindness. Next, she was aware of herself only to the extent that she felt a lack of self. There was no sensory perception of any kind. She was also highly aware that if not for her high level of magical ability or her own natural blindness, this experience would have felt a lot worse.

It only took half a moment and then there were on the Plateau of Light. Rosalie glanced at the Crone and noted the low level of discomfort on her face. "We don't have to do that again if you don't want."

Matlinda made a dismissive gesture. "Whether I want it or not, I imagine we may have to do it again to get back. I'm not sure how much power this ritual will drain from me."

Rosalie nodded in understanding and then looked around. They were standing at the foot of the specific plateau that was Aura's Sacred Shrine. She peered upward, trying to see the top clearly. She couldn't see Aura herself and the shrine seemed to be dim. Turning back to her companions, she grinned and made an all-encompassing gesture with her arms. "Welcome to the Plateau of Light."

Matlinda smiled back at her good-naturedly but Erik just squinted and grumbled under his breath. "Can we just get out of here?"

Rosalie glanced around the realm. She'd sensed that this plane had the clearest path to the Realm of Fluidity, the territory of the Prince. So, that meant there had to be a...

There it was!

About a hundred yards east of where they stood was a tear in the plane that vaguely resembled a jagged rip. It was recent and sluggishly closing. Every minute or so, white light flashed at its edges, giving away that there was someone on the other side keeping it open. Rosalie arched an eyebrow at the rip but moved toward it just the same. The others followed her just a step behind, Erik's guard up. He was well aware that no matter what the realm seemed to contain, they all had something that could hurt them.

Before much time had passed, they were stepping through the rip, carefully avoiding the white flashes of light. Rosalie was rather sure that Aura was the one of the other side of the planar tear holding it open, something she was likely doing for her own sake. While the Oracle of Light would normally balk at harming anyone, there were few creatures on the Plateau of Light that could be allowed into the Prince's Realm.

On the other side, they now stood in the Realm of Fluidity, where nothing was solid and everything changed, usually more often than expected. Unlike a week ago, she chose not to crest the hill but to skirt it. She was not in the mood to get drawn in to the Prince's whims, which was likely to happen if he managed a glimpse of her through the walls of his flickering palace. In fact, she had ignored all of his summons in the past seven days. Matlinda had been including her heavily in the making of this ritual, explaining everything and teaching her what she didn't understand. If asked, she would eventually tell him that she just hadn't had the time but the truth was that she didn't think she could stand to look at him without malice and betrayal echoing inside her head.

She only glanced at the palace once when she had the clearest view. At the time, she couldn't even see Prince Darrin but she knew he was there. The walls flickered and she could see that the dais that held his throne was surrounded by a multitude of beings, a lot of them she recognized to be Oracles of different realms. She tilted her head at the scene for a moment but shook herself and moved forward. She would have time to think about it later. Right now, she needed to look for the entrance into the Fey Realm.

*Or Realms, rather,* she reminded herself. They hated it when she referred their "intrinsically connected yet separate multitude of realms" as a single plane. She hoped with desperation that just this once she could avoid interacting with the King and Queen.

As they edged around the south edge of the hill, Rosalie saw the arch. The apex of the arch was at nine feet, she approximated. It gleamed white, somehow proud and gentle simultaneously, and managed to hide partially in the foliage near the Prince's hill. As she led them closer to the arch, she see the glowing Celtic knots that seemed to be etched into the very stone of the arch. She reached out and pressed the tip of her index finger roughly against one of its sharp edges. Pulling her hand away, she glanced at her finger with medical indifference. The cut was clean and had been almost painless. As blood welled to the point that it was about to drip off, she flicked her hand in the direction of the arch and let fly a medium-sized drop into the entryway. It stopped at the barrier, causing a surreal-looking ripple to echo through the arch.

"Rosalie? That you?" The voice that responded to her call was familiar. Rosalie had hoped that he was watching the gateway today.

"Yes." She pitched her voice clear and loud enough that it could be heard through the barrier. She noticed that many things on the other side tended to come through muddled. "Myself and two companions. I request entrance, Seamus."

A masculine hand reached through the barrier and Rosalie grabbed it as well as reaching behind her to grab Erik's hand, who in turn grasped Matlinda's arm firmly. The hand pulled them through securely and Rosalie breathed a sigh of relief.

A throaty chuckle greeted her. "You been avoidin' people, missy?"

Rosalie looked down at Seamus, a four-foot-tall satyr with an Irish brogue. "Maybe," she hedged in response to his inquiry.

Seamus arched an eyebrow. "Prince says you been ignorin' his calls. Her Highness misses your visits."

Rosalie snorted. "And the King?"

"Remains unconcerned, he does," he commented. "Where you been?"

Rosalie rolled her eyes and looked back at Erik and Matlinda. "This is Erik and—"

Before she could introduce Matlinda, Seamus stomped his foot impatiently and interrupted her. "I know your blood fiend and I'd know the Crone anywhere." Whereas he glared at the vampire, he presented the witch with a pleasant grin.

Matlinda inclined her head slightly, her eyes solidly on the satyr. "Pleased to make your acquaintance."

Seamus turned his attention back to the young planeswalker. "So, you wouldn't bring the fiend through here unless you was in a hurry. Why would that be?"

"We need to get to the fairy ring near the middle of the Great Redwood Forest. On the Material Plane."

Seamus nodded. "I see. They won't be happy that you came through here without them knowin'."

Rosalie knelt down to be closer to Seamus's level. "I know and I'm sorry. It's kind of urgent."

"Alright, follow me." Seamus began to lead them in a pattern that suggested that he was skirting a particular area.

"Wait!" Erik stopped and glared at the satyr. "What's wrong with me?"

Seamus didn't pause his pace or even turn to look back at the vampire. "Demons ain't allowed in Tir na nOg. Just like fey ain't allowed in the Hells."

Erik slowly started walking again, if only because the Crone nudged him forward. "This is the Valley of the Young?"

Seamus grunted. "We'd best hurry before the Guard comes. They been itching for violence lately. Everyone be itching for something, it seems."

"Probably the aliens," Rosalie commented idly.

"Don't be so sure," Matlinda returned in a soft voice.

Seamus glanced back at Rosalie and then Matlinda. He didn't understand what they were referring to but it was just as well. "Her Highness says change is comin'. She don't know if it be bad."

"We can only hope," Rosalie whispered.

After they'd followed Seamus for about half a mile, he stopped. In front of them stood what seemed to be an unending line of bright yellow stalks. Seamus gestured them forward. "Just follow the silverweed. It'll take you out."

Rosalie was silently filing all of this information for future use. It was a way to get in and out of the fey realms with the muss and fuss of dealing with the Prince. As they followed the line of silverweed, she noticed that under closer inspection the stalks were actually a silvery-gray but covered with small yellow flowers.

The time seemed endless but she knew that time flowed like that on the fey realms. Time was a flowing, undulating, changing thing. In what was actually a short amount of time, they found themselves in a fairy ring of mushrooms that seemed to be vaguely blue. As one, they stepped out of it. Rosalie was relieved to be free of the stress that being so near the Prince brought on, Erik was ecstatic to be free of the madness that was the foreign realms, and Matlinda was happy that the time for this ritual had finally come.

The Crone glanced up and gauged the height of the moon for the time. "I have an hour," she announced. "I'll prepare." She stepped away from them, aware that Erik was keeping an extremely alert eye on their surroundings. The power display would come soon enough and he would have something to do. For now, though, she needed to find the leyline.

Matlinda reached out with her senses and searched, simultaneously looking into the distance and deep down into the earth. After a moment, she smiled and pulled her preternatural senses back to herself. Three leylines crisscrossed about fifty yards from where she stood. It wasn't quite a power sink but the closest one was in Quebec. She was afraid she wasn't built for that level of travel anymore.

She moved in that direction with smooth grace. As she approached it, she fully realized that she could feel the earth power emanating from it. It would help amplify her own natural magic but she would more than likely be nearly drained. Perhaps she would have just enough oomph to teleport them back. Maybe.

The Crone knelt down at the point that the leylines crisscrossed. She envisioned the circle around her and pulled a small packet of sea salt out of a hidden pocket within her robe that she would use to sanctify it. She traveled the line of the circle, laying down the salt and calling down the Guardians of the four Cardinals as she did so. As she made her space sacred, she found her way to the center of it again and began her entreaty to the Goddess by addressing the Holy Trinity.

"Maiden, Mother and Crone, I humbly plead for your aid in our endeavor..."

As the Crone began her preparations that would continue until the midnight hour, Erik investigated every near corner of the forest while surreptitiously keeping a close eye on Rosalie. As soon as they were back on the Material Plane, she'd sat in a lotus position and put herself in a deep trance. He imagined she was working on repairing what damage she may have caused to her control. He knew what to do, though she had not said a word to him. Once the actual ritual began, he would nudge her out of the trance so that she could watch. She had a desperate kind of thirst when it came to learning about magic. Until that time came, he continued his survey on the area.

There was still time yet.

# CHAPTER TWENTY-EIGHT

Cara Jones glanced up at the wall clock above the entrance to her café and idly noted the time: eleven o'clock. She had officially been closed for an hour but she wasn't able to lock her doors until half an hour ago. There was always that one customer that she could never quite get to leave. However, there was still one more person left in her shop.

"So, you're what, exactly?" She grinned at the strange woman who was sitting on a table in the middle of the shop as she swept the floors.

V'Let smiled softly at Cara. "What makes you think I'm anything but human?"

"The coffee," she responded simply as she disappeared to retrieve her mop and some scalding water.

V'Let clucked her tongue. "But I didn't have any coffee." She couldn't help the disgust that rolled off her tongue at just the mention of the word.

Cara reappeared, pushing a plastic bucket with the handle of her mop, and grinned broadly at the woman. "That, right there. Just the way you say 'coffee', I can tell you despise it."

"Aren't you observant?"

Cara watched the woman's face smooth out slightly, knew that somehow her attention was a little bit somewhere else. "What did you say your name was again?"

"V'Let." The answer was simple, the way someone would say their name when they're not thinking about it. It was who they are.

"I thought you said 'Violet' earlier."

V'Let snapped back to attention and focused on Cara. "You have to admit that 'Violet' sounds more normal." She paused, taking in Cara's idle nod and smile. "Are you a... banshee?"

Cara glanced up, her smile growing broad. "Good guess. Yeah. I'm one-sixteenth banshee, the rest is human."

"So, what does the coffee have to do with my inhumanness?" V'Let glanced down at the floor and decided to stay on the table. She could smell the harsh soaps and thought it would perhaps be better to wait for it to dry.

"You hate it. Only the Others hate coffee." At V'Let's arched eyebrow, Cara continued as she scrubbed at the last bit of floor. "There might be humans that dislike coffee but only the Others have that level of disdain for it. Whatever repels everything else seems to draw humans in."

V'Let decided to tell Cara the truth. *She seems trustworthy down to her core.* "I'm an alien, Cara."

"Oh." She glanced at V'Let a moment before disappearing to the back again. "As in, 'take me to your leader'?"

For a moment, V'Let wondered if her judgment had been flawed. "Actually, I'd prefer the opposite."

Cara reemerged, a small smile on her face. "You look kind of human, though."

V'Let heard the question in the statement. She concentrated for a moment and let the glamour fade, revealing her true form. "Are you looking for something like this?"

Cara seemed shell-shocked for just a moment. "Something like that, yeah." She reached out and touched V'Let's hair, feeling its fine quality. "Why are you here? You know, humans tend to associate aliens with invasion."

V'Let's bright blue eyes hardened. "Yes, I know." She glanced at the shop's entrance and then back at the petite shop owner. *The time for truth was over.* "My brother and I are actually here to study what you call Others, the nonhumans."

Cara grinned brightly. "So, it's like specimen research, right?" After a moment, she frowned. "There's not going to be icky experiments, right?"

V'Let saw the images of people Cara knew torn apart just for the sake of research. She shook her head in response. "No, nothing like that. We have scanners. It's just surface research."

Cara nodded idly. "Oh, okay. That's good." They both sat in silence for a short moment before Cara jerked slightly. "Oh, I know!"

V'Let smiled in amusement as she watched the girl disappear to the back again. When she returned, she was carrying a map. "What is that?"

"It's a map of the city. Now, most of the demons keep to downtown." She ringed out a large area on the map with her index finger, then pointed at an intersection at the northern edge of that area. "The Crone lives here. She could probably help you with the whole finding-nonhumans thing."

V'Let nodded at her in gratitude. "That would be helpful. Who is the Crone?"

Cara's eyes widened considerably. "You don't know...?" She smacked herself lightly on the forehead then. "Right, alien. She's the oldest and debatably strongest of all witches, according to my mother. Mom goes to her for potions and the like. Crone is a title for older witches."

"Magic," V'Let murmured.

"Yeah," Cara replied. "Anyway, she lives there. She should be able to help."

V'Let nodded. "We'll go there first, then." She moved gracefully from the table to her feet. "My brother should be here soon and he's not... social."

Cara smiled and held out the map to her. "You need this?"

V'Let shook her head and tapped her temple. "It's all up here. I've got a good memory." With that said, she turned around and left, slipping out the doors without a sound.

Cara frowned at the door. "I thought I locked that."

V'Let smiled to herself as she made her way back to the spacecraft. All the shops were dark, so she felt no need to reconstruct her glamour. She rounded the corner into the alley and hopped upward when she noticed the shimmering air. In an instant, the vaguely unstable air turned into the very solid metal of the spacecraft. Upon entrance, she almost ran into her brother.

He looked her up and down. "Are you insane?" he inquired, a dangerously high note encroaching on his voice.

She smirked at him. "Not that I've noticed, but who am I to judge?"

He shook his head and turned away, leading her through the cargo area and to the bridge. *You really are too happy for your own good.*

V'Let arched an eyebrow at D'Las's back. He'd switched from verbal to mental communication seamlessly without any type of help or coercion from her. She reached out and closed the airlock with a twinge of afterthought and scurried to follow her brother.

*You'll never believe what I found over the... Pacific Ocean, I think?*

V'Let smiled at her brother's back. Something was going on. *Well, I know where we need to go next. That extremely diluted banshee was very helpful.*

D'Las turned around to face her, coming to a dead stop as he did so. *Did you reveal herself to her?*

V'Let nodded slightly, refusing to feel guilty. She hadn't done anything wrong this time, not even according to the regulations under the Council's own "preferences concerning planets that remain technologically disinclined and thus uninvolved with Council policies". *I did. And everything was fine. She didn't spiral out of control or anything. We had a civil conversation. She'd already guessed I wasn't human anyway.*

She watched as D'Las arched an eyebrow at her purposefully. When he responded, she noticed that his mental voice had gotten less audible inside her head. *Can this new destination wait until the new day? I believe what I found requires your sight.*

*Fine, okay. We'll go see this Crone tomorrow.* She let forth a mental sigh. *Lead on.*

He continued to lead her to the bridge. Upon reaching the central console, he input a set of coordinates that would take them roughly twenty minutes to reach. When he turned his attention to her again, she greeted him with an open visage. *Why did you switch to mental communication?*

V'Let tilted her head at him. He sounded genuinely curious. After a moment, she got it and it felt like a slap in the face. He was opening up subconsciously at an exponential rate, it seemed, but he was consciously and desperately hanging on to that last thread of repression. *I didn't switch until you did, D'Las.* She poured as much truth into those seven words as she was able.

*Say what?*

# CHAPTER TWENTY-NINE

Erik perked on the edge of the clearing when he began to feel the power mount. He glanced across the clearing to look at Rosalie. She was gazing back at him with clear hazel eyes. She tilted her head very slightly in the Crone's direction, a question in the gesture. He nodded once in response and watched as she stood to move closer to Matlinda, though not too close, to watch the ritual carefully.

Matlinda made an involuntary but slight jerk as she felt movement outside of her circle. She stilled and waited, though a part of her was still deep in the process of drawing power to her. The movement stopped, barely a foot beyond her power circle, and she relaxed enough to continue with the ritual. The girl would remain safe from her raw power and the vampire would keep them safe from everything else.

The Trinity had responded eerily quickly, as if even the Goddess had sensed this earthly urgency. For the last twenty minutes, she had been drawing power and creating connections. She was now firmly bound to both the spirit within the Earth and her sisters across the globe. There were gatherings of witches in Canada, South America, Europe, various parts of Asia, two specific points in Africa, Australia, and even another on the other coast of the United States. They were all ready, continuously drawing power until the moment arrived.

Matlinda listened to the earth to the best of her ability. There was a deep thrum inside the earth, echoing through the root system. *Now or never, Mattie,* she commented to herself.

Almost instantaneously, all the witches committed to this ritual halted their power gathering. The invocations were done and it was time to start the actual spell. They were fully connected to their respective leyline, which was an essential part of this ritual. Every iota of concentration needed to flow down into the earth. The moon was at its peak at the Crone's location.

The ritual began.

Matlinda took a deep breath and called out in imperfect Latin, "*Advoco tu adiuvo per hora difficultas!*"

Outside the circle, Rosalie watched, enthralled, and translated the words idly in barely a whisper. "We call on you who we have invoked in our hour of need."

"*Apud multi locus, exsisto!*"

"At many different locations, we stand."

"*Procul, iugo!*"

"From a distance, we connect."

"*Contego quoque complexo terra!*"

"Protect and encompass the earth."

"*Contego de omnis periculum!*"

"Protect from all harm."

"*Volo peractio!*"

"So mote it be."

In a smooth movement, Matlinda wrapped her hands around the hilt of her silver athame and plunged the dagger into the point where the leylines connected. The implement glowed white and flowed smoothly into the ground.

Rosalie watched in concern as Matlinda sagged to the ground. She didn't dare break the circle, however. She had no clue what that might do. She wasn't even completely sure that the ritual was really over.

"Well, well, aren't you a perfect little *rose*," a voice said from behind her, a very dangerous-sounding emphasis on the last word.

Rosalie craned her neck slowly, not really wanting to see what she knew was behind her. It was a vampire minion Erik had told her was called Lenny, formerly Leonard Franz. He stood at six foot, five inches tall and was deeply encased in muscle. Erik had called him a mechanic with a laugh. Later, he'd explained that he was the gang enforcer, which she knew meant he killed a lot and enjoyed it.

Not that most vampires didn't enjoy killing.

"Erik!" she called out in pure panic.

"Kinda busy!" he yelled back with what sounded to be a grunt following the words. Rosalie looked fully at where the vampire was, though she had begun to back away from Lenny. Across the clearing was Erik against three other vampires. She glanced back at Lenny and cringed at the molester's smile on his face. Glancing back, she tried to get a quick read on Erik's situation. She noted a flash of silver and one of the vampires hindering Erik's stance fell away. A fraction of a moment passed and there was another to take his place.

Rosalie jumped when she felt a crackle of energy. Hopping simultaneously away from the energy and Lenny, she turned her attention to what zapped her. It was the Crone's power circle and it was very slowly inching outward in all directions. While she was still instinctively moving away, she couldn't look away from the circle and Matlinda in the center of it. She wasn't moving.

"Come on," she whispered fervently, subconsciously trying to transmit energy at the prone witch. "Come on, Matlinda. Get up. It's not finished." She eyed the growing circle dubiously. "I think."

After what seemed like a very tense eternity, she saw the Crone move at a painstaking rate. She was lifting herself up using the hilt of the dagger. After stopping to take a breath, she gave the dagger a hard twist and pulled it out of the earth. Looking up, she smiled weakly at Rosalie and fell back down, this time on her back.

Rosalie looked back at Lenny. She saw that the vampire had a mixture of confusion and malicious intent on his face. When he focused on her after glancing at the power circle, which she imagined had to be troublesome for a vampire's power-seeking senses, that delight for whatever he intended to do to her overwhelmed everything else. She gave him a cocky smirk and took off in a dead run in the opposite direction, trying to aim in her panic-fogged mind for Erik's general vicinity.

She had been running for less than two seconds when she started to take in what was happening around her. They were surrounded, the entire clearing starting to crowd with vampires. A lot of them moved like newborn vamps without clear instructions. Apparently, the gang had been busy.

"What are we going to do?" she murmured softly. It didn't even occur to just planeswalk away from this nightmare. She refused to leave Erik alone in this. If he was going to die, she was happy to be the damsel he died for.

Suddenly, as quickly as she realized the odds were extremely against them, everything stopped. Rosalie glanced back, automatically checking on the Crone because Erik had already been in her sights, and noted that the power circle, the dome of crackling energy was gone. It was as if the earth had inhaled it.

If that was an apt analogy for what had happened, then sneezing was just as fitting for what happened next. The dome had been like a filmy white cover filling up with energy being drawn from the Crone herself but now green light was exploding out of cracks in the earth that Rosalie would swear on her parents' graves hadn't been there before. It filled the air and covered the ground, spirals upon spirals of green energy.

Mere moments later, she felt herself forced to the ground, though not painfully. Also, she could have sworn she heard a voice before everything went black.

*"Contego!"*

# PART TWO:
## Deals of Healing

"Give nothing of yourself. They'll make everything up anyway."
*- Madame Marina DuPont, on dealing with press*

# CHAPTER THIRTY

"I'm not saying I don't believe you."

"Oh, really?"

V'Let sighed audibly. They were back above the city that she had decided would be a good study of both humans and protected species. They'd gone out to that awesome expanse of water where there was a stretch of static reading. She saw it, openly admitted to seeing it but she wasn't sure it was as significant as he was making it.

"I do believe you. And I do admit that it was all kinds of weird."

"Um, V'Let—"

She cut him off. "Just... let me say this, okay? We'll check it out, somehow. I just don't know what to do about it being underwater."

"V'Let!"

V'Let looked at her brother sharply. "What! I'm trying to apologize here."

D'Las smiled softly at his sister. "Yeah, I got that part. But there's something coming at us." He punched a button and the screen was replaced with a radar system, which showed that something was enveloping the planet at a disturbing rate. "And it's coming fast."

*Down!* V'Let snapped mentally at her brother. In response, he flattened himself against the floor of the bridge without a second thought. She glanced at the radar system and reached out with her senses, trying to gauge what its purpose was. But it was coming too fast and she needed to react.

She curled herself down into a ball, making herself as small as possible. She pulled her senses in to wrap around the spacecraft and thought one Looran word with as much power packed into it as she could manage.

*"Yabusu!"*

Translated to common English, it meant "unbreakable".

Whatever it was finally reached the spacecraft, causing it to rock gently like a willow tree caught in a breeze. However gentle the rocking was, it was still disturbing the spacecraft. It frightened V'Let somewhat. Whatever this thing was, it was massive.

"What's going on?" D'Las whispered from his prone position, very careful to not move. He could feel the fear rolling off his sister in waves.

V'Let mentally shrugged at her brother. Every piece of her was enveloped in protecting the shell that was their spacecraft. She would not, could not fail.

*"Let go, little friend."*

V'Let's hold on the protective shield around the ship faltered slightly and she grunted as she reaffirmed her concentration. She pulled a thread of her power separate and called outward in an attempt to respond. *Why should I do that?*

*"I won't hurt you. Can't."*

V'Let thought furiously for a moment, which was a bit of a challenge seeing as a large chunk of her concentration was currently occupied. *Who are you?*

*"Mm. They call me Gaia, Terra, Mother Earth. But I think you would know me as the Earth entity."*

*Oh,* V'Let thought idly, her mind slightly dizzy. *Oh!* As instantly at the realization came to her, she felt herself being filled with a different sort of knowledge, something that had to be straight from the entity itself. At the moment, she couldn't sort it all out. She didn't know if there would ever come a time when she would be able to. However, there were bits and pieces of information that seemed urgent and she pressed it upon herself to sort through that knowledge to the best of her ability.

Without further thought, she pulled her power back to herself, dropping the protection around the spacecraft instantly. She pulled herself up and stretched slightly, her mind racing.

"D'Las? We're good."

D'Las pushed himself to his feet with a strong flex of his forearms. As he moved to the central console, he did his best to gather his shreds of dignity. "Okay. Where to?"

She smiled weakly. Glancing up at the radar that still occupied the viewscreen, she noted that the Earth looked like a very large, bright green ball but the energy was slowly fading. "Do you think you can find the nearest origin of the blast?"

"Sure thing." He typed in a few commands and the systems began a modified long-range scan. "Why do you say 'nearest'?"

V'Let moved to the secondary console and instructed the viewscreen to replay the blast from when it was first registered. "Watch the pattern," she instructed her brother softly.

D'Las watched the green pervasive blast as it repeated again and again in a loop. "It spreads fast. You think there were several origins?"

V'Let nodded as she stopped the loop and cleared the viewscreen. "Yes. Whatever happened, there were several different places from which it was being orchestrated."

"You think it was dangerous?"

"No, not really." V'Let sat back in the chair at the secondary console, rubbing her eyes with a type of exhaustion. For a moment, she felt that it was possible that she had used way too much power protecting the spacecraft. "I think it was the plan."

The entire spacecraft hummed for a moment. "Power origin found. Possible destination fifty-five miles south of current location."

"There?" D'Las asked. When she nodded confirmation, he typed in the coordinates. "What do you mean, 'plan'? For whom?"

"You know they knew." Her eyes were piercing as she gazed at her brother. "Apparently, while we were deep in stasis, they came up with an idea. Protecting the whole planet."

D'Las arched an eyebrow. "I thought we established that their tech is seriously lacking."

"It is." She stood again, feeling nervous energy pump through her veins. "There's something else happening here." She glanced at D'Las before looking back at the viewscreen. "The Earth entity talked to me."

D'Las stood to join his sister, trying to do his best to alleviate her anxiety and knowing that he wasn't much help. "I thought you couldn't. You said it was too big, on a higher level?"

She nodded. "It is, except apparently when we're there. On that higher level, when we use large amounts of power."

"You," he corrected her. "You mean 'you', not 'we'."

For the moment, she ignored him. "It told me it can't and won't hurt us. It wants our help." She nudged him slightly with her shoulder, attempting to lift her spirits. "Apparently, they were protecting the planet and it drew a lot of nasty creatures that are attacking."

D'Las looked down at his sister. "It told you all of this?"

V'Let winced slightly. "Sort of. Half of it was shown to me, like pictures in my head, or just suddenly knowing."

"You want to help them?" He grabbed her shoulders and turned her to look at him. "These people could hurt us. For all that we know, they're perfectly capable and probably *want* to hurt us."

V'Let nodded, straightened her back in a subtle gesture as she did so. "I want to help, Lasso. I'm tired to destroying and I'm tired of hurting because of it."

D'Las grinned. "Okay, let's do it."

V'Let smiled up at her brother, feeling some of the weight slide off her shoulders. "Good, because we're here."

Together, they walked down to the cargo area. The closer they got to the airlock, the more tense V'Let and D'Las became. For once, they were going into a situation completely unprepared. The so-called "nasty creatures" could be unbeatable, unkillable. The people they were attempting to help could turn on them in a heartbeat. V'Let was the only one with a real grasp on their natural power. But they were determined and, for once, their decisions weren't being controlled by someone else or even a group of someone elses.

They had very nearly reached the airlock when V'Let halted suddenly. She turned, said "Excuse me" to her brother, and bolted up to the bunk area very quickly.

"Change your mind?" D'Las called out clearly.

"No" was the faint response but he could feel her indignation echo strongly through their link.

"Fine," he muttered, crossing his arms over his chest in a sullen manner. "Don't tell me."

He heard a huff through the link and got the feeling that she was rolling her eyes. Three seconds later, he heard the muffled thuds of her hurrying back down to the cargo area. He looked back and noticed that she was carrying two palm-sized devices in her hands.

"What are those?"

V'Let grinned broadly at her brother. "Laser swords."

D'Las arched an eyebrow. "Laser swords?" he echoed doubtfully.

She tilted her head and widened her eyes at him meaningfully. "Yes, laser swords. I used metals I kept from planet Voo to make the 'hilt', or rather the origin device. The Bartians had nearly finished their research into making cutting laser finite, or at least shapeable. I merely took the leap to finish it."

D'Las flipped the device and looked at the base of the "hilt", where there was a symbol. As he knew there would be. "And this?"

V'Let chuckled. "It's a Looran power word."

D'Las traced the symbol cut into the metal. It resembled a upper-case "L" and a lower-case "h" with a starburst neatly incased between the two. He smiled. Most of V'Let's experiments were peppered with some kind of Looran tech, even if it was just a small detail. "What does it say?"

"*Dwan*," she replied simply.

"Sever," he echoed softly. "It'll help."

"Yes, it will." V'Let reached out with her free hand and pushed the airlock button, opening the hatch to the clearing the computer had chosen. She frowned as the scene outside their spacecraft started to make sense to her. Two females that seemed human were prone, one very large man was prone as well, and there was a man fighting off a never-ending stream of other men with a silver blade. The clearing was becoming choked with these men.

There was something very familiar about the men. They weren't human, that much was obvious to V'Let, but they could very definitely pass. After a moment, it occurred to her what they were.

*Vampires.* They seemed familiar because she had recently been in a vampire's mind. However, they were all angry as could be and their numbers gave away the intent to ambush.

D'Las gave a low whistle. "There's a lot of them, Letta."

She patted him reassuringly on the shoulder. "No worries, Lasso. Just... try to cut off their heads."

As one, they leaped off the hatch and landed near-soundlessly on the ground. "What?" D'Las tilted his head slightly to glance at his sister. "Why the head?"

V'Let shrugged. "If it doesn't work, I'll think of something else."

D'Las pressed a black button on the side of the device and a finite laser flowed out and back in again in such a way to create a sword, specifically a cutlass. It glowed white and looked to have a mean edge. He grinned at her happily. "You're the best," he whispered.

V'Let chuckled. Her gadgets always gave him a thrill. "I know," she murmured back.

"You got a plan?"

She nodded. "We start hacking at the enraged vampires until they back off a little and then I turn them away."

"You mean—"

"Yeah."

D'Las nodded decisively, a clearly vindictive gleam shining in his eyes. "Let's get to it, then." With that said, he moved forward to where the majority of the vampire were clumping.

*I'll let you have the big one,* he told her through the link.

*Gee, thanks.*

At that, she let their link fall away to a very soft murmuring and marched to the very large but apparently very unconscious vampire. She glanced at the female near him. The girl was small, a pale petite human with brown hair. A part of V'Let tugged gently, assuring her that something about this girl was not quite as human as she looked. Like Cara.

Without another thought, V'Let grasped one of the girl's ankles and started dragging her toward the older woman. Once there, she left the girl just outside what looked to be burnt grass in the shape of a circle outside of the old woman. She was tempted to kneel down and examine the circle when she felt a flash of pain through the bond with her brother. It was just a scratch exacerbated by D'Las's adrenaline but she got the picture. She needed to get her head back in the urgent parts of here and now.

With a sigh, V'Let made her way back to the bulky vampire. He was still completely unconscious and she was particularly curious about this whole scene. It was time for her to employ traits of malicious species that she hated, traits of species that were alive in her every day. She tilted her head and then delivered a swift and effective kick to the ribs of the vampire.

He turned over on his back, subconsciously trying to get away from the leg that kicked, and groaned in a slightly whiny tone.

"Wake up," she snapped harshly. She followed it with another kick to the ribs.

"God," the vampire muttered. "You hit harder than Darius."

V'Let's eyes flashed as she idly picked up surface thoughts. Darius was apparently the leader of Luna Morte. *Erik's gang?* she thought to herself before shaking the thought away. It was irrelevant for the moment. "What's your name?" she demanded of the still-prone vampire.

"You gonna kick me again?" He was sneering at her now. She reared back her kicking leg in an obvious manner. He winced and held out his hands. "Okay, it's Lenny."

She smirked in return. "Okay, *Leonard*," she began, stressing the name his mind said he hated. "What happened here?"

Genuine confusion flashed across his face and his brain went blank, almost literally. "What do you mean?"

V'Let stopped for a moment. It was obviously too broad a question and she needed answers quickly. She glanced up, searching for her brother and his distinctive blade. He had already cut a chunk out of the vampire ranks and he was staying well out of range of the vampire with the silver blade. She needed to ask this thug questions that were simple but would bring her answers in the surface thoughts. "Are these all new vampires?"

Lenny nodded. "Yeah. The others stayed behind. Safety." V'Let distinctively hear him mentally spit *lazy* in place of "safety".

She smirked to herself for a moment. "Hmm, what about your 'safety'?"

V'Let felt his mind harden and it resembled anger. "I had to kill the girl," he ground out.

She glanced back at the petite girl, who was stirring every so often but not waking. "And the army?"

"Distraction. Erik is very protective of this girl, God only knows why. Newbies are expendable."

V'Let nodded to herself. "Very well." She looked down at the palm of her hand and pressed the black button on her own device. Her cutlass laser glowed lavender. She grinned when Lenny's eyes widened. "Thanks for the info."

"What is that? What are you?"

The smile fell from V'Let's face and she swung her sword down in a decisive arc. Lenny's head separated neatly from his shoulders and she watched emotionlessly as both the head and the body seemed to sink in on themselves, leaving nothing but clothing and accessories behind. She glanced up to gauge her surroundings once again.

The newborn vampires were obviously becoming cautious, less eager to just jump into the battle. D'Las had trained every moment available to him for an opportunity like this and he was obviously a force to be reckoned with. The other vampire, the one with the silver blade, was nearly as efficient, cutting a bloody swath through the vampires. However, the newborns were swarming him in particular, probably under direct orders, and that was keeping him from noticing the presence near him that was not vampiric.

*It's time, brother,* V'Let projected to D'Las after a moment of deliberation. She needed to do this now before she lost any more energy. *Grab his blade. The noble vampire will follow.*

D'Las sneered good-naturedly at his sister in response but otherwise did as she directed. He pulled seamlessly away from the melting body of a vampire he had just felled and moved between two vampires that were approaching the man that he now dubbed the "Vampire Knight", following V'Let's comment regarding the vampire. He moved forward to take up the bladed vampire's range of sight, knowing that just the view of his face alone would knock him off-balance just long enough. As the vampire's eyes widened in a weak moment of shock, D'Las yanked at the hilt of his silver katana-like sword. It came easily, though he felt the vampire's grip on the hilt return at the end. It wasn't enough.

D'Las flashed a grin at the vampire and took off at a dead run toward his sister. He felt fingernails graze the back of his collar and his grin broadened. He picked up his speed and shoved his laser sword device into his pocket after switching it off.

*The chase is on!* It was a code phrase. It directed V'Let to begin whatever it was she had decided to do.

V'Let smiled mirthlessly and gazed past her brother and the vampire that was close behind him. There had been a group of five vampires that had just noticed her but they'd been shocked into immobility at the sudden change that D'Las had caused. However, that didn't last long and they were moving again. She narrowed her eyes and directed her power at specifically those five vampires.

"*Tinei sarenwo!*" she called out, lashed out with her power in the same instant. After a terrifying split-second, their screams filled the air as their bodies lit into flame. However, the flaming vampires were no longer an interest to her. She watched the reactions of the other fifteen or so vampires, instead. A few of the remaining vampires fled, flight having now become the reasonable course of action. Most of them stayed on the edge of the clearing with the clear intention of moving forward once their brothers had burned away.

V'Let harrumphed and a large amount of sadness and disgust washed over her countenance. She had hoped that the display of power would be enough to send them away in fear. She'd had enough of violence for the night; she felt now as she generally felt at the end of a mission, as if the violence she had committed would taint her forever.

"No more violence," she murmured under her breath. After a moment, she lashed out with her power again, this time with a completely different intent. "*Shishegui juzenpose, zhuzo!*"

She turned her gaze away from the vampires after she confirmed that they all turned and walked away in the opposite direction from her. She glanced down and realized she was clutching her still-activated laser sword in a very tight grasp. She forced her grip to loosen and slid her thumb to the black button to deactivate the laser.

She glanced up again to see her brother and the vampire beside him. D'Las was on edge, keeping his alert high so that the vampire could not retrieve his very sharp sword. The vampire seemed to be standing still and calm but V'Let knew he was waiting for her brother to give him the tiniest opening so he could strike.

"Stand down, Erik von Telford," she declared calmly.

The vampire stilled even further and shifted his attention to V'Let. He glanced at the women behind her and she heard his low growl. "Do I know you?" he ground out.

D'Las eyed the vampire in a new light. "This is Erik, the protector of a planeswalker?"

V'Let sniffed softly, showing her amusement. "That one, I would wager," she murmured and pointed at the petite brunette behind her. She nodded at Erik again, sending an obvious signal to her brother. "Watch him. I'm going to release the old one."

Erik sighed roughly. "If I promise not to attack, can I have my daikatana back?"

D'Las looked to his sister, who nodded. As he handed the sword back to its owner, she edged around Rosalie and knelt down at the edge of the circle.

Erik glared at D'Las but attempted to watch V'Let carefully as well. "What is she doing?"

D'Las glanced at the vampire curiously. There was a slump in his shoulders, signifying that he was probably much more tired than he was letting on. He then shifted his gaze back to his sister, who was now tracing the grass just outside the circle that had seared itself into the ground. After a moment, she pushed her hand against the air above the outlined circle. He could see a shimmering dome of white come into focus as she did so. Her entire body shuddered slightly and he suddenly knew that she had probably pushed herself too far tonight.

"D'Las?" she called to him after a moment.

He pursed his lips slightly, wanting more than anything to just leave these people to their own devices. He glared at Erik then. "She's trying to release the old woman. Whatever that circle is, it's keeping her trapped inside, probably sapping the woman's power to do so."

Erik's brow furrowed. "How do you know that?"

D'Las made a gesture at his sister and rolled his eyes. "She told me." That said, he moved over to his sister. He glanced at her when he was down at her level. "What do you need me to do?" He kept his voice low.

*I can push through but I don't have the strength left to carry the woman,* she admitted through their link. *I'm going to open a weak spot and you will slip inside.*

*Then what?*

She sat still for a moment, thinking. Then her eyes caught on a glint of silver. *I'm assuming this barrier might cut off our link, make it muffled. However, there's a silver blade in there. Drag its tip across the circle's edge.*

He turned slightly and looked her in the eye. *That's an act of power. I don't have any power.*

She arched a skeptical eyebrow in return, which he expected, but didn't comment on his lack of power. *I can feel power coming from it. It's tied to the old woman, somehow.*

D'Las nodded his assent and turned to face the circle again. *Let's do this.* He placed his hands on the edge of the circle's barrier, idly noticing that the dome was shrinking marginally. V'Let pushed on the barrier lightly with one hand and then struck sharply with the fingertips of her other hand. The dome trembled and D'Las fell through, barely managing to keep from collapsing fully on the old woman.

He looked around and realized that from the inside, the dome looked a lot more threatening. It crackled with white light that, while very pretty, looked equally dangerous. The woman was still unconscious but he made quick work of finding her dagger. It was partially obscured by her robes. When he grasped the hilt, he felt the power working inside this circle. There was a kind of draining sensation that made D'Las's skin crawl. He just wanted it to go away.

He plunged the dagger downward just enough that the tip was slightly under the ground. He dragged it outward until it sliced through the line of seared ground. There was a slight pop and the dome disappeared. D'Las glanced at his sister and smiled. Her weak smile in return was still enough of a reward for him.

D'Las turned back to look at the old woman. He knelt down close to her because he wasn't sure if she was alive. When he was a few inches away from her face, he finally heard her very shallow breathing. That was good; they didn't need to die.

"What is going on?" D'Las arched an eyebrow as the vampire's outburst but remained facing the woman, trying to find the best way to carry her without disturbing her too much. He had a feeling she needed all the sleep she could get.

"Sheath your blade, vampire." That was V'Let, of course, and there was a lot of venom in her voice. She didn't do well when she felt she was being threatened.

"Not until you tell me what just happened. What are you? How did you make the Luna Mortes just... go away?"

"You know what I am."

D'Las snickered softly to himself. The vampire didn't realize it yet but he wasn't going to get any straight answer until he backed off and they got somewhere safe, either inside the ship or a house. V'Let hated to be out in the open when she was as weak as she was now. After another moment of deliberation, D'Las slipped one arm under the old woman's neck and another under the crook of her legs.

He turned slowly and made his way back to their spacecraft, being very careful as not to jostle the woman. He smirked at his sister as he passed by her and she gave him a very slight nod.

"Get your planeswalker, vampire. We're leaving."

D'Las smiled wider as he realized the power reverberating in her voice, making the statement just over the line from a suggestion to a command. He knew she only used a little push, so small that he was ambiguous as to whether it was actually a solid command. However, the vampire was at least marginally surprised enough that he sheathed his sword and picked up the young girl, following them three paces behind.

After a few minutes, they reached the spacecraft. D'Las felt V'Let's smile echo his own from Erik's muffled gasp. The spacecraft was magnificent if you were seeing it for the first time. D'Las couldn't even imagine what it would be like if you hadn't been around spacecrafts your entire life. It was huge, though only a fraction as tall as the trees that surrounded them, and the outer panels shone like black silver. It was actually a bio-organic material that originated on Loora. Both he and V'Let cherished their culture and did everything they could to keep it alive. The hatch was still open, so D'Las moved the woman to rest against his shoulder and pulled himself up with just the one hand. He turned and offered his hand to his sister, who nearly snarled at him in return.

"I'm not helpless," she muttered, using both of her hands to push herself up and rolled the rest of the way inside with the momentum she created.

"This is... You're the aliens!" There was the accusation they were waiting for. "You were in my head!"

V'Let shook her head slightly. "Not my brother, just me." She sneered at the vampire before directed her gaze at D'Las. "I'm putting in the coordinates."

D'Las stared at her in open confusion. "For where? Where are we going to take them?"

She made a dismissive gesture with her hands, already turning away from them toward the stairs. "There's not a one among them human. I imagine the Crone's home would be the best." With that taken care of in her mind, she ascended the stairs and disappeared toward the bridge.

D'Las frowned. He wasn't sure what good going to the Crone's would be. She sounded like an old woman, perhaps not even able to help them. He sighed. However, they needed to start somewhere. That's how it always was.

Erik was moving toward him, a movement which turned D'Las's guard back up. "How did she know?" he hissed.

"Hmm?" D'Las pretended that he hadn't a care in the world, that he was barely paying attention. Just because he was alert didn't mean the vampire had to know it.

The vampire set his girl down in a semi-comfortable position and scooted closer to D'Las. "How did she know that she's the Crone?" On the second female reference, the vampire gestured to the old woman in D'Las's arms.

D'Las's lips curled slightly into a bemused expression. He knew that his sister had not known that they had the Crone but the vampire was under the impression that she was all-knowing. Their nonverbal communication earlier about breaking the circle couldn't have harmed that image at all. He decided his response should be nonchalant. "Oh, you know, she just does."

The vampire looked thoughtful and then his body language just settled. It was possible that he finally realized he was fighting a losing battle with them, D'Las wasn't sure. "So, what's all this stuff?"

D'Las looked at Erik closely. He looked genuinely curious but he wasn't sure if the vampire knew their reputation. He kicked himself mentally. No, how could he? How could the destruction of more than a dozen planets become known on a backwater planet like this one? He smiled good-naturedly at the vampire. "I think V'Let should explain that. Y'know, when everyone's conscious. Besides, she's the one that collected most of it."

Erik has been reaching out, letting his hand flow over the edges of a shapeless statuette. V'Let called that one the Goddess of Creation. "Is all this from the planets you've destroyed?"

D'Las jerked slightly and then forced himself to still. He was still very careful to not harm the woman he was holding. "Say what?"

# CHAPTER THIRTY-ONE

Dmitri scurried around the inside of the Looran speed glider, checking various settings. The glider hadn't been as prepared for a roundtrip flight to Zeta Sector as he'd assumed. Of course, as he well knew, this type of spacecraft wasn't really built for long-term flight but he also knew that it was able. However, all of the settings had to be changed, it was in extreme need of fuel and it was not helping with his son having a panic attack every few minutes.

As Dmitri scurried around the spacecraft, Marcus's face was on the viewscreen, talking to him all the while. He finally found what he was looking for at the forward console, a series of switches that would change the remaining settings on its own, shifting the capabilities of short-distance to intergalactic travel. He flicked the switched happily. They were over two hours behind his original schedule and as much as he poked and prodded at the Head Council Member, he did not want to be the object of his wrath during this very long trip.

"Okay, hush, Marcus." Dmitri cut off his son's current babbling tirade efficiently. Marcus quieted immediately and looked at his father with wide eyes. "Are you really truly worried? Or are you just trying to rid yourself of all this anxiety?"

Marcus smiled in a self-deprecating manner. "The second one."

Dmitri nodded to himself, having assumed as much. "Well, make sure you do what needs to be done. I need to contact V'Let before I allow Mallik and Gralug inside." He watched Marcus nod silently, although his face contorted slightly. He arched an eyebrow at his son but said nothing and waited for Marcus to end their communication.

After a moment, the viewscreen went black. Dmitri shook his head as he punched in the communication sequence and then the twin's spacecraft code. He knew it would take a moment to go through so he sat himself at the console.

He knew his son accepted the twins scientifically, knew that they were essentially controlled by a contract that could literally kill them. However, like everyone else in the Central Planets, he had been hearing Galaxy Killer propaganda since he was very small. They had completely obliterated one planet a year for the last fifteen years, one for which the Adepts had barely kept a bounty off their heads. Dmitri thought that maybe Marcus could come around completely, even in that irrational part of his mind.

He sighed roughly. "I hate psychology!" he muttered with malice.

His viewscreen flickered to life, showing V'Let sitting at the central console of the spacecraft. He noticed that she seemed pale and her pupils seemed larger than normal. "Hello, Dmitri." She sounded exceedingly weary.

"V'Let." He inclined his head slightly in greeting. "Things have gotten a bit complicated on this side."

She smiled at him, her entire expression becoming amused. "Not just on your end."

Dmitri arched an eyebrow before relaxing his countenance again. She would explain, he assumed, but he needed to tell her what happened before he got distracted. "Gralug and Mallik have insisted that we come to stop you from destroying Earth."

V'Let snorted. "I have no intentions of destroying Earth. The humans, however, are another story."

Dmitri was marginally surprised. He had been right. After a moment, he decided that that really hadn't been much guesswork. As much as the twins outwardly seemed to want to destroy everything in sight, they both knew the rules and had in fact fought the Blood Contract to the best of their ability. "What can you do to the humans without destroying Earth?" He was truly curious.

V'Let shrugged half-heartedly, her exhaustion obvious. "I'll think of something, after I've had a rest. They need to be dealt with."

Dmitri nodded, his mind thinking about that. He had seen the reports. The humans were truly one of the most malevolent species he had ever seen. Something needed to be done about them. After a moment, he focused on V'Let again. "What happened there?"

V'Let's smile turned quickly to a frown. "Some nonhumans are confused or maybe quick to judge. They assumed we were here to destroy the planet."

"Well…"

V'Let glared at Dmitri to the best of her ability. "I'm not sure what happened but they managed to allow the Earth entity to become proactive."

"The Earth entity?" Dmitri had never heard of this.

V'Let chuckled. "The Council has a file on it. However, they don't know what it is, just that it's the size of a planet. D'Las and I figured out that it *is* the planet." She watched him silently as his mind worked the knowledge in with logic and found that it fit. "I used an abundance of my power against some demon-human hybrids. I should probably approach the nonhumans before I can make a solid decision concerning course of action with the malevolent humans."

Dmitri nodded. "Good. I should be leaving the Central Planets within minutes. We'll be there as fast as this glider can take us."

V'Let nodded in return and ended the communication at that. Dmitri sighed. Apparently, she already had a plan. Maybe even a good plan, but he wasn't entirely sure that Gralug would be happy with it.

Dmitri smirked. That didn't mean he had to tell him about it.

He stood from his seat at the forward console and moved to exit the speed glider. There were certain things that the spacecraft would not adjust until all living creatures were absent from its contents. After a few moments, he had exited the speed glider and was facing a highly irritated pair of Council Elders on the platform.

Gralug growled softly. "We've been waiting."

Dmitri nodded idly. He turned to watch the spacecraft. The metal it was made of strongly resembled the Earth metal tungsten—dark and shining but nearly indestructible. However, the Looran metal was different in the fact that it was also highly malleable. V'Let told him it was a living metal, able to change and adjust at will. The Looran race was the only one that could communicate with it.

"Dmitri!"

Dmitri's lips curled into an impatient snarl. "I am aware that your endless patience has been tested, Gralug. The glider is in its final stages of adjustment. We will be leaving within the hour."

He heard the man harrumph but neither of the men behind him really spoke after that. Dmitri's snarl shifted into a tight-lipped grin. These Looran vessels were magnificent, especially the ones capable of transition.

The speed glider merely extended another five hundred feet and the front came more to a point while the area where the bridge was stationed became translucent. It was no longer a speed glider but an intergalactic express vessel. It wasn't quite as fast as the twins' cargo ship but it was a very close second.

Dmitri chuckled. "All aboard. I have to sign some papers, then I'll be boarding as well."

Gralug and Mallik glanced at each other in what they probably thought was a covert manner. Dmitri knew better. He had spent a good deal of his time with two people that had nothing better to do than to exploit the weakness in others, after all. No matter that all the while, they were creating their own weaknesses. However, he still needed to sign that requisition form that Maya had prepared. Otherwise, they'd be chased across the Sectors by the police force for theft of scientific research and possibly kidnapping the Head Council Member. Sometimes his luck worked out that way.

Dmitri was back in his offices, finishing signing all of the paperwork that his secretary has prepared, when the device hanging from his belt loop made a very decisive noise. He rolled his eyes and handed the paperwork to Maya. She smiled at him and promised to file it immediately. He wished her a good day and reminded her to clear his schedule for the next four to six weeks. She nodded and he turned away.

He lifted the device, unclipping it from his belt in the same movement. V'Let had assembled it for him when he'd complained about his research with the Looran spacecraft, had reminded him that he didn't speak Computer and that the ship's computer could only roughly understand the Central Language, Galactic Standard. It allowed him to communicate with the ship directly and from a remote location, if need be.

There was a blue light blinking on his surface. He grinned slightly. He had a feeling he knew what was going on. He pressed a button on the side and the computer's rigid voice filtered through.

"Unauthorized being attempting flight sequence. Permission to exit port?"

"Permission denied."

The blue light stopped blinking and faded to black. The computer was used to people without authorization trying to access its controls, what with various new interns taking it on another needed test flight. That was the reason for the device, in Dmitri's mind. He had to authorize every use of the spacecraft and it helped to be the only one that could communicate with this particular ship; that is, until they got in range of the twins.

After a couple minutes, he was back on the platform, staring at the spacecraft. He was really doing this, he was really finally rid of his old life and now traveling to Zeta Sector. He understood his son's apprehensions, especially when you took into account what Marcus would have to do while he was gone. It would be a difficult time for the boy but Dmitri truly believed that he would be stronger at the end of it.

Dmitri nodded to himself and finally resigned himself to this little trip. It was unneeded and costly but they all did for Gralug when they could. The man could be very scary when he was angry.

He entered the spacecraft, his face a serene mask. He made his way to the bridge soundlessly, aware that what he might find there would make him feel quite the opposite of serene. Upon reaching the bridge, he found Mallik and Gralug moving around the bridge in a borderline skittish fashion.

Dmitri smiled wanly at them when they saw him and suddenly halted all their movements. He moved languidly to the forward console and pressed a blinking red button.

"Initiating flight sequence. Fingerprint of Dmitri Andian accepted."

With barely a shift in the air, the viewscreen showed that they were exiting the R&D's open hatch through which all aerial mechanisms departed. Within moments, they had ascended past the planet's atmosphere and hovered almost indecisively in orbit. He sat at the console and input the coordinates for Earth and opened a hyperspace window. The spacecraft darted into the window and began its very long journey.

Dmitri leaned back and closed his eyes. Within days, the stress of being an Adept would fully alleviate and that tight knot that he had been carrying around with him would be gone. He would be free, though it was marginally depressing to realize that his young son was caught in the same trap, possibly a trap for which the boy was not prepared. However, it could not be helped. What Marcus had to do was something that had to be done.

After a moment, he stood and faced his two guests. Their eyes were filled with suspicion and calculation. They would probably never figure out his motives, though they would wrack their brains with any idea. They would assume that everything he did was a trap. He didn't care to wait for their trust or attempt to prove himself. He was not a dog waiting for scraps of affection.

"Now, we should get ourselves in the stasis pods," he told them after less than two seconds of study.

Mallik gulped visibly. "Stasis pods?" he echoed. Dmitri almost laughed. He should have pegged the fidgety man for claustrophobia. Not that it helped to have it in space.

"Don't worry." Dmitri moved past them and started toward the rear of the spacecraft. "The pods are quite roomy. Besides, going into stasis will cut travel time very nearly in half."

At that statement, he knew that two of them would glance at the viewscreen. It showed the current expected travel time of twenty cycles in the lower right corner of the screen. Dmitri knew that stasis in this ship was unlike the system aboard the twins' ship. Their bunks were hermetically sealed during stasis, but it was a ship built to have them awake for the duration of travel. This particular ship was actually built to run itself with a very complex artificial intelligence and a fluid nature that still boggled some of the most intelligent minds of the Central Planets. The stasis pods ensured that on longer journeys, the passengers would feel as if almost no time had passed.

He led them to a line of three stasis pods, one for each of them. He held out his hand in a wide gesture, inviting them to take a pod, but they remained immobile. Dmitri shrugged and touched the edge of the seal on the first pod, watching for a moment as the top half lifted.

Suddenly, he felt a hand on his arm. He glanced behind him and up at Gralug's face. He arched an eyebrow at the large man. "Yes?"

"Why should you trust us? Or we you? You could kill us in those pods."

Dmitri scoffed, as he well should. He idly reminded himself that these two knew next to nothing about Looran devices or how their minds worked. He honestly couldn't kill them while they were in the pods, even if he really wanted to. The pods were impenetrable and equipped with a very capable filter. The air they would breathe would be almost impossibly pure and once you were in the pod, nothing but your full consciousness would allow it to open.

"Truly, Gralug, I couldn't. And you can believe me or not. I do not care." He ground out the last four words with careful enunciation, making sure the large man understood how deeply his apathy ran. "However, you can either go into stasis or you and Mallik could spend twenty whole cycles with each other because I'm taking a pod." With that said, he gently removed Gralug's hand from his arm and laid in the first pod, pulling down the top. He quickly slipped into a deep sleep, hoping that the ship would stay on course.

Almost immediately, both Gralug and Mallik claimed a pod and followed suit.

# CHAPTER THIRTY-TWO

V'Let rubbed her forehead wearily with one hand and attempted to smooth her hair with the other. Too many acts of power caused the ends to frizz sometimes. Apparently, now was one of those times.

She had been truthful when talking to Dmitri. After thinking about it, she realized that she had to be diplomatic with these nonhumans, especially since most of them were protected. The Earth entity could also become a complication if she decided on the wrong action. Somehow, it had become very proactive. V'Let realized that she needed to find a way to confer with the planetary being.

How had everything gotten so blown out of proportion?

"Coordinates achieved. Landing sequence adjusted to allow for small fourth-dimensional structure."

V'Let snapped out of her introspection immediately at that. "Fourth-dimensional?" she echoed, communicating with the computer.

"Question not understood. Rephrase."

"Where is this structure?" V'Let moved her hands to her temples, trying to soothe a coming headache away. She knew that the computer couldn't always understand the nuances of speech but it was grating after a night like this one.

"Fourth-dimensional structure at exact coordinates given."

V'Let nodded. She had a feeling she might understand everything more when that old woman was awake. "Are you certain it is using a fourth dimension?"

"Yes."

"How?"

"Question not understood. Rephrase."

V'Let growled softly. "How do you know this particular structure has a fourth dimension?"

"Interior has a capacity tripling the size of the exterior."

V'Let nodded to herself. Something largely odd was going on here, on this planet. She obviously couldn't explain it yet but she would.

After a moment, she heaved herself up from the central console and made her way down to the cargo area. They were at their current destination, temporary though it may be. Once they were all off the ship again, it would slip back into its idle mode for a while.

As she exited the bridge, she started to hear muffled sounds below her in the cargo hold. It sounded like an argument, one side loud and the other quite low in volume. She arched an eyebrow, intrigued, and slipped down the stairs as quietly as possible. Her thinly clad feet made barely a whisper on the metal stairway.

"Could you lower your voice?" Her brother, obviously, worried that the other would wake the unconscious women.

"You destroy planets! How can you tell me to calm down?" The vampire.

V'Let completed her descent and eyed her brother, who looked very nervous but clutched the old woman to him in a protective manner. She glanced at Erik and her fists clenched tightly in response. He was holding her goddess statuette that she had collected three planets ago in a very threatening manner.

"What exactly do you think you're doing?"

The vampire turned to face her and she could see the fear hiding in his eyes, well hidden by the anger in his face. She tilted her head at him, imploring him to answer her question. "The two of you are dangerous. I should kill you right now." There was a tremor in his voice now and she could feel that his resolve was breaking.

V'Let stepped closer to him, keeping her eyes glued to his. "Are you sure about this assessment?"

Erik shifted his body, subconsciously easing out of the threat zone. "No," he replied truthfully.

V'Let relaxed slightly, the knot of tension in her abdomen slowly unraveling. "Good. Because if you did kill us, you'd be responsible for killing the last of a species." She turned away from the vampire and strode across the cargo hold to press the button to open airlock and the hatch beyond it. "I would also appreciate it if you returned the statue to its place."

She moved to exit the spacecraft, trusting the men with their unconscious women. Within moments, she was padding across a small expanse of grass that was all that separated her ship from the very interesting house. She gazed at the bulk of the house, feeling exactly what the computer's readings had told her. This A-frame house was a tad on the small side but she could feel the interior pushing past the boundaries that seemed to hold it.

"There's an extra spatial dimension," she murmured, realizing what the anomaly was. She smiled to herself and then started to focus on details. This house had a porch, which currently contained a medium-sized blue creature. She tilted her head. It was reading a book of some kind; she assumed it was sentient. "Hello there!"

The creature looked ready to jump out of its skin as it jerked to direct its gaze at her. Its flat black eyes looked emotionless but its body language gave away its anxiety. It took in the sight of her and she could swear that it become more anxious.

*Calm yourself. You can't assume every odd-looking thing you may or may not have seen before is an alien.*

V'Let frowned slightly. This creature was obviously very afraid when it came to the thought of an alien. She shook it off and continued approaching the house. "I'm V'Let."

The creature attempted to give her a smile, it seemed, but it came off as a painful grimace. However, V'Let took it for what it was meant to be and smiled brightly back at him. "Name's Quin." Even with just those two words, his voice sounded distinctly male.

"Quin," she murmured. She ascended the stairs and took the liberty of sitting down next to him. What she was about to attempt was nothing short of stupid but it was almost worth the risk. "So, you're a demon, right?"

"Yeah, how'd you know?" She arched an eyebrow at him in return. "Right. The eyes and skin give it away."

V'Let shifted her smile into a come-hither grin. She was playing coy and she knew she was bad at it. However, she knew she didn't have to play at it for long because her brother and the vampire would be coming into view soon. "So, what do my eyes and skin say about me?"

The demon looked uncomfortable for a moment. "Um... Wait! What's going on?"

V'Let craned her neck around to see the appearance of D'Las and Erik carrying the old woman and the planeswalking girl. "Damn," she murmured. She directed her gaze at Quin, hardening the look in her eyes. "Don't run."

The demon scurried away from her and off the porch. V'Let watched him with keen eyes, ready to react if he did run. Quin stopped in front of D'Las. "Give her to me, please." The demon's voice quavered but he remained adamant.

After a glance in V'Let's direction and her resulting nod, he turned to old woman over to the demon. They watched as the demon shot a glance at Erik and made a gesture for the vampire to follow him inside.

D'Las jumped onto the porch as they made their way inside the house. He gave her a meaningful glance full of questions.

She harrumphed softly. "The demon, name of Quin, is extremely afraid of us." She glanced at them just before they fully entered the house. "He's taking Erik to lay down the women and find out what happened."

He gazed at his sister, searching her face and seeing the exhaustion that she was refusing to give in to. "What did happen out there, V'Let?" He sighed. "There were so many vampires. What did they want?"

It was V'Let's turn to search her brother's face. "The big one, he was there to kill Rosalie." At the blank look on his face, she clarified, "The planeswalker. All the other vampires were to distract Erik, to keep him from noticing what was really happening."

"How did they know where they were? They were a long way from the city."

V'Let held up her hand to hush her brother. "They're talking now." She glanced at D'Las and saw the plea in his eyes, so she laid a hand on the top of his head.

There was a slight pulling sensation and then they were there. It was as if they were just standing a few feet away from Quin and Erik inside the house, although the view was smoky and the voices were slightly muffled because V'Let had very little power left. They were standing in a hallway and there were two open doors. They assumed the women were laid down comfortably in these rooms. However, there wasn't much more time for thought because the two men were talking.

"What happened out there? Who are they?" the blue demon hissed, roughly gesturing to the porch where V'Let and D'Las were physically.

"They're the aliens." Erik's voice was harsh and blunt.

"Oh, God."

The vampire straightened his back, looking like he was trying to work out tense muscles. "They helped us. We were attacked in force."

"Why would they help?"

Erik shrugged. "I don't know. I just know that we all could have died out there. There were too many vampires for me to handle alone."

Quin gasped. "Well, what happened to the girls?"

Erik chuckled. "I wouldn't call Matlinda a girl, myself. All I know is that they were unconscious when I got back to the circle. The aliens said the Crone was trapped inside the circle, that it was draining her. Rosalie was already unconscious."

Suddenly, light crackled on the edge of their vision and they were back, separate and outside the porch. V'Let inhaled a large breath, reached up to clutch her head and screamed.

# CHAPTER THIRTY-THREE

D'Las felt the pain inside his sister echo and reverberate inside him. He bit his lip against the need to scream. He waited a moment, allowing himself to adjust to the pain, before he pulled his sister to him. He wrapped his arms around her in a tight embrace, rocking them both forward and back repeatedly.

V'Let was crying into his shoulder, feelings of pain arcing through her entire being. However, he knew she was desperately trying to stay awake.

"Sleep, sister. I can take care of it."

With a final shuddering sob, V'Let let herself lose consciousness and D'Las could feel the pain fade away as well.

"What happened?"

D'Las stood, directing his gaze to the vampire that had asked the question. "I'll return momentarily." With that said, he leaped off the porch with V'Let in his arms. She needed rest, a lot of it.

"Where are you going?" The vampire again. He could feel both Erik and the demon following him.

"V'Let needs rest. I'm taking her to her bunk and then we can talk."

"We could talk on the ship." The vampire's voice sounded strangely hopeful.

"No." Passing seamlessly through the barrier of the cloak, D'Las hefted himself onto the hatch and scurried to put his sister in her bunk.

"Hey, where'd he go?" He laughed softly at the demon's comment.

D'Las moved quickly up the stairway and to the bunking area. He passed his own bunk door and was nudging hers open with his foot within seconds. The door swung into its hollow niche in the ceiling before he could grab it, making a muffled thunk as it landed. He winced at the sound but hurried across the room to put V'Let on her bed. He nudged the blanket loose of its tight wrap around the bed and covered her with it.

He rubbed his hand roughly across his forehead and gazed out into the corridor that crossed in front of their bunks. It would be so easy to just go to the bridge and get as far away from these people as he was able. However, he knew he would just be postponing the inevitable. V'Let would have them turn back as soon as she woke. As hard as she could be sometimes and as much as she probably knew that associating with them would like cause her to expend far more energy than was absolutely necessary, she did care. She cared far too much about people she barely knew.

He glanced back at his sister, noting idly that the crease in her forehead was slowly easing. Flicking his eyes up, he caught sight of the holo of their mother. The holo showed her happy and laughing mostly, though sometimes it did have that stern look that she got when they weren't paying attention to their lessons or when they came home covered in flybird feathers. He smiled to himself. It was as if he could hear his mother chastising him now.

The decision made, he exited his sister's bunk, pulling the door back down into its original place with a soft whisper of sound. He picked his way back down to the cargo hold and leaped off the hatch quietly. He landed on the ground soundlessly, letting his body flow into a crouch to minimize any sound. Glancing up, he saw Quin and Erik looking down at him from a few feet away.

Quin's brow furrowed. "Okay, now I'm really confused."

D'Las stood gracefully, idly brushing himself. "Now, we can talk." He walked past them and regained his seat on the porch within moments.

Both Erik and Quin sat near him, both of them making idle skittish movements before settling.

D'Las nodded at them. "Ask your questions."

Erik opened his mouth but Quin raised his hand almost immediately to quiet him. "The most important thing is to find out what happened in the clearing."

D'Las's eyes became distant as he remembered. It had only happened an hour ago, if that, but it still felt as if more time had passed than that. "We were directed to the clearing."

"By what?" This time, it was Erik asking.

D'Las shook his head. "I'll come back to that. When we landed, V'Let just told me to behead everything to looked to be attacking. Close to fifty vampires were swarming the clearing. I told V'Let she could have the big one."

Erik furrowed his brow. "I never saw a big vampire."

D'Las smiled. "V'Let interrogated and killed him. He was there to kill the planeswalker, she said. All the other vampires were there to distract you." His gaze was solidly on Erik at that statement.

"What about the Crone?" Quin asked anxiously. "What happened?"

D'Las shifted his gaze to the blue demon. "Mind you, I only know what V'Let has told me." When Quin nodded, he continued. "The old woman was trapped in the circle and the circle was draining her power and strength, keeping her unconscious. V'Let ripped an opening in the power to allow me inside so that I could break the circle."

"What about the other vampires?" Erik asked suddenly. "There had to have been twenty left when you took my sword."

"About that, yeah," D'Las agreed. "V'Let told me to lead you away. I gather that she set some on fire and made the others go away."

The three of them were silent for a moment before Quin spoke up again. "What happened to her?"

D'Las's eyes were hard. "She had used too much power tonight but she wanted to listen to what you were saying inside." He scoffed as Erik and Quin looked at each other. "It doesn't require much to do, especially for V'Let, but it took what she had left. When a Looran uses too much power, it sizzles the nerves. She also wanted to remain awake. If she had, it would have eventually fried her brain." D'Las sighed and passed his hand roughly over the top of his head. "As it was, I could barely keep from screaming myself."

Quin's black eyes looked hard at the alien. "Why?"

D'Las smiled mirthlessly. "We're twins, forever bound to each other despite my lack of power."

"You and your sister are the Galaxy Killers, though, right?" Erik asked, now getting to what they all wanted to know.

D'Las's blue eyes darkened slightly and he sighed roughly. "Gods above, I hate that name," he muttered.

"You do destroy planets," Erik rebutted in a vaguely snide tone.

D'Las snapped his gaze at the vampire, his face set in an angry grimace. "We don't have a choice!" He stood with the power of his outburst but withered as both the demon and the vampire flinched at the movement. "We've never had a choice," he repeated in a softer voice, slowly lowering himself back down to his seat.

Quin gulped. "You always have a choice."

D'Las tilted his head at them. "Ever had your blood boil? Your bones lose so much mass that they might as well be disintegrating? Lose your ability to see because your optic nerve's been fried?"

Erik arched his eyebrow. "Have you?"

D'Las nodded curtly. "Yeah. And she's gone through worse."

"How?" Quin whispered. He couldn't even wrap his mind around those things happening, much less the mechanics of it.

"V'Let says it was a Blood Contract, illegal even then. It exacts biological punishment on us when we don't follow the letter of the agreement."

Erik looked over at Quin, who was biting his lip in concentration. "What was the agreement?"

D'Las shook his head, feeling exhaustion washing over him. "We're sent to planets that do not yet have the means for space travel. If we find the dominant species either malevolent or dangerously indifferent, we destroy the planet."

Quin stood up, attempting to puff himself into a larger persona than he actually was. "We'll stop you from destroying this one."

D'Las chuckled. "That's not an issue."

Quin wilted slightly. "It's not?"

"Earth is protected by the Intergalactic Council. It cannot be destroyed because of creatures like you and the fey outside the city."

Erik arched an eyebrow at the alien. "Then why are you here?"

D'Las smiled vaguely. "That's yet to be determined." He stood gracefully after a moment. "However, for now, I believe we all need rest. V'Let and I will return soon." His voice brooked no argument and he turned away from them to return to their ship. He could hear them murmuring behind him idly but his exhaustion was currently taking precedence.

V'Let would be proud of him. He had fought his own instincts to do what she would have done instead. However, he thanked what gods might look down on him that they forgot to ask what directed them to the clearing a second time. As much D'Las understood the planetary being inside his own head, he was afraid that he couldn't explain it to them. Besides, he could feel that V'Let knew what they had done to the planet and she was so much better at explaining things than he was.

# CHAPTER THIRTY-FOUR

Marcus Andian stood on the edge of the courtyard owned by the Council. There was a large three-story house, dark and foreboding. He had never been able to get his father to tell him what it had originally been built for, but he did know that it had formerly been used as a type of barracks for single Junior Council Members. Now, it was equally owned between the families of Andian, DuPont and Trellick.

With a heavy sigh, he ascended the stairs that led to the front door. When he reached the door, he raised his hand and placed it on a shiny black panel on a high center panel of the door. A blue vertical line of light crossed the panel and just at his eye level, a circular eye lit up and shone into his retina. He remembered once his father complaining about the retinal scan that he had to endure with every trip to the Adepts' headquarters.

The doors opened silently and Marcus rubbed at his left eye, realizing that his father had been right. That damned light did sting like a bitch.

Walking through the doorway, he remembered the only other time he'd been here. Five years ago, when his father had decided he was old enough and began to tell him the truth about everything, he had brought him here. It was a shock to realize that the so-called Galaxy Killers were technically under the command of those he considered family, those that openly chastised them for their actions in a public forum. Even more shocking, his father had told him that he would, under no uncertain terms, take his place eventually.

After that particular revelation, he barely spoke to his father, attempting to rail against this piece of fate as much as possible. It was relatively easy, considering he was barely home from a fast-track scholarship at the finest psychology university the Central Planets had to offer. When he graduated with the highest honors and a promised occupation within the Intergalactic Council at the very young age of nineteen, most of the Adept revelations had lost their sting. He was an adult now. He could take anything life could offer.

Except, of course, for the next flurry of revelations his father would reveal to him. After his graduation but before joining the Council, his father took him to their home planet in Beta Sector, as was the tradition among their race as a type of coming-of-age ritual. They all had to return to their roots eventually. It was then that Dmitri told him of the razing of Loora, of the truth beneath the truth, a knowledge hidden even from Marina and Xavier. When asked why they returned to the home planet for this, his father had only smiled and told him two birds with one stone. He didn't understand at first but later remembered that the ritual was required and that their planet was also heavily guarded against interference that wasn't their own.

It was then that he first started to think tactically. He started to know that certain truths can only be known when in hiding and how to maneuver the people around him in a fashion that began to emulate his father. He had been appalled when Dmitri had pointed it out to him. He didn't want to be like his father; he didn't want to be an Adept. However, his father knew him well enough to know his thoughts. Marcus had always had a highly expressive face, something he was desperately trying to control. It was then that Dmitri reminded him those that fight what they don't want to become are those that cannot escape it. Acceptance, his father told him, was the first step to make the world bend to you.

In the last year, he had done heavy research in all his spare time, research concerning Loorans, Blood Contracts and absolutely everything he could find that linked to the Adepts. He accepted being an Adept but openly dreaded the day when he had to start acting as one.

Like today.

Shaking his head to clear away the memories, Marcus moved forward in the dark house. There were lights shining in various parts of the house, he could already tell, which meant that either one or both of the Trellicks were here. That could put a slight damper on things.

"Marcus?" That was Railey, obviously having heard the house allow someone entrance. If his was the first name she thought to call out, then Xen was probably with her. "Is that you? We're with the Separator."

Marcus rolled his eyes for a moment, casting a momentary glance at the staircase. What he needed was kept on the third floor but he needed to appease his partners. He continued smoothly to a large room at the end of a nearby corridor. That particular room contained the very large and intimidating Separator and the long-range communications system. As he approached the room, he tried to channel his father, that ice-cold and impenetrable persona he used every single time he went to meet with the other Adepts.

Peering into the room, Marcus instantly spotted his so-called comrades. He idly wondering if they had been told anything about the whole Adept business. He doubted it, he realized, because Xavier and Marina had known so little. They stood facing the Separator, their backs to the com system.

Xen turned away from it first, flopping into a nearby seat. He managed to exude disdain and grace all at once. Marcus knew for a fact that it was a cultivated movement, just as every other facet of Xen's flamboyant behavior was honed until it shone flawlessly. "I've got no clue, Ray-Ray. Maybe Marc knows."

Marcus watched Railey grimace at her nickname but she didn't comment on it. She turned to face him and twitched her head at the silver device. "What do you think?"

He looked closely at her face and saw the calculation there after a moment. He truly believed that Xen actually had no clue but Railey was testing him. Perhaps it was a test of loyalty but one could never really know with her. "It's the Separator. It was a device based of my father's research into mental capacity. It was created as another foolproof way in which to keep the so-called Galaxy Killers under control, according to the document of this facility."

A tense moment passed, one in which Railey closely scanned his face. He wondered if perhaps he had included too much detail but refused to let the worry show on his face, schooling a bland expression. Then she nodded and turned back to the device. "I'm thinking about having it destroyed."

Marcus jerked minutely, his face openly showing disbelief. "Why?" His voice was tight with stress. Was this another test?

Railey smiled over her shoulder at him and he realized her face was relaxed now, no calculations and no expectations. "Aunt Marina believes it's not working as well as it should." She chuckled under her breath. "Of course, that's about the only lucid thought I could get from her. She's still deep in the wine binges."

Marcus nodded idly. Most of the Central Planets were aware of Marina DuPont's wine binges, something of which he believed both his father and

Xavier had perhaps taken advantage. However, the spectacles the woman had made of herself publicly were her own fault.

"I think it's overkill."

Xen snorted playfully. "Ray, you're the militant one here. You're not supposed to believe in 'overkill'. Marc's the one that's supposed to bring that up."

Marcus flicked his gaze over to Xen and then back to Railey. She shrugged before continuing her line of thinking. "Well, it is. The Blood Contract is ironclad and essentially holds them under our thumb. Causing them pain every time we talk to them is just asking for trouble."

"Oh, a peaceful militant figure," Xen snickered.

Railey smiled at her brother. "Wouldn't Father roll over in his grave?" She moved to sit beside him, lowering herself with a level of measured control. "I'm glad the bastard's dead."

Marcus moved forward and touched the cool silver of the device. "So, we're agreed?"

Railey nodded and looked over at Xen, who in turn shrugged. "What should I care?" he added in a mutter.

"I'll have someone remove it tomorrow," Marcus offered.

At that, Railey stood again and strode to the rear of the machine. "There's actually a button back here, a type of self-destruct. I think it causes it to collapse on itself." He heard a muffled beep and then a sound like the air was being pulled out of something. As he looked at the machine, it began to shrink and dents began to pit the surface of the metal as it warped. "You haven't spent much time here, have you?"

Marcus shrugged his shoulder noncommittally. "I've been here one other time, when my father told me. I was mad for a while and then I was at the Psych Academy. For the past year, I've been getting used to working for the Council."

Railey nodded, her eyes softening slightly. He could tell that she was reminding herself that he was just a kid. He was twenty, not really a kid anymore technically, but Xen was twenty-five and she was over thirty. "Well, Xen and I were about to leave anyway. We've all got Council stuff, I guess."

Marcus nodded, smiling a tight smile at her. "Of course. I don't have another appointment for a while so I'll just reacquaint myself with the facility."

Railey nodded and exited the room without a word, Xen following suit languidly. After a moment, Marcus followed soundlessly at a short distance, just at the edge of earshot.

"So, what do you think?" Xen asked his sister.

Railey slowed her brisk movements slightly. "About which part? The fact that we have no clue what all this Adept business is about? Or if Marcus is trustworthy?"

Xen shrugged. "Either or."

She sighed roughly. "We'll watch him. Besides, he's only twenty. I'm sure we can find a way to control him, if need be. The other stuff, we'll have to research."

Xen smacked his forehead. "You know I hate reading."

Railey snickered as they reached the front door. "Except for holomags." She opened the door and they exited the house, the door closing slowly behind them.

Marcus stood less than five feet away from the staircase, his mouth hanging slightly open. "What is going on?" he muttered to himself. He gazed at the door, his mind working to incorporate the Trellick siblings' current motive. It seemed unreal, this nice side of them, but it did seem entirely plausible that Marina and Xavier had never told them the truth behind controlling the Galaxy Killers.

He rubbed his hand across his forehead, trying to clear away his thoughts. He was going to have an anxiety-induced nervous breakdown if he keep thinking too much about the truth behind the truth behind the truth of an entirely false propaganda. He hated politics.

He began to ascend the staircase, solidly making his way to a particular room on the third floor. It was the showcase room, holding a specific artifact. Unlike the bulk of the house, this room did not boast camera surveillance. His father had told him that they couldn't risk members of the Council setting eyes on the items within that room.

Inside of another minute, he was looking at the door blocking entrance to the room. He reached out and turned the doorknob to reveal the dark room. He stepped into the room, reaching to his right for the light sensor. An overhead light began to turn on, the light brightening in staggered phases.

Marcus knew this was the room of Galaxy Killer artifacts. His goal for coming to this house today was in the center of the room, contained in a plexiglass display case. There were no alarms in this room, not that he thought there would be. You had to clear a print and retinal scan just to get inside the house. Once inside, everything was open to you. As a whole, that was the most paranoid you could get on Council property.

He gazed at the Blood Contract in its preservation case and decided he should do this now before he lost his nerve. He moved forward and lifted the plexiglass container carefully so as to not disturb the contract too much. Setting the glass-like case gently on the floor, he removed the contract and gently set it on top of the case. After making sure it was flat and every detail of the paper was clear visible, he pulled two pebble-like devices with matching styluses out of his pocket.

He set the first device atop the paper, a vaguely pearlescent stone, and chose the correct stylus. Smiling, he had almost touched the stylus to the device when he suddenly stopped. With a frustrated sigh, he settled the other device in his palm and gripped the stylus with the other one between two fingers. He reached into his pocket again and pulled out a slip of paper. After scanning the contents of the paper, he nodded to himself and slipped the paper back inside his pocket.

He grabbed the stylus with the pearlescent tip again and began to mark the device. As the left edge, he marked with a vertical line with a long accenting mark atop it and horizontal line across, under which he marked with something resembling a lowercase "h". Finally, he marked it with a small accent mark above the horizontal line. He removed his hand, leaving the stylus there standing vertical against the stone-like device.

Marcus watched as the stylus melded into the device and the device itself seemed to melt and flatten out. It became the same color as the paper beneath it, yellowed with age. What look to be fresh ink spilled onto the page from no source and then arranged itself into the letters of the contract itself. The signatures slowly appeared on the paper, eventually appearing as if they'd always been there.

He picked up both sheets of paper and looked at them closely, citing the differences. Someone unskilled in nuances would not be able to tell the one from the other. However, both Marcus and Dmitri could cite the tells. The new paper did not have quite the feel of aged paper; the ink on the page looked just a little bit too fresh; finally, something that was glaringly obvious to Marcus and a relief, the twins' signatures were no longer that of blood. It didn't have the thickness that blood seemed to leave behind. Instead, it simply looked as if they had used a ballpoint pen with blue ink.

He grinned at his handiwork and set the copy in the original's place. Setting the original Blood Contract on the floor, he picked the plexiglass case and set it carefully back in its place. He looked at the remaining device and stylus in his hand. It was time, he decided.

Kneeling down, he placed the device, this one of an electric blue color, on top of the original contract. Closing his eyes, he reminded himself of the second symbol. He opened his eyes and touched the stylus to the stone. He began marking the stone with lines and accent marks, boxes and crosses. In the end, it seemed to resembled a type of complicated mathematical equation. He placed the tip of the stylus in the center of the device.

He stood and stepped away from the device as it crackled and spit electricity. After a moment, it let forth a sound of combustion and all that was left behind was a pile of dust. His face broke out in a grin of excessive relief and happiness at his success at the sight of the mess.

Marcus's moment of self-satisfaction was broken rather abruptly by a whirring sound. He focused on his surroundings and noticed a cleaning bot enter the room at a steady pace. It moved directly for the seemingly inconsequential dust, making marginally intelligent beeping sounds among its whirring. It cleared away the dust in serene and efficient movements.

So engrossed in the final eradication of the Blood Contract was he that he nearly jumped out of his skin when his pocket vibrated. The bot halted its cleaning, beeping in alarm at the sounds Marcus made, but resumed its task almost immediately. In turn, he reached into his pocket almost desperately and pulled out his communication device. It was narrow and small, made of cold silver and enough power to employ video share with a holographic screen.

The call was coming from the DuPont manor, which was disconcerting. He nimbly pressed a couple buttons, opening the conversation into two-way video. Before the holoscreen rose, he schooled his face into an almost perfect mimicry of his father's blank expression.

"Master Andian?" squeaked a small creature on the other end of the call. It was a member of a species called Parvini, captured from the dying planet Parvus in the Gamma Sector roughly a hundred years ago and brought to the Central Planets as slaves. The slave status hadn't lasted long as they had been smuggled there by a group of then-unknown pirates and the Central Planets did not allow one's status to be held superior to another. However, most Parvini still employed themselves as housekeepers and other servile positions, for which they were usually well paid. Marcus arched an eyebrow. He remembered hearing a rumor that Marina didn't treat her own servants well at all.

"Yes?" Marcus responded to the Parvini's inquiry.

"Where is the other one?" The creature was shaking visibly and Marcus felt his opinion toward these creatures soften further.

"Father is away on vacation. I've taken over his post on everything in his absence."

"Everything?" the creature echoed in query.

"Everything," Marcus confirmed.

The creature's shaking stilled somewhat, though it did not completely stop. "Okay. The elder Andian told us to inform him when Mistress DuPont was on her last bottle of wine from the infamous Voo. She started on it twenty minutes ago. Myself and the other Parvini servants are leaving so as to not be blamed. Can you assure we will not be blamed?"

*Blamed for what?* Marcus thought idly but he knew it was best to reassure the creature. If his father promised it, then it was probably already taken care of. "I assure you, no Parvini will be blamed."

The Parvini nodded and just before it ended the conversation, Marcus noticed about three other Parvini in the background, looking like they were vibrating with nervous energy. Then his holoscreen shut down again and his communication device lay still and cold in the palm of his hand.

During his conversation with the Parvini, the cleaning bot had exited the room, leaving behind an asymmetrical spot on the floor that was slightly cleaner than its surroundings. The Blood Contract was now irrevocably eradicated because the bot would eject what it collected into the house's incinerator. The twins were free of everything that bound them to the Adepts. While he intellectually knew that he'd done the right thing, years of Galaxy Killer propaganda made him wonder why they shouldn't keep them under a tight rein.

For the first time, he honestly wondered if his father had told him everything.

# CHAPTER THIRTY-FIVE

Xen Trellick gazed at the screen in front of him, more interested in how his eyes blurred from too much exposure and concentration than the information in front of him. He and his sister had returned to the house after lunch to find a note from their fellow Adept, informing them that he wouldn't see them for a few days because of his full schedule. However, that had been over five hours ago and the words on the screen no longer made sense.

Between Xavier, Marina and Dmitri, all the information concerning the Looran twins was organized and quite a bit more thorough than Xen liked. He cringed slightly when he thought of how Marina would berate and belittle him for thoughts like that. Information was an important part of the media, even more so when controlling it, she had told him before. No matter how condensed, it was always better to know what was happening than to be in the dark.

Since they'd arrived, however, he'd learned a lot more about the Adepts' agenda than he thought possible. The elder Adepts had been part of a strike force a little over twenty years ago when they were ordered to stop by the current Head Council Member. As it turned out, they had destroyed a species they thought to be dangerous but actually wasn't. Now, the last of that particular species was the Treasury Council Elder and currently dying of some kind of terminal virus. Dmitri Andian described the razing of Loora as a last hoorah before the strike force was dismantled.

V'Let and D'Las had been five, found wandering the planet listlessly. At this point, the boy would not talk and the girl would only speak to them telepathically. They believed it to be a show of power. Five years later, they tricked the twins into signing what remained of their lives away with the Blood Contract. Marina wrote that she believed that the twins had actually signed the contract willingly rather than being under the influence of Dmitri's prototypes of mental control.

For the last fifteen years, the twins had destroyed a planet a year, one of the planets a protected one. They never came to the Central Planets. Xen thought maybe they knew what Marina put in the media about them, about how she had convinced the populace of an entire sector that they were dangerous and destructive. From the last reports, they were on planet Earth in the Milky Way Galaxy in Zeta Sector, a planet so highly protected that it was almost considered to be classified.

A few hours earlier, Railey had found that some of Dmitri's files were encrypted. She had been working on them since then. Every time she made a muffled screech, he knew that she had been dumped out of the system and had to start from scratch again.

A muffled melody interrupted his musings and he pulled his com device from his pocket. He glanced at his sister as the sound became louder, no longer muffled by the fabric of his clothing, and could see the signs of a deep frown marring the side of her face. He quickly answered the call, pressing specific buttons for audio only.

"Master Trellick?" The voice on the other side of the call was a familiar one, that of Marina's personal butler.

"Hello to you, Jeoff. I told you to call me Xen."

"Yes. Very good, sir." Xen nearly laughed at the pinched stiffness in the butler's voice. "You are needed at the manor immediately, sir."

Xen glanced at his watch. It was slightly past six. On the way back from the manor, he could get dinner for Railey and himself. "Yes, Marina will probably want to see me."

Jeoff hemmed softly. "You'll see when you arrive, sir." With that, their connection had ended and Xen sat there looking at his com device.

He stood then, glancing at her sister who was still very determined with her current course of action. "Ray-Ray?"

She stilled immediately and spun her chair around to face him. "Yes?"

"I gotta go."

"Yeah, I heard."

"I'll bring food on the way back." At that statement, she nodded briefly and turned back to the computer. "Bye," he said softly on his way out.

Xen let himself quietly out of the house and found his hoverbike on the side of the house. With the upgrades in it, he could make it to Marina's manor in a few minutes. Jeoff may have had this uncanny ability to make everything seem as if it could wait but there had been something in his voice that made Xen want to know what had happened. It had sounded almost urgent.

Marina's manor was just a few miles out of the Council courtyard. They had offered her a house on their grounds but she had apparently required something a bit more grandiose. The manor was on a sprawling expanse of land that also boasted stables, a massive pool and training fields at which Xen never looked too closely. The house itself was large, though it only had two floors. Marina once told him that intoxication made stairs highly difficult and she didn't trust the hovertubes with which her home had been built.

Xen set down his bike in the circular driveway and walked quickly to the door. Before he could even reach for the doorknob, the door opened to reveal Jeoff. The butler gave a shallow bow and gestured for him to enter. Xen did as suggested and then followed Jeoff without a word, though he began to get hesitant when it became clear that they were heading for Marina's personal quarters.

"Um, Jeoff, I'm not allowed in Marina's room. It's her, and I quote, 'personal space'."

"No matter now, sir."

Xen waited for the butler to expand upon his comment but when he didn't, he just sighed and continued to follow him without another word. Within moments, they were standing in front of the door to her bedroom, which Jeoff pushed open.

Xen scurried into the room as soon as he saw Marina. She seemed to be lounging on a semicircular couch in the middle of the room, her head tipped back and an empty bottle of wine held loosely in her hand. He came to a stop in front of her, taking in her pallor and noticing that her chest was definitely not moving.

He spun around to face the butler. "Is she...?" He couldn't quite say the word.

"Yes, sir. She is dead. I found her briefly before I called you. There's no telling how long, though. She had a tendency to keep to herself of late." The butler sighed. "We have record of one of the Parvini giving her this bottle a little under six hours ago."

Xen made himself stop the frantic panic that had ensued under his mentor's death and made himself think logically. "What about the Parvini?" he asked. "I didn't see any of them. Could they have done this?"

Jeoff shook his head. "No. Today was their last day, to end at midday. We were outbid for them two weeks ago by Tactical Elder Andian for his son."

Xen furrowed his brow. Something highly odd was going on here and he wasn't certain what to do about it. "So, it wasn't poison, then?"

Jeoff shrugged. "I checked her already. She showed no signs of any poisons of which I have knowledge." He gazed on Xen with a flicker of sadness in his eyes. "I believe this is merely a case of reaping what you sow. The body can only take so much."

Xen nodded. "I'm going to leave. Report it to the Council as soon as I'm gone." The butler nodded back. Xen quickly moved through the house and out of it, fluidly hopping on his bike once he was back to the driveway. Within seconds, he was clear of the manor.

Once he was back inside the border of the courtyard, he cut down on his speed and allowed himself to think. The authorities would contact him in the morning, after the autopsy and a thorough questioning of the butler. He would have to school himself in the proper attitude, the exact kind of spectacle that Marina would have wanted.

Shaking his head, he veered his bike toward the Council cafeteria. Railey would most likely not even notice what she was eating, though she would ingest it. He landed his bike and hurried inside the building, scurrying through lines in an attempt to be seen as little as possible. Within moments, he exited the building with two plastic cases of Kretoran comfort food, easily digested without a need to actually look at it.

Xen turned slightly when he heard what he thought was a frustrated sigh. He darted to put the food in the bike's storage and then hurried to where the sounds seemed to originate. Peering around the corner, he saw Marcus Andian surrounded by six Parvini. The psychologist was locking up his office and heading to the cafeteria, though extremely impeded by the Parvini.

"Master Andian, we can make much better sustenance than they serve there," one of the Parvini argued. Xen had heard of the housekeeping skills of the Parvini, had even wished that the Trellick household had employed them. However, Xavier had been extremely prejudiced against the small creatures.

Marcus rolled his eyes. "My house is not big enough to keep six of you busy."

Xen stepped out from his spot and began walking toward them, doing his best to not reveal that he had been eavesdropping. "Marcus," he called out.

Marcus's face lifted in a wry smile. "Xen," he greeted. "How are you?"

Xen watched in amazement as the smile melted away and Marcus's face became devoid of all emotion. In turn, Xen chuckled softly, slightly alarmed when nervous energy began to wrap around him. He did his best not to show it. "I was just in the cafeteria, getting food for Railey and me. They only have Kretoran food left."

Marcus grimaced, deeply marring his features.

Xen continued before he could say anything. "I'm sure there's a kitchen in the house. Besides, you could help us research."

Marcus was silent for a moment longer than Xen was comfortable. The quiet stretched before the psychologist looked at him directly. "I suppose." With that, he continued walking toward the cafeteria.

Xen spun around with wide eyes. "Where are you going?" His voice was high and tight in confusion.

The smile was back on Marcus's face and Xen could feel the nervous energy loosen. "There's a Council transport tube around the corner. It'll deposit me a couple blocks away from the house."

"Oh. Right." He smiled back at Marcus and moved to hop on his bike. With a punch on the ignition, he was in the air and zooming toward the house. Perhaps, he thought, with Marcus there, they could finally decrypt Dmitri's journal.

Xen laughed. Railey would hate that.

# CHAPTER THIRTY-SIX

V'Let could only see blue. She stared at it, tilted her head curiously at the sight, but jumped slightly when a flash of red arced across her vision. Soon, silver and white added into her sight and she knew what was happening.

She was in her dreamscape again. She hadn't been here in five years, since the last time she'd completely tapped out her power. Her vision soon broadened and she was surrounded by windows and bubbles while the red lightning struck in the distance, a significant sign. It showed that her power and the damage it had done to her brain were healing at a magnificent rate.

Inside, she felt free and more capable. She knew something had happened, something trapping her had been removed. A semisolid bubble floated near her and came to a slow stop, hovering at her eye level. She gently placed her hands on either side of it and whispered, "Show me."

The surface of the bubble was suddenly awash with color, vague at first but soon with clear and precise images. It showed a brief image of Dmitri's son with one of his father's Looran power devices, geared to react to a Looran character once marked on its surface. Further detail showed the device to be destructive and set upon the Blood Contract. A mere moment later, the contract and the device were nothing but inconsequential dust.

"Sweet boy," she murmured softly as she released the bubble, which in turn moved on its way. She began to move toward the windows, reaching up to pass her hand over random bubbles on the way. She received flashes of images, most of which made sense but some that did not. Soon, she was standing in front of a window. She placed the flat of her hands against it and just allowed herself to see.

The window focused on people as they flitted through her mind. D'Las was sleeping in his bunk not fifteen yards away from her physically. The planeswalker, the vampire, the demon and the old woman were asleep within that house near the ship. Dmitri was accompanied by Mallik and Gralug most of the way across the sectors, all of them currently locked in stasis pods. *Boring*, she thought to herself.

She arched an eyebrow. Xavier was dead and Dmitri was on his way to her location, but what about Marina? The window focused, briefly showing a gaudy mansion before changing the imagery to Marina's inner quarters. The scene was only marginally alarming. Marina's body seemed to be unconscious on the couch but her butler stood to the side talking to the authorities. V'Let focused on Marina's body, the position of her hands shifting slightly to indicate a closer image. Her skin was much paler than normal, though that could be attributed to the wine of which she was so fond. She also didn't seem to be breathing. Deduction ruled that she was dead. Moments later, a couple of professionals were putting her into a black bag and zipping it closed.

"Well, he did say he would take care of them," she murmured to herself. "But what of the younger ones?"

The window refocused, seemingly to physically turn away from the manor and face a large, dark house on a discreet corner of the Council courtyard. From Dmitri's surface memories, V'Let knew this was the Adepts' headquarters. It peered inside their room for communications, causing her to cringe in anticipation. However, the sight inside was as much a revelation as her first sight through the bubble had been. The magnificent Separator was now a crumpled pile of useless metal, laying on the floor and waiting for the incinerator. As she gawked at the sight, she watched two of the larger cleaning bots enter the room, lift the remains of the machine and disappear from the room.

The view turned away from the room and continued through the house. It focused when it noticed movement and began a trail to what looked to be the kitchen. The view inside made V'Let let forth a small but delighted gasp. There were six Parvini scattered throughout the kitchen, hard at work but the happiest she had ever seen any of the creatures before. She vaguely remembered lessons on the death of their planet and how pirates had smuggled them into the Central Planets as slaves, how the Council of that time had deemed Parvini slavery illegal and freed them. She knew from other research that they had remained in the service of others. When questioned, one of the Parvini had stated that they were built for service and simplicity.

The window again turned its view away, this time moving toward what Dmitri had called the Hall of Knowledge. It was actually a large library where they kept research materials as well as all reports that had been written. Inside the room sat the middle and youngest of Xavier's children and Dmitri's son. Earlier, she had picked up from Dmitri's mind the fact that the successors had been moved into place. She wasn't sure what they were doing in the Hall so she immersed herself further into the scene, almost feeling that she was actually there. Now she could hear them.

Railey, the middle Trellick child, shoved herself away from the computer angrily. "I can't break the stupid encryption. I've tried everything, even your name in various different ways," she exclaimed, pointing accusingly at the man behind her.

Marcus, Dmitri's son, backed away from her accusations and glanced over at Xen, Xavier's youngest, who seemed to be eating rather hungrily. Marcus chuckled and gestured at the cleared table. "Maybe you should eat. I'll try it in the meantime."

Railey grumbled audibly but did as suggested.

Marcus sat in the chair she had vacated and sat gingerly down on it. For a moment, he just stared hard at the screen. V'Let twisted her hand slightly and the view of the window closed in on Marcus and the computer. He typed in a series of characters, something that she knew was two Looran words written in Galactic Standard. She smiled softly as the computer accepted the code and allowed him entry into Dmitri's private journal.

Marcus gasped. "I didn't think that would work."

Railey spun around and stomped her foot angrily, more resembling a young child than the age she was sure to be. "What was the code?"

"Tongzi tian," he responded in a monotone.

"What is that? I don't recognize the language."

"It's Looran. It means 'sweet boy'."

Railey harrumphed. "What, did your father call you that when you were little or something?" She leaned over him and deftly punched in a command to send copies of the extensive document to two other terminals.

"Or something," Marcus whispered as Railey moved away to the nearest terminal.

Railey glanced back at him. "Did you say something?" When he shook his head, she turned back to the terminal with a fierce determination. "This might explain a few things."

V'Let lifted her hands away from the window, pulling herself away with a few backward steps. She didn't know if Dmitri's plans would come apart or if the Trellick siblings would side with their new partner. She could only assume that both the Blood Contract and the Separator were Marcus's doing, which would make his father proud.

More importantly, she and her brother were free from that which had bound them. They no longer had to destructive. They could go home. The pressure on her to commit to certain actions were gone. However, it was still clear that the humans were a malevolent species, entirely too dangerous to remain as they were.

One part of her really wanted to go home, to hide from the things she had done and wrap herself in the comfort of a place she could call home. Continuing in that hopeful vein, she began to think maybe there could be others. They couldn't have been the only ones to survive. There were the Southern nomads and the Eastern oracles, after all. Both had to have contingency plans against destruction attempts.

Shaking her head, she desperately tried to clear her head of that kind of deadly hope, hope that needed to be crushed before it became dangerous to her. Because, as a matter of course, there was the other hand, in which they needed to do what had to be done. While it was judgmental and cruel to maintain that the humans were too dangerous to allow to live, it was also logical. They destroyed more than they made. Also, they made things with the exact purpose of destruction.

V'Let pressed her hands against her eyes, clenching them shut. Her mind was whirling with indecision and confusion. She didn't know what to do and in her current state, she was cut off from all of her active power. In the end, she laid down and curled into a ball, crying at injustice and loneliness. Her heart and brain hurt intensely. But she was healing.

When she woke again, two days had passed. She opened her eyes, waiting for her eyes to focus on the blurry ceiling. Her head throbbed with a light ache but she could feel it slowly easing away. She groaned loudly, using one of the vertical metal posts of her bunk to pull herself into a sitting position. For a moment, she just sat there, gently massaging her temples.

"Never again," she muttered.

"Well, that's a relief." She jerked her head to see her brother, though it caused the pain to jump alarmingly inside her skull.

"D'Las M'Kaz!" she yelped. "You scared me!" She gripped her head again, trying to refrain from hiding her skull between her knees. "Oh, pain."

D'Las was quick to sit beside his sister, pulling her hands away from her head and cradling her against his body. He shushed her softly as she whimpered. They stayed that way for a while as V'Let's pain lessened and the remnants of her power hangover drifted away.

"Okay," she said, pulling away from him. "I'm better. Ready to face the day."

D'Las grabbed her hand and pulled her with him as they exited her bunk. "I told them some but they want to know everything. I think we need to prove that we're not a threat to them."

She arched an eyebrow at him as they slowly moved down the stairs into the cargo hold. "What exactly did you tell them?"

D'Las began to tick the items of discussion off on his fingers. "Clearing, big vampire, turn vampires away, release old woman from trap of her own making, Blood Contract," he ended with a soft growl in the back of his throat.

Nodding to her brother, she stopped him as they reached the cargo hold. She broke contact with him and moved to her shapeless statue, picking it up and checking for marks that didn't belong. "The contract's been destroyed and Marina is dead."

"I know." At her backward glance, he backpedaled slightly. "About Marina, I mean. It was on the news feed."

"Ahh. Marcus destroyed the Blood Contract almost two full days ago."

D'Las furrowed his brow, following her as she set the statue down and moved to exit their spacecraft. "How do you know? You've been unconscious."

V'Let scoffed at him, a gentle half-smile gracing her face. "I was in my dreamscape for a few hours. One of the memory holders showed me that Marcus destroyed the contract and the viewer window showed me that the Separator has been destroyed, incinerated as well by now. They also managed to unlock Dmitri's private journal."

D'Las sighed and stopped his sister, still some distance away from the house and its porch. "What about Dmitri? I mean, Xavier and Marina are dead. That had to be his doing, right?"

V'Let sighed, wiping her hand over her face. "Most likely, it was." She turned to fully face her brother. "I forgot to tell you something."

Alarm flashed across his face. "What?"

"Dmitri's on his way here with Mallik and Gralug." She sighed. "The ship read him as being on a transitioning Looran vessel."

D'Las's eyes had widened and remained that way. "How long?"

"Seven days now, maybe as much as ten."

"Why are they coming?"

V'Let reached up to rub her forehead. "To stop us from destroying Earth." She started to walk toward the porch again when they saw the demon Quin leading the old woman outside. "Gods, how I hate Marina."

"Well, at least she's dead now."

"Yes, there's that."

Together, they moved up the stairs and sat themselves on the porch. V'Let gazed at the old woman, smiling gently. "So, you're the Crone?"

The old woman smiled. "You're the aliens?"

D'Las gazed closely at the woman. "You look blind." It was a statement but a slight lift in his tone at the end almost made it a question.

"Yes and no." After that statement, she maintained her silence.

D'Las looked over at his sister with wide eyes. "I don't understand," he whispered in a low voice.

V'Let gazed back at her brother with a smile similar to the one that graced the Crone's face. *She constantly uses power to maintain a type of second sight. She thinks of it as "magic".*

*I don't get it. Is magic the same as our power or different?*

*Kind of both. I'll explain it later. The others are coming out.*

D'Las looked up to see Erik and the planeswalker emerge from the house. He remembered that both the vampire and the demon had referred to her as Rosalie. That left him to assume the Matlinda they'd mentioned over two days ago was the Crone. He crowed internally. He had deductive knowledge, without V'Let's aid.

V'Let gazed at each of the people before her, receiving different emotions from each of them. Quin, the blue demon with the flat black eyes, was fearful but she was slowly getting the impression that fear was a default for him. Matlinda, the one the others called the Crone, was serene, almost happy in the outcome of things. The young planeswalker, Rosalie of the flat brown hair and tired eyes, had anger coming off of her in waves, directed at V'Let. Erik, the very protective vampire, was full of trepidation as his eyes flicked between Rosalie and the aliens.

V'Let's smile broadened, which she felt Rosalie did not like, and directed her gaze back to the Crone. "I understand you performed some type of ritual."

"Yes," the old woman replied. "We did. A protection spell of sorts."

"Is that how it happened?" D'Las was directing his questions at his sister. "Was that the wave, the entity?"

V'Let inclined her head. "I believe it was."

At that, Rosalie exploded, wild anger flaring. "What the hell are you talking about? We did that spell to protect Earth from you!"

Anger flashed across V'Let's face as she glanced at her brother again. "Did you not tell them?"

D'Las held up his hand, palms outward as if to deflect accusation. "I did. I told them Earth is protected by Council ruling."

"I don't believe your lies," the planeswalker growled.

V'Let stood, looking the vampire in the eyes. "If you can't control her, take her away."

Erik laid a hand on the girl's shoulder and shared a meaningful glance with her. She calmed down slightly but V'Let could still feel her quivering with wrathful energy.

V'Let gazed into the girl's eyes. Vaguely, she could sense something, someone on the edge of Rosalie's thoughts, a person that caused her distress and anger but who she still somehow managed to trust. "Little girl, you need to realize that maybe it's not me that is feeding you lies." She felt the anger mount further but Rosalie said nothing. V'Let returned to her seat and her conversation with the old woman. "How specific was your ritual?"

Matlinda sat there for a moment, thinking of how she had worded the spell. In retrospect, the spell had been achingly vague. "Not very," she replied in response to V'Let's question.

V'Let rubbed her temples. "Okay. By all technicality, you made the entity within Earth proactive. It can now do whatever it wants."

The Crone gasped. "What have we done?"

V'Let chuckled, sharing a glance with her brother. "No worries. It cherishes life, despite the fact that some lives grant their own destruction. It will not hurt anyone, I assume. I will leave to contact it soon."

This time, Rosalie spoke. "What about you? We don't know anything when it comes to you." Behind her, Erik shrugged slightly.

"We are V'Let and D'Las M'Kaz of the planet Loora. We are *tiancai*." The Looran term did not translate into English, which surprised the twins.

They shared a glance, their faces a mirror of frowns. V'Let shrugged and moved on. "Our planets was razed, its inhabitants murdered, as the last act of the Intergalactic Strike Force twenty years ago, some time after our fifth birthday. We were the last ones alive in our city. The three people that later came to be the Adepts took us with plans to mold us."

"Mold you into what?" Quin asked suddenly, as if he couldn't hold in the words. "What was the Strike Force?"

"Essentially, they were trying to mold us into them. The Strike Force traveled the galaxy, following tips on specific species. If these species were thought to be a threat to the Council or the universe as a whole, then they were to be eradicated. This detail was pulled when they eradicated the species of a Council member." V'Let sighed, passing her fingers through her hair. "The razing of Loora was supposed to be fun, not an assignment," she spat.

"Who are these 'Adepts'?" the Crone asked softly.

"No real need to know now. Two are dead and one is on his way here," V'Let replied idly. After a moment, though, her eyes widened. "I didn't mean to tell you that."

"What?!" Rosalie screeched.

D'Las chuckled. "No worries. He's the good one."

"The good one?" Erik echoed. "How is that possible?"

V'Let looked down, her hands clenching each other as she remembered. "Shortly after we were brought back with them to the Central Planets, his son was born and he changed. I know it sounds cliché, but it's true and it was a real change. D'Las wouldn't talk at all, he was almost catatonic, and then I was hearing these thoughts about freeing us. While it was a nice thought, it was unrealistic."

D'Las reach out and rubbed a circle on his sister's back. "The good one is Dmitri Andian. The others were Xavier Trellick and Marina DuPont, may the gods above forever curse their souls." V'Let sent him a sharp glance, the warning in her eyes. "Okay, I'm sorry," he said in a soft voice to her. "They were or are all members of the Intergalactic Council."

V'Let then continued her vein. "What Dmitri was thinking was dangerous. Even if he could get us free, they would kill him. We needed a longer ranging plan. He needed to remain the same to them. I had a feeling some bad things would happen. However, Loorans are a strong race. We could deal with things as they came."

The Crone gazed at V'Let with those cloudy blue eyes. "What happened? Quin said something about a contract?"

Rosalie sat up straight. "Contract?" she echoed. She glanced at Erik, whose eyes V'Let saw showed a measure of sadness.

V'Let's lips turned up in a mirthless smile that more resembled a grimace. "The Blood Contract, signed when we were ten. Dmitri would have nothing to do with it. Besides the fact that it was inhumane, it was highly illegal. As much as he could force himself to do a large range of heartless things, the Blood Contract was far beyond what he would ever do, even before Marcus was born." She paused, glancing idly in the direction of their ship. "Loorans can heal, among many other things. However, their biological punishments were still quite excruciating."

At this point, D'Las picked up the conversation while V'Let sat silent again. "The Blood Contract is exactly what it sounds like. We sign it with our blood and they with theirs. Whenever we would try to defy the contract, something would happen, more often to V'Let than to myself. She took the brunt of the attacks."

"Why?" Rosalie asked. "You look stronger."

"Looks can be deceiving," D'Las remarked with a smirk.

V'Let looked up at the girl, tears swimming in her eyes before she blinked them back. "Looran strength and power is equivalent to how much our minds are open. D'Las does his best to stay shut down. When he has his power, he is much stronger than me." D'Las scoffed in response, mostly out of habit. "What? I remember."

"So you tried to stop?"

V'Let smiled at the girl. "Of course. All those things dying, some that didn't quite deserve it, it hurts." Her voice became soft as the alien gestured to her chest. After a moment, her resolve strengthened. "However, the dominant species did deserve it."

"How can you be so judgmental?"

D'Las gaze hardened. "Have you looked at the humans?"

"I'm a human!" she cried indignantly.

V'Let laughed out loud. "No, you're not. You're like her," she said, pointing at the Crone. "Except for your power being bound."

Rosalie's eyes narrowed on some unseen object. "What about the humans?"

D'Las laughed a mirthless chuckle. "They're entirely too malicious. Not only do they destroy the nonhumans and each other, they destroy the very ground beneath them, that which is meant to nurture them, that which gave them life!"

It was V'Let's turn to rub circles on her brother's back. "Calm, brother."

In turn, he bowed his head deeply in apology. "However, just recently, we've hit a snag. The humans are too malicious and dangerous to remain as they are and yet we can't destroy the planet. Council decree is above the Blood Contract. But then," she giggled, "briefly after our incident in the clearing, the Blood Contract was destroyed. So, we're no longer bound."

The Crone's brow creased deeply. "What are you going to do?"

"We could go home," D'Las murmured hopefully.

"We can't assume that there's anything there," V'Let replied in a soft voice. She continued louder to the rest of them. "The entity needs to be convinced to return to its passive state. I'm not sure what is happening to all the nonhuman species while it is active. Also, the humans have to be dealt with." V'Let glanced over at Rosalie, who seemed to have that pesky anger building again. "However, much of that can wait. I believe some of us have our own personal things to deal with."

Rosalie looked up at the alien and mouthed, "Thank you."

*Come see me when you're done with him, please,* V'Let whispered into her head. Rosalie eyes widened considerably. After a moment, she shook Erik's hand off her shoulder, nodded at V'Let and disappeared.

"Nifty trick," D'Las muttered.

# CHAPTER THIRTY-SEVEN

Rosalie found herself on the Prince's realm, anger still rolling through her like a massive tsunami. First, she'd been angry with the aliens. For their lies, for their calm as well, but mostly because apparently they had gotten to Earth some time before the ritual had been performed. Erik had kept insisting that if they hadn't shown up, they would all be dead. Well, except for Quin because he had stayed behind.

The aliens were skilled, he said, fighting off the vampires better than he ever could. When she'd woken that morning with her head still very fuzzy, he said he thought that the vampire ambush was a setup, that the male alien (*D'Las,* she reminded herself) had said there was a big vampire there to kill her. She'd had to agree at that—Lenny had been there and he hadn't looked like he was there to help.

The aliens that destroyed planets were their saviors. It was difficult to wrap her mind around it. They knew for a fact that these aliens could get inside your head. When she returned to the Material Plane, she would make herself talk to V'Let and try to be open-minded about it.

With a rough sigh, she focused on her surroundings again and found herself on the knoll, just outside the Prince's palace. She was almost ready to burst with emotion. Maybe V'Let had been right. The aliens certainly didn't act like they were lying and she had someone in her life that had lied to her before, probably more times than she was aware.

As soon as the palace walls flickered away long enough, Rosalie darted inside in a way that kept her against the walls in the throne room. Inside, Prince Darrin was talking to both Aura and Senka. Arching an eyebrow, Rosalie did her best to remain silent and unseen.

"The twins arrived before the ritual was completed," Aura stated in such a way it seemed as if she were reporting to the Prince.

"The ritual wouldn't have worked anyway," Senka replied snidely. "Not against them."

"But we knew that. The ritual wasn't about protecting Earth from the aliens," the Prince added, sounding tired.

"Then what was it about?" Aura sounded confused.

"It was about releasing the Earth's spirit, making it strike out."

"I'm still not clear on how a protection ritual did that," Aura whined.

"Don't act stupid, sister. Will it kill the humans?" Rosalie cringed at how delighted Senka sounded.

At that point, Rosalie decided she had heard enough. For the Prince, this had never been about the aliens or the possible invasion (which was, granted, a moot point now). This had been about destroying the humans, maybe all of them, and using a being that had to be more powerful than him to do it. He was never one for getting his hands dirty.

"It won't," Rosalie stated, stepping away from the wall.

Darrin rolled his eyes. "Great, the child's here. Did the invasion go well?"

Her eyes narrowed at his snide tone. "Somehow, you knew they wouldn't destroy Earth. You didn't tell me. You just let me believe the end of the world was coming with E.T. at its fore. So that what would happen? Mother Earth would kill her precious humans?"

Darrin looked thoughtful for a moment. "Yes, that's essentially it."

"Well, you overestimated something. Both of the aliens says she's a life-giver, that that's what she does."

Darrin made a dismissive gesture and the Oracles faded away, both of them giving Rosalie a smile of some kind before disappearing. "No, she won't just strike them down where they stand. However, she sent out a protection wave and it's disrupting a lot. The humans will eventually kill each other."

Rosalie threw her hands into the air. "Eventually! You arrogant bastard," she accused as she marched determinedly up to him. "More aliens are coming. And the ones that are here are highly unhappy with humans." She growled when he grinned triumphantly. "It doesn't even matter as long as they're gone, does it?"

"No, it doesn't." He tilted his head at her in a challenge.

"What do you have against humans? You could care less what happens to the planet. You wouldn't live long enough to see it die."

"They're weak," he spat, glaring at her in a way that made her very aware of the fact that he lumped her in a box with them. "They're sentimental bags of flesh and they're in my way."

Rosalie harrumphed, glaring at him with indignant fire. She was much too angry to try to figure out what exactly the humans were in the way of. Without another comment, she disappeared from the Prince's flickering realm and found herself back on the Crone's porch. She collapsed on the porch bench and sighed, placing her head in her hands. After a moment, her strong emotions spilled out of her eyes, the tears bitter and steady. She kept her eyes clenched shut and her hands over them. This type of loss of control usually reflected in her planeswalking. She was still physically on the Material Plane but if she opened her eyes and looked, she would see far more than someone her age should have to.

Part of her had really trusted Darrin. Sure, she didn't like him or most of his opinions, not to mention how he dealt with problems, but she thought he could be trusted. As it turned out, the aliens she had spent the last two weeks building fear and anger against were probably leagues more trustworthy than the ruler of the Infinite Realms. She suddenly hated the way she'd bent for his every whim over the years.

She didn't know how much time had passed but she felt someone sit next to her. She wanted to find out who it was but she wouldn't dare pull her hands away from her eyes. The person placed a hand on top of her head. After a very brief moment, the person moved from next to her to kneel in front of her, moving the hand to two fingers on each of her temples.

*Come back.*

It was odd. She could feel her control building and her emotions spiral down to a manageable level. After a moment of feeling her control reconstruct itself, she pulled her hands away to look straight into the bright blue eyes of the alien, who smiled back at her.

Looking at the alien now, she could see the oddities. Their eyes were slightly larger than normal and almond-shaped, the blue of their eyes a little too bright to be normal and their pupils barely a pinprick. She wondered idly if their pupils dilated at all. Both of the aliens had seemed tall, their skin a deep violet and their hair a gentle lavender shade. She realized that they could easily pass for fey with their slight and slender features.

V'Let returned to her seat next to the girl. "Was it bad?" she whispered with what seemed to be a large amount of concern.

166

Rosalie nodded, wiping idly at the tears that still leaked out of her eyes. "Oh, and how," she muttered in response. She turned her head to look at V'Let. "What did you do?"

V'Let's lips curved into a smile. "I helped heal the cracks." At Rosalie's blank expression, she explained. "I understand that your power is bound totally and completely in walking the planes. However, power, control and emotions, they're all tied together. I can't unbind your power but I can heal your emotions until you can find it in yourself to be whole on your own."

Rosalie gazed at the alien, her eyes soft and a half-smile gracing her face. "You're not what I expected."

V'Let's smile morphed into a wide grin. "That's good. I knew you expected some kind of mass invasion by hairless grey men."

Rosalie let forth a watery giggle. "I blame television?"

"And him, of course. Whoever he is."

Rosalie's face hardened. "Yes, he let me believe you were bad. He just wants the humans dead."

V'Let's smile wilted, her forehead creasing in concern. "I take it not for the same reasons we do."

Rosalie shook her head. She knew it wasn't a question but V'Let needed to know why. "He hates them, always has. I'm not sure why."

The alien tilted her head at the girl. "No, you know why."

Rosalie looked hard at V'Let and then looked hard at her own impression of the Prince. How he reacted to her presence, how he reacted to humans, even his words. "Prince Darrin is a semi-corporeal creature, wispy as the morning fog. Humans are solid and so am I. I think he's jealous. Maybe?"

V'Let smiled encouragingly. "He might take it too far one day. However, that day is not today and can be dealt with at a later time." After a moment, she changed the subject, her serious tone crystallizing. "I need you to understand something, Rosalie."

Rosalie straightened her back, half-fearful of what V'Let would say next. "Yes?"

She sighed. "Loorans, we're not a naturally destructive species. What the Adepts have made us do, it's wrong and I have endured a lot of pain trying to defy them. So, when we have to judge a species, we take it very seriously."

Rosalie rubbed her hands over her upper arms. "But, y'know, people make mistakes."

V'Let inclined her head. "Yes, that is true. However, humans are deadly. They're also keeping themselves in evolutionary stagnancy. Their lives are too short to see how bad things really are."

"You're only twenty-five," Rosalie accused softly.

"That's true. That doesn't mean I don't see a bigger picture. This planet is divided far more deeply than it should be. Humans hurt the planet just to get ahead, just for progress."

Rosalie nodded. Maybe it was from being around demons and other things on various realms that were decidedly not human, but she did have a certain distaste for humans. If she thought about it, she understood. Despite the exceptions, humans destroyed everything they touched.

"I want to see the entity today," V'Let said suddenly in a hard, determined voice. Rosalie snapped her focus and realized that they had been joined by her brother, who looked at V'Let with a type of sadness. "I'll go whether you help me or not."

Rosalie relaxed against the bench and resigned herself to watch the two of them. It didn't involve her and she didn't really want to draw attention to herself by standing and purposely removing herself from the equation.

"You just woke up two hours ago, Letta. Now you want to power up to talk to some all-powerful entity?"

"Well, it's probably not *all*-powerful," she hedged.

"What if you exhaust yourself? What if you die this time?"

In return, V'Let rolled her eyes. "Don't be so dramatic. It doesn't take so much power that it'll drain me. It has to be done."

D'Las cast his gaze downward for a moment before looking back at his sister. "At least let me take you there."

V'Let nodded her consent. Then she glanced back at Rosalie. "So, planeswalker, how about it?"

Rosalie looked back into the blue eyes of the alien. "What? You're serious? You want me to go with you?"

V'Let chuckled softly. "Yes. You are an integral part of my current plan."

Rosalie grinned at the alien, though she still remained somewhat confused. "So, why do you suddenly want to talk to the 'entity'?"

V'Let's eyes twinkled. "I can multitask."

Rosalie rolled her eyes. "That wasn't vague at all."

D'Las grinned at the statement. "What my dear sister means is that while she was trying to convince you of our genuinely good intentions, she was arguing with me mentally about talking to the entity."

Rosalie nodded and stood. "So, when are we leaving?"

V'Let stood as well. "Right about now." She jumped off the porch, followed closely by her brother and at slightly greater distance Rosalie. "Before they notice we're gone."

After an uncertain pause, Rosalie rushed to catch up to the aliens. At the edge of Matlinda's property, they disappeared, causing Rosalie to bring herself to an abrupt halt. "Okay, what just happened?" she murmured to herself.

She waited, keeping herself very still and feeling ridiculously out in the open for almost an entire minute before half of V'Let appeared before her. Rosalie squeaked in alarm in response to seeing only the upper portion of the alien.

"You coming?" V'Let asked, holding out a hand for the planeswalker.

Cautious and slightly skittish now, Rosalie reached out and clasped the hand, following when the alien pulled her through what she assumed was a type of invisible barrier. Beyond the barrier was something the like of which she had only seen in science-fiction television shows. V'Let led her through a cargo hold after pressing a large button that closed the hatch that they had climbed to reach this point. Everything seemed to be made of a metal that she didn't recognize, a type of dark silver that made her think of tungsten, which in turn made her think of her father.

"Positive thoughts," V'Let said suddenly in a singsong tone, breaking Rosalie from the very vague but completely sad last memory of her father.

Rosalie chuckled self-consciously. "Do you do that a lot?"

V'Let looked at the girl with a searching look, not missing a step as she led them up the stairs. "Probably. Surface mental reading comes natural to Loorans. We've been able to do it for thousands of years. For some, it's the first step in evolution. Some days, it's hard to shut it off."

"Can your brother...?" Rosalie trailed off, remembering a little too late about how V'Let had said that he shut himself off on purpose.

"No, nor would he want to." V'Let released the girl's hand, trusting her to follow now. At the top of the stairs was a long metal corridor that went in both directions. V'Let turned left and so Rosalie did as well, though she craned her neck to try to see what was in the other direction. She could only see doors. Within moments, they approached an open doorway and Rosalie could see the door itself pulled inside a crevice in the doorway. V'Let spread her arms wide. "This is the bridge. How long, D'Las?"

He sighed, punching buttons on his console. Suddenly, the screen at the fore of the bridge brightened with color and there were numbers and symbols at the bottom right corner of the screen that Rosalie didn't understand, "What does that say?" she asked, pointing at the symbols.

V'Let glanced at the girl and then at the screen. "Oh!" she exclaimed after a moment, followed by a self-conscious chuckle. "It's in Looran. Two more minutes."

"Until what?"

"Until we're back in the clearing."

Rosalie's eyes widened so much that she felt they were about to fall out of her skull. "We already left?"

V'Let's face broke into a soft smile. "Yes."

"And we're going to the clearing?" Rosalie hoped that V'Let could hear the hidden question under that jumble of words.

"The easiest way to contact the entity is to return to one of the sites of the ritual. The closest one is the clearing. It may very well be the best as well, considering that the old woman made a power sink."

D'Las twisted his body so that he could look at them, seeing as they stood behind him. "Really? A power sink? That's what that was?"

Rosalie's brow furrowed as she gazed at V'Let in askance. "What's a power sink?"

"Okay, using that instance as an example, Matlinda started out with an area that was slightly more powerful than average, using lines of power that wrap around Earth."

"Leylines," Rosalie interjected.

V'Let's smiled widened. "Right. It helped her tap into the entity and complete the ritual. Did she draw power to her beforehand?"

Rosalie had a feeling that V'Let actually already knew the answer to her own question. "Yes. When we were planning it, she said that even during the ritual, she would be continuously drawing power from the things around her."

The alien nodded. "Because it was a massive, complex ritual. She needed as much power as she could summon. However, the downside to that is when the entity was allowed to become active, it took all of that power."

"Was that why she passed out?"

"Quite right. And again, because of the ritual's purpose, the first thing the entity did was put a protective filter around the planet. Because Matlinda lost consciousness, the entity kept drawing power, turning that area into a power sink. A power sink will draw in your own power and return it to you almost tenfold." V'Let sighed. "It's what will allow me to communicate with the entity with little to no power loss."

Rosalie gulped slightly. "If it kept drawing power from the Crone, could she have died?"

V'Let nodded solemnly. "It's possible."

"Do you think it happened to the others?"

V'Let's brow furrowed slightly. "I'm not sure. That would be a question for the entity, I suppose." She glanced at the screen again. "We're here."

With a slight flourish of a turn, V'Let led the girl back down to the cargo hold, reaching out to glide her fingers over the Goddess statuette as she passed it. What she was about to do was a little bit of a bigger complication than she was letting Rosalie or her brother know. Especially her brother with his overprotectiveness and ability to persuade her when she had doubts. Besides, she reminded herself, this was something that needed to be done.

Craning her neck to glance over her shoulder, she made sure that Rosalie was following, which she was. In the deepest parts of her, she wasn't sure why the girl was so important but she could feel it in a way that she wasn't sure she could even explain to her brother, much less anybody else. Yet another thing she needed to ask the entity about...

V'Let eased herself down to the ground, moving with a calm grace that belied her inner thoughts. Once she was actually free of the ship and aware of her surroundings, she could feel the pull of the power sink. She clenched her eyes and whispered a few words to herself, something the Looran oracles had thought to teach them at a very young age. It was an incantation so old that they said it couldn't be found written anywhere. It was used to tie the Looran power and the power of all other things to sight.

When V'Let opened her eyes again, the world had become brighter and even more colorful. A few feet ahead, she could see the power sink clearly, a wobbly mass of alternating light with three bright green lines of power crossing at its center. Frowning, she stopped, glancing again back at the planeswalker that followed her. As she had expected, the girl was wrapped in massive power, blindingly bright and somehow prismatic, but the power itself was binding, coiled around her and squeezing every so often. In the middle of a power squeeze, V'Let noticed the girl wince and decided that later she would ask what happened during those moments.

She held out her hand in a halting gesture. "Stay here, Rosalie. Don't come forward unless I tell you aloud."

Rosalie's brow creased, though she did as she was told. "Why?"

V'Let nodded at the power sink, which somehow still showed the seared ground. "The entity may be a life-giver but that doesn't mean that it cares who dies. The power sink can still be dangerous for someone unprepared." She didn't mention that since Rosalie had no real control over her own power, the sink could just take and take until all that was left of the planeswalker would be a lifeless husk.

Rosalie nodded idly. "I can see that. Death is part of the life cycle."

Without another word, V'Let immersed herself in the power sink, watching at the power flashed at her and somehow shrank away. It would be something to think about later but now she knelt at the point where the lines of power crossed and touched the center.

*I want to talk to you.* She pushed the thought through with power and felt it as it latched onto the massive being that seemed to somehow be everywhere.

*"Speak, child of Loora."*

It was daunting, the feeling of an incomprehensibly large entity suddenly turning its attention to her. She swallowed thickly, her mind awhirl with disjointed thoughts. *What happened?*

There was a massive laugh echoing inside of her head. *"You know what happened, child. You even informed the witch of what was so obvious to you."*

V'Let inhaled and exhaled, trying to cut through her growing frustration. She absolutely hated talking to entities of this magnitude; they always were just a little nonsensical and loved to play games a little too much. *Why did it happen?*

However, her question was not to be answered just then. *"Oh, good. You brought the Guardian."*

V'Let could hear the importance in the word, a seeming type of personal importance for the Earth entity. She frowned, however, because she hadn't realized she'd brought something of import with her. Then the entity seemed to reach out behind V'Let but stopped short.

*"She remains bound."* There was anger in the words. *"Why would you tempt the world with salvation but keep it out of reach?"*

V'Let's forehead creased deeply, trying to work her way through the entity's words. They carried a hint of insanity and she could feel the very essence of what made the entity being stretched beyond what it could handle. Very much beyond. *Are you talking about the girl, the planeswalker?*

Again, the entity flooded her with images and knowledge, much of it making little to no sense. There were fires and a marching body of men in medieval armor, women screaming nonsense and men clutching their head with fear in their eyes. *"Rosalie McGrath comes from a long line of Guardians, my Guardians, those that stood against the humans and their so-called righteousness. A long time ago, the power was tainted by jealousy and dark power. The human seed was allowed to spread and I was condemned to destruction, slow and painful."*

V'Let clenched her hands into fists, her fingers digging into the ground in a way that was almost painful for her joints. The images came with the entity's own very large feelings and V'Let had a hard time coming back to herself. *Why don't you just kill them? Destroy in turn?*

The entity turned away from the thought of its Guardian and answered the alien. *"It is not in me to do so. Life is life, no matter what cruelty a soul can sow in another."*

V'Let stared into the distance in front of her, watching the shadows move in the trees as her mind worked through what the entity had stated. There was something there in the words, a possibility of sorts. "But can you?" she whispered aloud.

*"Yes, I can. I can kill but I find claiming their souls in death distasteful."*

The entity's particular phrasing stuck with V'Let, yet another thing that she would have to dissect at a later time. However, at this moment in time, she knew that the being was open enough to strike a deal. *How could I convince you?* Her mental voice carried a note of openness in it. V'Let would do almost anything to rid the universe of the human plague.

*"I cannot condone xenocide."* The entity's voice was hard and firm, brooking no argument.

V'Let rolled her neck. She herself was not trained in diplomacy, though she had memories of some of her race and their scant dealings in politics. *What about thinning the herd? Humans are extremely dangerous, after all. They taint everything they touch.*

The entity made a sound that somehow combined a sigh and a growl. *"How thin?"*

V'Let felt herself relax finally. Maybe she wasn't so bad at the whole diplomacy thing, after all. Or maybe, the Earth entity knew it couldn't be active forever and something truly needed to be done about the humans and their endless governments. *For every human you allow to live, you must consume one hundred thousand of them.*

There was a long moment of silence. It stretched between them, making V'Let doubt herself. She refused to break the silence, mentally or physically. She locked herself in position and waited for the entity to speak. *"There will be less than seventy thousand humans remaining on the surface of the planet."*

*But there will be humans left alive. They won't be extinct.*

*"I find these terms acceptable."* V'Let's face broke out in a grin, her body flowing in its normal loose lines again. *"I have a condition of my own. I will not do what you want until this condition is fulfilled."*

The smile fell off her face, leaving her limp rather than loose. *What condition?*

She heard a chuckle from deep within the earth. *"Unbind my Guardian. Only then I will thin the human herd."*

*But I don't know how. I don't even think I can!* V'Let's mind was alive with panic. Without the entity's consent, destroying the humans could do a lot more harm than she could foresee.

*"You can and you will. It's the only way."* That said, the entity turned its attention away from the alien and back to whatever it had been doing before.

After a moment of desperate contemplation, V'Let stood slowly, her joints aching vaguely from the time she had spent on the ground. There was a nagging thought in the back of her mind that the entity was not quite done asking nearly impossible tasks of her but she swiped it aside. There was already quite enough to think about without her own mind adding to the pile.

Rosalie stepped closer to V'Let when she stood unsteadily, watching with curious eyes. The alien held up a hand in a halting gesture, however, and she obeyed. V'Let stood still and seemed to just breathe for a moment but Rosalie could tell that something was wrong. The alien's pupils had apparently dilated somewhat, no longer pinpricks but wobbling black discs across a blue surface.

"You're the key," V'Let said, finally looking at the planeswalker.

Rosalie furrowed her brow in thought. "How am I the key?"

V'Let moved out of the power sink's reach and closed her eyes, pressing the heels of her hands against her eyelids. When she opened her eyes again, her sight had returned to normal and her pupils had returned to barely visible dots midst the blue irises. She shook her head and gestured for the girl to follow her back onto the spacecraft.

Rosalie scurried after the alien, her confusion continuously rising. "What's going on? What did the entity say?"

Again, V'Let shook her head, this time emphasizing her decision with a dismissive gesture. Rosalie could feel her too-ready anger rise again before she squelched it firmly. She reminded herself that she couldn't possibly attempt to guess the alien's motives for anything. Something had obviously disturbed her. It just bothered Rosalie, the not knowing. She was very much like Erik in that way.

V'Let hurried up the steps to the bridge, mentally pressing the airlock after she was sure the planeswalker was inside. She noticed idly that the girl stayed in the cargo hold but paid it no extra attention at the time. She burst onto the bridge with all the urgency all her mind could muster.

"Back to the Crone's," she told her brother without preamble.

She moved around the central console to be in a position to face her brother as he punched in their former coordinates. He looked up at her, his eyes asking a specific inquiry.

"I'm fine."

"You were down there for over an hour," he chastised gently. "Excuse me for being worried."

"We have a problem." V'Let's voice was hard, determination crystallizing her words.

D'Las's eyes lit in concern, an eyebrow arched in a clear question. She connected her own eyes to his, her gaze solid and unwavering. She told him what had happened along their link, as well as sending him what the entity had shown her, something that she now knew was images from witch hunts from centuries ago. He inhaled sharply when she disconnected her gaze and she knew his mind was making the same trek hers had.

"I need you for this, D'Las," V'Let declared as she turned to face the viewscreen. "I can't do it alone."

D'Las stood from the console and moved to hug his sister. "I'll try my best." He laid his head on her shoulder, staring into the distance and not quite seeing the viewscreen. "I haven't been able to use my own power since we left home."

V'Let sighed. "Maybe I can." She moved her arms to return the hug and her head to rest on top of his. "Why can't this all just be over?"

# CHAPTER THIRTY-EIGHT

Marcus entered the house quietly, his mind whirring with paranoia. Today had been Marina DuPont's funeral, a spectacle of death that not even the military could match. There had been publicity whores and media vultures and Xen Trellick at the forefront of it all. Marcus had unknowingly mimicked his father as Dmitri had been at Xavier's funeral, hiding from the procession and completely aloof a few dozen yards away from the gravesite. He hated funerals but every Council member was expected to attend when "one of their own" died.

Over the past two days, he had tried his best to read as much of his father's private journal as he could manage. It was convoluted with tactical observations and bits of information of which he had been told before, so those he skipped. However, he paid close attention to his accounts of conversations with V'Let, such as the one in the first entry. That had been a disaster the first day, having to face up to the others. While Marcus wanted to believe that the Trellick siblings were not as manipulative and controlling as their predecessors, he forced himself to remain neutral. He had told them he refused to discuss anything until they finished the journal and decided between themselves.

Decided what, they had asked at the time. He told them that they would know in the end. Then he'd left, taking his Parvini and a copy of the journal on an info-drive with him. Early this morning, he'd received an alert from Railey about having finished her "research" and how she wanted to talk to him at the house before Xen returned from the funeral.

Idly, he wondered how she'd gotten out of going to the funeral and if she was going to kill him when he arrived. In all honesty, he wasn't sure if he should fear for his life or hope that they would understand.

Sighing desolately, he moved through the house to the library. He was just wasting time by standing in the foyer and speculating. As he walked, he could vaguely hear the Parvini somewhere in the house. Every morning after making sure his own house was up to their standards, they came to this house and it managed to keep them much busier than his own small, one-bedroom house.

When Marcus entered the library, he noticed Railey pacing agitatedly between two terminals, her lips pressed into a thin line. In the back of his mind, he realized that she didn't seem angry, just merely disturbed and deeply so. He made his way to the table with soft thuds echoing his movement and waited for the Kretoran woman to say something.

"Did you do it?" she blurted out suddenly.

Railey had stopped her pacing and gazed at Marcus with wide eyes. In return, he gave her a wry smile, having only the smallest inkling to what she was referring. "Depends on what you're asking me about."

She sighed roughly, jerking one of her hands through her shoulder-length black hair. "The Blood Contract," she clarified. "Did you destroy it?"

Marcus inclined his head in affirmation. "It was illegal and beyond inhumane."

Railey nodded to herself. "Then what's in the Artifact Room?"

"A surface mimic." He tilted his head slightly, narrowing his eyes in an attempt to examine something about Railey more closely. "You're not angry about it. *He* would have been."

At that statement, she stiffened and glared back at the psychologist. "I am not my father," she declared firmly between clenched teeth.

Marcus nodded again, his smile never having left his face. "I am aware."

At that, Railey deflated and sat across the table from Marcus. "Did you know about all of this?" she asked, spreading her arms wide in a gesture meant to include more than just the house.

"Some," he admitted. "A lot of it, apparently, but not all." He let his smile fall away and looked into her eyes sincerely. "I didn't know what he had planned for your father. Or Marina."

Railey shrugged her shoulders idly. "They would have done the same to him for less. It was really for the best."

Marcus frowned, his forehead wrinkling in a crease. "He killed them. And he got away with it."

"Who got away with what?" Xen had flounced into the library, still in the fabulous outfit he had worn to Marina's funeral. It was grief in an explosion of color and glitter, meant to draw attention away from any behavior that was out of place.

Railey looked up at her brother and then glanced back at Marcus. He nodded almost imperceptibly. "Dmitri got away with killing our mentors."

Marcus had expected Xen's face to darken but, on the contrary, it brightened further. "Really?" He collapsed bonelessly into a nearby chair and proceeded to attempt to peel himself out of the colorful contraption that was his outfit. Marcus cringed, expecting to see skin, but relaxed when there was another layer of muted material underneath it. "How did he do it? Both of their autopsies had expected results." Xen paused, grunting softly as he pulled the last of the bright material free and then proceeded to toss it aside in disgust. "Did he bribe the medical examiner?"

Railey shrugged. "Maybe."

At the same time, Marcus scoffed. "No." Both Railey and Xen turned to him and simultaneously arched their eyebrows. The sight of it caused him to chuckle, a reaction that he swallowed after a moment. "It's just... Dad thinks bribing authorities is tacky."

" 'Tacky'?" Xen echoed in shock. "I thought bribery would be the political thing to do." At the look he received from his sister, he continued in a smaller voice. "You know, tactically speaking."

Marcus shook his head at their interaction. "No, he always said that if you're going to do something illegal, you should do it so well that it never leads back to you."

Railey's brow furrowed deeply. "But it did lead back to him. He admits to it in his journal."

Marcus laughed bitterly. "In a journal only he or I could open. No one else knows that nickname."

Railey rolled her eyes. "Anyone that knew a little Looran could figure it out eventually."

Marcus shrugged. "V'Let said it wasn't a common nickname."

"I don't get it." Xen stared hard at the psychologist. "That's a Galaxy Killer's nickname for you?"

Marcus stopped, deciding to take a moment to analyze everything. As much as it was hard for him to reconcile the harmless Looran people with the picture that Marina had painted of the Galaxy Killers, he knew rationally that the Galaxy Killer propaganda was very far from the actual truth. When his father talked about the twins away from the other

Adepts, he'd always been peaceful, a smile on his face that maintained that everything was still all right with the world. Marcus was well aware that he needed to move past his emotions when it concerned the twins and it was entirely possible that a lot of Railey's and Xen's reactions had more to do with the propaganda rather than with what they actually knew about them.

"More importantly," Railey interjected, "are they going to come after us?"

At that remark, Marcus's brow smoothed out into disbelief. "Why would you think that?"

Railey fidgeted for a moment and Marcus figured she almost started to get up to start pacing again before she settled for staring down at her hands. "Well, we're the successors of the people that forced them to destroy fifteen whole planets and more people than I could ever think to rationalize."

Again, Marcus shrugged. "I really don't think they're the type to hold a grudge." At the look he received from Railey, he clarified. "My father once said that grudges hurt the soul. It's honestly more something a Looran would say, not a tactical advisor."

"I still don't get it," Xen interrupted, his face still crinkled in thought. "Why would she call you 'sweet boy'?"

Marcus grinned. "Dad always said that I melted his heart of ice and she was the first one to notice."

Railey scoffed. "What are you talking about? Dmitri Andian still has a heart of ice."

Marcus clucked his tongue softly. "Ah-ah," he chastised. "To the public eye, he's still the same because he had to be. At home and away from the others, he was full of soft gooey goodness."

"Ew," Xen murmured softly. At the looks he received from Railey and Marcus, he explained. "I just pictured Tactical Elder Andian as a gummy treat."

At that, they all broke apart into laughter. For the rest of the day, their conversation veered into less dire events as they tried to avoid thinking about what might happen if the twins were to become angry.

# CHAPTER THIRTY-NINE

A few hours had passed. D'Las stood outside their spacecraft, standing guard with strict instructions to let no one pass. Not that they hadn't tried. Oh, how they had tried…

Rosalie had been escorted off the ship as soon as they landed with a glare that had sent her scampering to the Crone's house. Only moments passed before she returned, flanked by the vampire and the blue demon. The elderly witch had joined them as well but she stood back by a few feet. That damned serene smile had been pasted on her face while D'Las had rebuffed all of them. Rosalie had been massive levels of angry because V'Let had yet to explain what had happened. D'Las himself could care less if they knew, idly wondering if it were better that they didn't. It was entirely possible that V'Let could unbind the girl's powers without actually being in physical contact with her.

The passing time had become dull but D'Las was well aware that his sister was not quite finished yet. For the past four hours, she delved through their genetic memory banks, sorting through rituals of binding and how to undo them. Almost an hour ago, he felt her emotions rise and he figured that she might have found something. However, he also knew that she would keep going until she exhausted every angle of this equation.

"Do you eat meat?"

D'Las glanced up to see Erik moving cautiously toward him, holding a plate of what looked to be thinly sliced meat encased in wheat-rich bread in one hand and a clear plastic container with leafy greens and oddly-shaped red vegetables. "Sometimes," he replied in return. "More than V'Let at any rate. I require the protein more."

Erik smiled welcomingly. "She can have the salad, then."

As the vampire approached, D'Las snagged the plate and began taking large bites out of the sandwiches. He hadn't realized how hungry he was until he actually saw the food. He watched as Erik continued past him and then paused uncertainly at the edge of the cloak. "Go on," he encouraged the vampire. "Set it next to her but don't disturb her."

With a nod, the vampire continued beyond the cloak. He reappeared a few seconds later. "What's she doing?" Erik inquired of the male alien softly.

D'Las swallowed a large chunk of sandwich, wincing in minimal pain as it traveled the length of his esophagus. "Does it matter?"

Erik shrugged, his eyes glancing back to the hidden spacecraft before returning to meet the alien's gaze. "Not really, I guess."

D'Las's eyes keenly studied the vampire, clearly seeing the relaxed stance and the vague almost-smile. Memories from time spent on other planets came rushing back to him, memories of the animals to which his sister connected always unerringly finding her and staying by her side. Once, he'd asked her about it in irritation. In response, she'd told him that she just assumed that being near the source of the connection made them feel content. He'd left it alone then but now, he wondered, what did they feel?

"You feel better?" he asked the vampire.

Erik snapped out of the daze, focusing on the alien. "What do you mean?"

"Being near V'Let. Does it make you feel better?"

Erik's dark blue eyes shifted slightly up and to the right as he thought about it. "Yeah, actually. I feel almost… happy."

D'Las nodded, taking another bite out of his sandwich. Maybe V'Let would know better how it worked, he figured, and he doubted it would ever go away as long as both of them lived. He smiled softly as he thought about it. Neither of them were likely to die for a very long time.

After a while, as D'Las finished his multitude of sandwiches, Erik began to hum a song. D'Las's sensitive ears twitched, listening closely to the melody. The alien glanced over at the vampire, subtly enough that the movement was not picked up by the hybrid, and noticed that he was in a daze again. Another moment passed and D'Las could pick up words that Erik had begun to sing, words that sounded very typical of Looran speech and song.

"Can I ask you something?" the alien inquired softly, keeping his voice at a volume and pitch so as to not break the daze but still earn responses.

"Hmm?" the vampire breathed in response, his voice signifying that he was listening.

"V'Let says you were part of that vampire gang that attacked before. Why did you leave?"

A smile graced Erik's face, seeming to float across his countenance. "Luna Morte captured Rosalie one night, shortly after she moved to the city. They were attracted to her power." At this, the vampire frowned slightly. "There was something about her, something grounded and earthy. I wanted to protect her. So I took her and ran."

D'Las smiled. If he hadn't trusted the vampire before, he certainly did now. He showed a strong protective streak. "Why did you want to protect her?"

Erik sighed. "Despite her amount of power, I could feel a block in that power. She was helpless. Something reached out and made me keep her safe."

*The entity,* V'Let whispered into D'Las's head. He jerked slightly, casting his gaze behind him just in time to see her step through the boundary of the cloak.

In return, D'Las arched an eyebrow at his sister. *Are we sure it was the entity that made him protect the girl?*

V'Let smiled softly. *He was already highly protective. He just needed a little push.* She flowed gracefully past Erik and then turned to look at the vampire, the question clear. *What's with him?*

D'Las chuckled softly. *He's near you, sweetling.* He maneuvered himself to put an arm around his sister's shoulders. *You're the one that told me the connection never really goes away.*

V'Let smiled at her brother, obviously happy that he'd remembered one of her lectures, and grabbed the vampire's hand as they headed back to the Crone's house. "Are they mad?" she asked her brother in a quiet murmur.

D'Las laughed out loud in a way that bordered a hysterical cackle.

V'Let sighed softly. "Oh."

Quin stood on the porch, his mind a million miles away. The Crone had set Rosalie down in the living room some time ago with a tea suffused with herbs to keep her compliant. Erik had disappeared to the edge of the Crone's property with lunch for the aliens the better part of an hour ago. He'd been out here, staring into the distance and trying to sort through his thoughts.

There had been large amounts of fear, indescribably huge. Despite his own status as a demon and a large knowledge of the things that surrounded him, Quin had to admit that he was highly afraid of the unknown. Besides which, he had a bad habit of jumping to conclusions of the worst kind. Being around Rosalie and Erik hadn't helped any—the two of them both had very deep wells of anger. Aliens with nicknames like "Galaxy Killers" also didn't do well to instill confidence about their good intentions.

That was before, though. Before he had personally heard D'Las talk about the Blood Contract. Quin would admit freely that he couldn't comprehend the science or need behind such a contract but he could tell that their pain had been real and intense. There had been some fear as well. Not a lot, but enough for his paltry senses to pick it up. The way they acted, he doubted they felt or acknowledged the fear consciously anymore but it was something that kept them wary. Both of them had held themselves tense beneath the loose and relaxed lines of their bodies.

Quin's focus snapped back to his surroundings when he heard the almost soundless thuds against the wood of the porch. She caught sight of the Crone in his peripheral vision as she moved to sit next to him. She smiled, her mask of serenity cracked with worry. "Where are your thoughts?" she inquired softly.

Quin smiled back tightly. "On them. The aliens."

The worry leaked through more. "You're not still thinking of running?"

Quin shook his head, his smile becoming more genuine. "No. They're good people. I just... I'm not sure what's going to happen. They're so secretive sometimes."

Matlinda nodded. "I can still feel it coming."

Quin arched an eyebrow at the witch. "The cataclysm?"

She nodded. "It's something big and everything will change. The more I try to concentrate on the cataclysm itself, the more I'm sure it has to do with Rosalie."

"That's because it does." Quin glanced quickly at the intrusion, which was V'Let. She stepped gracefully onto the porch, followed closely by her brother and Erik.

Quin peered closely at the vampire, seeing the dazed look in his eyes. "What happened to Erik?"

V'Let gestured dismissively and turned to the vampire. Gently, she laid her hand over his eyes. She pulled herself up on the tips of her feet and whispered something into the vampire's ear before slowly turning away.

Quin watched in amazement at Erik's eyes cleared and focused, his eyes landing on V'Let briefly before flitting across his surroundings.

"That was... refreshing?" Erik seemed slightly confused.

V'Let shrugged and settled herself near her brother, who had already seated himself with a bored expression plastered across his face. It was as if he'd seen what she had done a dozen times before.

"What just happened? What did you do to Erik?"

V'Let gazed at Quin after he asked the question, her pupils seeming to dilate very slightly. After a moment of scrutiny, she smiled softly. "I connected with Erik during the journey to Earth. Those that I connect with can fall into a contented daze when I'm near." She shrugged. "I think I balance out the anger."

Quin nodded, about to open his mouth to respond, but Erik interrupted his attempt. "Where's Rosalie?"

Matlinda nodded at the entryway. "In the living area, too stoned to be of use for now."

Quin turned to face the Crone. "You gave her the opioid?" His voice was a mixture of shock and amusement. "Why?" Out of the corner of his eye, he could see V'Let and D'Las looking at each other in that way that suggested that they were having a conversation separately, despite the fact that they were not talking.

Matlinda shrugged. "She wouldn't calm down. I didn't foresee her deflating any time soon. I gave her something that would numb her enough that seeing the other planes wouldn't scare her witless."

V'Let cleared her throat softly, capturing their attention again. "Is that what happens?"

Matlinda tilted her head very slightly at the alien. "Is that what happens when?" the witch echoed with a tinge of reproach in her voice.

Quin watched as the alien's skin darkened almost imperceptibly across her cheeks. "Sorry," she murmured in response to the Crone's tone. "Before I spoke to the entity, I saw Rosalie's power. It coils around her like the venomous reptiles on our planet and squeezes her every so often. She cringes when it happens."

Erik was the one that answered this time. "She's said before that sometimes her control slips and that causes her to see some of the planes, some of them very unpleasant. She doesn't know why it happens."

V'Let nodded, seeming to just file it along with other information in her head. "I suppose one of you can tell Rosalie about what happened after this is all over." She looked at Matlinda, her eyes piercing. "These herbs you gave her today, they make her what? Unafraid? Numb?"

Matlinda's brow furrowed, trying to follow the alien's line of logic without any clues. "Numb, almost completely."

V'Let nodded again, this time decisively. "Good." She glanced sideways at her brother, who gave her an encouraging smile in turn. "After our talk this morning, I waited for Rosalie to return." The alien smiled idly. "There's something about her, something important that I didn't know before. It is, perhaps, why things have gotten so out of control in the last thousand years."

Quin snorted loudly, making much more noise than he had initially meant. "You say that like it's a short amount of time. A thousand years is a long time!"

D'Las chuckled. "For your kind, maybe," he replied in a murmur.

V'Let hushed her brother softly. "It's enough time for the humans to continue to swarm the globe. Rosalie's line was what stood between the humans and everything else. She's capable of powerful magic. She is, in essence, the guardian of this planet."

Erik frowned. That didn't sound like Rosalie. Sure, there were those times when she felt she had to help, needed to be there. Her lack of usable power kept her far away from the battles, whatever they happened to be. "Are you sure about that?"

Quin became even more interested as V'Let's eyes flashed in indignant anger. "Yes, I'm sure." The anger faded away, replaced by calculation and memory. "Does she ever want to learn more magic even though she can't execute it herself? Have a protective streak? Anything like that?"

Matlinda grinned at the vampire. Quin echoed the woman with a ghost of her smile when Erik inclined his head slightly. During this latest crisis, Rosalie had nearly torn the hair out of her skull to try to help. Idly, he wondered if any of them actually knew the planeswalker at all. Even Erik hadn't met her until she was wrapped in layers of control. Quin's smile widened slightly. It was possible that the only person here that knew Rosalie was V'Let, with her strange ability to know what they all were thinking.

Quin forced himself to focus on what the alien was saying now. "... agreed to thin the herd."

" 'Herd'?" the demon echoed softly.

V'Let gazed at Quin with an understanding and amused glint in her eyes. "When I spoke to the entity this morning, I got it to agree to thin the human herd."

"How thin?" the Crone asked, having leaned forward in her seat.

"We agreed that less than seventy thousand humans would remain." Quin watched as V'Let straightened, her eyes becoming cold and distant. As D'Las reached to put an arm around her shoulders, the demon realized that she was distancing herself from them, from their reactions. Quin wasn't entirely sure that was necessary.

"Wow," Erik breathed. Matlinda's eyes merely widened. Quin said nothing for a moment, allowing them to fit the idea into their concept of the world.

The moment passed and Quin shifted slightly. "What do you have to do?" he asked V'Let. There had to be something in return. He remembered her saying that the entity inside the planet was a life-giver and there had been that mention of what Rosalie really was.

The skin around V'Let's jaw tightened as she clenched her teeth together. She forced herself to relax and replied, "I have to unbind Rosalie's power to flow in its natural state."

"How exactly will you do that?" the Crone asked, having come back to herself.

"It's why I was meditating in the cargo hold and why D'Las wouldn't let anyone disturb me." She smiled softly, though there seemed to be a type of hardness to it that Quin couldn't identify. "I was searching my genetic memory."

"Your what?" Erik asked incredulously.

D'Las chuckled quietly as V'Let responded. "The Looran race has genetic memory. What any one Looran has known, we all know. It was been part of us since the first Looran had the ability to learn and reason. It's as much a part of us as… oh, a vampire's photosensitivity."

The vampire nodded as D'Las looked closely at his sister. "How far back?" he asked quietly.

V'Let's smile hardened further then, losing all of its softness. It worried Quin vaguely, not in a fearful way but in a concerned way. "I had to search back over three thousand years, which put me in the middle of the Separatist Wars." Quin's interest piqued with D'Las cringed. "Some Loorans cast binding rituals in these wars, so many different types. But there are ways to undo every single one of them inside our memory." The alien gazed at all of them in turn. "Once I know the specifics of Rosalie's binding, I can unravel it. Of this, I am quite sure."

Matlinda straightened slightly. "Did the entity show you anything about the binding?"

V'Let shrugged. "Images and such. Large beings such as the entity tend to think on a higher level than me. I had to sort through it for a while. I believe it was during the wars referred to as the Crusades." Though her voice sounded unsure, she shivered slightly. "There was a witch hunt, but not by humans. It was by a group of witches aligned with black magic. There was something about a belief that the guardian was too powerful." V'Let sighed. "It's all really demoralizing."

Quin nodded. He remembered learning about the Crusades when he had been small. Not that he thought about it, he could have sworn that the first witch hunt hadn't been until the fourteenth century. However, V'Let had said that this particular witch hunt had been witch against witch, something that he certainly never heard of before.

V'Let's lips curved into a smile, a glint shimmering in her eyes as she gazed at the demon. Quin watched her stand and cast a meaningful glance to her brother. He stood gracefully at the obvious command. Without another word spoken, the two of them began to walk away.

Both Quin and Erik stood almost immediately. "Where are you going?" Quin asked, an unintentional sharp tone in his voice.

D'Las turned back to face them while V'Let continued to their invisible spacecraft. "The unbinding is a difficult ritual. My sister and I must trance together so that she may tap into my dormant power." Quin smirked at that. He saw how the brother acted. Like Rosalie, he acted as though he had no power. He believed the same was true for D'Las as it was for the planeswalker—he simply couldn't access the power on his own. "She has decided she will perform the unbinding in two days. One full day to access to my power and another to rest and cleanse." Quin noticed as a spark of confusion entered the alien's eyes. D'Las turned again, this time to fully face the direction in which his sister had gone. She was standing at the edge of whatever it was that made their transport invisible, edges of her body closest to the ship shimmering and parts of her gone. After a moment of what Quin could only guess had to be intense conversation between the two of them, he turned to face them again. "V'Let wishes that you would not tell the girl about this ritual but she had agreed that in all reality she needs to know. As long as she takes the opioid drink on the day of the ritual."

Erik took a small step toward the alien. "Why does she need to drink the tea?"

D'Las shrugged slightly, casting a glance over his shoulder at his sister. She was gone, having disappeared through the invisibility barrier, but Quin got the impression that they were still talking. "She says it has to do with her self-control. She had to completely let go for this to work and I don't think she can do it without something forcing her." That said, D'Las turned away, following his sister's path in slightly hurried footsteps.

Quin sat down again, glancing over to look at the Crone. "What do you think?" he murmured.

She smiled softly. "They're not lying, if that's what you're asking." She tilted her head slightly, watching as Erik slowly placed himself back in his seat. "The hard part is going to be convincing Rosalie's to take the tea again so soon after having forced her to take it once."

Erik shook his head in an idle gesture. "She's not going to be happy."

# CHAPTER FORTY

D'Las passed through the cloak in time to see V'Let clearing a large space in the cargo hold. As an idle afterthought, he reached out and pressed the button to close the airlock and the hatch outside it. Now, there would be no way they would be disturbed.

"You think this is enough room?" V'Let glanced at her brother with clear eyes.

D'Las passed a hand over the top of his head, barely disturbing his very short hair. "I'm not even sure that this is a good idea."

V'Let shrugged. She knew that D'Las would always be the one that wanted to run home and keep away from the rest of the universe, the mindset of a true Looran. However, she was like her mother – she believed in responsibility. It also helped that planetary entities scared her deeply. "It has to be done. It *needs* to be done."

D'Las nudged the toe of his boot at the floor of the cargo hold. He didn't look at his sister as he asked his next question. "What if it doesn't work? What if I really have no power left?" The real question, the one that he feared was true, was: *What if I repressed so much that it all faded away?*

V'Let came up next to her brother, lifting his chin with the crook of her index finger. "It's still there," she whispered confidently. "I can feel it every day and I still don't know why you can't and won't access it." She turned away and sighed. "I will find out, though, because this time I'm looking for it."

He frowned at his sister. "It won't be like last time, will it?" A thrum of fear echoed through his voice.

She shook her head gently. "Nowhere near," she reassured him.

"However, this will solidify our bond, strengthening far more than we're used to for a while."

D'Las's frown deepened when she turned around to face him then. "Do you know how long that will last?"

V'Let shrugged idly, her features smoothing out into an almost expressionless mask. "Not really. I can't imagine it will be for long." She gestured to a spot directly across from her about five feet from where she stood. "Now, sit. We have a long trance ahead of us."

D'Las gazed at his sister for a moment before dropping to the floor, folding one leg to lay on top of the other. He trusted his sister implicitly but sometimes he worried that she kept too much to herself. The truth of it was that she was most open with him and he knew this very well. But D'Las was highly aware that she kept things even from him.

"Now, I need you to be fully in a trance state before I can follow."

D'Las glanced up at V'Let and looked into eyes that were almost unreadable. He arched an eyebrow but closed his eyes. "Why?" he asked idly.

V'Let sighed roughly. "I'm trying something new. Just... concentrate on your power." She smiled slightly when D'Las merely scoffed softly but continued to do as he was bid. The smile slid off her face slowly as she knelt down in front of her brother, just outside his proximity range, and watched him drift into the trance as easily as she could.

She shifted slightly and landed softly with her rear on the floor, pulling up her knees and tucking them under her chin. It would still be some time before she could follow him into the trance, before he was deep enough inside himself for her to do what had to be done. She shifted her head to lay it sideways on her knees and let her eyes close.

V'Let could still feel the conflicting emotions below everything, buried under the very urgent responsibility that was the Earth's agreement with her. Dealing with what the entity asked was simple compared to what she had to face within herself. However much she hated it, she set the burden of this planet aside while she examined her own conflict.

It wasn't the deep-seated feelings that she kept buried, the ones that only arose during a deep trance to form a new connection. It was a refresher in her feelings about being free, about being able to return home. As if it happened recently, she could remember the destruction the Adepts had rained down on their home at the Strike Force. She could remember her *mama* dying to protect her from a rogue shard of flying glass that should have pierced V'Let's neck rather than her mother's heart. She remembered her mother telling her to be a good girl and protect her brother. In the next instant, her *mama* was gone, her wide blue eyes portraying no emotion, and her brother ran into the room and witnessed the carnage. With the wisdom that comes from experience, she had cringed and watched her brother closely. D'Las, with his phenomenal amount of power, had become known for his tantrums that could tear a house apart. However, he'd just stood there and she had felt nothing through their birth-bond. She had released her mother and approached her brother. He didn't even look at her then.

After that, a lot of what followed was very vague. She remembered that the house had begun to collapse and she had a hard time dragging her brother out of it. Free of the house, however, he followed her without complaint, verbal or physical. The Adepts found them soon after, trailing idly through a ravaged city.

"I miss you, *mama*," V'Let whispered to herself, the voice floating and fading through the cargo hold. "How can I face them?"

The truth of everything was that she didn't feel pure enough to be a Looran anymore. For the past twenty years, she'd taken the brunt of all the pain and responsibility so that D'Las wouldn't have to. She didn't know how he would take being the hand that destroyed an entire planet. She would always protect him from everything that came their way as long as he was there to protect her from herself.

There was also a possibility that their planet was still populated. She'd wrapped herself in the belief that there was nothing to go back to, for there was certainly no home and no family beyond her brother. She believed that despite their short time on the planet, the Adepts had destroyed everything. They had believed completely in the way that self-involved people can and she had clung to that belief. She knew it was a fallacy, though, these thoughts of being the last of a species. There were survivors on the planet and threads of power had been pushing at her genetic memory since they had landed on this wretched planet.

Soon, she would have to let the threads of memory that were not her own win. She shivered slightly, feeling the fear thrum through her body. She didn't want them to know what she had done, making the humans an endangered species on a planet they ruled at present nearing the bottom of a very long list. However, it would wait until she had finished the ritual in a couple days. Maybe even longer.

V'Let seamlessly shifted her body into a position that mimicked her brother's and forced herself to relax. When they woke from the trance, she promised herself that she would inform D'Las that they would be returning home after this piece of badness was finished. But no sooner.

Without another thought, she followed her brother into the trance. Following someone else into a trance was something she'd never tried before, though she had plenty of secondhand memories of the act. With every one of them, it was a little bit different. For V'Let, it was like falling into a dark hole, consumed by inky black until she noticed a pinprick of light at the bottom. Once noticed, the light grew and grew until finally it overwhelmed her sight, blinding her with burning white before fading away.

When her eyes adjusted, she was floating in a dark blue space. She glanced around, seeing only the dark blue nothingness at first. She was patient, though; she knew that sometimes awareness came in phases. After a moment that seemed both instantaneous and eternal, she saw her brother. His eyes were clenched shut and everything about his body language was closed.

With a frown, she waved her hand in front of her face, wondering if she was closed like her brother but seeing with another kind of sight. Her small hand passed across her line of vision, ensuring that her eyes were indeed open. Her frown deepened and she cast a glance downward to examine her own body language. The frown and creases smoothed away at the sight. Her body language was most definitely open, though there was a forced diffidence and genuine shielding as well. It was to be expected, of course. Deep down, she knew who she was.

There was also a lavender cord, erupting from the center of her chest and connecting firmly to D'Las. With each heartbeat, it thrummed with life and pulsed signals in both directions. She knew it was their bond, twice the size of the average Looran heart. Examining her brother more closely, she noticed that other bonds erupted from him. However, they were black and dead, sending and receiving absolutely nothing.

Glancing around herself, she could see thin cords of bonding shooting off in the same direction that her brother's were. There weren't dead, though. She could see information coming from somewhere else but right before it reached her, it stopped dead and vanished. She knew it was further proof that Loorans were alive and well but she turned her head away from the sight, knowing that there was still a large part of her that didn't want to know, didn't want *them* to know.

V'Let caught sight of another cord of bonding, deep purple in color and thrumming as steadily as the bond with D'Las. She tilted her head slightly and listened hard. The cord was very thin, nearly as thin as twine. It received more than it sent, letting her know that it was a connection with someone of lesser mental ability. It was the bond to the vampire Erik, she knew. Marginally alarming, though, was the fact that he could receive things from her.

*Oh, well,* she thought, shaking the worry and concern away. *That's for another time.*

She focused on her brother again, intent on finishing this trance before any more revelations came. Slowly, she willed the bond to pull her almost flush with him. She felt the cord grow in size minimally in response to her action, her very direct pull on the bond itself, before settling back to its original size.

She gently placed her hands on either side of his face and stared intently at his clenched eyelids. He twitched slightly, his face scrunching slightly in an effort to do nothing. Sighing softly, she whispered one word, pushing hard through the bond as well.

"Open."

Almost immediately, D'Las's eyes flew open, blazing bright white. V'Let knew she was seeing locked power, power that was more than ready to spill out at the seams. She knew that sometimes Looran power didn't do very well when it was confined. Once you'd begun using it, it built to the point that you need to expel some of it almost daily. Their bond kept D'Las's power well and truly contained but it had never stopped building.

By using this command, V'Let knew she had changed something at the core of her brother, something that he had worked very hard to maintain. However, it was necessary. That much they had agreed, despite how much he hadn't liked the thought of it. She also knew he had underestimated how much this would change his power.

They would have to return to Loora very soon.

She tightened her grip on his face and pulled them closer to each other. They filled each other's vision, were all that the other could see. That wasn't all that was required to finish what had to be done, however. She had to say the right words.

"See only me."

Slowly, D'Las's eyes dimmed to their natural blue and she smiled. Then she felt it. A burning sensation, like something that wasn't her own forcing itself inside. It was painful, she admitted idly, but she kept herself physically attached to her brother. Glancing down, she gasped.

The bond was expanding at a radical rate. Twenty years of confined energy and power couldn't pour into her fast enough, not at the size the bond had been. It was growing, had already grown to cover their torsos. As it grew, so did the pain. However, she didn't cry out. She just allowed the power to find room in her body wherever it could.

Moments later, the pain stopped, filling V'Let with a type of emptiness. She glanced down and found the bond had grown to encompass their entire bodies. Both she and her brother were glowing with a type of ethereal lavender light. It suddenly occurred to her that maybe she had underestimated what this trance would have done to them as well.

She released her brother and drifted away. She sighed, trying to remember how to pull out of the trance, when she noticed the look on her brother's face. His eyes had remained open and he was looking around, his body language opening. He smiled softly.

V'Let sighed and blinked her eyes, her will strong behind the action. In the next instant, her eyes opened and they were back in the cargo hold, reality having bled back into their awareness. The dark gray of the spacecraft, their surroundings the remnants of dead cultures, the end of everything she had known for so long looming over her head in an almost physical way now—it was a bit too much.

"Is it always like that?" D'Las still had that goofy smile on his face.

V'Let frowned and stood, wiping at her chemise to remove nonexistent dirt. "Sometimes."

D'Las stood as well, looking at his surroundings with a type of awe. "Why didn't you tell me?" He seemed to be looking at everything in a new light, in a new way.

V'Let huffed softly, striding across the cargo hold to the stairs. "You knew," she snapped before ascending the stairs with a purpose.

D'Las watched his sister disappear to her bunk, the smile falling from his face. She was right, he knew. He had known, in a way. He knew everything she knew and this knowledge about the beauty in everything, especially their own power, was often what made destroying planets so hard on her.

Following her lead, he began to ascend the stairs. He wasn't sure how but the trance had taken quite a bit of energy out of him. He knew that V'Let's mood would fade, although he had a sneaking suspicion that there was an underlying cause to her snippiness. He didn't know where the thought came from but he knew it was true.

He had just reached his bunk door, had just reached out to push the door open when he was forced to his knees. There was a massive feeling pressing on him, a lot of it translating as pain. He could feel of rush of something he couldn't identify before falling into a heap on unconsciousness on the floor, his body mere inches from his bunk.

What he hadn't known was that his newfound openness had reactivated every bond he possessed, opening links to every Looran he had ever known and quite a few he hadn't. Also, as he fell into a forced sleep and while V'Let lay on her bed drifting in the same direction, his sister's very carefully erected shields against Looran minds was crumbling.

# CHAPTER FORTY-ONE

Z'Tem woke abruptly, his large blue eyes snapping open. A mere two seconds later, his head was filled with new knowledge, direct from the two people he had spent the last twenty years trying to find. The knowledge, however, forced him to his knees with a phenomenal sadness.

Much of the memories were tainted by negative emotions. Planets destroyed, followed by weeks of crying jags and unbreakable sadness and comfort from a sibling. A contract that caused unreasonable pain and such cold, hard faces. Worry and shame and guilt...

However, there were some high points. Building things and watching a new invention become useful in the capable hands of a brother. Feeling a sister marvel at the beauty of a new world. Memories of the homeworld before... well, before.

Z'Tem broke himself out of the memories, trying not to let his memory of finding his best friend's house demolished or learning the news of his own father's fate become fresh. He was one of many that had to spend years studying with the Gurus of the West to deal with the negativity that came with the destruction of one of their larger cities and the deaths of so many Loorans. Through it all, he never forgot about D'Las or V'Let. The lost *tiancai*, Loora's own "gift from the gods". D'Las had been his best friend, despite their differences. Before they'd disappeared, Z'Tem and D'Las had just reached the point in their maturity where they would leave V'Let behind.

Now he knew that because of that particular habit, she had been home with her mother when she died. She'd kept them from dying, although it meant they had been wandering the streets of Datong when three people of assorted species that she thought of as the "Adepts" found them. This

196

memory was tied almost directly to the contract and the destruction of so many planets. It was connected, somehow.

There was movement outside his home and then his front door opened. He stood and peered out of his bedroom and sighed in relief when he saw Marta. She carried a bag similar to a rucksack and looked around idly before she noticed him. He darted back inside his room and quickly dressed for the day.

As he donned his clothes for traveling, he could hear her soft footfalls when she entered the hallway that led to his room. His own travel bag had been packed the night prior, so that he wouldn't have to suffer Marta's wrath about his sleeping habits. He was lacing up his boots when she opened his door.

Marta glanced around Z'Tem's room before collapsing almost ungracefully on his bed. He glanced at her, noticing the new weight in her shoulders, and knew that she had received the memories as well. He was almost certain he had been among the first to receive their memories, as he had been their only friend and their mother and most of their teachers had died in the attack on Datong. He also knew that within days, these memories would fade into the general consciousness of the Looran genetic memory.

Marta stared at her hands and then glanced up at Z'Tem. "How could they?"

Z'Tem smiled at Marta. She was barely eighteen now, the thought of her only beginning to form when the twins had been taken. She had spent much of those years studying everything she could find, the long hours in confined positions causing her bones to stop growing earlier than usual. Z'Tem found that her studies had also blocked her ability to see certain equations from all sides. Most of the time, she was clinical and practical, rarely showing the emotion she exemplified now. Physically, he always thought she must be similar to what V'Let looked like: clear violet skin, long lavender hair, big blue eyes. Of course, Marta was much shorter.

In response to her question, he shook his head. He couldn't understand it too well himself, he knew. "I'm not sure." He hefted his rucksack onto his back. "We should be going. The oracles are expecting us."

Marta levered herself into an upright position and followed Z'Tem out of the house. "I really want to understand," she said behind him in a soft, almost pleading tone. "I need to."

Z'Tem smiled to himself as they continued to walk to the edge of Taicheng. The nearest oracle was fifteen klicks from that particular city.

However, he now knew that the emotion Marta had been showing just a minute ago was more than likely not her own. It was possibly a byproduct of the memories. "It's another reason to see the oracle," he told her softly.

Marta harrumphed almost inaudibly but continued to follow the taller man with long strides.

A mere fifteen klicks from Z'Tem, another Looran opened his eyes. Sadness and concern etched across his face. He glanced around, his movements slightly hurried, and spotted a stone bowl on a nearby boulder. He stood and retrieved the bowl silently, peering inside to assure himself of the presence of the very sharp stone within. He moved to sit again, folding one leg to lay upon the other, and placed the bowl on the ground in front of him.

He sat still for a moment, forcing himself to be still inside. He closed his eyes, seeing the twins in his mind's eye, and smiled softly. Opening his eyes, he reached into the bowl and pulled out the deadly-sharp shard. With a deft movement developed from long experience, he sliced a shallow cut along his wrist and let his arm hang over the bowl. Dark blue blood leaked from his wrist, filling the stone bowl very shallowly, before the cut healed itself. With the shard set aside, he dipped his fingers into the bowl. One hand marked his face with his own blood, a dot on his forehead and each of his cheekbones, while the other painted complex symbols and lines on the stone floor.

"*Fuxian, shen Loora,*" he murmured in a soft, unused voice.

Slowly, a form coalesced less than three feet in front of him. At first, it seemed to fill the entire cavern in which he lived and slept with a deep purple haze before it shrank and began to take a semi-physical form that resembled a female Looran, though still quite a bit taller. Even at a height that touched on eight feet, the being was now well out of range of the cavern walls.

"*Ah, K'Sar. How are you?*"

He stood languidly, looking up at the being. "They're coming back." His rough voice was low as he glanced past it to the cavern's opening where he could see the light of the beginning day. "Their memories have joined the greater memory."

The being, this essence of Loora, frowned. Her wispy form turned and faced the opening as well. "*So they know. Are you the closest oracle to the boy?*"

K'Sar nodded. In another couple of hours, two Loorans would darken the entrance to his cavern and he would have to accept them. He would take the girl to the elders and they could decide if studying with the oracles suited her path. He would also answer the boy's questions.

*"Will you tell him?"*

K'Sar bowed his head in obeisance to the entity. "If you so wish." He closed his eyes, breathing cleansing breaths, and pushed away the renewed willfulness within himself.

A glance at the entity would have noted a smirk on her face. *"I do. More than that, I will it."*

He nodded. He returned to his position, one folded leg on top of the other. "She's breaking. She'll be close to broken by the time they arrive."

The smirk fell from the entity's face, replaced by concern and a distanced sadness. *"I know. We will help them."* With that said, the entity dissipated, returning to the planet beneath them.

K'Sar remained still and waited.

# CHAPTER FORTY-TWO

Rosalie came to slowly, her head a foggy mess of pain and nightmares not clearly seen. The last thing she clearly remembered was ranting wildly in anger about V'Let keeping secrets from her and the Crone handing her a mug of tea. After that, everything was fuzzy and completely unclear.

She reached up to grab her head, expecting some centralized head pain after all the blur. However, none came. Something that was confusing in and of itself.

"No pain will come."

Rosalie looked up to see the Crone watching her with a smile. She reached out and retrieved the mug that sat on the table in front of her, walking away to the kitchen. For half a moment, Rosalie debated standing, wondering if she was steady enough, before she stood on strong legs and followed the witch. "What did you do?"

"I gave you tea, my little rose, to calm you down."

Rosalie missed a step, stumbling slightly before she caught herself. She was so used to vampires referring to her as a "little rose" that she hadn't expected the words to come from the Crone. "What was in it?"

Matlinda shrugged idly, setting the mug in the sink and running water into it after a glance at the tea leaves. "Kratom leaves. A strong, natural opioid. A gift from my sisters on the other side of the world."

Rosalie got the feeling that when she said "sisters", she meant Sisters of Aradia. Other witches, ones in the Eastern Hemisphere. "But why?" The Crone gifted her with a strong look, one that said she'd already answered that question once. "You drugged me to calm me?"

The witch shrugged, that damnable smile still firmly in place. "A test," she replied.

Rosalie didn't know whether to laugh or to growl. More tests, which made her angry, yet she could never seem to get too angry around the Crone. Maybe a fear mechanism or the way the witch always exuded serenity. She sighed roughly, transmitting her frustration strongly. "Did something happen while I was out?"

Matlinda led her out to the porch, where she saw both Erik and Quin talking softly. "We should perhaps discuss it together," the witch decided, sitting next to her demon messenger primly.

Rosalie glanced in the direction that the aliens' spacecraft resided before settling down. She looked at Erik, a question clear on her face.

The vampire sighed softly. "To get it out of the way, the entity made a deal with V'Let."

Rosalie arched an eyebrow. "What kind of deal?"

The Crone cleared her throat. "Our dear Mother Earth has agreed to thin the humans out quite a bit if our powerful alien friend agreed to unbind your power."

The sentence washed over Rosalie, sending her into a slight state of shock. "No more planeswalking?" she whispered. It didn't feel real. She'd been walking the planes since before she could remember and it seemed like such a permanent part of herself.

Erik nodded with a smile on his face. "No more constant guarding of your control either," he replied encouragingly.

After another moment, Rosalie came back to herself, her shrewd nature rearing its head. "Why me? What's so important about me?"

At that question, Matlinda grinned. It was the first time Rosalie had seen her smile in a way that showed her white, even teeth and projected happiness rather than serenity. She nudged Quin lightly with her shoulder. "See? I knew I needed those texts." Without another word, the Crone disappeared into the house again, moving at a speed that Rosalie wasn't aware that she possessed.

Rosalie arched her eyebrow again, her eyes following the witch until she was completely gone from her sight. Then she turned her gaze on the vampire and the demon. "What's going on?" she inquired with a confused lilt in her voice.

Erik glanced at Quin, who nodded in turn. The demon turned to face Rosalie. "To put it bluntly, you're the guardian of this planet." At the look she gave him, he continued to clarify. "The entity told V'Let that your lineage was the thing that stood between the nonhumans and the spread of what the demons call the 'human plague'. You were supposed to maintain some kind of balance between them, I guess." The demon sighed, his black eyes glistening from the late afternoon sun. "From what V'Let said, a group of dark witches cursed your family line with some kind of constrictive binding. She believes she can undo it."

Rosalie inhaled slightly, trying to keep herself from gasping in a type of joyful shock. She wouldn't planeswalk anymore and she wouldn't have to lower herself to be under the Prince, which was a point in the win column. However, from the sound of it, there was a lot of responsibility involved. She frowned. That thought was sobering. "I... I don't know."

Matlinda reappeared, an open book in her arms. "I'm not sure you have a choice." She sat down, her gaze directed on the tome now in her lap, and continued to turn pages with determination. "When our dear alien friend mentioned you being a guardian, I remembered something. I hadn't heard anything about it since my obsession with lost histories but then I remembered this book."

Rosalie's interest was piqued. "Really? What is it?"

Matlinda glanced up at the girl, a tight stretch of lips marring her normally serene face. "It's a compilation of things lost or forgotten through history that have been caused by witches."

Rosalie winced slightly, her lips turned downward in a slight frown. "Nice," she muttered sardonically.

"Aha!" Matlinda's lips turned into a more genuine smile. "Here it is. The Guardian of the Realm bound. At the time, it was a male guardian, which might explain the attack a little better."

Rosalie's frown deepened. "It does?"

The Crone's face crinkled a little in an emotion that Rosalie couldn't identify. "It was near the end of the twelfth century." She glanced down, peering at the information in her lap. "There were rumors of the Church attacking witches. Witches were using increasingly dark magic to protect themselves from the fanatics or to attack in turn." Matlinda sighed and turned the page, her eyes clearly showing her sadness. "An unknown man turned up, using magic to deflect the witches' attacks. The same group of witches found him again weeks later and bound him with a family curse."

Rosalie twisted her hands in her lap, her eyes wide. "What kind of curse?"

Matlinda glanced up at the girl, her lips having returned to that tight line. " 'To know death and pain and loss of mind and to walk where others cannot follow'," she quoted directly from her tome. For a moment, she read further. "That can't be right," she murmured.

Rosalie's wide eyes returned to their normal state as piercing orbs. "What is it?"

The Crone looked at the girl again, her unseeing eyes now conveying a type of horror. "After the curse was cast, the earth swallowed them whole."

Rosalie's brow furrowed in confusion, feeling vaguely as if she was missing something that she should have been getting. "Is there some significance there?" In the corner of her eye, she could tell that Erik was just as confused as she was.

Matlinda chuckled softly, though the sound itself seemed a little hollow. Next to her, Quin frowned, a look of serious comprehension on his face. "This is a sign that the thing that V'Let calls 'the Earth entity' needs or wants the family curse undone."

Rosalie frowned. "What has to happen?" She paused for a moment, forcing herself to clarify the statement. "What does V'Let have to do to me?"

Matlinda stood, taking the book with her, and nodded at Quin before disappearing into her house. In turn, the demon smiled wanly at the witch, his face seeming to stretch tight. "Somehow, she's going to find out what kind of binding you're cursed with and then she's going to unravel it. She said this will happen in two days." He stopped then, his jaw tightening in such a way that Rosalie knew he was clenching his teeth.

Rosalie arched an eyebrow at the demon. "Is there anything you're not telling me?"

"We think you have to let your guard down for the duration of whatever it is she's going to do." Erik was the one that answered her now, his voice soft and low.

She glanced over at her vampire friend then. "What makes you think that?"

The vampire smiled now, his face very nearly mimicking that of the demon across from him. "She thought you might need that tea again. To numb your control."

Rosalie sat very still after that. Personally, she wanted to have the choice—to be bound to this curse or to be free... Not that it was really a choice. She had had more than enough of this planeswalking hell, trapped under the thumb of a jealous and spoiled Prince. However, if she truly was the Guardian of the Realm, the thing that stood between the humans and the Others, then that was a lot more responsibility that she was used to. If she were truthful to herself, it really scared her, the new massive level of unknown things about her.

She stood abruptly, her eyes glazed in deep thought. Deep down, below the onslaught of too many thoughts, she could feel her very solid control slipping, unraveling slightly against the thought of this new part of herself. She turned away from her friends and moved to enter the house.

Erik reached out quickly with his inhuman speed and grabbed her arm loosely, knowing not to set off her punch-the-intruder instinct. "Where are you going?"

Rosalie smiled down at the vampire, though her face didn't really convey a particularly positive emotion. "To think and to meditate. No matter what I decide, my control still needs to remain intact. For now."

Erik nodded and released her, casting a slightly worried glance in Quin's direction. Rosalie continued back into the Crone's living room, smiling at the witch as they passed each other, and began to focus on her meditation. After that, she had some very heavy things to think about.

# CHAPTER FORTY-THREE

Z'Tem and Marta approached the cave with some apprehension. During his time with the Northern Shamans, he had been informed repeatedly that the oracle closest to Taicheng could often be difficult. However, he was also the most devoted, the most talented of all oracles. Z'Tem remembered asking a shaman why this oracle wasn't one of the Elders—hewas certainly old enough. With an odd look in his eye, the shaman had replied that this oracle preferred his solitude, something which could not be abided by the Elders.

Marta shivered involuntarily. She'd heard many stories about this oracle, growing up as she had among the shamans. He was reputed to have an abnormal amount of power but there was no physical description of him. Her guardian, Shaman Trell, once said that to describe him would be to do him an injustice. There had always been something else as well, something of which none of them ever spoke.

Suddenly, a lank shadow fell over them both. Startled, Z'Tem and Marta gasped in a way that suggested they might shriek in fear.

Their reply was a soft chuckle. Z'Tem mentally shook himself at the sound and focused on the man that stood before them. He was tall, even for a Looran, his height topping out at six-and-a-half feet. The blue of his eyes and the shade of his skin seemed extremely pale, as if he spent a lot of time in the darkness. However, the chuckle had been good-natured and the man had a slight smile on his face.

"K'Sar?" he inquired, failing at keeping the skittishness out of his voice.

The man inclined his head in a tilted fashion, the smile broadening.

"Do the two of you need a rest or can you continue another five klicks to the Elders?"

Z'Tem glanced over at Marta, who nodded in the direction they need to continue. "I'm good," she said softly, pulling her water bottle out of the side of her rucksack.

K'Sar began to lead them away, his kind eyes smiling at them. "Can we ask you something?" Z'Tem inquired haltingly. There was something about this man that seemed massive, though his body was lank almost to the point of being gaunt.

K'Sar gazed over his shoulder at the two following him, the smile gone and his eyes searching and flat. The soft kindness was gone, replaced by keen perceptiveness. "Is it about the new memories?"

Marta apparently couldn't stop herself. "I don't understand how they could destroy so much life," she blurted out.

The man laughed, the sound erupting as a surprised guffaw. His gaze shifted to Z'Tem after a moment. "Do you understand?"

Z'Tem shrugged his shoulders lightly. "Some, I guess. A lot of the memories are muddled, like the twins are trying to block them."

"Okay." K'Sar paused for a moment, though he still led them in long strides to the City of the Oracles. "I want you to concentrate on their emotions the last time they destroyed a planet."

Marta held up her hands in apology. "Sorry. I don't do emotions so well. I don't understand them usually."

K'Sar nodded. "I expected as much." He eyed Z'Tem with a significant look. With a nod, Z'Tem placed a hand on Marta's shoulder and closed his eyes.

Marta huffed indignantly. "What do you mean, you expected as much?" Her voice was shrill with the only emotion she usually felt: annoyance.

K'Sar smiled to himself. "You're a child of the shamans," he answered simply.

"Oh." Marta paused. "What does that mean?"

Z'Tem hummed softly, effectively hushing his friend in the process. She would ask questions incessantly until the oracle's good mood turned sour. On the other hand, he understood her agitation. Raised around the shamans, she had put much of her faith into power and knowledge, less on the emotion involved.

He dug deep into the new memories, digging deeper than he usually searched in memories that were not his own. The emotions felt during memories were harder to find than the memories themselves. He searched back about thirteen or fourteen days, his mind tied as directly as he could manage to D'Las.

The people of the planet had been nice enough but their corruption had spread deeply, finding root sometimes as early as pubescence. The verdict had been clear in the first months but V'Let had insisted on the full year, desperate to find enough goodness and purity to support continuing life on the planet. She had failed, same as the planets prior to this one, and D'Las had a sneaking suspicion that she was dragging it out to prevent this fate on other planets just as deserving. As V'Let planted the device to turn this planet into an empty void, D'Las felt nothing but the echo of his sister's emotions. Tendrils of heavy guilt and regret floated across the bond before he buried it just as deeply as the others. There was the thought that "they" would never let them stop and very real sadness as he felt V'Let cry herself to sleep. Again.

Z'Tem gasped and opened his eyes. They were at the edge of the City of the Oracles now, something he had only seen once before in a holopic when he was very young. His eyes were clouded with sadness and hollow rage, directed at someone with no face—the undescribed "them" within the twins' memories. He took a deep breath and reached behind him to grab his own water bottle. Calmly, he took a small sip and shook the bottle, watching the liquid slosh mutely in its container. Grabbing the bottle in both hands, he let his currently roiling power flow, freezing the bottle and its contents almost instantly. He turned around and chucked the frozen container as hard as he could toward the edge of city limits, watching in idle satisfaction when it shattered like weak glass against steel.

"What in the Seven Hells was that?" Marta asked shrilly, her eyebrow arched in agitated confusion. Off to the side, K'Sar waved a hand in a low circular movement and Z'Tem saw the shattered pieces of his bottle melt into the ground.

"They're being controlled," Z'Tem spat out, the disgust in his voice obvious. "He doesn't feel *anything* and she cries herself to sleep most nights. They don't want to."

K'Sar's face broke out into a wide smile. "Exactly." They now stood in front of a large building, noted to be the Hall of the Elders by the engraving over its double doors. He turned to Z'Tem. "You must remain outside, as you are neither an oracle nor wish to study their knowledge. You must not speak to anyone until I return." At his nod, K'Sar turned back to Marta. "Come, child, if you wish to know as the oracles know."

Marta scoffed softly and entered the building without a word, the doors barely making a sound. Z'Tem sat quietly on the outside steps of the building, attempting to quiet his rage. The release of power had helped, as well as the destruction of something. The gurus had taught him to expel power during heightened emotional moments, especially when those emotions were negative. They said that too much power unchecked could be dangerous to him, could turn around and control him in turn.

Z'Tem felt it as much of the anger faded, dissipating like fluid down a drain. He got the impression that the emotion was being pulled forcibly away from him and fed elsewhere like the unraveling of a loose thread. He frowned deeply and glanced to his side.

"Negativity is hazardous to your inner power," K'Sar told him softly, repeating the core lesson Z'Tem had learned from the gurus during his grieving. The tall man sat down next to him, his movements delicate and jilted.

"That was quick," Z'Tem replied, a low note of shock threading through his voice.

The oracle shrugged, a smile quirking his lips. "An oracle must attend the knowledge seekers through the doors but they must face the Elders on their own. She'll be busy for days while they test her knowledge and her devotion to learning our ways."

Z'Tem chuckled softly. "Oh, she's devoted."

"But stunted," K'Sar added. "In more ways than one."

Z'Tem tilted his head. "Would it make a difference?"

K'Sar shook his head to the negative. "Only the gurus and the nomads are supposed to place importance in the emotions of our species. Oracles and shamans are only supposed to care for knowledge and power."

Z'Tem arched an eyebrow at the oracle. "You think differently?"

K'Sar smiled at the younger man, his eyes shining. "Emotion is as much a part of Loora as our power." The lank man stood suddenly, holding out his hand to Z'Tem in aid. "We should leave until her tests have been completed."

Z'Tem frowned, disgust marking his face. "We're going to that cave?"

K'Sar chuckled. "We can return to your home. You live on the edge of Taicheng, correct?"

Z'Tem's eyes widened, his mouth opening slightly in a gaping gesture, as he stood and followed K'Sar down the building's steps. "How'd you know that?"

Eyes twinkling, the oracle tapped his temple, insinuating the omniscient presence of all oracles of Loora. "Now, you might want to hold your breath."

Z'Tem adjusted his rucksack to sit comfortably on his back again and watched the oracle. The man grabbed his hand in a tight grip and half-knelt to the ground, touching the ground beneath them in a light touch.

"*Diban* Taicheng." Idly, the Looran power word echoed through Z'Tem's mind, something about "earth transport". That had to be important somehow, right?

Without warning, the ground beneath their feet rumbled and reached out to swallow them, causing the young man to gasp. Then there was only darkness and a very loud moving sound. Mere moments passed, though the moments felt like thick slices of eternity, before there was light again. The ground ejected them, making a strange sound that sounded both like spitting and retching.

Z'Tem laid on the ground, gagging at the taste of soil in his mouth. He pulled himself to his knees, vomiting a large amount of dirt and some of the breakfast he'd eaten hours ago. There might have also been a little stomach bile, he wasn't sure. Glancing up, he saw that they were a quarter-klick from the city limits of Taicheng.

"What was that?" he gasped, his eyes shooting bloodshot daggers at the oracle.

K'Sar shrugged. "I'd rather not spend a large chunk of my day traveling by foot. I told you to hold your breath."

Z'Tem grumbled, pulling himself the rest of the way to his feet. He led them to his house, attempting to pull his remaining dignity together. His home was in sight before he spoke again. "How did you do that anyway? I've never seen anything like that."

K'Sar's lips twitched in another almost-smile. "I'm not very much like the oracles. I have a strong connection to Loora itself and I'm older than most of them."

Z'Tem arched an eyebrow, pushing the door to his house open as they reached it. "How old, exactly?"

"Almost eight hundred years, come the cold season," the oracle answered idly.

"Huh, what?" the younger man sputtered, spinning to face the oracle and dropping his rucksack in one movement.

K'Sar chuckled, moving around the other to seat him on a sofa in the living area. "It's not unheard of," he replied.

Z'Tem shook his head and followed the oracles, sitting near but by no means close to him. He decided to change his tack, putting aside the thought of the oracle's age for now. "I'm getting the feeling that you're not just here because you felt like making me ingest dirt."

The oracle inclined his head slightly. "First things first. We must check something and I do not have the ability." He cleared his throat. "Whose memories did you read before?"

"D'Las's, of course," Z'Tem answered immediately, automatically.

"Of course," K'Sar murmured. "Because he was your best friend, so your bond to him is stronger than your bond to V'Let."

Z'Tem nodded. "But how did you know...? Um, you know, never mind."

This time, K'Sar laughed outright, the sound filling the room. "Okay, I want you to try to read V'Let's memories."

At that, Z'Tem paused. At the heart of it, he didn't really want to, afraid to peer into the girl's memories. She wasn't closed off like D'Las was, that much he could tell from the male twin's memories. "Why don't you?" he asked the oracle.

The smile on K'Sar's face drooped slightly and a muted sadness seemed to dull the shine in the man's eyes. "I've always known... I could always feel them and know what was happening to them. If either one of them is shielding now, I don't know it."

Z'Tem was prepared to make a snarky remark about oracles supposedly knowing everything but he didn't when he fully noted the distant, increasingly mournful expression on K'Sar's face. "Okay," he answered in a soft voice. "I'll try."

The younger man closed his eyes, reaching out for an unused bond. He hadn't paid much attention to V'Let when he'd been younger and never actively attempted to know what she knew. D'Las had been the powerful one. Though they had both been *tiancai*, D'Las had been considered the prodigy. If they had remained on Loora, he knew she would have always been "D'Las's sister" with barely an identity of her own.

Outside of himself, he vaguely felt the oracle shift closer to him and thin fingers touch his temples.

Suddenly, he was hit by emotions, ten times stronger than when he'd felt them through D'Las, the very thing he'd been fearing. Worry, shame, guilt, regret, sadness, pain—quite a lot of pain—buried under solid layers of determination... Things slowly became clearer. He could see flashes of many of the planets moments before their destruction, the image replaced by those same damnable faces he had seen before, that image in turn replaced by a contract with V'Let's and D'Las's names marring the bottom in what looked like Looran blood. V'Let talking to something that seemed massive but Z'Tem couldn't actually see it; V'Let speaking with a stout, dark creature and the words "I'll take care of them"; the knowledge of freedom... Z'Tem tried to follow the line of freedom but was overwhelmed by a bright white light. The light pushed at him hard and he yelped.

K'Sar sighed softly. "That's what I thought," he murmured.

Z'Tem pressed the heels of his hands up against his forehead, digging into the skin hard to attempt to force away the sudden headache. "What? What did you think?"

The oracle stood. "She rebuilt her shield."

Z'Tem frowned, the action causing the pain inside his head to flow fresh for a moment. "Is that why we didn't know?"

"Maybe." The oracle shrugged, beginning to pace in languid movements. "I only see moments, albeit important ones. I just *know* about the rest."

The younger man closed his eyes, this time against the light of his surroundings, and waited for the pain inside his skull to subside. After a long moment, his eyes snapped open again. "I keep seeing a contract, with what might be blood at the bottom."

The oracle nodded. "A Blood Contract. The one they signed fifteen years ago."

"What's a... Blood Contract?" he asked uncertainly.

K'Sar exhaled roughly. "Illegal is what it is," he answered with that same roughness. "Causes all kinds of pain if you don't obey. The kind of pain that Loorans, especially the *tiancai*, can heal from. Eventually." What had sounded like it meant to be a reassurance ended up being much less.

Z'Tem gulped audibly. "I don't want to know, do I?"

K'Sar shook his head. "You really don't."

"What can we do?"

"Nothing, really. They're returning in a few days."

Z'Tem frowned very slightly. "How do you know?"

The oracle merely smiled.

# CHAPTER FORTY-FOUR

Rosalie opened her eyes to find that she had shifted planes yet again. This happened sometimes during heavy meditation. This was the first time it had happened since she'd signed herself out of the mental hospital, though.

All around her was light and softness within. It wasn't like the Plateau of Light where the light seemed to penetrate and agitate. Rather, here the surroundings tended to envelop and comfort. Idly, Rosalie wondered if a darker creature than herself would see something entirely different.

"They do."

Rosalie turned at the voice's declaration and found that she didn't fully have control here. Sure, she still turned to face the feminine owner of the very female voice but she had a distinct feeling that she wasn't doing it under her own power. "What's going on?"

The owner of the voice looked distinctly female, even standing within the warm ethereal light as she was. She seemed ridiculously tall with slender limbs but her hair was dark, which was a large contrast. When she smiled, Rosalie felt subtle warmth coil in her chest and something dark inside of her let go. "A little rose has joined my garden."

The anger in Rosalie snapped, crackling with indignant energy, before melting away. Her face shifted to a vaguely goofy grin. "I remember you," she murmured.

The woman nodded, moving to sit next to the girl. "You have aged, as mortals do."

Rosalie still smiled, though now she no longer saw the woman. She looked inward on past memories, trying to remember the exact moment she had seen this woman before. "I was seven and Daddy left. I was afraid."

The ethereal woman smiled softly, her head bobbing in a single affirmative nod. "Frightened child needing help. I was needed."

"Daddy kept me safe for so long but he left." A tear slid unnoticed down Rosalie's cheek but drifted away before it could reach the line of her chin. "It was hard on him, the planeswalking. He was gone and then there was you."

Rosalie could remember it clearer now. It was fifteen years ago and her father had disappeared the night before. She'd cried herself to sleep, frightened at the things she was seeing. When she woke up the next morning, she was in the exact place she was in now. At the young age, her lack of control hadn't been as much of an issue, seeing as how things had pretty much been out of her control her entire life up to that point.

"You told me to go outside and find another grown-up, tell them Daddy was gone and my head was wrong."

The woman's smile broadened vaguely. "To find the balance you need, you must first face your own imbalance."

Rosalie knew that the woman probably knew everything—that she had spent ten years after that day inside a mental hospital working on her control; that maybe now all her hard work was for naught. "I don't know what to do," she whispered, her eyes looking into the woman's own light gray orbs.

The woman stood again, her arms stretching out to include the environment. "This is the Plateau of Light in the Dimension of Balance."

Rosalie jerked visibly, her body now rejecting the warmth it had collected. "I jumped dimensions?" she asked in a shrill voice.

The woman chuckled. "Certainly not. I brought you here." She offered her hand and Rosalie grasped it, allowing the woman to help her to her feet. "In most things, we all must find our own balance. My advisors said you would bring the change, allow your dimension to come more closely aligned with our own."

"Are you an oracle?" she whispered in a breathy voice. She felt like something was happening, something that she couldn't quite grasp yet.

"Many call me 'augur'," she responded. She tilted her head very slightly to the side, a thoughtful expression crossing over her face. "I gather I would be similar to your oracles."

Rosalie followed the woman as they began walking, heading to what looked to be a small body of water. "Why did you bring me here?"

The augur brought her head back to its original position, giving the girl a vague smile. She refused to speak as she led them the rest of the way to the water. It was then that Rosalie realized that it was a large tide pool with a smaller one cordoned off from the rest. She smiled as she gazed at the variety of colors within the pool, blues and greens and red. A large blue anemone opened up to reveal its inner color of deep purple and the augur chuckled softly behind her. The pale hand shot into the water and passed gently over the anemone, which immediately closed up and caused bubbles to float to the surface.

"What was that?" Rosalie asked softly, shifting her gaze from the tide pool to the smiling woman.

The augur's smiled broadened. "It was trying to tell you something. I don't think you would understand the meaning yet." The woman grasped Rosalie's hand lightly and placed it to lightly touch the water before pulling it away again. "Now, tell me. What do you see?"

Rosalie looked at the tide pool again, watching as all the beautiful colors turned dark. The many colors dimmed to varying shades of black and gray and drab white. She frowned slightly, glancing very briefly at the augur again, and tried to focus. "I don't get it," she murmured under her breath.

The woman did not speak, only waiting. Rosalie's frown deepened, her anger spiking yet again. Wasn't she here because she needed help? Wasn't this oracle-like woman supposed to help her?

*Find your own balance...*

Then there was a voice that sounded distinctly like V'Let's, something she had said earlier that day. Or was it the day before?

*That doesn't mean I don't see a bigger picture...*

Rosalie grinned. That was it right there—she needed to see the bigger picture. The tide pool was like an optical illusion... or like one of those puzzles that only become jumbled when you focus too closely.

She forced her eyes to cross, resetting how she was seeing the pool, and then made herself look at the image the pool made as a whole. Slowly, the image began to coalesce. She saw the Prince pacing his little palace, every once in a while allowing his impotent rage to take hold and tossing something across the room to crash into the momentarily solid walls.

Rosalie blinked and shook her head. "It's the Prince. Why are you showing me this?"

The woman moved her hand to hover just over the water, a frown of sadness on her face. "The corruption of the Immortal Guardians is directly tied to your family curse. The Guardian of the Realm and the Immortal Guardian of the Planes—their lineage cannot exist without the other. Thus, when your family was cursed to walk the planes of existence, their family was forced to become a mere shadow of what they were."

Rosalie sat back on her behind, her eyes distant in thought. "Does Darrin… Do they know what happened to them?"

The woman shook her head. "It's very doubtful, as the Guardian of the Planes traditionally have no foothold on the Material Plane. That is the place that the Guardian of the Realm must maintain peace."

"If I allow V'Let to do the unbinding ritual, will the Prince return to the state he should be in?"

"It might take time, as adjusting always does, but I believe he will become whole again."

Rosalie's brow furrowed and she pressed her lips together in a thin line, her thoughts working at a furious pace. Deep down, she knew the decision was already made. Now, it was just to face up to that fact.

"Send me back," she told the woman softly. She was still deeply ensconced in her own thoughts, so she barely noticed when the Crone's living room reformed around her. Moments passed before she concentrated on her environment again. She stood, uncoiling herself from her meditative position, and turned around.

At which point she squealed a muted scream.

The Crone sat on the couch behind where she had been meditating, smiling that semi-permanent serene smile. The mahogany table in front of her was cluttered with books and she had two open across her lap.

"Where did you go?" she asked idly as she closed the book on her lap and place them to join the pile on the table.

Rosalie arched an eyebrow. "Was I gone?"

Matlinda chuckled. "Your body was here but your spirit was elsewhere."

The girl's face returned to normal, her lips twitching in the ghost of a smile. "Where are Erik and Quin?" she asked, hedging around the question for a moment.

The Crone tilted her head to the hallway, silently denoting the direction of the bedrooms. "They've been asleep for hours."

Rosalie nodded idly, moving to sit on the loveseat near the couch. "Okay. I was pulled into another dimension."

Matlinda's smile broadened instantaneously into an open grin. "Really? Which one?"

"She calls it the Balance Dimension." Rosalie shrugged. "I was there before, when I was younger. The woman, she said she was an augur, said she was helping me find my balance."

Matlinda nodded. She knew that the augurs stayed away from the dimensions that didn't align closely enough with their own. They believed in balance and almost nothing else. To coerce Rosalie in the way that they probably did during her jaunt meant that Rosalie, or rather the curse upon her lineage, was the key to bringing this dimension closer to balanced.

"What are you doing anyway?" Rosalie asked suddenly, piercing through Matlinda's thoughts. "Researching?"

"Exactly." Matlinda awarded the girl with a full close-lipped smile. "I'm making a timeline of sorts."

Rosalie arched her eyebrow again. "Does this have to do with my curse?"

The Crone nodded, moving to open another book and revealing a page full of notes underneath that particular tome. "Yes. I believe that cursing you brought darkness to this dimension. Not to mention, making the Earth spirit extremely angry."

Rosalie frowned, her brow furrowed in deep thought again. "Why didn't it affect the other dimensions?"

Matlinda hemmed for a moment. "I believe it did but only some of the dimensions. There are many dimensions that don't have the problems we have, such as the humans or the technology. The dimensions are like planets, constantly but subtly changing."

The girl nodded in vague understanding. "Okay," she replied. "So, likely, the ones that didn't have an abundance of humans weren't affected. Because they didn't need the Guardian to maintain the balance in the first place?"

The Crone nodded. "In this dimension, however, it began to alter even some of the nonhuman species. Some of them are corrupted, having adapted to humans just to survive."

Rosalie passed a hand through her hair. "I want V'Let to unbind me. I want everything to regain some semblance of balance. Will you help me learn magic?"

Matlinda smiled. "I'd be honored."

The girl sighed, her eyes far away. "There are going to be a lot of problems. This is a world where demons and vampires attack to get what they want. It's what they've always had to do." She focused her eyes on the Crone. "Luna Morte is going to be a big problem."

Matlinda gazed down at her books and then back at Rosalie. "More than just the vampires and the demons. There are fey in this city that live to be problematic."

Rosalie shifted her gaze to the hallway, her lips twitching as a thought occurred to her. "I think I have an idea."

# CHAPTER FORTY-FIVE

V'Let woke slowly, fighting the process the entire time. She slowly opened one eye and groaned, feeling like someone had opened her skull and poured in a bucket of sand. Grabbing the underside of her bunk, she rolled and attempted to place her feet firmly on her floor. It worked in a way that resembled clumsiness.

She was inspecting her eyes in her mirror when there came a loud clanging at her bunk door. "What?" she called out.

The door opened with a whoosh of air and a soft clink into his ceiling crevice. D'Las stood there, a large smile pasted on his face. "Are you ready yet?"

V'Let leaned over, placing her elbows on the edge of the sink and her hands over her eyes. "Gods," she murmured to herself. "I forgot how annoying you are."

His grin only broadened in response. "I feel great," he proclaimed. He spun once in a half-circle and collapsed gently on her bunk. "Even though I didn't sleep in my bunk."

V'Let uncovered her eyes and gazed at her brother's face in the mirror. "Did you sleep?" He nodded, his gaze unfocused and his smile assuming a vague goofiness. "Well, where?"

He made a dismissive gesture at the door. "On the floor, outside my bunk." He leaned over and picked up the device that showed the shifting holopic of their mother, his smile slowly fading. "Do you miss her?"

She smiled at him, her lips curving in nostalgic sadness. "More than I could ever put into words," she assured him. She moved to her door and gazed at the corridor outside their bunks before moving back to the mirror. "What happened?"

"Passed out, I guess." He shrugged and returned the holopic device to its original spot on the edge of V'Let's bunk. "Why don't you ever talk about her? About what happened?"

V'Let sat down gingerly next to D'Las and mimicked his shrug. "You were catatonic for a long time, Lasso. I didn't think you wanted to know and I'm a little certain that you didn't."

He rewarded her with a half-smile. "Not then, at any rate," he replied smoothly. "Will you tell me now?"

She nodded, echoing his smile and remembering how infectious his happiness used to be. "Okay, but after I do, we need to find Rosalie and start the ritual." He inclined his head in acquiescence. She inhaled deeply and thought about that day twenty years ago. "It was the middle of the warm season and you and that boy had left without me again. I remember being sad—I wanted to play but I was afraid to wander by myself. *Mama* was busy preparing food for the festival, the celebration of the Great City, and told me I could practice with our studies. I wanted to show her how I made one of the singing flowers dance when there was a big explosion. The kitchen window exploded inward and *Mama* jumped in front of me. She had a shard of glass in her chest and she was bleeding too much. It would have gotten me in the neck. She told me to be a good girl and protect my brother and then she was gone."

"Z'Tem," D'Las murmured when she stopped talking.

V'Let breathed deeply again, arching an eyebrow at her brother's comment. "What?"

"That boy," he replied. "His name was Z'Tem." He shook his head slightly and focused on his sister. "We *are* going back, right?"

V'Let inclined her head slightly. "As soon as this ritual is done. We can leave this planet their aftermath. I just want to stop for a while."

D'Las nodded and stood, holding out his hand to help his sister. She grasped it and he pulled her to her feet. "Well, then, let's get this over with already."

V'Let scowled slightly. That beaming smile was back. Just great. She shook her head and they both headed out of her bunk, D'Las pulling down the door behind them. At the stairs, they parted ways, which caused to V'Let to stop at the third step and look back at her brother.

At her arched eyebrow, he bounced from one foot to another and back again. "I'm really too wired to just sit and watch right now. I'm going to put in the coordinates for Loora and send a long-range message." He shrugged slightly at the question in her gaze. "If we're lucky at all, we'll get a response before we leave."

V'Let smiled at her brother. "Don't break anything," she called over her shoulder as she continued down into the cargo hold, obviously remembering what he had been like before the Adepts. She was momentarily glad that she had essentially drained almost all of his power the night before.

Once she reached the cargo hold, she turned around, scanning the upper level to make sure her brother was in the bridge now. As he was nowhere to be seen, at least in her own line of sight, she scurried to a shadowed corner of the open area. One of the crevices there hid a smuggler's hold, where she stowed very specific things.

Right now, she only needed one very specific thing: her mother's pendant. The necklace was a lopsided heart pendant in the same dark silver as the ship on a silver chain that shone like mithril. On the back of the pendant was an inscription that read, *With eternal love, K'Sar.* V'Let had always found it both profoundly mysterious and very romantic. Her mother had given it to her when she and her brother had begun their studies, saying that it would bring her luck. Since then, she wore it every time she planned to perform a powerful ritual of any sort.

She removed the necklace from its hiding place and donned the accessory. The pendant itself fell to lay just below the hollow of her throat, an odd dissonance against the violet of her skin. She smiled, her face now echoing her brother's beaming smile.

She was ready.

V'Let stepped out of the spacecraft and broke through the cloak moments later. Matlinda, Rosalie and Erik were sitting on the porch again, the girl sipping at something in a porcelain mug. V'Let sighed, passing a hand through her long hair and then touching the pendant lightly with the tips of her fingers. The ritual could take hours or it could be instantaneous. Personally, she hoped for the latter—a large push of power and the following exhaustion. She didn't like it here.

Erik shifted slightly in her seat and caught a glimpse of the alien, which caused him to smile slightly. She grimaced deeply, quickly forcing the expression and the feeling tangled with it away. She needed to find a way to release the bond between herself and the vampire. Or at least, a way to dampen it.

V'Let tilted her head at the vampire. However, the vampire could come in handy later, though she wasn't entirely certain how. The distance soon to be between them could also help him adjust to the bond.

She grabbed the railing and gracefully leapt over the barrier. Once her feet touched the floor of the porch and she steadied her balance, she leaned against the railing, surveying each of them in turn. Rosalie's eyes were beginning to glaze over, though she still drank obediently out of her mug. Every once in a while, she would bat at the air and her face would contort into a confusing array of emotions. The Crone was tense this time, keeping a close eye on the girl next to her.

V'Let arched an eyebrow at them. She made a gesture of inquiry, which the vampire answered.

"She just started drinking the tea a few minutes ago," Erik told the alien. "Mattie said during this first stage, she might do things to hurt herself."

V'Let nodded in response. She could feel Rosalie calming at a very rapid rate but she would intermittently twitch, causing her calm to crack. Every time she batted the air or visibly twitched, Matlinda would reach over and put her to rights.

The elderly woman glanced up at V'Let in apology. "She's taking it a little worse this time. You're not supposed to take kratom in close intervals like this."

V'Let responded with a slight inclination of her head, indicating that she would wait until the tea's effects settled fully. She glanced back at the vampire. "Where is the demon?"

Erik's smile broadened at her question. "Quin is out on the town spreading rumors."

Rosalie giggled, the laugh conveying a sense of lunatic absenteeism. "The world's ending."

V'Let smiled softly, sensing that there was more to this. "Why?"

Erik chortled, his deep voice making the laugh more sadistic than she assumed he intended. "It was Rose's brilliant idea." He turned his bright smile to the girl, making V'Let think for once that maybe stripping the vampire of his anger was a good thing. He turned back to V'Let, his eyes serious again. "Quin has always been a messenger demon around here, spreading around information to pretty much anybody. So, Rosalie thought it would be effective if he started warning everybody about the upcoming apocalypse. She hoped the good demons would hide and the bad ones would be out wreaking havoc when your entity strikes out at the humans."

V'Let's lips curved into a smirk, her blue eyes bright. "That's actually impressive."

Erik snorted. "Thanks," he muttered with a soft overtone of sarcasm. She quirked her head at the vampire. "I try."

Matlinda cleared her throat softly, grabbing at their attention. V'Let turned her head and focused on the girl again. She was completely still, unblinking and silent. "I think she's ready," the elderly woman murmured. She waved a hand idly in front of Rosalie's eyes. "She's pretty much gone."

V'Let closed her eyes, exhaled her exhaustion and inhaled a pretense of certainty. Opening her eyes again, she pushed off from the railing and knelt in front of Rosalie. "Let's do this," she muttered.

On the spacecraft, D'Las hummed a jaunty tune idly. He had sent the subspace message first and then proceeded to input the coordinates for their homeplanet. Now he sat at the central console, energetically drumming his fingers against his legs.

This particular change in his core attitude was quite drastic. He could feel everything and now he remembered why he had been the child prodigy between the two of them. He'd always had what always seemed like an endless supply of energy, constantly expelling it in some form or another. However, as emotional as V'Let could be, she was also highly controlled even from a young age, something D'Las assumed she did to emulate their mother. He'd thought before that she had found a way to keep a large reserve of power without having to expel it, even though expelling massive amounts of power exhausted her quickly. They were twins after all—her power had to be somewhat similar to his own.

Even now, he could feel his power growing, filling up the spaces she had emptied. All at once, he suddenly realized that she had taken on this massive amount of power. V'Let had been full of her own power, hadn't expelled anything in the past few days except whatever it took to communicate with the being that normally existed within this planet. However, she had taken on his power, what had to be a substantial amount of untouched but contained power stored over the last twenty years.

D'Las suddenly had a much higher level of respect for his sister.

"Incoming transmission from Zeta Sector, Milky Way Galaxy, Planet Loora." The computer's monotonous voice broke through D'Las's musings.

The man grinned, his serious thoughts giving way to the realization that they would be going home very soon. "Accept communication."

A bored voice erupted through the speakers, the viewscreen showing a Looran male with short hair that was just beginning to curl around his ears. "Loora home transmissions answering message from Looran vessel *Tiancai*."

"So, Loora wasn't destroyed?" D'Las wasn't aware of the facts his sister had come to understand during their trance bonding, wasn't fully aware of the lies that the Adepts had told them were just that. Lies that incompetent Council members with delusions of grandeur had told themselves and their charges to make the monstrosities seem justified.

The unknown Looran glanced up at his own screen, his face marginally alarmed and confused. "No. Who told you that?"

D'Las tilted his head at the screen. In one corner of his mind, he could tell that V'Let had started the trance that preceded the ritual with the planeswalking witch-girl so she could not be bothered with his inquiry. Looking at the Looran on the other end of this transmission, he realized that this particular Looran had not yet reached the twenty-year mark. "Do you have a supervisor?"

The Looran ran a hand through his hair, the alarm and confusion increasing at the question. "Yeah, sure. I'll just get him." His eyes widened slightly, a different kind of fear entering his big blue eyes. "Her. Sorry, it's a her now. F'Gar retired last season."

D'Las shifted his expression to one of understanding and nodded. "I'll wait," he answered, watching as the now skittish man disappeared from the screen.

During the time that passed, D'Las turned his attention to what his sister was doing. Idly, he hoped this transmission would be over by the time she finished the ritual. She would be monumentally tired by the end of it.

Seeing through his sister's eyes was always a disorienting experience at first. Especially this time, when she was locked mentally onto another person. At first, he saw more than his mind could organize, slowly realizing that he was seeing what the girl saw when she was not under control. It was layers upon layers of different planes, some confusing and others warped or twisted, many of them holding species of creatures he'd never seen before. He could feel V'Let forcing herself to focus and the foreign realms of existence slid away like water. Inside the girl was something similar to the Looran genetic memory but much more primal. It was pure knowledge and need, to stand up and between, to be the thing that was strong. This particular essence was stronger in this girl that in some of others of her ancestry, he knew. V'Let now examined the curse and the afflicted simultaneously, trying to find the link that would shatter the curse.

"Sir?" The soft feminine voice broke D'Las out of his sister's trance almost too easily.

He shook his head to clear the images he'd received from his sister's mind. The skittish boy was back, now with what looked to be a slightly older woman. Her structure was similar to that of his sister, except there were faint lines on her face that came with frequent frowning and narrowing of the eyes and her hair was cut very short away from her face.

"Yes?" D'Las answered, allowing his lips to curve into what he assumed was a charming smile.

At the expression, however, the woman's face contorted into what he could now tell was an expression she used often, likely the very one that caused the faint wrinkles. "I'm the supervisor here, Sarra T'Lin. Can you tell me why you believed the planet to be destroyed?"

D'Las shrugged. "I was really out of it when it happened. My sister said our home was destroyed and I believe her. Twenty years ago, we lived with our mother in the Great City."

The woman—Sarra, he reminded himself—rolled her eyes and clicked buttons on the keyboard in front of her. "Which Great City?"

D'Las closed his eyes. He'd been so young then and most everyone had referred to their city as the Great City, usually as if it were the only one. With a sudden snap of memory, he remembered his sister and mother having a conversation one day when he returned from his day with Z'Tem. They'd been discussing politics, which was always so boring to him, and the Great City, except his mother had called it something else.

"Datong," he told her with certainty.

She glanced at him and continued to input the information. "Datong," she repeated, though she was saying it as if she was reading from the screen before her. "Great City of Unity, decimated by unknown parties twenty years past, site of shrine to presumed deceased *tiancai* and mother." She stopped reading and he watched as her eyes flickered up at him and then to another screen. "*Tiancai* is the name of your ship."

He smiled at her again, attempting to placate. "My sister and I, we are the *tiancai*," he told her.

Disbelief flowed over her face. "Really?"

Suddenly, he could hear his sister's voice hissing into his mind. *Don't tell them who we are, idiot!* He jerked visibly, turning his attention inward, but his sister had already returned her focus to the impending ritual. He knew exactly how much interrupting her could harm her in turn. As such, he obeyed her.

"No." He added a scoff and roll of his eyes. "They're obviously dead, right?"

Sarra arched an eyebrow, her face conveying that she noted this obvious change in his demeanor. "Right."

"Anyway, we're on Earth now and should be leaving before this cycle is over. We've been gone for a very long time. Since Datong has only the shrine, I assume, we'll touch down in Taicheng."

The woman nodded, glancing at her watch. "We will be expecting you approximately midday tomorrow."

D'Las rewarded the woman with one last smile, although this one was tight and forced, before he ended the communication. He sighed, feeling a good level of his happiness seep away.

Now, he reflected on V'Let's attitude when he had almost confirmed that they were the *tiancai*. Her tone had implied that it was something he should have known. Usually, when it was something that was obvious to her but managed to escape him, it had to do with politics. In all his years, he had still never understood politics or the motivation behind it. He might be the powerhouse of the twins but it was always V'Let that *understood*.

He hauled himself out of his seat and exited the bridge, pressing a button near the door to make the ship power down for now. He needed to join his sister. He could watch her, remind himself how to use his own power in a non-destructive fashion and be there to carry her to her bunk when she lost consciousness, as she undoubtedly would after the ritual.

D'Las paused halfway down the stairs, gripping the railing as the sudden halt caused him to lose his balance. Forcing himself to loosen his grip, he continued down the stairs. There was something missing or disturbed in the cargo hold. The awareness of it was slightly disconcerting after the absolute nothingness he'd dealt with for the last twenty years. However, despite the disturbance of order in the cargo area, he didn't feel concerned with it.

It was an odd feeling.

He had memories of V'Let lecturing him about the ship after they'd had it commissioned to be built. She always seemed to know everything that would happen months and sometimes years before it happened. When the Adepts held them captive and those Council members had still been largely faceless voices in his memory, she had been designing a spacecraft. He remembered her telling him about smuggler's holds, especially one specific hold in the cargo area that she said was for "memories and stuff". After signing that damnable contract, she had sent out orders and requisitions for Looran metal only. Their spacecraft couldn't be made of anything else.

D'Las found himself walking to the shadowed corner of the cargo hold, feeling like something was pulling at his bottom of his stomach. As his environment became darker, his pupils dilated to compensate. There was a panel level to his lower leg muscles slightly askew to the rest of the paneling. He knelt down on his knees and pushed the panel to the side.

He reached a hand inside the hollow hole and encountered some type of metal cube. Using his other hand, he pulled what turned out to be a silvery metal box out of its hiding place. The top of the box was slid away, revealing little treasures and trinkets inside. D'Las assumed the disturbance was because his sister had removed something from the box before she left the ship.

There were three holopic devices, which he removed from the box and set aside. Besides that, there were only a stack of sketches and a writing tablet. Skimming through the sketches, he noticed that they were the designs for V'Let's inventions—including the ship in which he stood—and sketches of people and animals and various other things from their homeplanet. He set those neatly back inside the box and picked up the writing tablet, turning it on with a tap to the screen with a stylus secured inside a crevice on the tablet's side.

The writing tablet was a small portable computer, pretty much all screen and not much else. It was highly limited, confined by a smaller amount of space and the only programs were a word processor and a drawing program that was mostly empty. He opened one of the documents and skimmed it briefly before closing it very quickly. With jittery movements, he placed the tablet back in its place and took a deep cleansing breath through his mouth.

It was V'Let's journal. She would kill him if she even knew that he had read anything out of it. Not that it was anything he didn't already know or couldn't guess at. However, it was a confirmation of some of her deepest and most secret thoughts. It was an invasion of privacy to even open any one of the documents in that writing tablet.

Shaking his head slightly, D'Las turned to the holopics with a slight smile. He knew they hadn't actually managed to escape their home with any of the actual holopics, so these had to be manipulations. He turned on the first one and gasped. It was almost exactly the picture that had hung in the living area of their home on Loora. D'Las and V'Let were in their fourth year, clinging to their mother's legs with one arm and waving with the other. Their mother was standing tall, her hands clasped together in front of her.

It was a very good manipulation.

The other two weren't quite as good but they came very close. The second holopic was of Z'Tem at five years, shorter than D'Las had been by a few inches and a stance that seemed by convey his shyness. The last holopic was of someone he didn't recognize, a very tall and skinny Looran with a stoic face. This was the only one with a word on it. Carved into the device in the same way that V'Let carved Looran power words into her inventions were a set of Looran characters that spelled out a name. "K'Sar," D'Las read softly. "Who's that?"

Suddenly, D'Las felt a different type of pulling sensation, something much more urgent than that which had pulled him to this box of memories. He hurriedly replaced the holopic devices in the box and the box back in its smuggler's hold, placing the removable panel just slightly askew from the rest of its surroundings. Confident that everything was returned to the way he had found it, he turned and rushed off the ship toward his sister.

He broke through the cloak seamlessly and bounded across the ground between their spacecraft and the old witch's home quickly. Upon reaching the porch, he grabbed the railing and heaved himself over it gracefully, unknowingly mimicking his sister's earlier movements. He scanned them all quickly, reading their open faces.

The demon wasn't present. Both the old woman and the vampire looked concerned. The girl, Rosalie, was oddly alert and settling V'Let into a seat gently. His sister's head lolled to the side and her eyes were closed. He focused on her then, knowing something was off and that the pull had been significant.

She was gone.

Rosalie smiled at him. "She passed out," she said with a shrug. "I think… I think I'm back to normal. If this is what normal is." The old woman smiled at her and nodded.

D'Las frowned deeply, anger creeping and darkening his bright blue eyes and his lips thinning into an almost nonexistent line. He closed his eyes and turned away from the females to face the vampire. Erik still looked concerned and, now that D'Las took more time to notice, largely alarmed.

"Is she dead?" the vampire asked softly.

D'Las felt something inside of him crystallize and he clenched his jaw to control the sudden urge to lash out with what power he had managed to accumulate in the last day. "If she is," he said in a controlled voice, "then so is she." He pointed a single slender digit at Rosalie, turning to face her. "This planet and all in it be damned, girl. If my sister doesn't return, I will kill you."

Rosalie's eyes widened, knowing with certainty that D'Las was not bluffing. She shrank back into the Crone next to her. "I thought... you couldn't."

D'Las narrowed his eyes. "Things have changed recently." He sneered at the girl. "Because you *had* to be returned to your natural state, my sister forced me open. I have nowhere near the control she has."

Rosalie gulped audibly and looked over at the Crone. "I don't know what to do," she murmured.

D'Las collapsed in his sister's lap, that crystal thing inside him shattering as he sobbed. "Come back. I can't do this."

The others looked on at him as he cried in his sister's lap, wondering what was happening. Erik placed his chin in his hands, his dark blue eyes projecting a deep sadness. He hoped that everything would turn out okay, for once.

# CHAPTER FORTY-SIX

She was surrounded by green. That sickly color of growth and life enveloped her and she wanted to retch. She'd had enough of this planet before they'd even landed. Was this the entity attempting to hold her prisoner?

"I did what you asked!" V'Let declared loudly into the green. "I want to go home now."

*"Is it really home to you now?"*

V'Let scoffed and turned around, coming face to ethereal countenance with the entity. It had taken the green around them and formed a humanoid body. It stood slightly shorter than V'Let, its skin spring green and its hair hunter green. It was clothed in a flowing A-line dress of sea green and its eyes glowed white. Its form was much more feminine than masculine and it was smiling.

"It's the only home I have," she answered the entity finally. "The ship is not home."

The entity chuckled. *"I need you to do something else for me."*

V'Let threw her hands into the air. "I released your precious Guardian. Will you never be done with me?"

The entity inclined its head. *"This will be the last thing I require... for a while."* It sighed heavily. *"This will go a long way towards completing the balance."*

V'Let sighed, echoing the entity's own gesture mockingly. "All right. What do I have to do now?"

The entity's face broke into a smile and waved an arm behind her in an encompassing gesture. Behind her, V'Let could see that the green had parted but the entity was blocking much of what had been revealed. *"I just need you to readjust the attitude of my Realm Keeper."*

Now, V'Let was suspicious. Something about this seemed vaguely familiar and... off. "Who is your Realm Keeper?"

The entity took what seemed to be an impossibly large step out of V'Let's line of vision. Through the parted curtain of green was an angry, semi-corporeal man, pacing with furious intent throughout his equally incorporeal environment. After a moment, he heaved a temporarily solid vase across the room in which he stood and it flew through the wall at the exact moment that it flickered out of existence.

*"His name is Darrin, the Guardian of the Infinite Realms. As Rosalie is the thing that stands between the humans and all others, Darrin is the thing that binds all other realms together."* The entity frowned. *"The curse that you lifted off of Rosalie should have returned him to normal but his rage seems to block all else."*

V'Let tilted her head at the scene. "Isn't this the guy that Rosalie's been avoiding? The one that hates humans?"

*"Turn him away from his anger and everything else will fall back into order."* The entity moved around behind V'Let and nudged her roughly in the back. Without another moment passing, she found herself on the other side of the curtain...

In the room with the very angry man who lacked solidity merely because he was stubborn.

"Well, this is just great, isn't it?" she muttered darkly.

Darrin turned sharply at the sound, his eyes narrowing on the being that was in the palace with him. "Who are you?"

V'Let merely rewarded him with the fakest smile she could make. *If I do this, that damned entity better return me to my body,* she thought to herself as she wandered around this room into which she had been forced. *Lasso must be going crazy right about now.* As she thought about her brother, she turned inward toward the bond to find that it felt very far away. She attributed that to two things—she wasn't in her body and she was most definitely on another plane.

Finally she faced Darrin, her eyes narrowed. "Let's get this straight, okay? I'm not here because I like you. I'm here because it needs to be done."

The man's face seemed to clench, the skin tightening in an unflattering fashion. "Who are you?" he asked again through teeth that seemed to be grinding together.

V'Let tilted her head at the Realm Keeper, her narrowed eyes looking deeper. She knew that she was completely incorporeal without having to look at herself. Darrin, however, was a flickering solid that for some reason made her think of dry ice. He shifted from solidity to a type of gaseous, semi-transparent form similar to her current state so quickly that there almost didn't seem to be a difference. Maybe he had been shocked at her arrival, enough to lift some of the anger, but he seemed to be building it back quickly.

"What are you looking at?" The grinding demand grated on her nerves.

V'Let looked inward again, trying to gauge her power level. Maybe she could force some kind of fake happiness on him until he returned to normal. She sighed after a moment. Her power level was too low to affect his emotions, almost completely drained after shattering that eternal curse on Rosalie's lineage. She would be lucky if she could float a feather until she rested.

"You're a nasty little person so full of rage that you can't see what's happening around you," V'Let spat out snidely, moving toward a wall idly. "You're angry, so angry that most of the time you can't think about anything else. As a result, you can't bring yourself to care how your decisions can affect others." She reached out to touch the wall in the half-moment that it flickered solid.

The wall glowed lavender for a moment, coming into focus, and its flickering state faltered before becoming completely solid. The glow spread, soon covering the entirety of the throne room and bringing it all to a solid, unchanging state. V'Let frowned as the glow faded, feeling like a part of her had slid into place. As the room became solid, she felt just a little more whole.

Darrin turned around slowly, frowning at his throne room. It was solid, constant, comforting because of those things. He felt the shock rock through him for a moment before it was followed by a blast of anger at this mysterious violet-skinned woman who managed to do what he couldn't.

V'Let felt the anger flow through him and rolled her eyes. Maybe nothing would do. She took a deep breath and sat in the middle of the room suddenly, folding one incorporeal leg on top of the other. She needed a different tack. "Come. Sit with me."

She smiled when he sat down across from her a few feet away. He didn't look happy at all but now she knew what the entity had been thinking earlier. Of course Darrin could have been left alone and perhaps he would have simmered down given time. Introducing an unknown variable, however, was forcing a quicker solution, forcing the Realm Keeper to forego his anger for other emotions that could help return him to a state of normalcy.

"Tell me about it." V'Let sat very still, her bright blue eyes boring into Darrin's gray eyes. She remembered that psychology was like an infestation on this planet and she knew personally that just knowing what bothered you helped you to get past it.

The Realm Keeper's response was not surprising, if not exactly expected. He sneered at her with a certain kind of darkness in the gray depths of his eyes. "Why should I tell you?"

V'Let ignored that deep part of her that twitched in momentary fury at the condescension in his tone and smiled amiably at him, making an all-encompassing gesture with her hands. "I'm here and I'm stuck here until you return to normal."

The furrowing of his brow conveyed his confusion while the scowl gave way to his obvious thoughts. "What do you mean?" The scowl deepened. "This is normal for me."

Her lips curled upwards into a slightly wicked grin, realizing that he really didn't know that this semi-corporeal state in which he was stuck was extremely abnormal for him. Again, she had to remind herself that this world didn't share her species' genetic memory. At least, not in a way that was easily accessible.

V'Let shook her head. "It's not, actually." At his arched eyebrow, she continued. "I've been told that you hate the humans, although the truth is that you hate pretty much anything that has a solid form."

Now he was tilted his head at her very slightly, the darkness in his eyes creeping away. "Who are you?" There was no anger in his voice now, though the fury was still running rampant through his system.

She smirked at him, openly conveying good-natured amusement. "You know who I am," she answered. "I suppose I was to be your solution to the human problem."

Darrin's brow furrowed, his lips beginning to part to form a circle of realization. "You're an alien."

V'Let chuckled lightly. "Of course. Doesn't the skin give it away?"

Embarrassment floated over the man's face, marring its structure for a moment. "Um, well, my vision hasn't been consistent lately. It's made me agitated."

She clucked her tongue softly. "What can you see?"

"It's shapes and blobs most of the time. Usually, when I can see clearly, there's no color. Just black and white and gray."

"For how long?" V'Let leaned forward, gazing into his gray eyes. Were they supposed to be a different color?

The Realm Keeper shrugged. "Maybe about five days, I think."

She sighed, exhaling a large amount of air. That was roughly the time of their arrival, when the entity had been released. Idly, she wondered where this place was in coordination to what Rosalie referred to as the Material Plane. If she were to be transferred to that plane from here directly, would she find herself near one of the new power sinks?

V'Let smirked at herself, at her wandering thoughts but continued to follow their line. It was highly possible that they were a triumvirate of power and protection of sorts. The Earth, the Guardian and the Keeper so tied to each other that breaking one shattered the others. After a moment, she shook her head. She could ruminate on this another time.

"Anyway, the point of me being here is that you really need to let go of your anger," she stated softly.

Darrin scoffed. "Why should I?"

V'Let rolled her eyes. Darrin held on to his anger like a dog with a bone. It was something with which he was comfortable and he wasn't likely to release it any time soon. Except that he had to. "Because if you don't, this planet's essence will not be able to kill the humans."

He jerked visibly, the revelation shocking as it was. "But she won't! She can't!"

She chuckled. "Not even considering the fact of the wars and the idle destruction of the humans' so-called 'progress', she has been without her Guardian and Keeper of the Realms for almost a thousand years."

"Her what?" Darrin sounded really confused now. "What are you talking about?"

V'Let smirked again, the gesture soon melting into a genuine smile. It was like lecturing her brother on how something worked. Sure, before he shut himself down, he was the one that could make something work. But she was always concerned with the how, something that enabled her to fashion new devices rather than use crippling displays of power.

"Okay, I'll start from the beginning." While they had been waiting for the numbing tea to set in to Rosalie, V'Let had picked up some interesting tidbits from their minds, not to mention the primal memory just below the surface of the binding curse. "Almost a thousand years ago, this world was in balance, though the humans were becoming stronger and more convicted. The search for the Holy Land had begun, wars started in its name and hunts for real witches were being whispered even though the Church denied the existence of witchcraft."

Darrin opened his mouth to speak but V'Let laid two fingers across his lips, effectively hushing him.

"It was dark, dangerous times and witches were afraid, so much so that they often resorted to forbidden magic to defend themselves. Soon, it turned to outright attack against the human fanatics." V'Let sighed, her blue eyes darkening as she spoke memories that were not her own. "The Guardian of the Realm at that time was a man, a powerful mage that had stood between a group of particularly dark witches and the men they were trying to kill. Many weeks later, these witches found the man again and cursed him and his family line very specifically. He was to know insanity and to be able to go where humans couldn't follow. Almost immediately, the earth swallowed the witches whole in a massive earthquake."

Darrin had waited for her fingers to fall away, which they did after a while. "What does any of this have to do with me?" He was trying to force his anger to mount again, but every time it seemed to fail him, fizzling away under the onslaught of the alien's smooth voice.

V'Let held up a hand and he quieted again. "That man was Rosalie's ancestor. In forcing her ancestors to planeswalk, the entity tells me your role was stolen, leaving you and your ancestors since then an incorporeal husk of what you should be. Without the two of you, it could not protect itself. So, a few days ago, we struck a deal."

Darrin's face was open and questioning. V'Let could almost feel his rage leaking away. "What kind of a deal?"

"Legally, I can't do a thing to this planet. But the humans are really despicable, right? So, the entity eradicates them at a very high ratio and leaves less than seventy thousand of them alive. In return, I remove the curse, thus freeing both you and Rosalie at no small cost to myself."

Darrin huffed softly. "Then what's wrong with me?"

V'Let watched in fascination as his gray eyes bled out, leaving behind bright green orbs, and the smoky essence of his body hardened and became real. She reached out to touch him, knowing that for some reason her incorporeal state was flexible here. When she touched him, he was solid, permanently so it seemed. "Nothing anymore."

He arched an eyebrow and then glanced down at himself, a soft shriek erupting from his mouth. "Oh, Gods, I'm solid." He looked back at V'Let. "Is this real?"

She glanced around her at the very solid surroundings. It had switched like magic, instantaneously permanent and somehow comforting. She opened her mouth to answer him when her world suddenly tilted on its axis. Everything wobbled and for a moment, she thought she could see the Crone's porch and house before her vision started to dim.

She pulled together what energy she had left into a tight ball and used it to lob a single message of six small words at the Realm Keeper before her entire world went black.

*Make sure I'm in my body.*

Darrin was still marveling over this new development when it hit him like a brick. The message was so clear and hit him with such massive intent that he felt a sharp pain at the corner of his left eye. He reached up to lightly touch that particular area, still amazed at the physical contact and sensation, and felt something vaguely liquid. Pulling his hand away, he found his fingers marked with red, something he realized was his own blood.

"Gods, she's strong," he murmured to himself.

*Make sure I'm in my body...*

Darrin stood and walked idly around his throne room, finally settling after a moment in his throne. How exactly was he to make sure she was in her own body? He tilted his head slightly. Why did he care?

He forcefully turned away from the question, not wanting to face it at the moment. The point was that he did care, for once in his hundred years of life. But to track the alien? That was something else. He thought back on the little story she'd told him, noting that every time she'd mentioned Rosalie it had been in a familiar tone. She also had good, clear insight into the minds of witches of the Dark Age, something that leant toward the Crone of Witches. He should likely start there.

The thought barely managed to pass through his mind before he was there. Standing with solid presence among witches, aliens and a vampire. Out of the corner of his eye, he noted a demon approaching the house at a fast clip.

Rosalie sat near the Crone and a decidedly male alien was hovering over the body of the female that had broken him out of his unforgiving rage. Darrin stepped forward, the soft sounds of his footsteps pulling attention to his presence, just as the violet-skinned man seemed to collapse in front of what had to be his sister to lightly slap her face. There was an odd outburst of happiness when her eyes fluttered open.

"Was that really necessary?" she grumbled in a low tone.

The man pulled her up, hugging her fiercely. "What happened?" Darrin heard him ask very softly.

She nodded over his shoulder. "I had to help him."

It was odd, the sensation of scrutiny when they all turned to him. The alien woman was smiling kindly, softly but it was Rosalie's expression that chilled him a little. It was cold and tinged with fury. Everyone else just looked decidedly confused and blank.

Darrin watched as the aliens looked at each other, sensing that there was a conversation happening there, and she squeezed her brother's shoulder. In response, the man moved them toward Darrin, supporting her obviously exhausted form the whole time.

"I don't even know how you're still awake," he heard the man murmur to her.

She rewarded him with a beaming smile as they reached Darrin. When they stopped, she looked into Darrin's eyes intensely. "I'm sorry about before. I'm V'Let and this is my brother D'Las. I believe you know Rosalie," she finished with a smirk.

"I think she's mad at me," Darrin commented in a stage whisper.

"That's because I am," the girl all but growled, standing in the process.

V'Let gazed up at her brother. "Calm her," she murmured. With a nod, D'Las held his hand up like a vertical line and then swayed lightly. Darrin felt a rush of power and Rosalie very nearly melted back into her seat.

Darrin tried subtly to force the tension out of his body. He would have to apologize to Rosalie sometime but not while she was likely to strangle him. "That was impressive," he commented to D'Las.

In return, the alien just shrugged and shot his sister a look. She smiled and nodded. Darrin frowned, his brow furrowing. He opened his mouth to ask something about these internal conversations but V'Let spoke before he could utter a syllable.

"We're leaving before the fun starts," she declared in a loud voice, meant to reach all of them. "We need to go home."

Darrin's eyes widened. This was the one person that had been able to help him see things clearly in… well, ever. "But…" He didn't know how to say what he wanted without sounding like a frightened child.

V'Let's soft blue eyes turned to him. "If you need me, just think of me," she told him cryptically. "Besides, I have some political tangles to unknot." That said, she shot a dirty look at her brother.

Without anything else said, D'Las and V'Let stepped off the porch, walking in a beeline to the edge of the Crone's property. A few moments later, they seemed to merely disappear and Darrin frowned.

"What just happened?" he murmured to himself.

That was when the ground began to shake and Darrin thought it would be a better idea if he were back in his throne room, a couple planes away from the disturbance.

# PART THREE:
## Consequences and Fate

"You have to reap what you sow. There will always be something to pay for."
*- Doctor Dmitri Andian, on a tactical endgame*

# CHAPTER FORTY-SEVEN

"Hurry," V'Let murmured softly when her brother quickly deposited her on her feet in the cargo hold. With a brief nod, he pulled himself up the stairs, more using his arms and the railing rather than his feet and the stairs. She slowly and deliberately moved to the airlock button, her steps uncertain but firm. Just as she felt the whirring that signaled the ignition of the ship's engines and a deeper rumble underneath that, she reached the button and pressed on it with her body weight rather than force of strength. The airlock and outer hatch closed smoothly and she rested on the panel, careful to avoid the button.

That was how D'Las found her when he returned, her head resting on the cool metal of the airlock paneling and her breathing a little shallow but even. Her eyes were open, though heavy-lidded and slightly glazed. He stepped up next to her and looped her limp arm around his neck, moving them both carefully through the cargo hold.

"Bunk?" he inquired.

"Bridge," she answered in a soft, breathy voice.

D'Las shot a look of concern at her but she merely laid her head on his shoulder and forced her feet to move. To her, the brief journey seemed longer than usual, if only for the effort she now put into it. The stairs were difficult, as was the lip she had to step over in order to enter the bridge. Her brother deposited her at the central console and moved to stand a few feet in front of her, facing her.

"What's going on?" He eyed her seriously, his pinprick pupil widening very slightly. "What's so important that your rest has to wait?"

V'Let rolled her eyes. "You told them we are *tiancai*, Lasso."

He sighed exasperatedly. "But I took it back when you told me not to tell them. I played it off like I was joking."

She chucked derisively. "Have you ever listened to yourself? You're a terrible liar." He shrugged. "Technically, I've broken some Looran laws."

D'Las frowned deeply. "What laws?"

"The laws against destruction," she replied smoothly. At his confused look, she explained. "While you were out playing with Z'Tem, our mother was explaining politics to me. She said I was more suited to it than you." At that comment, D'Las nodded vigorously. "After the Separatist Wars three thousand years ago, there was a treaty put in place that eventually evolved into the only law the Loorans follow. It essentially says to not destroy without reason."

Throughout that particular lecture, D'Las's face had been smoothing, understanding clearing the creases of confusion away. At the last sentence, however, it twisted in deep confusion again and a type of panic. "But... There was reason! All of those species were horrible."

"I'm the only one that truly knows that, brother."

He shrugged. "So?"

"Look inside yourself. Are there memories other than ours?"

As she instructed, D'Las looked inward. He clearly perceived both himself and his sister, though there was something odd about his perception of V'Let. She was there, consistently present, but even he couldn't access any of her memories. Filing the obvious question away for later, he turned to his other bonds, which were there in abundance. Memories of the last twenty years on Loora filled his mind, the most vivid of which were those belonging to Z'Tem.

He pulled out of the internal wandering, pushing back the Looran genetic memory for another time, and pinned his sister with a hard stare. "Why can't I see your memories?"

V'Let sighed heavily, her exhaustion making itself known with a painful pounding in her temple. "I'm shielded. I taught myself how, around the time we were taken. I didn't want anyone to know."

"Know what?"

"Maybe I didn't want to know myself," she muttered under her breath. "I didn't want them to know what we would be forced to do, to know how utterly horrible these other species could be to each other."

D'Las nodded and sat in front of the secondary console. "What will happen?"

For a moment, V'Let's head lolled to the side and she forced herself to remain conscious. "When we land, they'll detain me." He frowned darkly. "And you will let them."

"Why?"

"Law states that they must hinder or confine forces of destruction. However, they cannot keep me, for we are *tiancai*."

"Okay…" D'Las could hear that there was another point to be made.

V'Let smiled wanly. "An oracle must prove that I am *tiancai* for them to release me."

"What if… What if the oracle won't say it because of the things we've been made to do?"

Her smile turned bitter, knowing that some of the species they'd seen had affected D'Las's reasoning. Not that his point wasn't valid. She had a feeling that some of the oracles could be just as selfish as any one of the lesser malevolent species. "I've thought of that. That's why you absolutely have to find K'Sar."

"K'Sar?"

V'Let fingered the pendant that she still wore idly. "I know you saw the holopic I made. He's one of the oldest living oracles and he was a friend to our mother." There was a twinkle in her eyes that he couldn't interpret.

D'Las and V'Let sat quiet for a few moments, his mind racing and hers shutting down. Then he asked, "How will I find him?"

A light snore answered him.

D'Las smiled softly at his sister, knowing the exhaustion couldn't be delayed any longer. He stood, stretching his tense muscles, and checked all the settings. The route was unchanged and they were still moving at the same speed. He moved to his sister and hefted her onto his shoulder, moving smoothly out of the bridge. He would settle her on her bunk and then nap beside her.

He had a feeling that after they landed, they would be separated for a while.

# CHAPTER FORTY-EIGHT

The lid to the stasis pod opened very slightly, leaving a crack for oxygen to fill Dmitri's lungs. Slowly, over the course of five minutes, the Council member reached consciousness. He inhaled deeply and pushed weakly on the pod lid. In response to the action, the lid swung the rest of the way open but Dmitri merely laid there and breathed.

"Something's wrong," he murmured. He glanced down at the device that allowed him to communicate with the ship, pressing the button while he tried to find the energy to pull himself out of the pod. "Report."

"Looran vessel *Tiancai* had altered course. Set course indicates destination to be Loora. Continue to Earth or follow to Loora?"

Dmitri cleared his throat and forced himself into a sitting position. Now he remembered why he hated going into stasis. His species just wasn't built for that kind of shutdown. "Status of Earth?"

"Unstable."

Dmitri huffed. "What does that mean? Is it destroyed?"

"Planet is intact. The surface is covered in spatial disturbances. Natural disasters."

Dmitri frowned. "Natural disasters?" he echoed uncertainly.

The computer, however, took that to be a question. "Tornadoes, earthquakes, hurricanes, monsoons and tsunamis."

The words themselves didn't make any kind of sense to Dmitri, as his species lived on a temperate planet where the earth did not feel the need to strike out at its inhabitants. "What about the humans?"

There was a pause in which Dmitri assumed the ship was scanning the planet. "Dying by the thousands."

"Any Looran tech on the planet?"

"None distinguishable."

Dmitri hopped in place before forcing himself to subside. Whatever the twins did, they did it without any evidence drawing attention to them. "Follow Looran vessel *Tiancai* and send a subspace transmission to the Looran government."

"Instant or interactive?"

"Interactive."

Dmitri sat in front of the controls, waiting patiently for the transmission to be accepted on the other end. He had an idea that something was happening, a low level of panic emanating along the edge of his mind. Whatever it was, it certainly couldn't be good.

The screen in front of the elderly Zillian flared to life suddenly. "Looran authority of Taicheng D'Tar Yash answering call from Looran vessel *Jhiri*." The so-called man of authority was small and stout for a Looran, though he did somehow project a presence. His skin was a chalky lavender, denoting the fact that he was probably often inside, and his pupils were wider than Dmitri could ever remember the twins' being. Vision problems, Dmitri guessed.

He stood then, bringing his own small stature in full view of the screen. "Hello. My name is Dmitri Andian, Tactical Elder of the Intergalactic Council. Myself, the Council Head and the Diplomatic Elder are en route to your planet. You should expect us in five galactic cycles."

The man—D'Tar, Dmitri reminded himself—grunted softly and reached for something just out of view on his desk. "We don't do business with the Council."

Dmitri inclined his head, expecting as much. He knew that the attack by the Strike Force twenty years ago could not be easily forgotten, though he was congratulating himself internally on the adjustment to the thinking that there were Loorans remaining. "We understand. That's why we have come. We hope to change that." Dmitri cleared his throat, having no clue what was about to happen. "There is also the matter of your Gifted Ones."

D'Tar's face immediately hardened, creases appearing across his countenance. "They will be dealt with. It is an internal matter."

In turn, Dmitri shook his head. "Actually, jurisdiction would fall to the Council if an investigation were to occur. In this matter, we wish to make sure nothing happens to them. Recent events have revealed that their minds were being controlled."

The man on the screen jerked visibly, his reaction so strong that he actually stood. "There is nothing like that in their memories."

Dmitri smiled gently. "There wouldn't be, would there? They have only recently been released from this control through the very brave actions of my own son."

"Oh..." D'Tar's voice had a note of sudden understanding in it, making Dmitri very curious.

"What?"

He sighed deeply. "We only recently received the twins' memories. It hit all of us like a brick." He glanced down, rifling through some papers. "Oh, they'll be arriving tomorrow." He looked back at Dmitri, his blue eyes darkening in a type of sadness that the Zillian recognized. "At least one of them will have to remain incarcerated until you arrive. It will likely be V'Let, as she committed almost all of the destruction."

"Incarcerated?" Dmitri echoed. "Isn't that a little harsh?"

It was D'Tar's turn to give the gentle smile. "We don't have detention confinement here, as our only law prevents destruction. She will remain under my care and will be required to talk with an oracle."

"About what?"

"Anything. Everything. She is still *tiancai*, so she cannot be punished. Not really."

Dmitri nodded. "Alright, then. Five days," he reminded him.

"Oh, Elder Andian?" Dmitri had been leaning over the controls, a half-second away from ending the communication, but looked back at the Looran man. "What of those that had controlled them?"

Dmitri's face hardened, his eyes glinting ice at the thought of Marina and Xavier. "They're dead." With that said, he did end the communication. He then sat down roughly, letting his head fall into his hands. Thinking about his former partners didn't help matters much or thinking about the fact that he was solely responsible for their deaths. It had been scarily easy, using that device he'd created so long ago, so similar to the prototypes that had been used to nullify the communication between the twins when they were so young. This device, fine-tuned over many years, was designed to stop brain activity, which would stop everything else.

"I'm a killer," he murmured softly.

Her voice came, as it had every other time he doubted himself. *It had to be done.*

Dmitri jerked visibly, having forgotten how massive the twins' abilities were. "God, V'Let. You scared me."

*Nothing new.* He could hear the smile in her voice as she said it. *You do realize it had to be done?*

Dmitri inclined his head slightly. "Yes. If I hadn't killed them, their thinking would have been pushed on our successors. Marcus just isn't strong enough to do what I did."

*Oh, I think you underestimate the boy. He did do some very dangerous things for being so young.* There was a pause and Dmitri could almost feel her distraction, as if she was listening to something else. *Speaking of the junior Adepts, you might want to encourage them or something. They're freaking out a little.* That said, he could feel her mental presence dissipate and he smiled goofily.

He pressed the button on his device again. "Record holo-message and send to Council Court, care of Marcus Andian." He paused and cleared his throat. "Altered route to Loora. Planet Earth not destroyed, planet Loora still thriving. Explanation to follow upon return. Side note—V'Let says to stop freaking out. Be well, all of you."

"Transmission sent," the ship's computer intoned. "Continuing route to Loora."

Dmitri nodded sharply and returned to his stasis pod. By the time he woke again, he knew he would lose control of the ship. He smiled. Everything was good.

# CHAPTER FORTY-NINE

Z'Tem woke suddenly, craning his neck to glance at the clock near his head. It was barely past sunrise and part of him desperately wanted to disappear back into unconsciousness. However, as soon as he registered the shadow standing over him, sleep was no longer an issue.

He jerked spasmodically and fell out of his bed, carrying a good portion of the sheet and blanket with him. "K'Sar!" he called out harshly. He stood with as much dignity as he could muster, the sheet and blanket falling away to reveal him to be bare-chested and wearing lounge pants. "Do you ever sleep?"

K'Sar tilted his head to the side, his eyes rolling away in the same direction in thought. "Not often. I don't require much rest."

Z'Tem moved smoothly past the oracle and found a shirt to wear, pulling it on as he turned back to face him. "And why are we up at the crack of dawn?"

"They'll be landing at the port... soon."

"The docks?" the younger Looran corrected idly.

K'Sar shrugged. "It's all the same thing."

Z'Tem frowned deeply as they moved their conversation to the living room, his thoughts a little deeper. He knew from the memories that the twins had literally done the unforgivable, broken the only law the Loorans cared about. However, they were also the Gifted Ones, the progeny that cannot be punished. They were the salvation, the key evolutionary step.

"V'Let will be held."

He arched an eyebrow at the oracle, the day before having taught him to stop asking how the older man knew the inner questions that he always had yet to ask. "Just V'Let?"

K'Sar bit his upper lip momentarily. "She is the one that actually committed the 'atrocities'," he replied. He tilted his head again, this time his eyes staring ahead at something Z'Tem couldn't see. "Something happened recently but I can't see what it is. Yet."

Z'Tem frowned up at the tall Looran. "Why not?"

The oracle reached out in front of him, seeming to grasp the air in front of him before lowering his hand. "Whoever made a change, their mind is blocked somehow." He tilted his head very slightly and his pupils widened with a kind of precision. After a moment, his mouth formed a small "o" of understanding. "He's in Looran transport."

Z'Tem's frowned deepened slightly. "That's... unexpected."

K'Sar merely responded with an enigmatic smile.

That was when the front door burst open.

# CHAPTER FIFTY

They had arrived three hours early, pushing the engines in an attempt to elude the Looran authorities. It had been D'Las's idea, a last-ditch effort to save his sister, and V'Let had let him with a small smile on her face the entire time. It had irked him.

Upon their arrival, there had been a short Looran man waiting, echoing his sister's own small smile. Seeing it on more than his sister, he recognized it for what it was—serenity. The same smile the old witch always had on her face.

After a moment, the man's face shifted, twitching to show pleasant surprise, and V'Let giggled. She then turned to face her brother. "You should have known better," she murmured into his shoulder as she hugged him. "This is Loora. Someone always knows." She stepped back, giving him an encouraging nod. "I have to stay at Governor D'Tar's home until our friends from the Council arrive."

D'Las's pupils widened slightly. "They're following us here?"

V'Let inclined her head slightly and made a vague gesture toward the governor. "Apparently, he's already spoken to Dmitri." Her face softened slightly. "You have to remember that Loora isn't like other places we've been. Our species has long evolved past criminal punishment and cruelty. You can come see me anytime but I really need you to have K'Sar come see me."

D'Las smirked. "Tall guy from your vid manipulation?" As she nodded, something occurred to him and his smiled slipped. "Where can I find him?"

She smiled that vague, knowing smile and turned away. *Find Z'Tem. Everything else will follow.*

248

D'Las growled softly. *I hate it when you do that.*

*I know.* The comment was followed by a laugh, making him smile.

He watched as his sister took the governor's hand and they boarded a land transport, speeding away before he finally turned. Staring at the roads before him, he tried to remember where Z'Tem's family home in Taicheng was. After a moment, he sighed and closed his eyes, forcing himself to stop thinking. His memory of Loora was very vague and faded, only boosted by V'Let own memory. However, she had only been to Z'Tem's home in Taicheng once and she had been deep in her studies then.

He opened his eyes and realized he was walking, that he had been walking for a few minutes now. He allowed himself to continue at a relaxed pace, glancing to the south to see the sunrise. The light skim of clouds at the edge of the horizon added lavender to the progression of orange and yellow cast across the sky. D'Las smiled slightly and urged himself to hurry to a house that he knew was near but couldn't properly remember.

He turned a corner and suddenly memories flooded fresh into his mind, as if someone had refreshed an InfoNet page and forced him to really look. Three lots down, there was a modest house, a house that seemed to scream "home away from home". Without allowing any other thoughts to interfere, he ran to the house and began to knock frantically on the front door.

In his excitement, he didn't notice that his power opened the closed door.

*Calm,* his sister murmured into his head. *Control.*

D'Las stopped then, pressing his hands into the skin above his eyes, and watched as the door rebounded off an adjacent wall. A violet hand reached out to stop it from closing again from the other side. It seemed that there were suddenly two people in view—a Looran with his similar build but a leaner structure and then another, much taller man. Everything about the latter man seemed stretched. His skin was sallow and very pale and something about him seemed very old.

Another memory assaulted his senses in that moment.

{D'Las and V'Let were barely three years of age when he left. V'Let had tried to make him say goodbye, tugging him with one hand while clutching her stuffed singing bird with the other. "You have to say bye, Lasso. We won't see him again for a long time."

Even at a young age, D'Las had the arrogance of a prodigy. Everyone said he was because he had more power than his sister. When he wasn't acting with what he would later recognize as foolish behavior, he knew the truth — that his sister was just as powerful as him but in a different way. She was different and had learned from a very early age how to hide that from the others. However, they could never hide from each other.

"He'll be back in a few years. He said so. He promised." D'Las secretly hated how much like a child he had sounded then.

V'Let had only shaken her head and left him in peace. He'd noticed even then but paid no mind. She'd seen something very far away and she was always very good at making connections. It was a skill he didn't care for.

He watched through a crack in his bedroom door as his mother and sister said their farewells to his father. His father had always been very tall, taller even than their mother. He always thought that maybe one day he would be that tall.}

In all those years, he'd never changed. His skin was that sallow mauve that both of the twins' skin tended to turn when they were on the ship for too long. However, that very tall man seemed so very comfortable in that pale tone.

Had he been living in a cave or something?

As the thought flowed through his mind with a kind of unending clarity, D'Las saw the tall man—K'Sar M'Kaz—smile as if in response. "I have."

D'Las rushed forward as if he couldn't control himself, his arms wrapping around the man in an instant reaction that he had cultivated by spending a lot of one-on-one time with his sister. "Oh, Gods above. It's been so long."

Z'Tem cleared his throat after a moment, suppressing the smile that was threatening to blossom across his face. It was odd, how familiar it seemed. "Excuse me. What's going on?"

With a nervous laugh, D'Las detached himself from K'Sar. "She knew," he murmured softly. He reached out as if to touch the taller man's face before forcing himself to pull away. "She knew even then that we wouldn't see you for a very long time."

K'Sar smiled gently. "How is she? Last I felt, she seemed so fragile."

D'Las scoffed. "She's stronger than you know. Definitely stronger than me."

Huffing in exasperation, Z'Tem placed himself between the two Loorans. "You know each other?"

D'Las cast a sharp look at K'Sar before returning to face his best friend. He looked so defensive. "K'Sar is my father. He left to return to the Oracles when we were three."

Z'Tem took a step back, arching a thin eyebrow. "Say what?"

# CHAPTER FIFTY-ONE

V'Let laughed softly. D'Tar glanced at her sharply as he unlocked the door to his home. She was an odd creature, this *tiancai*, and he suspected her brother was the same. Once they were inside, he had some questions for her. Of course, she didn't have to tell him anything. She was only required to speak to the oracle she chose but he idly hoped she would allow his curiosity to be sated.

"This is a nice home," she commented, her voice as low as her laughter had been. She gazed at her surroundings, her eyes still dancing.

"Thank you." He placed a hand at the middle of her back and led her to a very organized sitting room. It was covered in deep blues and greens, colors that calmed the governor. "How would you feel about a chat?"

V'Let inclined her head slightly in the affirmative. "Of course." She allowed him to lead her to a high-backed green chair while he sat in a blue chair of similar make. She looked at her surroundings again and he realized that she was actually looking for something specific. "No wife?"

D'Tar felt the familiar lump rise in his throat, blocking his speech for a moment, and the pinpricks of pressure at his tear glands. "She died." He winced slightly at the roughness of his voice.

V'Let frowned deeply. "My condolences," she murmured. "Datong?"

He nodded, the gesture urging a single tear to roll down his violet face. "A shopping trip in the Great City of Unity. It was her first time there."

She closed her eyes, letting his pain flow over her. "Did everyone in Datong die during the strike?"

D'Tar nodded. "Yes. Every living Looran barring you and your brother."

Her eyelids squeezed together harder, internally aligning the information but trying to push the truth of it away at the same time. "Gods above," she murmured softly under her breath. After a moment, she opened her eyes and D'Tar could see the black pupils had overwhelmed the rest of her eyes. "Was it the Oracles that made the Strike Force believe it was the entire planet?"

D'Tar nodded, belatedly realizing that she couldn't see him. The dilation of the pupils to that extent was like temporarily blinding yourself. "Yes. How can you do that to yourself?"

V'Let cleared her throat and allowed her pupils to return to their natural state. It was an odd sensation for the governor to suddenly see all that blue in her eyes, quite a difference from the black. "Governor Yash, there are some things you have to understand. Being out there and forced to do those horrible things, I have changed. In truth, I probably more belong to the Intergalactic Council than to Loora. I have seen horrible things, things that make the completely false memory of my burning planet pale in comparison." In the heat of her statement, she had stood and towered over the shorter man. Realizing her position, she forced herself to move to a nearby window so as to not physically undermine the governor's authority. "I won't be able to stay here but D'Las needed to come home."

D'Tar barely maintained his calm but managed to stay seat. "But... You're *tiancai*. You belong on Loora."

She turned to face him again. "I remember what it was like then, Governor. D'Las is the powerhouse, the prodigy. I'm so much less."

He clearly heard the sadness in her voice, the thickening of the lining of her throat. "No one ever said that."

In turn, V'Let laughed bitterly. "Definitely not. However, it was in everyone's head." She stopped, bowing her head slightly. "They're right. I can't wield power on his level. My talents lay elsewhere."

The governor's curiosity piqued at that. "Where would that be?"

She smirked knowingly. "That would be telling." Her eyes skirted her surroundings before settling on him again. "Do you have a subspace communicator?"

D'Tar nodded. "In the guest room."

Her lips smoothed into a genuine smile. "Thank you. I'll remain there until K'Sar arrives."

The governor watched the girl leave the sitting room for her guest room and mouthed "K'Sar?" before putting his head in his hands.

# CHAPTER FIFTY-TWO

Marcus was pacing in the library when one of the Parvini approached him. "Master Andian?" it called out softly.

He nearly tripped on the next about-face when the Parvini's voice broke through the fog that was Marcus's panic. Regaining sure footing, he cleared his throat and cast an expectant look on the small creature. "Yes?"

The Parvini scuttled closer to him. "There's a message from your father. I have it waiting for you in the communications room."

Marcus sighed heavily and followed the Parvini out of the room. They separated in front of the com room when he had to continue inside and the smaller creature disappeared to other corners of the house, supposedly to clean and organize. He knew that one had an unusual form of Parvini obsession-compulsion in regards to cleanliness, something the others assured him was quite odd but not debilitating to their species.

Once he was in front of the large console that the room contained, he punched the command to listen to his father's message. After that, he tilted his head and squinted his eyes slightly in confusion, idly ordering the message to be played again. And then two more times after that.

"Wait, what?" His question was soft but echoed in the room that was much too large after the Separator had been removed. His mind worked frantically as he filed away the message to show the Trellick siblings later and allowed the com screen to dim.

He had turned away, his feet having already taken him halfway to the door, when the screen flared to life again. "Incoming transmission. Sender and location unknown."

Marcus spun on his heel, glaring slightly at the computer. "How is that even possible?"

"Insufficient inquiry. Rephrase."

Marcus rolled his eyes and clenched his teeth, unknowingly emulating the Looran sibling that he so feared. "How can you not know the name and location of the transmission?"

"That information has been blocked."

He sighed and sat in a nearby seat, the worry of the last days obvious on his face. "I thought the Council saw everything," he muttered.

"All passcodes have been accepted. Will you accept the transmission?"

He shook his head, belying his actual answer. "Sure."

"Hi!" The chirpy voice on the other end of the transmission was not what he had been expecting. A glance upward told Marcus that it was V'Let and he consciously gripped the underside of his chair so as to not fall off of it in shock. He realized quite suddenly he hadn't ever heard her voice before. He recognized her, however, from the propaganda posters plastered around the Central Planets.

A part of Marcus desperately wanted to run screaming from the room but the largely rational portion of him forced a completely phony smile on his face. "V'Let. How are you?"

The Looran girl tilted her head slightly, her bright blue eyes seeming to pierce in his mind. He idly remembered his father commenting on how eerie she could be sometimes. Now, he was thinking that "eerie" was an understatement. She didn't speak until the smile slipped off his face.

"How's the new regime of universe-changing individuals?" He detected a hint of hardness in her voice and something else. Something that trembled. Could she be afraid?

Marcus took his turn at eerie, narrowing his eyes in concentration at the Looran. At close scrutiny, he could tell she looked drained and fear showed in her eyes beneath a thick layer of hardened worry. Her skin had a definite grayish tone and the whites at the very edge of her eyes looked bloodshot. He also noticed her pupils kept changing size.

In response, he shrugged, an attempt at nonchalance. "They're not their predecessors, that's for sure."

V'Let laughed weakly. "So they're not planning to take over the universe and destroy everything that stands in their way?"

He knew it was a joke but he was also very aware that she was searching for assurance. "They're really not." The irrational fear that flooded his system any time either of the twins were mentioned melted a little when he saw the relief cover her face. Maybe this was the solution to that fear. "If anything, I'd say they're kind of ashamed."

She chuckled softly and pressed her hands with firm pressure on her eyes. "I think I should tell you that my brother and I are not plotting on some kind of revenge on the second generation."

Marcus arched an eyebrow. "How did you know about that?"

She answered him with a heavy sigh. "I just do."

"You look tired."

An ironic look passed over her face. "Thanks," she muttered sarcastically. "I can't sleep. My Oracle should be here soon."

Marcus frowned, the term familiar but her usage odd. "Oracle?" he echoed.

"On Loora, they're like lawyers." She rolled her eyes and then launched into an explanation. "They can still see the future, although it's more like seeing the connections that lead to the future. But we don't really need laws per se on Loora. We just have one unbreakable code, which I broke."

Marcus leaned forward, his interest in Looran culture obvious. This was a species that had formerly been believed to be nearly extinct and now here it was, blossoming before his eyes. "What code?"

V'Let smirked. "Destruction is forbidden."

Marcus coughed, choking on almost solid surprise. Almost everything she had done was legal by Council standards, he knew. He'd read the case reports himself, combing through them to try to understand them once. That had been during his education when he had been possessed by this need to explain those that were supposedly the Scourge of the Universe. However, Council law clearly stated that any species that showed signs of forceful dominance or dangerous bigotry had to be eliminated before reaching star travel; if they reached this technology before these tendencies were found, treaties and restrictions had to be made.

"Why?" he finally managed to ask.

Her smirk transformed to a slight curve of her lips, a gentle condescension conveyed there. "Destruction hinders evolution and that's what our species cares about. You must complete the evolutionary path, despite the fact that that path never ends." She sighed and her eyes flicked off-screen suddenly. "Oh, gotta go."

The screen went blank.

"That was a revelation."

Marcus squeaked shrilly and jumped out of his chair, whirling to come face-to-face with Xen. The effeminate Kretoran chuckled at his reaction. "How long have you been there?" Marcus demanded.

"Long enough," he answered simply. "I thought you were afraid of the twins."

Marcus laughed nervously. "I am." After a moment, he narrowed his eyes at Xen. "If you don't remember, we were all panicking just two days ago. We shouldn't."

Xen arched an eyebrow. "Why not?"

The psychologist smirked slightly. "Their planet's not dead. They're not the last of their kind. They'll more likely than not stay on Loora."

Xen frowned deeply. "That doesn't make sense."

"What doesn't make sense?"

Marcus refrained from jumping out of his skin once again when Railey's voice followed her brother's voice, walking smoothly into the room. She still wore her military officer's uniform, a dark red and black ensemble with clean lines. Her eyes pinned them in askance.

Xen cleared his throat in such a way that it was clear to Marcus that she had startled him as well. "Apparently, the Looran planet wasn't destroyed."

Immediately, frown lines cut deeply into Railey's forehead. "That's odd. Even Dmitri was sure that the planet had been razed completely."

In that moment, certain facts connected inside Marcus's head. Loorans had been known for their ability to affect the brain; the report that Dmitri had buried about the attack on Loora said that they had been on the planet no more than an hour whereas the attack on other species had taken at least six hours; the Looran vessel in which his father traveled now was found more than five years after the attack.

"They made them believe that," he murmured softly.

The Trellick siblings turned to gaze at him as one. "What?"

Marcus cleared his throat. "The Loorans are mentalists of an astronomical capability. They could've made the ISF believe the planet was razed, that everyone was dead so that they would leave. In the amount of time that they were likely there, they probably only actually destroyed one very large city, maybe some of the surrounding area."

Railey's eyes went wide. "That does make sense."

After that, they went their separate ways for a while. Marcus didn't mention his suspicion that V'Let wouldn't stay on Loora. There was something about her that couldn't be held down. Internally, he hoped they could talk again.

On a similar subject, how could he kill the Galaxy Killer propaganda?

# CHAPTER FIFTY-THREE

As they walked across the residential district of Taicheng, K'Sar eyed D'Las. He walked behind him and Z'Tem, watching how they interacted. In a way, it was like they had never been apart, chatting easily as only best friends could. Of course, there was the other side of that coin. Every once in a while, Z'Tem would ask a question and D'Las would shut him out, closing like an angry clam. K'Sar was relatively sure that these questions either had to do with V'Let or the memories.

It was understandable, the boy's reaction. He had aided somewhat in the destruction in multiple other planets and most kinds of destruction were completely unnatural to a Looran. K'Sar wasn't entirely sure how V'Let had managed, taking the brunt of pain and destruction and ending up almost completely unscathed.

At heart, he knew that V'Let was no longer what the Elders would call a true Looran. They might even go so far as to demand that she leave. However, her status as *tiancai* meant that she didn't have to listen to anyone apart from her brother and her chosen Oracle. All in all, this was a complicated mess. The *tiancai* were unimpeachable, the law stated that clearly, and this was the first time any Looran had openly defied the Code in two thousand years.

D'Las turned to look at him. "Stop worrying."

K'Sar inclined his head, chuckling internally at the simplicity of his statement. After twenty years of his son having been a dead link, it was refreshing and somewhat unnerving for him to be an open receiving line again. Not that his powers could ever reach as far as his sister's...

"We're here." Z'Tem's voice broke through K'Sar's cloud of thought.

At that point, K'Sar paid attention to his outer environment again.

The house in front of them was magnificently large and built from the cold stone found in the far north. The governor's home conveyed both his expensive taste and the majesty of his authority.

The older man led them inside. Whereas Z'Tem had been the only one that knew how to get to the governor's home, K'Sar was the only one with the authority to freely traverse its interior. Even the oracle had to admit that even the furnishings were marvelous, but the feel of the house matched the temperature of its stone. He knew that D'Tar probably would never move past what happened to his wife, roughly the same thing that had happened to K'Sar's own.

K'Sar closed his eyes, clenching himself against the memory that threatened to assault him at that thought. He had returned to pleasantly smiling when they found Governor Yash in his sitting room, idly tracing the edge of a crystal glass that held a golden liquid. The oracle cleared his throat softly to break through whatever thoughts in which the governor was trapped.

D'Tar glanced up at the noise, a small smile blossoming over his face at the sight of his guests. He clearly saw the question on K'Sar's face. "Guest room, west wing."

V'Let's location answered, K'Sar turned around and began his journey there, only stopping when he realized D'Las and Z'Tem were following him. Facing them, he shook his head negatively. "I have to talk to her alone first." He gestured back to the sitting room. "Keep the governor company." He laughed sharply when they both grimaced, each face an exact mimicry of the other.

He continued down a hall, reaching out with his senses to find his daughter. There was a tentative response, light as a feather, and he noticed a door at the end of the hall open. He frowned to himself as he hurried to the room beyond the door. Despite his many years, K'Sar remained one of the most sensitive to power usage on this entire planet. However, he had barely felt V'Let use power to open her door.

Very interesting.

He entered the room, trepidation showing in his movements. Whereas meeting D'Las had been a surprise, he was nervous about meeting V'Let. He wasn't entirely sure as to the reason but he knew that the feeling closed up his throat.

"Hi, Dad," she greeted softly.

K'Sar could only stare. She was almost an exact copy of her mother, slightly taller with a narrower structure. After a moment, he cleared his throat. "I understand you chose me as your Oracle."

He could only watch as her expression dropped, almost as if someone had slapped her. After a moment, though, hardness presented itself in her eyes and she gazed directly at him. He felt a slight pinching under the surface of his mental shield and suddenly knew what she was doing. The pressure that had begun building left before he could react and her mouth formed a small, breathless "o".

K'Sar reacted in the only way he knew how. He was heavily shielded and had spent more than five years alone in endless caverns. "Find what you were looking for?" His voice was terribly hard and sharp, so much that he almost cringed at the sound.

For a moment, she reacted as if she were still just a little girl, wincing visibly and taking a step back. Then, lightning-quick, her expression hardened again. "You can't scare me." She cleared her throat and the untouchable look melted away. "I didn't know I looked like her," she murmured softly.

K'Sar frowned. "Don't you have memories of her?" He moved around her to sit on the bed. He was antsy at the sudden dynamic change.

V'Let sighed and had to repress a yawn. "My clearest memory of my mother is the worst kind of memory."

He nodded. "We need to discuss your trial with the Elders."

She scoffed lightly. "They can't do anything. I'm not sure there's anything they could do if I weren't *tiancai*."

K'Sar laughed softly and then smothered it by clearing his throat. "They can ask you to leave."

She shrugged and finally sat next to him. "I probably will anyway."

He turned his head sharply to look at her. "Why?"

Her laughter was soft and hard at the same time. In a way, that was an answer alone. Loorans weren't hard really. Yes, the Oracles didn't put much counsel in emotion. However, no Looran living had endured true malevolence. The last time Loorans had been violent to one another had been during the Wars. Cruelty and sadism just weren't in their nature.

Her voice was soft when she finally spoke. "Part of it is that I'm not like the rest of them. I've always been different, more like you and I know they barely respect you."

He grimaced at the statement, true as it may be. "And the rest?"

At that, V'Let smiled broadly. In that moment, he could see who she really was. Confident and almost enthusiastic, she was like a subdued version of her brother. "I've seen a lot of the universe and there's still so much I haven't seen. There's something odd about it all." After she noticed his look of askance, she continued. "It's like the universe isn't complete."

K'Sar gazed at her, his eyes curious. As he spoke, he forced a note of skepticism into his voice. "Well, the universe is always expanding. I dare say, it will never be complete."

She sighed roughly. "Stop being intentionally dense." She stopped for a moment, her eyes darting slightly as she pulled her thoughts together. "When we were on Earth, before Marcus destroyed the contract, I discovered the planetary entities."

"Entities?" K'Sar echoed uncertainly. The spirit of Loora had never really mentioned others and he had never left the planet. But why wouldn't it tell him about this?

V'Let gazed at the deep frown on her father's face. "The entities are selfish and usually look down on lesser species. The Earth entity only told me what I needed to know but it was weak enough to make a deal." She watched alarm flash across his face and wondered at the story behind that expression. "Don't worry. The Earth is a life-giver. It needed me to remove a binding."

"What kind?"

"A lineage binding with disturbingly far-reaching effects." V'Let remembered the look on Rosalie's face when the neverending vision of alternate realms stopped. "The Earth has two Guardians. When one was bound, it affected the rest. The Earth had been holding everything together for almost a thousand years."

At that piece of information, K'Sar's frown shifted, sending a different kind of message. "How did it happen?"

V'Let giggled. "Witches." Her father's eyebrows went high at that. "They call it magic. It's actually advanced science." She shrugged, her smile slipping away. "They cursed a man who had stopped them from doing something horrible. The binding carried down through the ages, was in the body of a girl about my age before I unbound her. It completely undid the balance of the planet, essentially turned the other Guardian into a useless shell and the entity broke. Sort of." She sighed again. "It's difficult to explain."

K'Sar put an arm around her and squeezed lightly. "Try."

She rewarded him with a slight upturn of her mouth. "Even after the binding was released, the entity was still very sad. I think it was supposed to fix something that was lost a long time ago." She put her face into her hands and groaned. "It's like I can almost make the connection. I don't have enough information."

Pulling her into a loose hug, K'Sar smiled softly. No matter how hard she had gotten, V'Let was like the rest of her family. She wanted to fix things, even if she had to leave everything she knew to do it. There wasn't much to fix on Loora, hadn't been for millennia. "I think I have an idea how to get that information," he told her. "First, though, we really need to talk about how your trial will go."

# CHAPTER FIFTY-FOUR

"How much did you hate Marina?"

Xen was shocked at the sudden question. He had just returned from a long day of straightening out the mess his predecessor had made of her contacts and files and stood in the kitchen, silently watching four of the Parvini. He refused to answer the Zillian psychologist in favor of continuing to watch the small creatures.

He had never told anyone but he'd always been fascinated by the Parvini. They were the smallest sentient creatures he'd ever seen, though the Network confirmed that planets he had never visited had things that were smaller, tiny even. On average, the Parvini barely reached his hip and had a body type that made you think they were plump and slender at the same time. Their very long ears with rounded points were pulled back by large, thick elastic bands. Otherwise, they flopped around and got in the way.

"Come on." Marcus moved around to be in Xen's line of sight. "I know you hated her. Railey hated her father. I've spent years hating my father."

Xen rolled his eyes and saw one of the Parvini snicker almost silently. "I didn't really hate Marina, I don't think. She was a mess, an all-around horrible and soulless person." He shrugged. "I don't know. Maybe I did."

Marcus frowned at the man. "Do you not know?"

Xen sighed, his bright eyes agitated. "No. I mean, she was over-bearing for sure. But… hate takes so much effort. I don't see the point."

Marcus's lips curled into a smile. "Really?" The other man knew that was a rhetorical query, so he remained silent. "Then, are you even actually afraid of them?"

"The twins?" It was Xen's turn for rhetoric, for he knew very well to whom Marcus was referring. "Not really." It caught his attention, though, when the Parvini turned to listen to their conversation.

Marcus's back was to them and he blinked in the half-second that curious surprise flashed across Xen's face. He just tilted his head at the new media rep. "I don't get it. I was horribly frightened of them, even with a father assuring me there was nothing to be frightened of."

Xen fought the urge to roll his eyes again. The difficulty of repressing the gesture assured him that he would always be an adolescent inside. "That's because you're neurotic." He sighed roughly, now trying to divert his attention from the Parvini. "Why are we talking about this anyway?"

Marcus shrugged, a bad attempt at looking nonchalant. "I think we should kill the Galaxy Killer propaganda, trying to set it up as false. Or something."

Xen's anxiety began to show at that. He saw that Marcus noticed but apparently he filed the expression away for later. Maybe he even thought his anxiety was at the thought of destroying such a large, all-encompassing piece of media. However, his true anxiety was from the reaction of the Parvini behind the psychologist. At the mention of the destruction of that propaganda, the Parvini had smiled this small, slow expression, each of them echoing the rest. He didn't know if he thought it was cute or creepy.

"I mean," Marcus continued, unaware of the activity about him. He cleared his throat, slightly at unease at the growing wariness on Xen's face. "I know V'Let will not stay on Loora. It's not in her. She shouldn't have to endure social leprosy if she comes to Alpha Sector. And... I don't know how to deal with all this media complexity."

Xen laughed nervously, his eyes on the Parvini as they turned back to their various kitchen activities. The more he watched them, the more unnerved he got. He forced himself to concentrate on the conversation at hand. "Okay. I'll try to figure something out."

Marcus just nodded and left, his strides quick and sure.

Xen's eyes quickly darted between each of the Parvini, a nervous tic jumping on his upper cheek. "Did I imagine that?" His voice was low and sharp.

The sound of soft footsteps and brush of the weather seal under the kitchen doors against the floor caused him to look behind him. The other two Parvini had entered, one silently closing the doors and the other coming up to him and gesturing at a stool.

"Please sit, Master Trellick."

A feeling of vertigo rushed through Xen as he watched the Parvini gather around him. If he didn't know better, it would have seemed like some type of conversation passed between them silently. The Parvini weren't telepathic, were they?

In one odd moment, they all glanced at the camera that watched the kitchen and then dispersed to their various activities, leaving the two that hadn't been there to begin with. The one that had closed the door grabbed Xen's hand and urged him to a standing position, keeping an unnaturally tight grip on the man's hand. The one that had urged him to a seat gestured silently for him to follow and exited the kitchen.

Xen's gaze shifted to the small creature holding his hand. His face must have showed his anxiety, for the Parvini smiled and tilted its head toward the other. Somehow assuaged by that, he allowed himself to be led.

Within moments, they were climbing the staircase. In all the confusion within his mind, Xen felt a kind of calm. When he focused on the Parvini leading him by the hand, he realized it was female, a prepubescent girl in fact. With a shock, he remembered this one to be Marina's favorite servant, the only Parvini allowed to step inside her private chambers. "Because she's so small I can pretend there's nothing really there," the dead woman had told him once.

Xen swallowed a thick layer of bile that rose in his throat at the thought. The way Marina had treated her staff had always irked him deeply. He'd grown in a household that prided itself on strictures and discipline, always different, always two steps left of the middle. It was something that made him stand out against the comparison to his militant sister.

He had always loved the arts and he seemed to be perfectly in place in the media. He loved the attention and was very adept at leading their focus. The truth of it was that living with his father had prepared him for pretending. Pretending to be something else, to not understand, to not see or hear whatever he shouldn't.

But he did.

The sudden stillness was thick when Xen finally came back to himself and noticed it. He and the two Parvini were standing in front of a door on the third floor. He arched an eyebrow at the larger creature and tilted his head very slightly at the door. The Parvini, in return, merely gestured at the door and bent slightly at the waist.

Slightly apprehensive, Xen pressed the flat of his free hand against the door paneling. A small whoosh of sound and the door opened slowly, the lights within flickering on. Stepping inside, he realized they had led him to the artifact room, the only room in the entire house that didn't have a watchful camera.

Once inside, he turned to face the Parvini. The door closed languidly behind the taller one. "What exactly is going on?"

An odd noise erupted from the mouth of the taller Parvini. A moment of consideration let Xen know that it was a laugh, though muffled. "You see us, Xenith."

Xen cringed at his given name. He had shortened it legally to Xen before he was even in secondary education. To cover his reaction, he scoffed at the small creature. "Of course I do."

The smaller Parvini that still clutched his hand giggled in response. "Silly-face. Papa means you see us for who we really are." Her voice was high-pitched and childish, making Xen realize yet again that this particular Parvini was not yet grown.

The older Parvini made a hushing sound at what was apparently his daughter but for the Kretoran, confusion still reigned. He knew something in the statement was eluding him. "Who you really are?" he echoed. "What does that mean?"

The small man sighed and made an odd, somehow encompassing gesture with his hands. "What does the entirety of Kretor—the entirety of the Alpha Sector, for that matter—think of our species?"

Xen was slightly distracted by the fact that the Parvini had referred to this planet by its name. Most people referred to the allied planets within the Alpha Sector as the Central Planets or Kretor itself as Council Central. After a moment, he forced himself to concentrate on the Parvini's question.

"Servants. They all think of you as servants." He laughed a little. "Beyond that, I don't think they really think of you at all." There was a thick pause as Xen allowed the underlying meaning to become clear. "You're not servants?"

The little girl giggled again. "Not as such."

The older Parvini shot her a sharp look, softened somewhat by the love and humor in his own eyes. "The Parvini believe in the importance of subservience. Our sister race is the Loora."

Xen's eyes went wide. "But..." His mind went over the statistics of Loorans that his sister had been repeating over the last few days: slender and taller than Kretorans with a violet skin tone. The Parvini, on the other hand, were short and a touch squat with an odd skin tone similar to powder blue. "They're so..." His free hand rose to a good half-foot above his own height. "And you're…" He pried his other hand free of the girl's and hovered it above her head at what was approximately the other's height.

The older Parvini frowned at Xen softly. "Suffice to say that it is hard to explain and that we can feel the Loorans as much as we can feel another member of our own species." He cleared his throat softly. "There was a girl born some time ago to Loora that can realign the connections on which the universe depends. She needs to be free to do this."

Frown lines creased the Kretoran's forehead. "What connections?" He paused, the hint becoming clear as his brain worked further. "V'Let?"

The girl giggled again. "See? I told you he'd get it… eventually."

With a glance at his daughter, the older Parvini answered Xen instead. "Yes, V'Let. She is the first Looran in many centuries to be able to withstand what your predecessors did to her and come out the other side intact."

Xen's frown deepened. "What about D'Las, her brother?"

The elder's lips curled into a thoughtful smirk. "He never endured anything personally. He felt the echo through his sister. She knew he could never survive it."

The planes of Xen's face smoothed out except for shallow lines of confusion around his brow. "He couldn't?"

"Loorans as a whole are not built to withstand pain. They are frail creatures, nearly on par with Serrian fragility." Marina was a Serrian, Xen knew, everything about her extremely frail barring her alcohol tolerance. "V'Let, however, has managed magnificent shielding at a young age. She did feel the pain of the punishments…" The Parvini paused and it looked like he was searching for the words that would make sense to Xen. "However, it was more like she felt an echo of an echo of the actual pain."

"So…" Xen looked back and forth between the girl and her father. "You're asking me to kill the Galaxy Killer propaganda?"

The Parvini's smirk smoothed into a genuine smile. "Yes. The quicker, the better."

# CHAPTER FIFTY-FIVE

Z'Tem stood in front of Governor Yash's guest room door, his hand halfway raised to knock on the door. It had been twenty hours since K'Sar had had his talk with her, after which they were given strict orders to let her sleep. The governor was instructing D'Las on basic politics—Looran politics, anyway. He had asked Z'Tem to wake up his sister.

After another unnecessary moment of deliberation, he finally knocked sharply on the wood of the door. Almost immediately, the door opened to reveal V'Let. He was shocked to see her height almost matched his own after years of being around Marta. Her skin and hair perfectly matching her brother's with the exception of the length of her hair. Looking at her eyes, though, he realized something was off.

V'Let arched her eyebrow at Z'Tem. "Where's Lasso?"

He shook himself mentally, deciding he would tackle the state of her pupils later. "He's talking to D'Tar in the sitting room. I think, about politics."

She snickered softly. "He's hopeless when it comes to politics."

Z'Tem shrugged. "Politics for Loora isn't really difficult. We officially separated from the Council after the attack on Datong. I guess it's more like looking after our own."

She sighed at the mention of the city that had once been her home. "It wasn't sanctioned, you know."

He gazed at her, trying to find the meaning in her words without her having to explain. After a moment, he gave up. In essence, V'Let was unreadable. At least, she couldn't be read in the way that he was used to reading others. "What wasn't?"

"The strike against Loora. It was supposed to be fun." She spat out the last word, her tone suggesting a different definition than the word itself implied. "The Intergalactic Strike Force was being dismantled, Council orders, because of an 'unfortunate accident'. However, Loorans were considered dangerous, especially in congruence to the Adepts' ultimate plan."

He moved past her into the room, taking the liberty of sitting on her bed. "Can you explain it to me, all the horrible memories?"

V'Let smiled softly and nodded. "The burning of Datong occurred just after our fifth birthday and I was alone with Mama. She died that night."

Z'Tem nodded. "In the wreckage, we found her body. We thought it was the structure had crushed her. Later, an examiner found a deep cut in her chest. She probably bled out before the house fell."

She bit back a quiet sob and nodded. "A concussion blast from a nearby explosion shattered the kitchen window. It would have been me." She paused and physically shook her head before continuing in a different vein. "We were wandering in the streets when they found us and took us."

"Who?"

"The Adepts." Her eyes rolled to the side in memory. "On the trip back to their trial, I called them that. They liked it, especially when I told them why." She caught his arched eyebrow and answered the obvious question. "They were very good at hiding their true faces from the rest of the Council."

Z'Tem nodded. "What about the trial?"

V'Let chuckled, a dry tone to the sound. "They were acquitted. They were always very good about covering all their bases."

He held up a hand, stopping her for a moment. "Why is it I can't see this stuff? The genetic memory's all destroying planets and some kind of contract and a lot of sadness and pain."

"First of all, you have to understand that both D'Las and I have very strong coping mechanisms. Lasso shut himself down hard after we were captured. It took me a year just to get him to talk. He blocks and forgets and denies. It took me this long to put him back." She sighed heavily. "On the other hand, I just shield myself from other minds. The only reason the genetic memory picks up anything from me is because when D'Las opened completely, it cracked my shields a little."

Z'Tem frowned but nodded in understanding. "How does the planetary destruction come into it? I mean, you were so young and I can't expect you to have known the law—"

"I did," she said sharply, cutting into the end of his sentence. "I was learning politics before it happened." She cleared her throat. "They tried for a long time to mold us a certain way, make us harder or meaner or maybe just jaded. It didn't work. That's when they finally resorted to something illegal."

"That contract, you mean?" he asked softly.

She nodded. "Blood control is illegal. The Council outlawed it fifty years ago."

He frowned. "That's not very long ago."

"It was kind of a lost taboo. It had been frowned upon for many millennia, considered to be savage and unnecessary." She rolled her eyes, watching his expression mirror what hers had been the first time she read those words. "Then, about sixty years ago, it started to pop up around Council-allied planets. In some cases, people died. The Council head of that time finally placed a law against blood control. He said blood control was too dangerous to be allowed, even in ignorance."

"But they made you sign a contract with your blood?"

V'Let nodded. "And theirs. It made a connection. When we refused to destroy a planet for any reason or tried to extend judgment, the pain came. They would cause the blood to rise to unbearable temperatures, the bones to lose abnormal amounts of mass, sometimes other things that could hurt more."

"Biological punishment?" Z'Tem asked, the sympathetic cringe on his face enough to cause her to pat his hand gently.

"The rest you know," she murmured. "Fifteen planets gone before the Blood Contract was finally destroyed."

"You don't sound too sad about it," he mentioned, an unintended sharp edge to his tone.

V'Let stood abruptly and put space between herself and Z'Tem, taking long strides to stand in front of the subspace com system. "You weren't there," she murmured softly.

Z'Tem stood as well but didn't dare move nearer. From his questioning of D'Las earlier, he knew this was a sensitive subject. "I just want to understand."

After a long moment, she finally turned around to face him. "The last planet was the worst. Maybe because there were more people there and it was so divided a planet. I know that the Adepts sent us to planets that the Council itself had jurisdiction to destroy if they paid attention. They were not nice planets."

"How not nice?"

"Violent, malevolent, sometimes so indifferent it was frightening. It was the indifference that scared Lasso. 'How can they not care?' he said." She paused, shifting her eyes away. "I couldn't answer him."

Z'Tem arched an eyebrow. "Couldn't?"

She shot him a sharp look. "Wouldn't. I could barely understand it and I was hearing it straight from their heads." She sighed, something in her deflating. "Despite our law against destruction, there are those out there that the universe would be better without."

"It's hard for me to believe that."

She harrumphed softly, her eyes sliding languidly away from his. Because he was actually looking, he saw the color of her pinprick pupil shift back to its normal black shade.

"Wait. That was weird."

V'Let darted her gaze back to his own again, her black pupil becoming white. "What was?"

Z'Tem made a vague gesture at his eyes. "Are my pupils white?"

She arched an eyebrow. "Yes…" She glanced over his shoulder at the door behind him before reattaching her gaze to his. "I thought that was normal for you."

"What's normal?" Z'Tem turned to see D'Las's delighted expression. Being back on Loora was good for him.

Not as such for V'Let, it seemed.

"Lasso, come here," she told her brother softly.

The other *tiancai* was next to her in less than a second. His reaction time stunned Z'Tem. Not that it was a large room, but it reminded him of how much even D'Las had changed on a basic level.

"Yeah?"

"This is so strange," V'Let murmured to herself. Louder and directed at her brother, she continued. "Look at our eyes but don't interfere with our line of sight." She reached out and grabbed Z'Tem's shoulders and looked into his eyes.

"Oh, that's so… Your pupils are white, both of you!" He laughed softly. "What's going on?"

V'Let sighed. "There was stuff in Mom's head about it. When she would think about Dad, she would think about things would have been so much better if they had shared the Gaze of Love or something. It has recognized authority over the Elders." She paused. "I think."

It felt like something was blocking Z'Tem's throat. It couldn't be. It was some obscure legends the gurus spread around, the story of your true love. Where the gurus had spoken of it like a legend they hadn't seen, the shamans spoke of it like science. They said the reports of the Gaze had dwindled when the travel stagnancy had set in after the attack on Datong. When he had asked a shaman if it was really true love, the response had been laughter. It was something about the same thing that enabled their genetic memory, something about a perfect genetic match causing the eyes to simulate glowing.

D'Las's bright smile widened further. "Well, this is just awesome. We're home and I have my best friend back and..." He sighed. "Everything's great."

Z'Tem watched at V'Let's head dropped slightly and he could almost feel a large pit of sadness under the surface. "Come on, D'Las," she said to her brother. "Let's sit down. I need to talk to you."

Despite the happy façade he was projecting, Z'Tem could tell that something dark had entered D'Las's eyes and the minute shake of his head. V'Let was right—he was a victim of denial.

# CHAPTER FIFTY-SIX

K'Sar was waiting. He had been waiting patiently for fifteen hours and said patience was beginning to wear thin. It was his fault, really. He had managed to arrive during the Elder's preparatory session that occurred directly before Marta's final test before the Elder tribunal. This particular test generally took about ten hours, at best.

After the session and the test and the probably half-hour statement that followed, the doors opened to reveal a very happy Marta, though she was trying very hard not to show it. Upon noticing K'Sar, she bounced up to him, conveniently forgetting that she didn't like him that much. He hazarded a guess that she was just delighted to see someone that wasn't an Elder. They didn't tend to look kindly on this kind of enthusiasm.

"I made it!" she squealed softly once she felt she was within his earshot.

He stood smoothly and smiled kindly down on her. Sure, he'd been shut away for years but the girl deserved at least one smile for her accomplishment. It wasn't easy to convince the Elders to allow you to study under them and maybe one day become an Oracle yourself. "I see that."

Over the small girl's head, he watched the many members of the tribunal exit the room, barely glancing over at them. He figured most of them were tired. There were very few Loorans that could match his age and only one on the tribunal itself. The Madam Judiciary was one hundred years his senior.

"It was kind of difficult." K'Sar tried very hard to listen to the girl's babble but it had been so very long since he had actually done Oracle studies. Apart from that, the Madam had just exited the doorway, leaning against the frame, and was now merely watching him and waiting. For what, he just wasn't quite aware. "I thought I knew everything, living with the shamans as I did. But there's so much more… Are you listening?"

The Madam made a soft sound, a gentle clearing of her throat. "Excuse me, Marta. I have some things to discuss with K'Sar. The steward will show you to your new room."

Marta's face flushed deep purple, an automatic reaction to being addressed by the Madam Judiciary. She nodded spasmodically and moved to take the seat that K'Sar had recently vacated. "Yes, Madam," she answered in a soft mumble.

The Madam made a gesture and K'Sar led them back into the empty justice hall. Behind them, she closed both of the tall doors, allowing them a modicum of privacy. "Am I to assume this is pretrial?"

"Are we really going ahead with this farce?" K'Sar was shocked at his own outburst and made himself notch down the volume in his voice. "Even V'Let, my daughter that was abducted at year five, knows that the *tiancai* are unimpeachable."

The Madam smiled gently and moved to take a seat in the audience section, her finger trailing along the stone railing in the process and drawing a line in the thin layer of dust. "We know. The Elders have refused to hold trial."

K'Sar jerked into stillness, his blue eyes attempting to bore into hers. "Under your guidance?"

The smile grew. "Of course. Besides which, the law isn't the problem. We've all analyzed your son's memories before Marta's trial began. We have an idea how bad, how malevolent those planets actually were. However, his memory is spotty at best."

He frowned deeply, finally seating himself in the chair next to her. "Then what is the problem?"

"V'Let is heavily shielded. The only thing that could pierce it, I assume, is a familial bond. Maybe even the Gaze of Love, if she's so lucky." She paused, the smile slipping away to cause her face to maintain an open expression. "We need a full account of the twenty years they were gone, from abduction to their return. I would prefer she give it to me. She is the only one that knows everything."

K'Sar deflated slightly. "That's certainly true." He paused, trying not to unleash the large sigh that was building in his chest. "You may have to deadlock the file. There's been a lot that has happened, maybe even more that she stopped from happening."

The Madam nodded. "Very well. I shall expect you both to be here, sunrise tomorrow."

With a shallow nod, K'Sar stood and left the large room. Marta was long gone, probably settling into her new room. The Elders pretty much controlled all of her time for the next two years, a fact which might cause Z'Tem a small amount of pride. Within moments, he was outside the Halls and navigating himself out of the city, steady strides leading him unerringly toward Taicheng.

He had thought that he could have the Madam Judiciary call a mistrial on account of their status of *tiancai*. The Madam had had such a status herself hundreds of years ago. The secret, however, was well-kept and he only knew it because he knew what the planet knew. He thought idly that she knew something he didn't, which was marginally possible. His link to the planetary being locked out the genetic memory the species shared, instead the essence of Loora feeding important bits of the massive interlink to him directly.

The Madam, whose given name was S'Ran Harn, had been born the female aspect of the *tiancai* more than nine hundred years past. The planet adored her in a way, choosing to see the revolutionary, the person that had encouraged them to separate from the Council politically during the attack. While she claimed to know that the attack was unsanctioned, the correct action had been to sever ties.

S'Ran always seemed to know more than everyone else, always lived in a semi-permanent state of secrecy. In a way, she reminded him of V'Let, open and closed at the same time. The Madam always knew what was best, he admitted to himself. His own knowledge and wisdom came directly from the planet, which even his own daughter knew could have its own agenda.

K'Sar flitted a glance over his shoulder at the City of the Oracles and then directed his gaze at the red sun peaking in the sky. Change was coming, he knew. V'Let knew something was wrong with the universe and if she was anything like her parents, she wouldn't rest until it was fixed.

# CHAPTER FIFTY-SEVEN

V'Let tugged at the garment she wore. After years of comfortable shifts of linen or cotton, the trial dress of Loora felt overly dressy. The fabric was finely weaved satin and the design of it covered her arms and hands while exposing her neck and collarbone. In a way, it was a statement to the tribunal, both shielding and accepting whatever decision was made.

She turned to cast a mock-pleading look at her father before letting her expression settle. "So, to review, I just have to tell the Madam Judiciary everything that happened to us?"

K'Sar nodded. He opened the door to the governor's house, ostentatiously gazing at the steadily lightening horizon. "Why is your brother sulking?"

V'Let cast her gaze downward momentarily. "I told him. About after."

His response was a shallow nod. After a beat, he changed the subject with another question. "You're sure the governor was fine with us using his transport?"

She sighed and gently nudged him out the doorway. "Yes, it's all fine. We'll be late if we don't leave now." She edged around him and sat in the designated passenger seat. "You have to drive."

He gave her an almost indefinable look, one that said too many things for her to want to translate. Settling into the driver's seat, he input the driving commands and the destination. "You know this could turn out very badly, right?"

Confidence filled her, the sense of following a pattern together to find something good for once. "You're right." She inclined her head in deference to her father's longer years. "It could all go very bad. But I have a very good feeling."

A massive feeling, much larger than anything either of them had capacity, rose around them. In reaction, V'Let giggled softly, the laughter itself containing a knowing quality. For K'Sar, it was the first time he had felt anything like it outside of the caverns.

*"Trust her."*

As quickly as the feeling had come down on them, it dissipated just as rapidly. His shock fading, K'Sar managed to chuckle a little. The entity had made its feelings known. He had no choice but to obey.

V'Let sat silent but smiling throughout the rest of the short journey to the City of the Oracles. When K'Sar had finally returned to the governor's home the afternoon before, he had assured her that she was not being charged with anything. He had been very clear about that point at the time. Now that the new day had arrived, however, he was jittery and paranoid.

She had managed to not let anyone else know about the Gaze between herself and Z'Tem. In a way, it was both awkward and completely unwanted. She wouldn't know a romantic feeling if it crawled up and spit in her eye. She tilted her head very slightly. It occurred to her that she could ask the Madam Judiciary.

Letting her mind wander, V'Let was not surprised when it chose to return to the puzzle that was her "incomplete universe" notion. She knew that the thought of it and the theory that lay therein had merit, she just wasn't exactly sure how it happened or how to fix it. In essence, all she really knew was that something was wrong at the core and she had a burning desire to fix it.

Oddly enough, when the Looran entity had interfered in their conversation and coerced K'Sar into trusting her, it felt like something had clicked together. Like the massive thing that was one planetary being was still just a tiny piece of an even bigger puzzle.

V'Let snorted to herself. *Talk about a big picture.*

At that point, they had reached the Hall of the Elders, a white building several floors high. For Loora, it was a very tall building. V'Let had never seen this building but could not make herself gape at it. Other planets that she had visiting had metal structures so tall that the population referred to them as skyscrapers and religious temples that attempted to overrun entire cities. In comparison, this building was quaint and modest.

As per usual, she kept her thoughts under wraps. Maybe being beyond this shell of a world had tainted her too deeply. Again, she scoffed at herself. There was no maybe about it. She was different and she wouldn't be comfortable again until she was gone from this place.

K'Sar stopped at the door, his body language loudly suggesting she stop as well. "I have to remain outside. The justice hall is the first set of doors inside." He reached out, his hand trembling slightly in anxiety, and brushed her hair with his fingers before planting a light kiss on her forehead. At the gesture, V'Let felt warm, another connection settling into place. "Don't be afraid to tell her everything."

She nodded and slipped past him into the building. Inside, the walls were the faded beige of desert stone. There was a set of tall double doors in front of her, one of the open to reveal a female figure. The female showed signs of deep age, the obvious signs of a Looran allowing herself to die. Her hair was white and her skin wrinkled deeply. She smiled when she finally noticed V'Let.

V'Let returned the smile with equal fervor, stepping up the pace to reach the woman more quickly. "Madam Judiciary Harn?"

The woman inclined her head in a polite affirmation. "You can call me S'Ran, if you wish."

S'Ran turned on her heel and stepped back into the hall, gesturing idly for V'Let to follow. After a moment, she realized that they were both wearing trial garments—V'Let in gray and the Madam in burnished orange. V'Let nudged with her mind and the tall door closed behind her.

Once fully inside the large room, they skirted a large, broad pedestal made from soft stone. Behind it, V'Let could tell there were seats carved into the stone, enough to seat twelve people comfortably. She turned away from the sight just as S'Ran opened a door.

"My private chambers," the woman said, an inviting gesture following the statement.

V'Let entered the Madam's chambers, the small dark-paneled room an adjustment after the large courtroom with its stone accoutrements. There was a large desk against a far wall. The walls, desk and chairs were all made of a dark wood but the wall beyond the desk looked like a double-sided mirror. She registered a slight urge to walk to it and touch the glass but ignored the feeling to sit in a chair facing the desk.

"So, how are we doing this?" She avoided the Madam's gaze, primly folding her hands in her lap.

S'Ran, on the other hand, smiled softly above her head and took the seat next to her. "Don't worry, V'Let. This room is shielded. Whatever I find out will stay hidden."

V'Let snapped her head up to pin the Madam with a hard blue gaze. "How?" That one word was as sharp as an ice shard.

The Madam remained unaffected, the smile constant. "I am nine hundred and thirty years of age, dear girl. I believe I might know a thing or two about everything, especially shielding." She sighed, her own faded blue eyes increasing incrementally in solemnity. "You just need to let your shields down."

In return, the younger Looran shook her head vehemently. "No. It's too horrible."

S'Ran reached out and took V'Let's hands in her own. "Don't worry. I've endured horrors of my own." She nodded, her smile encouraging and enigmatic simultaneously. "Just let go, let the walls fall away."

V'Let peered at the older woman, searching under layers of shielding just as she had done with her own father. She noted the flicker of surprise and smiled very slightly when the Madam's mind relaxed in response. There were horrors beneath the shielding, things S'Ran had endured of which no one else had knowledge, but not so bad as what planetary destruction could do to the soul of a Looran. All in all, she felt that S'Ran could handle her own fresh horrors.

She felt herself relax and forced her substantial mental walls to drop. For a moment, it was like feeling the ground drop away from under her feet. The threatening sense of vertigo caused her vision to wobble slightly before it corrected itself. There was only S'Ran and V'Let and this room but she could very distinctly feel everything else.

Something was wrong.

Revisiting her own memories was odd. She had a feeling that the room's shield rebounded the genetic memory back on her. She now remembered the moment her shielding had started. She had understood theoretically from the racial memory and from their instructors' lectures but she hadn't actually been able to build her mental walls until the moment their father left under orders from the Elders. Her mother's death, their abduction, signing the Blood Contract—these memories, however, she had gone over and over inside her own head. It was like seeing a stain on your carpet that no amount of cleaner seemed to be able to remove.

Beyond her memories that now seemed to fill this room, she could feel a glaring error. It wasn't like when she viewed the universe through her own eyes and found it lacking some unidentifiable perspective. In this case, she felt the wrongness like oncoming, unstoppable disaster, destruction wrapped in shards of accident.

She cringed visibly when the memories passed through the destruction of the planets. The Madam's face did not move, her eyes having long closed to take in the memories in silence and darkness. However, she heard the soft, almost nonexistent gasp when the first punishment for disobeying the Adepts entered the line of her mind's sight. It had been the third mission, a planet of deeply underdeveloped humanoids. V'Let had felt they were still too infantile as a species and said as such to their "masters", despite her brother's concern about such a move. The Adepts' response had been instant: they sent punishment in the form of extreme bone loss. Dozens of her bones broke over the course of two minutes and she did what they wanted. She had forced the planets' core to expand at a dangerous rate, breaking it apart as a result. It had taken two weeks for her body to fully mend and another month to stop the crying jags. That had only been the first of another seven attempts to defy them.

The sense of wrongness, meanwhile, was increasing, the pitch of it thrumming like a tuner fork inside her brain. The weird part was that there was something familiar there—not whatever was happening but the thing to which it was happening. Physically, something in her recognized it.

*Cold and untouchable... like ice is mean...* Her own words from a little over twenty years ago reverberated through her head and she gasped, the signs suddenly making sense. The recognition was like calling to like, she knew, because Dmitri was aboard the Looran ship *Jhiri*. Something had happened, something indeterminately bad. Knowing Dmitri's reliance on the capability of the machine and his irrational trust in Looran tech, he was likely in the stasis pod and the ship had followed their route, cutting corners sometimes closer than it should.

"Oh, Gods above," she murmured breathlessly.

She continued to wait, compelled by her own agreement to allow S'Ran access to all of her memories. Through the complex unbinding ritual on Earth to the Gaze of Love with Z'Tem, V'Let's impatience grew exponentially. She kept very still, clenching her teeth against the need to give in to a nervous tic.

After an excruciatingly long moment, the Madam opened her eyes. Something inside V'Let crumpled slightly, seeing the pain and horror of her life reflected back at her. "I'm sorry," S'Ran murmured, her voice barely audible. "I'm so sorry."

Just like that, V'Let's walls were back in place. "I know." She paused, her eyes flitting to the door that was between her and the oncoming disaster. "I have to go." With that, she was up and running, leaving the Madam and her sad eyes behind.

She didn't register the courtroom as she ran through it, expertly dodging anything she interfered with her path to the outside. Within seconds, she found herself on the steps and jerked harshly on her father's arm.

To his credit, K'Sar rushed to his feet and to the hovercraft, pushing it into gear a bit faster than the safety guides would suggest. He glanced back at the now receding Hall of the Elders, noticing that no one seemed to following his daughter, and moved his hand to slow down the vehicle to a more favorable speed. As soon as his hand touched the gear control between them, V'Let stilled his hand with her own and moved it forward, increasing the hovercraft's velocity.

He eyed his daughter curiously. "What happened back there? What are you doing?"

She gave him a look that contained a large dose of incredulity. After what seemed to be a long moment, she rolled her eyes and faced forward again. "Set the destination for the Taicheng docks. We need to get there quickly."

"How quickly?" The first question erupted from his mouth without him even thinking about it. However, it was quickly followed by the only explanation of which he could think. "Are you running?"

Not even turning to look at him again, V'Let rewarded his second question with a spluttering scoff of disbelief. "We need to be there inside of ten minutes. A ship is about to crash there."

K'Sar frowned at his daughter as he increased the speed a little more. "How do you know?"

Now she turned to look at him. "It's the Looran spacecraft designated *Jhiri*. That's how."

# CHAPTER FIFTY-EIGHT

D'Las stood very still, watching his friend pace. Z'Tem had started this recently, around the time they had both felt a sort of crushing sensation descend. His friend apparently did worry and panic really well. Or really badly, depending on how you looked at it. On the other hand, D'Las just assumed this pressure on his insides had something to do with what his sister had told him.

She was leaving. Very soon.

It was horrible to think about. They were never separate. He had wailed and begged and finally sulked. She'd said it was time. He was home and he fit here, she said, whereas she never could. The impending sense of abandonment was very nearly overwhelming, sometimes so much that it caused a heavy pounding in his head.

*D'Las, I need you to meet me at the docks.*

He ignored her and crossed his arms, that particular action the only indication that he had in fact heard the instruction. The movement, after being still for so long, caught Z'Tem's attention and the other Looran halted his pacing. D'Las had a sneaking suspicion that a sullen expression had given him away.

His sister gave a heavy mental sigh. *Lasso, please. Something's about to crash.*

Once he registered that bit of information, his sulky and stiff posture fell away. On the tail of her very specific and pleading statement were bits of information connected to it. Words like *Dmitri* and *spaceship* and *off-course...*

D'Las grabbed Z'Tem's arm and pulled him smoothly out of the house. "We've got to hurry."

The other man unknowingly echoed K'Sar's earlier expression of surprise and concern. Z'Tem matched D'Las's pace stride for stride. "What's happening?"

D'Las didn't answer. At the moment, he couldn't put the reasoning into words that Z'Tem would understand. He simply increased his pace and relied on the faith of their friendship that the other Looran would match it. How do you explain to a home-grown Looran that destruction was coming? His species simply couldn't grasp it realistically anymore.

He noticed, after a moment, that Z'Tem was matching his speed. He reached out with his mind, pleased that it was so easy, and found the governor's hovercraft was nearly parallel to them as they raced to the center of Taicheng. The pounding of their feet against the pavement and the knowledge that they were growing ever closer to a new destination lulled D'Las into a sense of complacency.

*I hope you have a plan, Letta.*

She responded haltingly with a relieved laugh. *Don't worry. You'll have ample excuse to flex your power.*

Seconds passed, blurring into minutes. Streets and houses and intersections lost geographical meaning. Soon, he could see the gleaming building that was the station that preceded the actual docking area. His speed increased even further at the sight of it, a maniacal grin lighting his face.

He looked up at the sky momentarily. If V'Let was in this much of a hurry, then the spacecraft was close. Maybe even close enough to see. The sun was still low in the sky, only one hour having passed since dawn. He glanced in front of him, making sure his path wasn't blocked by something hazardous, before casting another searching stare at the vaguely pink sky.

There was a dark glint that he almost missed, obviously miles above his head. He tilted his head slightly, idly wondering how it could shine like that, when the sky lit suddenly in orange flame, tiny at this point but clearly discernible. His frown deepened at that. Looran vessels didn't burn the atmosphere during reentry. Of course, they didn't crash either.

There was a sudden jerk to his arm and he was pulled to a stop. "You need to tell me what's going on." It was Z'Tem and there was a marginally angry look on this face.

D'Las sighed and glanced at the station, now a mere fifty feet away. "I don't know how. V'Let can explain it better." The hovercraft stopped in front of the station as he looked. His sister's lithe figure bounded out of her seat and ran to the door. With eerie timing, she just stopped and turned to look at him. He turned his attention back to his friend. "And look, she's right there."

Z'Tem jerked slightly and turned to look at V'Let. D'Las grinned as he watched his pupils turn white. In a way, it was very odd, watching the effect of the Gaze. Also, very interesting.

D'Las grabbed his friend's arm and led him to the docking station. As they neared, his sister gave them a soft smile and led them through the station. She looked pretty in the light gray garment, he thought, with it giving a soft dissonance to her light violet skin. Her hair was loose and slightly frazzled, telling him without their connection that she was stressed and anxious.

Once inside the station, he glanced around. Looran tended to use either their own dark metal, strong wood or the warm boundary stone found at the point where the mountains gave way to the desert. With the exception of the governor's cold stone manor, Taicheng tended to use a combination of all three. This station was no exception. The structure itself was made of boundary stone, the seats in the lobby of dark metal and the ticketing desks of wood. The overall impression, however, didn't seem mismatched but balanced.

On the other side of the station was three acres of open land. Not that D'Las could physically see all of the land but D'Tar had updated him on all of Taicheng's statistics recently. There were three nondescript cruising vessels and their own intergalactic cargo ship past that.

D'Las rushed to his sister's side when he noticed that she had finally stopped, her head tilted up at the fire lighting up the air above their heads. "Let's have it," he murmured, referring obviously to her plan.

"We don't have much time." She sighed. "I need you to shape this as K'Sar and Z'Tem freeze the moisture in the air." As she spoke the words aloud, she projected a large image to him mentally. It looked like an upside-down funnel made of solid ice. However, it was very tall, competing with the size of one of the tallest buildings he had ever seen.

He simply nodded, gesturing for the others to join them. "What are you not telling me?"

V'Let chuckled mirthlessly. "I need you to shape it over yourself." She grabbed his hands and guided him above five feet to the left and ten feet farther away from the station. "Its trajectory is headed here. When it hits the ice, I need you to throw the whole thing straight up in the air."

His brow wrinkled into a frown but he nodded again. "And you? What are you going to do?"

Her lips curled into a sly smile. "That's where I come in. I'm going to try something very… interesting. Not to mention difficult."

"What is it?" His frown melted away as curiosity overwhelmed him.

She chuckled again, a secret mirth emerging from the sound. "You'll see."

In response, D'Las pouted slightly. "No fair." She walked away, allowing him room for the massive size of the ice funnel, when Z'Tem and K'Sar stepped up beside him.

"What is going on?" his father demanded. Z'Tem's dark gaze echoed the sentiment.

"I'll tell you after," V'Let called over to them. "Just do as he says. I'll explain, I promise."

He watched as Z'Tem stared over at her for a long moment, the white of his pupils belying the seriousness of his gaze. He nodded finally and turned normal eyes back to D'Las. "Tell us what to do."

D'Las glanced at K'Sar, a tentative question in his expression. A moment, not quite as long as the one between V'Let and Z'Tem, passed and the older Looran nodded. "I'll do what you need."

He grinned brightly. Now that they were beside him, he decided they were safest close to him. He could merely shape the ice around them. "Okay, just freeze the moisture in the air. I'll shape it."

Z'Tem and K'Sar cast dubious glances at each other, having long since noticed something burning through their atmosphere. "That's it?"

D'Las's grin turned maniacal again. "Trust me, gentlemen. This is going to be much bigger than you think."

V'Let smiled as she watched the interaction. She feared she would never understand her brother's ability to bond to others so easily. She meant what she told him—he did belong here, like sliding a key into a lock, a perfect fit. The *tiancai* were meant to be unimpeachable leaders, the buffer between Loora and the rest of the universe. D'Las could easily fill that role but the essence of who V'Let was…

She knew she was tainted.

Shaking her head clear of negative thinking, she turned her gaze back to the sky above them. The orange atmospheric burn was growing, declaring the ship's steady progression. The thick atmosphere of Loora seemed to have slowed it down, for she could feel her own anxiety lessening as a response.

It was the light that caught her attention first. The ice funnel was growing at an exponential rate, showing her brother's skill and power in turn. The rising sun glinted rays of light off the ice, wave after wave of striking prisms. Time seemed to stop as D'Las's construct reached for the sky, freezing water stretching to meet the spacecraft in its destructive transit.

The dark ship was close enough that V'Let could see it as a black dot without manipulating her pupils. A brief mathematical calculation put it at six miles above the ground, whereas the ice structure was reaching for roughly a mile. She forced her pupils to cover half of her eyes, bringing the vessel into focus so she could examine its shape.

It was a transitional transport, an intergalactic craft designed to carry living beings rather than inanimate cargo. Its nose came to a sharp point for something of that size and it dove directly for D'Las's position. This vessel had the beauty of the sleek songbirds with the hidden ferocity of an angry stinging insect.

With its shape clear in her head, V'Let allowed her eyes to relax. Again, the prismatic light grappled with her attention again. What she was about to do was complicated—catching and shaping light waves was like trying to catch rushing water with your bare hands. She narrowed her eyes at the light that glinted off the ice and forced it to bend to a specific shape, a prismatic shell to encase the ship as it hit the makeshift structure.

By the time she had the shell in very nearly solid state, the ship crashed into the ice, pushing a deep crack into the prismatic encasement. It managed to shatter through nearly a third of the ice before D'Las's reflexes and power tossed the remaining ice into the air. As the ship destroyed the ice, the frozen shards created more light, more prismatic waves for V'Let to manipulate.

She used the wave of light to form a thick prismatic cocoon around the spacecraft. The energy was dense despite the illusive transparency. A twitch of her fingers led to the landing gear popping out of their niche at the base, short digging stems that were currently situated perpendicular to the ground.

V'Let narrowed her eyes even more, the blue of her large eyes shining through small slits. She tilted her head very slightly and the craft turned on an axis in response, slowly but surely positioning the landing gear for the top of D'Las's skull. She could feel something warm on her face, slippery and murky. In the back of her head, she knew it was some part of her, exiting her body and forcing weakness upon her mind.

*She's bleeding.* The small voice echoed inside her head, making the shock of it even more unbearable than if it had been said aloud.

*Let it go, Letta. I'll land it.* D'Las's voice soothed away the other voice, coating her inner turmoil with a numbing quality.

With some trepidation and steady concentration, she released her hold on the light cocoon. A film of gray covered her vision and there was a loud whooshing noise, very loud. After that, however, V'Let heard and saw nothing as her body collapsed into heavy unconsciousness.

D'Las twitched idly when his sister passed out. He cringed visibly as he waited for her body to hit the ground. Though a huge part of him was thickening the air around the vessel that was still falling, he turned around when he didn't hear anything after a few seconds. He smiled softly when he realized that Z'Tem had gone to her side at the slightest sign of her collapse. The sight would have been cute if he didn't know for a fact that it was something V'Let frowned upon—unnecessary cuteness.

He turned back to hardening the ever-thickening space between the skin of the craft and the air that it sliced through like a dull knife. The reaction caused a loud noise as Loora's slightly heavy gravity fought his own power. A moment of crystal clarity sliced through his concentration after a moment. The bend that seemed to form around the crashing but tremendously slowed craft was still heading directly for his own position.

D'Las pushed harder with his power, crystallizing the hardened space around the vessel, before abruptly letting go. With a reaction time born out of too many years of self-preservation, he tossed himself out of the way, just barely managing to grab his father's wrist in the meantime. A complicated jerking movement and D'Las was covering them both from what was about to happen.

The crash was sudden and very loud. It left a ringing in D'Las's ears. By the time he released his tight hold on K'Sar, a scattering of dust was settling over them. He stood, examining the ship with his eyes. The rough landing had shattered the crystal nothingness but he could tell that it had kept everything else pretty much intact.

A full minute passed before D'Las realized that nothing was happening. The hatch was positioned at the fore portside of the vessel, completely unmoving. He frowned slightly, a small part of him trying to figure out what his sister would do.

There was a soft murmuring behind him, much lower than his hearing could catch. A moment passed and Z'Tem's voice floated on the air. "She says they're still in stasis, D'Las."

D'Las whipped his body around as if it had been strapped to a tightly strung tether once the words registered. The vision of his sister resting bodily against Z'Tem with blue blood running down her face like tear tracks was not one he would be forgetting any time soon. The blood was too horrific and allowing herself to depend of another was too unlike her.

Was it the effect of the Gaze?

He mentally shook himself. V'Let would never be under the control of some biological influence, no matter how strong. The prism cocoon thing must have weakened her. He moved to kneel beside her. "How do I get in?"

V'Let rolled her eyes half-heartedly. "Override," she murmured softly, the sound of her voice crackling slightly.

At first, it didn't make sense. What override? Then, like a light switching on inside his brain, he remembered. The *tiancai* override command, it superseded everything on this planet. With that certainty now in place, he stood and walked with long strides back to the spacecraft. He noted and ignored his sister's soft laughter as he escaped earshot.

This vessel was made of the same materials as their own, the actively transitional metal culled from deep within the planet. However, whereas the *Tiancai* was on the bulky side because of the cargo space, the *Jhiri* was slim and a beauty to the eye. It likely only had a bridge, an engine room and the stasis pods.

Before accessing the panel next to the niched hatch, he turned his thoughts inward and focused on the link with his twin. *Why did it crash?*

There was laughter again, but this time it was contained within their link. *No worries. There's nothing wrong with the vessel.*

D'Las frowned to himself, the negative creases on his face growing deeper. Even V'Let's mental voice was rough and worn. How much power had she used? He didn't ask the question, though, but merely waiting for her to finish her explanation.

*No one was manning the reentry sequence. Now someone has to let them out of the pods.*

He rolled his eyes and punched seven digits into the panel, a simple alphanumeric code. The outline of the niche burned a little brighter than the dark silver of its make and two Looran characters glowed white on the hatch's paneling. The first character was a square with the vertical lines slightly longer than the horizontal and the second was a triangle with open points and an accent mark both within and below.

"Override authorization?"

D'Las smiled to himself. "Override passcode *tiancai*, generation twelve." In response, the lettering and niche both faded and the hatch slowly opened. He stepped out of its trajectory and waited for it to finish its ascent before stepping softly inside the vessel.

Inside the ship, it was very dark, the only light being the sunlight from outside. They had probably knocked something seriously loose while impeding the vessel's crashing descent. Beyond the hatch, he was faced with three horizontal stasis pods. He edged himself between two of them and found himself on a thick steel mesh catwalk. He figured it was a poor substitute for a corridor and made him miss the secure structure of the *Tiancai*. Looking to the right, he glimpsed signs of a too-clean engine room. A brief moment passed and he very carefully turned to the left and walked to the bridge.

As opposed to the rest of the ship, the bridge lit up like a tiny second sun once he entered. The viewscreen and every button on every panel had an iridescent backlight. He cleared his throat loudly, the shift between murky darkness and twinkling light making him feel like something had lodged there. However, the bridge responded immediately, the speakers humming somewhere just beyond a lesser being's range and something like a wave passing across the lights.

D'Las thought it felt like the ship was waiting for something. He closed his eyes, attempting to channel his sister again. He'd always known what to do before but everything had changed now. He didn't know who he was now. Until he did, V'Let tended to know best.

"Status?"

"Proximity and light sensors down. Engine stalled from atmospheric burn. Stasis holding."

"Release stasis."

"Stasis released. Pods depressurized and open."

D'Las smiled wider. This wasn't so difficult. "Self-healing capabilities?"

The energetic hum that had been emanating from the speakers suddenly turned dull. "Mechanic needed."

"Certainly." D'Las searched and quickly found the passcode panel on the broad console. He punched in the same seven alphanumeric digits. "Begin shutdown sequence." Almost immediately, all of the lights in the bridge began to dim, signifying imminent shutdown. There was a countdown on the viewscreen starting at one hundred fifty. By the time it reached zero, every living being needed to be gone from the interior.

His movements were quick and slightly jerky as he exited the bridge. Immediately as he crossed some invisible barrier, a steel door slammed shut, hard and close enough to ruffle his very short hair. A very brief glance showed that the same thing had happen to the space between the stasis pods and the engine room.

A soft whooshing noise denoted the final bit of depressurization from the stasis pods. D'Las rushed forward to help the Council members out. The sleep gas within stasis aboard a Looran vessel was specifically designed for the highly evolved Looran body. There wasn't much that could keep a member of the Looran species unconscious for days at a time. Even a power-weak person like V'Let couldn't stay unconscious for more than ten hours unless under the influence of stasis gas.

However, other species tended to react negatively. There was sluggishness and grogginess, blurry vision and sometimes nausea.

D'Las heard a disgusting retching sound from the far stasis pod. "There it is," he murmured to himself. There was no doubt in his mind that that particular pod contained Mallik.

"What happened?" Dmitri was pulling himself out of his pod with the strength of his arms. "D'Las?" There was a high note to his question that suggested idle panic.

He helped Dmitri the rest of the way out of the pod, gesturing idly at the open hatch. "We just have a couple minutes. We all need to be out of here before the shutdown sequence finishes."

The middle pod revealed Gralug, a bulky person that D'Las had never met but about which he had heard several stories. The almost impossibly large man grunted softly and removed himself daintily from the stasis pod. "What happened?"

D'Las rolled his eyes. V'Let dealt with the inevitably echoing questions much better than he did. He made another broad gesture toward the open hatch, wincing internally when he remembered servants and staff from the Central Planets making the same movement. However, when he spoke, he made his voice firm, pushing a little with his mind. "Out the hatch, gentlemen. Explanations will follow."

Dmitri shot him a look, the only one of the three Council members to be even a little aware of what he was doing, but they all flowed out of the vessel like a rushing wave. D'Las was the last to exit the ship and cringed visibly at the loud, rough sound the steel barrier made as it closed. The hatch began its slow descent and he input his seven-digit code into the panel to lock all mechanisms until a proper mechanic could be found.

"Help me up." The commanding sound of V'Let's soft voice caught his attention as he finished with the passcode.

D'Las turned to see Z'Tem pulling her gently to her feet and supporting her firmly at her elbow. The blood tracks still visible on her face were still vaguely horrific, though the effect of it was probably worse for the Council members. He realized almost immediately that her gaze was on him.

He arched an eyebrow and fought down a smirk.

She nodded and made a dismissive gesture. At the movement, Z'Tem leaned over and whispered something in her ear. While she had begun to smile, she immediately scowled at his attention. He heard her harsh, whispered response. "I'm fine."

D'Las turned away as the smirk finally broke out on his face. He didn't have to be linked to her to know that V'Let was actively fighting the biological imperative that was the Gaze of Love. However, it seemed that Z'Tem had already given himself over to it despite his initial misgivings, something that had been achingly obvious.

The days to follow would be interesting, he knew, even if the Council members hadn't had to be saved from their own crash landing.

# CHAPTER FIFTY-NINE

V'Let stood at the mouth of the network of caverns her father referred to as his Cave of Solitude, reflecting on the last week. D'Tar, Gralug and Mallik had been locked in one of the smaller banquet rooms for the better part of that week, much to Dmitri's amusement.

The elder Zillian had kept her company when both her brother and father had decided unanimously that she needed the rest. She hadn't complained much. After the barely audible argument she'd had with Z'Tem at the docking station, she didn't feel like seeing him again.

It seemed he was avoiding her as well.

Taking an unnecessarily deep breath, V'Let forced the thoughts away, not entirely clear and unwilling to pursue why they bothered her. This sacred space within the cave was important, one of the few places left on Loora that was still completely connected to the entity. This was the thing that brought her ever closer to the missing connection that growled harshly in her mind anytime she bothered to look at it.

"This is the culmination of too many lifetimes." K'Sar stood next to her, his thoughts far from and yet somehow very close to her own. His following sigh was heavy and she had seen something in him growing older as the days passed. A part of her knew that he was actively choosing to die and it had something to do with her being here now.

She didn't try to dig too deep to figure out what he meant. There was a niggling feeling that she was going to find out very soon. "I'm doing this solo, right?"

He nodded, driving the point home further by taking a step back.

She entered the cave with tentative steps, slightly ducking her head needlessly at the lip of the entrance. Oddly enough, it was as if someone had turned off the sun. The darkness was thick around her, an almost physical thing. She had almost begun the process of complete pupil dilation when she noticed something.

Her skin was glowing.

She bit back the gasp that threatened to escape. Forcing herself to remain calm against this shock, she examined her skin, wondering idly if there was something different on parts of herself that she couldn't see. Every bare inch of her skin glowed iridescent white.

*"Oh, it did work. I worried it wouldn't."*

V'Let glared openly at the air around her. She could distinguish a faint purple mist in the darkness, the glow of her skin giving a small amount of light by which to see. "What is this?" she ground out through clenched teeth.

There was a large rush of power and the mist solidified in front of her, taking the form of a Looran woman. V'Let tilted her head and thought that it looked a little like her mother. *"I supposed he didn't tell you."*

For her part, V'Let smiled wryly. "My father is too deep in the habit of hiding."

The entity chuckled. *"That's my fault."*

V'Let arched an eyebrow, unsure if this entity was trying to engender trust or genuinely taking blame. After a brief moment, she decided that the entity was going for the first but the truth lay with the second option. "Maybe you can explain." It took some time before she realized that this entity needed prompting to give her an explanation.

*"Long ago, the Elders would tend to me, for I was the key to evolution. Since the Wars, this race has gotten arrogant in its own abilities and I was not needed. That was before the Universe fractured."*

V'Let cleared her throat softly, breaking through the entity's line of thought. "Does this have to do with what happened on Earth? The thing I had to fix?"

The being smiled softly, though there was a hint of satisfaction and pride in that expression. *"Yes, the unbinding. When the Guardians were ripped from their roles, the Living Planet we call Earth had to turn away from the Connection."*

"The Connection?" V'Let eyed the entity curiously. She was about to break into a hysterical questioning fit when the thing that was Loora hushed her.

*"It is what ties the Living Planets together. In part, it is also a piece of the*

Universe that was ripped clean. Without the Connection, the Universe stops making sense."

V'Let huffed softly. "What does that have to do with me and my special glow-in-the-dark skin?"

*"K'Sar found this cave when he was twelve, just before his testing with the Elders began. The Connection was newly severed and I needed a way to fix it. He gave me his life and his free will. However, that made him sedentary. Besides which, I needed the pure power of the* tiancai *to bond with the power I bestowed him. It was many years before he finally met your mother."*

V'Let scoffed under her breath. *Many years—that's a fact.* It had to have been at least seven hundred years between the time her father gave himself to the planet and the day he met her mother.

*"I believe he would have shared the Gaze with her, had he not given so much of himself to me."* There was a massive sigh and V'Let felt overwhelmed with warmth. *"The power had to be stored in the female aspect, for it has always been the female of the* tiancai *that can hold more power. Within this power is the ability to restore the Connection."*

V'Let stared at the entity, the massive implications of just what had been done to her hitting her fully. After the destruction of the Contract, she was sure she had been finished playing to someone else's strings. This time, however, it was something that had been planned hundreds of years before she was even born and there was no way out. Sure, it was true enough that she had no inclination toward staying among her own kind. Also true was that the missing connection bothered her a great deal and knowing about it helped a little. She wanted to make these decisions of her own volition, though.

After a moment, she forced herself to square her shoulders and ask the burning question that would decide everything. "What would happen if I should choose not to restore this Connection?"

There was a glint in the eye of the physical form of the Looran entity, though its expression showed that it was unsure whether or not the question was a decision of itself. *"The Universe has already halted its eternal expansion. Many of the Living Planets died with the loss of the Connection. Eventually, maybe even within the breadth of your lifetime, everything will die before its time. New stars will implode and the whole of Creation will essentially be unmade."*

V'Let arched an eyebrow at the entity's melodrama, knowing that the poetic destruction within its words was yet another way to sway her decision. "Fine." She closed her eyes and breathed deep to clear away her negativity. "How do I do this?"

The physical manifestation of Loora beamed and disappeared. Well, more or less, it broke apart back into mist. *"Okay, I need you to bleed on the soil."* V'Let pulled a mildly disgusted face. *"The blood is everything. It's life and essence and the physical presence of your power."*

V'Let rolled her eyes. "Fine." She reached around the back edge of her left hip where there hung a lightweight blade from her cinching cloth. With a quick tug from its flimsy holster and a firm swipe, the inside of her wrist was bleeding. She held the hilt of the blade limply, not wanting the blood on the tip to stain her shift, and fisted the hand of the bleeding arm. Her thin blue blood dripped to the ground before slowing to a stop as her skin healed itself. Once the blood hit the dirt, it flashed bright white and the ground seemed to drink it like a desert flower with water.

"That was odd."

*"It's not all."* There was a vague smile in the entity's voice.

Suddenly, as if it was just that voice for which it was waiting, the cave filled up with light. It was so bright that V'Let had to close her eyes, clenching them against the brightness. In hindsight, it was the better thing to do for it allowed her to realize the light was coming from her. The moment she bled on the ground of this sacred half-hidden place, a part of her that had been locked away previously was now open.

Seeing this strong part of herself was beautiful. It was like the first time she saw a galaxy. There was so much and a small possibility of danger but she could only look on in awe. The light deep within swirled out of her like being pulled down a drain, exploding out of her pores and orifices. Instead of the weakness that followed a normal power drain, she felt the best she had in years.

The light died away, giving way to the darkness that dominated the caverns. V'Let felt a wide smile covering her face, not caring how goofy it made her look. After a moment, the grin faded as something occurred to her. "I have to go back to Earth?"

*"Yes. Wait a while before you go."*

V'Let arched an eyebrow, her eyes unfocused as she tried to figure out the reason herself. "Why?"

*"With what she did to the human beings, the former holy places are becoming sacred again."*

V'Let nodded and turned to leave, knowing the end of a conversation when she heard it. Halfway to the mouth of the cave, she halted as another question formed in her mind. "How will I know where to go?"

*"You'll know."*

# CHAPTER SIXTY

Three more weeks passed. They were back at the docking station, preparing to leave. All three Council members were filing onto the *Tiancai* as V'Let said her goodbyes. The treaty had decided that there would be a liaison from Loora to the Council and that Loora had ten years to lift the travel stagnancy. In her opinion, V'Let thought that enough time to allow for the tragedy of Datong to drift to the back of the Looran consciousness.

After many arguments with her brother, it was decided that Z'Tem would accompany her through her travels. She believed that he was trying to get her to admit to the biological imperative that pressed down on her more every day. D'Las insisted that she shouldn't be traveling alone and he didn't have a choice—he had to stay on Loora if she left.

*Don't stay gone too long.* D'Las's face was a picture of impending grief. Over the last weeks, he had begun to deal with his sister's leaving better. However, the separation itself was difficult and the slow anticipation of it somehow made it even worse.

A smile curled on V'Let's lips. *You know how to reach me.* Not only could their link stretch across vast distances, she had finagled with the com system in the governor's guest room until it contained a frequency that sent directly to the *Tiancai*.

D'Las glanced behind him, watching Z'Tem's idle fidgeting. *Go easy on him. Maybe it's not just, you know, chemical reaction.*

V'Let could feel her smile soften as she shifted her glance to match her brother's. Ever since the time she spent within the cave, she could feel herself change minutely when she looked at Z'Tem. Biologically, he was her match and the opening of that inner part of herself allowed her to accept that. However, no one else had to know that.

*I know.*

V'Let turned back to her ship. Not theirs anymore, only hers. It was sad in a way, leaving her brother behind. She knew now, though, that their paths had diverged from birth. He was the embodiment of the *tiancai*, the defender of Loora. On the other side, her genetics had been manipulated so that she could save the Universe. She knew that they were always meant to be separate.

She boarded the ship and smiled at the Council members congregating in the cargo hold. They were all staring at the various things around the room, Gralug and Mallik in some kind of awe. Dmitri smiled at her and followed her to the bridge. "They'll want to keep them."

She smiled wryly at him. "Want and have are very different things." Pulling herself up to the central console, she punched in the coordinates for the destination in the Central Planets. Her journey back to Earth would follow after she took them back to their Council. "Those cultures are dead and inconsequential. They'll figure that out."

The shorter man tried to look at her coordinates but couldn't quite see over her shoulder as she was over a foot taller than him. V'Let obliged by transmitting the information on her console to the viewscreen. "The Central Planets first?" Dmitri glanced up in time to see her nod. He noticed she was frowning at her own smaller, interactive screen. He looked back at the viewscreen, hoping to see what she saw. After a brief moment, he realized there was a series of complicated Looran characters on the bottom right. "What is that?"

V'Let jerked her head at the inquiry. She forced a small smile onto her face. "I just have a message. It's been here for over a week." Idly glancing backward, she noticed Z'Tem waiting silently and sighed. "Dmitri, check everything down in the cargo hold. We need to start the launch sequence."

Z'Tem stepped forward as the Zillian brushed past him. "What do you need me to do?"

V'Let passed a hand over her face, schooling her face into blankness, and faced him. "The engine room at the end of the corridor. Just monitor it and tell me if anything is wrong."

"Do you expect it to be?"

She shook her head idly. "Not really. Better safe, though."

He nodded and turned on his heel. She watched his back until he was too far away to see. Her attention diverted when a small beep sounded. It signaled the confirmation that everything was properly sealed. "Begin launch sequence." With that said, the ship audibly powered up and they began liftoff.

V'Let eyed the Looran characters on her screen and tapped the one to open the message. She smiled in relief when she realized it was from Marcus. The message contained two attachments—one was an audio newsfeed clip and the other a holobook from Central Publishing—and one sentence.

"Dad will be in for a surprise."

She uploaded both the book and the clip, tapping her fingertips against metal of the console. Immediately she opened the clip. Though there was no visual, she could tell that the reporter was a young Serrian woman.

"Central Publishing's 'Truth Behind Propaganda: Galaxy Killers' found its way to the top of bestselling lists. It is told through the eyes of one Dmitri Andian with a succinct foreword by his son, Marcus. It tells the true story of V'Let and D'Las M'Kaz, the twins most of the Central Planets known as the Galaxy Killers. After a long session with younger Andian as a witness, the Intergalactic Council confirmed the book's validity and removed the unofficial persona non grata status of the twins. The Council encourages everyone to read the book."

There was a scratchy sound as the clip stopped, as if it had stopped short. V'Let sat very still, not knowing what to do or how to react. Marcus had figured out how to reverse the propaganda, really and truly.

They were free now, free to publicly travel among planets until the Confederation's rule. However, the repercussions of this immediately filed themselves to eat away at the unexpected joy. Dmitri was an Adept, so he might be tried for treason or something equally punishable by execution. Gralug and Mallik had been investigating the twins without the knowledge of the other Elders and their crime would be conspiracy against the majority. Its punishment was long-term confinement at the worst.

With a heavy sigh, V'Let opened the holobook and began to read, silently convincing herself that everything would be fine.